WRAPPED TOGETHER IN THE BUNDLE OF LIFE

Bryan Webster

Bryan Webster

Second edition: October 2019

ISBN: 9781091252547

Bryan Webster Fair Havens Houndlaw Park EYEMOUTH TD14 5DA

My thanks to Collin for help with Oliver, Philip for help with Hercules, and Lisa for help with everyone else.

Thanks, too, to Lynne who read and corrected the text.

OTHER BOOKS BY BRYAN WEBSTER:

On Such a Tide: Kindle (2005); Paperback (2019)

Aida and the Soothsayers: Kindle (2011)

Time, Hens and the Universal Significance of Fiddle Music: Kindle (2013)

Eyemouth and the Hecklescar Stories (Short stories 1970s): Kindle (2018)

CHAPTER ONE

Hercules stood on the first tee at Hecklescar, adjusted his white leather driving glove and decided his best course would be to disappear.

Of course, his name is not Hercules nor has his name anything to do with his decision to disappear. His mother called him Harold after her own father, and the name labelled him through childhood and youth. But when he began to make his way in the world his snobby aunt Jacqueline fed his latent vanity by suggesting that the family name, Douglas, common in Hecklescar, was, in their case, a corruption of an old French name, and ought to be pronounced DuGlasse.

Harold adopted the new pronunciation with alacrity and talked about it in the street and down the pier of the small Scottish fishing town in which his family lived and worked. Was it by osmosis that he began to intone in French, or did the locals begin to imagine it? Whatever, the only Frenchman they had heard of was Agatha Christie's detective Hercule Poirot, so Hercule he became. Not all by-names stick, but this one did because it fairly described Harold's belief in his superiority. Where the 's' came from I do not know and have no way of finding out.

(Yes, I know that Agatha's Hercule was Belgian, but Hercule sounds more French than Harold, does it not?)

His decision to disappear has nothing to do with his

name. It has been bubbling up for months. Then today he heard that Peter Munro intends coming home. That has settled it. He must leave Hecklescar. There is no alternative. He cannot risk being in Hecklescar. when Peter Munro steps back into it.

The time had come to quit; to cut loose, to make a clean break; to move on - all of which phrases lobbied his mind and confirmed his resolve. He would put his achievements behind him and start again.

He called them 'his' achievements, but were they? Had not the bulk of them been earned and passed on by his father, Anthony? And had not Anthony been given a flying start by his father, Old Nero?

Give Tony credit, (and the name by which he was known down the pier), what he had taken over from Old Nero was a fish cadger's business, buying fish on the pier and selling it to shops in Hecklescar and in neighbouring towns. Out of it he had grown a small empire.

He had bought the shops and supplied them through contracts he held with several boats that fished out of Hecklescar, Brisset and The Shore.

When the Common Fisheries Policy throttled the white fish industry, Tony nimbly hopped into prawns and signed up boats in Ballantrae, Mallaig, Skye, even Lochinver, to supply his fish processing plant on the pier at Hecklescar. His large 44-ton articulated lorries, resplendent in livery of Douglas tartan, pounded the roads and motorways of Scotland, delivering prawns in cold water tanks to his fish processing plant on the pier. The same lorries then transported the prawns, now labelled langoustines, to the gourmet tables of England and the Continent.

That some of the old Hecklescar boats had had to be laid up and sold off did not trouble Tony much. He was not sentimental, which is just as well, for sentiment is a poor business advisor. Besides, some of the displaced fishermen became drivers of his trucks, and others, instead of gutting fish on heaving decks stood in his clean rooms carrying out the same task on static concrete floors.

Tony thought he had done his best for young Harry and no-one contradicted him. He had promoted Harold out of Hecklescar High School into Fettes College in Edinburgh to mix with the sons of the successful. When young Harry responded to this privilege with a decent set of Highers, his father funded him through a Social Science degree at Strathclyde followed by a Masters degree in Business Studies at Edinburgh. How could the lad fail? He was equipped, (was he not?) to take over the family business.

At age 23, he entered the office and sat in a chair behind a desk and watched his father manoeuvre his way through the days and weeks. The son thought the father pathetic: no strategy, no business plan, no objectives, no targets, no reviews, no monitoring, no control, just muddling through. OK, it made money, but God knows how; not the way to run a modern company.

These were his thoughts, but he shared them only with his fellow MBAs when he lampooned his father in the cafes and bars of Edinburgh and Glasgow. In Hecklescar he sat upstairs in the office and did his job. What was that job? Customer Liaison, a job that did not exist until it appeared on his business cards under his name. He checked invoices, soothed complaints, chatted to customers and made promises.

He was bored to tears but did not have the guts to say so. On the rare occasions when his father asked for comment, he mumbled platitudes. He transferred what little drive he had inherited from his father to devising a busy social life away from Hecklescar, furnishing a flat in Edinburgh, spending his father's money and reducing his golf handicap.

Then, in the summer of his thirtieth year, a phone call from his mother fetched him from the links at Gullane. His father had been struck down with a stroke and was unlikely to recover.

Thus Hercules inherited the Douglas business empire and had only the vaguest notion of how to run it. In that he is not unlike many top executives. Like them, he quickly learned that the business ran itself, as those who had done the work before kept on doing it. He drifted upwards into his father's office, answered the phone and e-mails, held meetings with Jakey who ran the yard, Fiona who ran the office, and Angela who looked after the girls, (the girls being the women (some of them older than herself, some them men) who gutted the fish, scraped the meat out of crabs and lobsters, and packed the fish and crab meat for shipping.)

Of course, he laid out strategies and plans as he had been taught at Business School. Not that these made much difference to the business, except to give Jakey, Fiona, Angela and workers in general the complication of having to give his notions enough attention to convince him that they were, in his words, 'driving the business'.

Jakey, Fiona and Angela did not conspire to run the operation in spite of him, but they soon became adept at implementing his strategies and plans without seriously altering what they knew worked best in practice.

Their growing expertise coincided with a spurt in demand for fish and worked its way onto the bottom line. The business flourished and Harold became convinced that he had a rare business talent.

It was about this time that Aunt Jacqueline infiltrated the notion that he might be French and he made the mistake of slipping it into his conversations down the pier. Within days he became Hercule; within a week, Hercules. When Angela, at one of the meetings, blurted out his by-name by mistake, the phrase 'business colossus' flickered in his mind and he forgave her.

Now he would attempt to stride the business world of this backwater, shake it up and drag it into the twentieth century before the century sputtered to a close in ten years' time.

(If I am overdoing Hercules' heroic fantasies, please forgive me. Back then, if you had met him in the street, whether in Hecklescar or Edinburgh you would not have found him detached from reality or talking business gobbledygook. No, provided you were important enough to merit his attention, he would have come over as an affable man who talked sense. What I am giving you is a glimpse of his dreams. Do we not all dream, especially when we are young? Do we not need our dreams to persuade us that we are not here just to make up the numbers?)

Twenty years have passed when we find him standing on Hecklescar golf course contemplating escape.

Had he had any doubts about disappearing they would have been scotched by the sight of four old men on the fairway before him. They were not so much playing golf, as amusing themselves knocking a ball along the grass in genial company. That had always irritated Hercules; now it firmed up his purpose. He would put up with fools no longer.

Yet these men were no fools. Each had been, Hercules conceded, successful in his own field; had got on, made something of himself.

He knew Maxwell had been Director of Social Work for the local council until he shuffled off into early retirement carrying with him a comfortable pension and a substantial lump sum. Some of this he had entrusted to Hercules to place in the Golden Opportunities Life Fund, an investment vehicle of Hercules' own design. (Do not be misled by the 'Life' in the title. It is not a life insurance, nor a life-long investment, nor has it anything to do with life at all. Hercules stuck 'Life'

9

into its title to make the acronym GOLF; a device he thought would tempt golfers to invest. It has worked well enough for Hercules to think it a stroke of commercial perspicacity.)

He had similarly corralled a thousand pound or two of another of the group, George. For twenty-five years he had been a sea-going captain shipping oil from the gulf to Australia. When he gave up captaining tankers, he became a pilot escorting them in and out of Hound Point on the Forth. At sixty, he too returned to the place of his birth, Hecklescar.

Michael had started his working life as a boatbuilder in Hecklescar Boatyard. He had then moved on and up to become a peripatetic inspector for the White Fish Authority. When ten years ago he returned with his wife to his home town, Hercules had been able to give Michael the satisfaction of holding a modest share in J.W. Spiers and Co, which company ran the Hecklescar Boatyard. Hercules is a non-executive director of J W Spiers. If this morsel of information leads you to suspect that J W Spiers & Co is one of those companies invested in by the Golden Opportunities Life Fund, I will not contradict you.

Hercules had not been able to persuade John Hendry, the other member of the quartet to invest, partly because John's money was already tied up before he ran into Hercules, but mainly because John had serious doubts about Hercules' financial acumen.

John had been a bank manager in the days when banks had managers who were allowed to do banking. They roamed freely and wisely over current accounts, deposit accounts, savings, mortgages, overdrafts, loans and investments. After reading the prospectus of the Golden Opportunities Life Fund, John had expressed his misgivings to Hercules. Now in his eighties and still sharp, John Hendry seldom missed an opportunity when meeting Hercules of enquiring how Golden Opportunities fared in the markets. He did not need to wait for an answer. He knew, and Hercules knew he knew. This had always troubled Hercules; now in the financial downturn, it frightened him. John Hendry was an open, sociable, talkative sort of man. What, fretted Hercules, did he share with his companions as they lined up their putts or sat together in the clubhouse afterwards?

To this disturbance add aggravation. With their achievements comfortably behind them these four relished their weekly game of golf in each other's company. They were determined to enjoy the game and not count over scrupulously the number of strokes required to put the ball in the hole. This disinterest irritated Hercules. He played off four.

The old men cleared the green and Hercules drove a sweet ball down the middle of the fairway. No need for rush. The withdrawal must be tactical. Napoleon was noted for his retreats. He knew when to quit, how to snatch opportunity from the jaws of defeat. That would take time. It was now the 11th of June. He must be well clear by Christmas.

'Pencil in 31st October. That gives me time to maximise my exit strategy.'

CHAPTER TWO

Hercules did not play a full round, just enough to remind him of his prowess and to clear his head of the fishyard. The fishyard had slithered its way into his dislike. He had come to despise it. It reeked not only of fish but of entrapment. It had been his passport to a larger, fuller life, a station on the road to somewhere, something bigger and better. That he had not moved on and up grated. He blamed circumstance, he blamed the banks, he blamed family commitments, he blamed Olivia, he blamed loyalty to the place and the folk of the place, and in all of these pigeon holes there may have been a smidgeon of truth. But what he would not accept, could not accept, was that he had achieved all that he was likely to, or capable of. In his heart he felt, in his bones he knew, that he was capable of more. He was made for bigger things.

He parked his golf mobile and, in the mellowing evening, loaded his clubs into the boot of his Mercedes. Hecklescar golf course sits high above the town to the south, across the river on land that heaves up in huge folds until it collapses into the sea in the towering cliffs of Hawk's Ness.

It had been Hercules' custom, when he came out of the clubhouse, to look out over the town, much as a farmer surveys his fields and anticipates his harvest. Of late, Hercules had stopped doing this. Now it gave him no satisfaction. Once cowed by his dominance, now it spat back.

The course at Hecklescar is relatively new, laid out ten years ago at the instigation of Hercules and fellow members of the club when the little old nine-holer was cut in half by the new road leading to the new fish market, ice-factory, and embryo industrial estate.

In most of these ventures Hercules had an interest, if not a stake. He had made more than a little on these developments and had contributed, he thought generously, towards the new clubhouse, a vulgar, in-your-face structure, that now dominated what was once a quiet green hill.

On this day, Hecklescar lay comfortably huddled around the bay at the mouth of the river, though it now drapes its ever-billowing skirts over the fields around it. Along the river ran the harbour, once so full of drifters or seine-netters that, the auld anes said, you could walk from one side of it to the other without getting your feet wet.

Now the glory had departed. A couple of prawn trawlers and a few crab and lobster boats do their best to claim the harbour. The Harbour Trust has betrayed them for gold, handing over the quay to pleasure boats of various descriptions. They are provided with comfortable berths alongside floating pontoons that now fringe most of the quay. Fishing is the past, tourism is the future.

Talking of pleasure boats, one of them belongs to Hercules, an ocean-going yacht called Olympian. You can pick it out easily; it is by far the biggest and its mast soars well above the others. Perhaps we are being unfair to class it as a pleasure boat. Hercules would argue, (and argue he did with HM Revenue & Customs), that it is used almost exclusively for entertaining business clients - and is therefore tax-deductible.

Hercules drove home but not to a welcoming meal. He did not live on his own but he would make his own meal; that was the arrangement. Except on Sunday, when, if, his daughter was at home. Then Olivia would make the meal, otherwise he would take it at his Golf Club; not the Hecklescar Club, but Gullane, where he was a member.

Hercules and Olivia are not separated but they live apart. He would claim they are not estranged, only that they have different interests. The double bed in the master bedroom is made up, but they never use it. Hercules would explain that this is a practical arrangement, born of his need to be up and about in the early morning, late at night, or even during the night to clear up logistical problems with a delivery in or a shipment out. But he has no need to explain for no one knows and no one asks.

Hercules is frequently away from Hecklescar overnight. If he is not, they breakfast together. Provided, of course that he is not up early sorting out logistics, which is not often; hardly ever, in fact.

You ask Jakey's wife, Ina, and she will tell you it is her man, who gets up in the middle of the night to unload a lorryload of prawns from Mallaig or despatch Nudge to Holland with boxes of langoustines. Not Hercules, the night phantom, she would add.

Jakey will be in the office at seven every morning regardless of his night shifts to report to Hercules what has moved during the night. Thus, Hercules can continue to control the business, provided, of course, that he is not in Edinburgh or London, or, more recently, more often, at the end of a mobile phone somewhere else.

If Hercules is not away and comes home early enough Olivia will make a little supper and they will eat it together before retreating to their separate rooms.

You may not think this is a happy arrangement, or a satisfactory one, but it suits both parties. They are still together in the same house after twenty-five years. That counts for something nowadays, does it not?

That's another thing - the same house! That rankled

with both of them. It is not what Hercules intended and not what Olivia had been promised.

To most folk in Hecklescar, Avignon is a grand house, a fine Victorian Villa in Alexandra Drive. Many who are invited to visit feel intimidated long before they reach the front door, for it glowered from a porch that brooded over a long rising front garden.

It is said in the town that Jessie Collin, when she and Dod were invited for a glass of wine and a mince pie just before Christmas one year, took fright at the bottom of the steps leading up to the porch and scuttled away leaving Dod to face the wine and Olivia on his own. Mind you, Jessie has a different explanation for her sudden change of mind. She reckons that she suddenly remembered that, with the tablets she is on, the doctor said she mustn't take alcohol of any description, especially wine.

Those, like Dod, who braved the front door found themselves in a spacious hall with a drawing room opening out on one side and a lounge on the other. They would not be invited to inspect the rest of the house, but had they explored on their own they would have discovered a dining room, study and Olivia's day room on the ground floor leading to an enormous kitchen that pushed out in conservatory glass into the manicured back garden. The kitchen bristled with equipment, glistened in stainless steel and quietly asserted its taste in laminate flooring and light oak furniture.

I make no mention of the downstairs 'facilities' for they can be taken for granted. The main bathroom upstairs boasts a sunken bath, surrounded by a black and white tiled floor, a walk-in shower, several basins and a panoply of mirrors and decorated tiled panels.

There are four bedrooms, one each for Hercules and Olivia, the double room aforementioned for guests who like to sleep together and Sally's room. Sally is their daughter, at present in Edinburgh studying to be a nurse.

We will not venture into the spacious garret. It is there that the two sons have their territory. What they do not rule over is occupied by yesterday's must-haves waiting for Olivia's recall. There are chests of old glassware, pictures and porcelain, found in the house when they moved in and stashed away by Hercules on the off chance that some of it may be valuable. But we will leave the door closed. We have nosed enough.

Hercules and Olivia are in the kitchen drinking coffee and eating salmon sandwiches when we join them. He says he doesn't like salmon sandwiches. The fish comes out of a tin and thereby undermines one of the pillars of his business strategy: that fish ought to be fresh. But Olivia has strategies of her own, and one of them is to avoid preparing food unless there are guests that need to be impressed.

As we know these two are not normally in the same place at this time of day. Even when they sit down to supper together, they remain apart. I mean that there is no friendly chat, no reviewing the day's twists and turns, no mutual interest in what the other has been doing. The standard routine is for each of them to pick up a newspaper or magazine and browse it as they eat and drink. Each one may occasionally issue a muttered comment in the direction of the other on what they have been reading or some snippet of local news, but generally it is a silent supper.

Tonight, however, Olivia has something to say to Hercules that requires a response.

'Sally is coming on Sunday,' she said after she had put down the sandwiches and handed him his coffee. Hercules set aside his Times and took a sandwich.

'I'll not be here; you'll make my excuses. I'm at Gullane.'

'She wants to see you'

'She wants to see me? What for?'

'She didn't say. Just that she wants to see you. It's important.'

'Tell her to tell you and you can tell me.'

'I thought of that. I told her that most Sundays you're at golf and not here, but she's insisting that she wants to talk to you.'

'You've no idea what it's about?

'No.'

'It'll be about her course. Has she made a mess of it again?'

'I don't know - and she didn't make a mess of it – they did. They lost her dissertation.'

'So she said!'

Olivia ignored the riposte.

'What time will you be back? You could see her then. She can catch the late train.'

Hercules thought about knocking back the question, of refusing to be hemmed in by family affairs. He wanted rid of all that. Had he not made his decision? For a while he sat stirring his coffee.

'She doesn't like me,' he murmured at length.

'She doesn't particularly like me,' Olivia replied flatly, 'but that's not the point. You are her father, and she wants to see you, so what time will you be back?'

Sally is a disappointment to her parents; always has been. She does not have her mother's looks or confidence, refused to abandon the local school for education in Edinburgh and made a best friend of Katie Smith, the fish cadger's daughter. They had wanted her to study medicine and become a doctor but she had more modest ambitions and is training to be a nurse. Next year she will qualify and hopes eventually to return to Hecklescar as a community nurse.

Olivia, impatient for a reply, put down her magazine and looked at him. All couples dance, particularly those that have been together for many years. I don't mean foxtrots or rock n' roll, I mean that they develop ways of moving round each other. These two were experts. They knew what moves to make when.

Hercules regarded anyone who questioned his judgement or commented on his decisions as an opponent. That included Olivia but he had long discovered that the techniques he used at the yard did not work here. Down on the pier if he thought he was being thwarted, questioned or even counselled, he would fix his gaze on his opponent and expect them to flinch. He did not often look into the eyes of the person he was talking to, but when he did, he expected a reaction; that is why he did it. He wanted them to know that he had them in his sights. This was not a technique he had been taught at university nor was it part of his managerial training; he had grown into it. It arose from who he is and what he thought of himself.

Blame his father if you must, but only of neglect. His father, brought up in the local school and subject to the withering climate of opinion in Hecklescar, knew instinctively that he must not rise above himself. But he had deprived his son of that education and so exposed him to other untaught lessons.

At his Edinburgh school and at university his son had absorbed the belief that he was a leader of men, one of an elite, to be looked up to, listened to and obeyed. That others did not share this valuation of him did not cross his mind. Had he heard Jakey's wife calling him a phantom boss, he would not take it as criticism, but classify it as a reference to the awe he evoked in the minds of his workers.

He had required the same respect from his daughter Sally, his sons, Alexander and Hector and, at least in his own reckoning, concluded he had received it. Not that he did not love them, nor indulge them. Certainly, he never changed their nappies or fed them their baby food, but he had been a good father; attentive, indulgent even, playful at times, and always the breadwinner, with cakes a-plenty. He loved them in his own way - from the throne. But tutored in irreverence by their mother, they had now begun to drift into insubordination.

Olivia repeated the question.

'What time will you be home? You are coming home, I take it.'

Hercules put down his cup and stood up.

'No promises,' he stated, 'I'll try to make it for seven.'

'Good, I'll tell her that.' said Olivia, and went back to her coffee and Vanity Fair.

CHAPTER THREE

Olivia and Hercules have tired of their comfortable, convenient house in Alexandra Drive. That is its failing. It is comfortable and convenient. It stands in a row of other equally convenient houses, though few of its neighbours are quite as comfortable. What Hercules had planned and Olivia had been promised was something much grander, something that made a statement about who lived in it and what they were.

Drive a kilometre out of the town, to where the Beanston road crosses the course of the old railway line and you will see an old farmhouse nestling comfortably into five acres of what used to be a market garden. This is where Hercules intended to build his mansion. He does not call it a mansion; country house is his name for it, but we may call it a mansion provided we don't get too carried away. In his study on the wall he has an architect's drawing of the house alongside an artist's impression of what it will look like when it is finished.

The house is a work of his own imagination: Arts and Crafts with overtones of Art Deco and Modernism. It has not been designed to live in, but to show off how sophisticated is its owner.

What will it cost? £1.5 million. Does Hercules have £1.5 million? No. Is he likely to have £1.5 million in the future? Not now, now that his Golden Opportunities Fund is sinking, now that Peter Munro is coming back. Now he has no option but to disappear – and leave the country house behind.

In the meantime, what about the other house, the farmhouse that now occupies the site of Hercules' plans and Olivia's dreams. On the map it is named Latchlaw, but locals know it as Latchly.

Certainly, Latchlaw is not the grand house Hercules has in mind, but it well serves its present tenants, Alistair and Alice Kerr. It is a stolid no-nonsense house, built a hundred years ago for a small farmer who couldn't really afford it by a local builder who never got all of his money. It stares at the Beanston road from a sloping hillside, the way a bairn's house stares at you from sugar paper, with a door in the middle, a window on each side, and three windows upstairs. It even has the child's curtains at each of the windows.

Round the back are the remains of the old steading, now mostly roofless and crumbling into rubble. But Alistair has rescued a couple of the smaller outbuildings to house the equipment he uses in the small market garden that surrounds the house.

Alistair is not a market gardener. He is a retired farm labourer, who grows vegetables and fruit that he sells to anyone who is prepared to buy them and knows where to find him. He has established a base of loyal customers from Hecklescar and beyond. It is said that there is a woman that travels down from Edinburgh every so often to buy his produce. But do not report him to the tax man; it is all cash in hand, nothing goes through the books for there are no books. If there were, I am pretty sure they would prove that he does not make enough to pay tax. But it is best not to probe.

You may well ask how a retired farm labourer comes to be living so well above his station in life, in such a house, on a market garden, in such a desirable location. The man has no private income or occupational pension - and no pile of savings on which he draws interest. Nor should you surmise that the wife has money. Alice, Alistair's life companion has shared his poverty all her life. She is the daughter of a farm labourer and remembers that her mother was bound to work in the fields at harvest time and at tattie-picking to pay for the house the farmer provided for them. Alice herself had spent many a cold day rogueing swedes in the fields up from Fairnieside through an unwritten obligation to the farmer who employed her husband.

Alistair holds the house and grounds by the kindness of Hercules. Let me say that again, this old couple live where they live and enjoy the life they enjoy (and they do enjoy it) by gift of Hercules. They pay rent, but it bears little relation to the value of the land they occupy, and Hercules expects and receives nothing from the proceeds of the sale of produce. But for him, they would be still living where they lived before, in a council house on the Poplace Estate, trying to grow a few tatties and lettuces in a plot not much bigger than a tablecloth.

If this largesse surprises you let me add a note of caution. Hercules is being kind. In some ways he is a kind man. Ask the workers in his yard about their Christmas bonus and the evening receptions Olivia lays on from time to time at the house. Then there's the cheap fish they take home on a Friday. Not all of this is calculated generosity, designed to draw loyalty to himself and the business. Some of it is genuine, arising from traditions he picked up from his father and continued by him out of patronage of the people who depend on him for their income.

In the case of Alistair there is another strand to Hercules' generosity. Alistair is the grandfather of Christine, girlfriend of Hercules' youngest son, Hector.

Hector, like daughter Sally, is a disappointment to his parents. He did quite well at school, taking three Highers, but showed no interest in taking it higher. He spent his youth in and amongst boats. He and his mate Craig had taken over a pooh boat that Hercules had impounded. Hercules reckoned that he had lent the owner, a retired fishmonger from Newbottle on the Tyne, the wherewithal to buy it.

It wasn't much of a boat, 5 metres, clinker built of wood, open, no wheelhouse, with a covered foredeck and an old Kelvin inboard motor that worked when it worked, but often decided not to. The Newbottle man had used it occasionally to throw a few creels into the sea amongst the rocks in search of a lobster or two, or a box, maybe, of crabs. When he tired of his hobby the boat lay in the harbour for three years until Jimmy Doo pointed out to the Harbour Master that the boat had sunk. When Hercules found out he claimed the boat, then not knowing what to do with it, gave it to Hector and Craig when they showed an interest.

The boys had worked hard on the boat and soon restored it to service. They then picked up the Newbottle man's trade and made a pound or two with the few creels they begged from the fulltime men.

Hector thus acquired a taste for the sea, and at sixteen when he heard that Michael D. had a berth on the Wandering Star, put in for the job. Hercules knew nothing about it until Michael mentioned it to him on the pier. Hercules instantly forbad it and made it clear to Michael that he would not handle any of his fish if he gave his son a berth. Olivia was horrified at the thought of her son returning home stinking of fish and diesel, and of living and sleeping alongside the Filipinos who made up the rest of the crew. She steeled Hercules' resolve and together they scuppered Hector's ambitions for a life at sea.

Hector responded by refusing to go back to school, or on to college or university. The stage was set for a long and damaging stand-off until Christine took a hand.

She and Hector have been friends for as long as anyone could remember. They attended primary school together, played together as children, attended the same parties and at Hallowe'en prowled around the town in each other's company looking for apples, sweets and a coin or two. They found themselves in the same class at High School, and helped each other with their homework. Hector assumed she would always be around when he needed someone to talk too, and she was always there. How far their acquaintance has advanced I do not know and have no intention of prying into it. I am sure they love each other and that their love runs wide and deep.

Christine's father is a builder, (and more than a builder if you read the sides of his lorry: Duncan Kerr, Builders, Plasterers, Tilers). Christine proposed to her father that he take Hector on as a sort of apprentice - and to Hector that he could work at building during the week and fish in his boat at weekends. Reluctantly Hector conceded, and even more reluctantly Hercules and Olivia accepted the compromise.

Hector has been working with Duncan for two years now.

CHAPTER FOUR

Hector has used the two years well. He has learned to plaster and learned to tile. He can mix cement, lay a path and build a wall if it is straight, not too long and not too high.

Hector's growing competence has excited an itch that has nettled Duncan for years, but he has never had the courage, the workers or wherewithal to seriously scratch it. Whenever a job needed a bit of joinery Duncan had called on old Tam Beesknees. (Tam's surname is not Beesknees, it is Spence. Years ago, he endorsed a power screwdriver he had used for the first time as 'the bee's knees.' After that he was called Beesknees. That is all it takes in Hecklescar.)

Old Tam is approaching retirement and truth to tell, he has slowed up. He is a good craftsman of the old school; often too good, for he makes every job a work of art. Duncan has a door in his house hung by Beesknees and will show you, if you ask him, how it will swing closed at the merest touch of a finger. Then he will tell you that Beesknees spent three days on it; he had had the hinges off seven times before it was 'just right'.

However laudable such standards are they rarely craft a healthy bottom line and Duncan often found himself stretched between charging what he had estimated and paying Beesknees for the hours he had spent on the job.

Now, thought Duncan, could it be that Hector might be

trained up to do the joiner work that Beesknees had done? The lad could go to college to learn the basic skills and Beesknees would teach him the practicalities and the quality. Then Beesknees could shuffle off into retirement leaving Hector to do the woodwork.

Duncan could then expand the business, and allow him, with the aid of Martin the plumber and Wull the electrician to build and fit out a complete house, something he had not been able to do in the past. Hector was shaping up. In two or three years he would be capable of doing all the Beesknees did - and quicker than Beesknees ever did it. Should he launch out? Now would be the time. Planning regulations had been relaxed and anyone with a bit of ground was planting a house on it. There was scarcely a farm in the county that had not built, or was in the process of building, a little executive housing estate alongside the steading.

For such a venture he would need money, but Duncan does not have money. He is a meticulous tradesman. That means two things. First, that people seek him out when they want a quality job, and, second, that they can never quite afford the time that Duncan has put into it. Almost everything that he undertakes takes longer than it should, and costs more than he had estimated. In addition, (or should it be, in deduction) there were those jobs, familiar to all small tradesmen where the invoice has to be chased for months or even years before it is paid, or, in some cases, written off.

On this, listen to Duncan's wife Janet, who does his books.

'It's a funny thing about them that has money: they can't pay. They can pay for holidays in Antigua, they can pay for their fancy cars; they can pay for their big houses and their fitted kitchens, but they can't pay for the work that's done in them.'

Duncan lives in perpetual hope of putting something

behind him, but whenever he had set aside a little stock it had been pilfered and lost. He remembers, and Janet never lets him forget, this couple from down south, (Basildon, Duncan thinks), who commissioned him to extend and enhance an old house half way up the brae at Brisset: new kitchen block, conservatory, double garage, balcony to sit on and take in the sea breezes, and a monoblocked patio to accommodate two cars and a picnic area. The budget was generous: £150,000, and the estimate accepted without quibble. Duncan beavered away for six months before the couple pulled the plug citing family commitments and the wife's bad chest. Duncan, true to his character and upbringing, finished the work in hand and hoped to recoup his outlay from the sale of the property. The house eventually sold for less than he had laid out on the improvements. Had the bank not stood by him, it would have been the end of the business.

That was 15 years ago. Duncan had scarcely recovered from the setback. For the new venture - of adding joinery to his building, plastering and tiling, he would need capital. He would do it properly. Duncan would not do anything he could not do properly. For a whole week he sat at the kitchen table and laid out plans. He talked to Beesknees about what equipment he would need, and Beesknees buried him in brochures.

Premises? Now would be the time to invest in premises. He had worked too long out of the unit up on the Industrial Estate. Every year the council imposed some new restriction; every year the rent went up. Yet every year in the East Border Gazette the Executive Member for Industrial Development. praised the council's 'Enterprise for Excellence Initiative', and wined, dined and wooed budding entrepreneurs to set up in Hecklescar and in other attractive locations in The Borders. Duncan believed, and his fellow tenants believed, that if you were setting up a business in the town you could rent a unit free for a year or more, particularly if you were one of those iffy businesses where nobody knew what you did, like Information Technology Services, Infrastructure Development, or Climate Change Consultancy. All of which had opened to the blaring of trumpets and the cutting of ribbons but had shut up shop when the free rent ran out.

Old tenants, tenants like him, were ignored or, at best, tolerated. It was time, Duncan thought, to possess his own workshop and premises, and he knew just where to find them: in the old steading at the back of the house at Latchlaw where his father and mother now lived. There, he could lay out new premises to accommodate both building and joinery. The fitting-out he could do himself but would need around £18,000 for facilities and equipment.

For a business, £18,000 is not a lot but Duncan did not have it. At least, he did not have all of it. There was about £5000 in an account at The Bank of Scotland; an amount that ebbed and flowed as materials were bought, wages paid out and invoices paid in. But he also had title to £10,000 plus profits in Hercules' Golden Opportunities Life Fund. It could come out of there.

He was sure that Hercules would let him have the old steading. There should be no difficulty about that, he told Janet. After all, it is for his own son.

'Should!' replied Janet, 'Should! But you never know with him. Watch him, and make sure you have all your buttons fastened when you see him.'

'No' be too hard on the man, he let fither hev the hoose.'.

'He let your 'fither hev the hoose' so he'd look after it. He's not daft. If he'd left it empty, what damage the rain didn't do would be completed by the vandals. He knew you'd see your father an' mother alright. So, he has a builder to look after his property without the expense.'

'Ah, you're an auld cynic. Anyway, if ye're right, he'll let me have the steading just to keep it wind and water tight.'

'He might,' said Janet, 'the Lord is full of mercy, and life is full of surprises.'

CHAPTER FIVE

It is not surprising that Duncan looks to Janet to keep him right. His mother, Alice, served in the same office for his father. Alice was born three years and one month before her husband and has maintained the precedence ever since. In the Methodist Church at Hecklescar in 1955 she promised to accompany him through life. She was twenty-two years old then. When we meet her, she has kept her promise for fifty- four years.

Alistair was not, as they say, academically inclined. He was, is, bright enough in a practical sort of way - fixing things, making things, working out what went where and why. But words between hard covers, written on a blackboard or scribbled in an exam paper did not interest him.

When he left school therefore, he faced a choice: the sea or the land. At first, he opted for the sea. He thought he would like it. The sea was in his blood, his granny had said, whose man had made big money on The Superb out of Peterhead. In the blood it may have been, but it wasn't in the stomach. For six weeks he lay on the deck or in his bunk moaning with sea-sickness. Eventually, the skipper told him what he already knew: that although he had the determination to be a fisherman, he did not have the constitution for it.

He became a farm labourer, at Fairnieside just outside Birsett, a couple of miles along the road from Hecklescar. After a year or two he began, if not to enjoy it, at least to welcome the opportunity to work in the open air, to become fit and strong and to discover that the men he worked with valued his work. He likes to tell of the time he saved a whole day's work by fixing the reaper with a wedge and a length of baler twine.

The pay was poor (and likely to remain so) but after three years he had saved enough to propose to Alice that they should marry and apply to the farmer for a house on the farm. Both Alice and the farmer were willing and the pair (Alice and Alistair, that is, not the farmer) set out on life together in the house on the end of the row at Fairnieside. For a while Alice continued with her job in Aitchison's shop in the Market Place at Hecklescar, but soon found work on the farm, or in the farmhouse.

While at Fairnieside, Alistair and Alice bore two children; one a frail little girl, Mary, who died when she was fifteen months old; the other, Duncan, the builder whom we have met, born the year his sister died.

If you want to see where they lived and the legacy they left, take the track that leads from the brow of the hill on the Hecklescar Road and follow it round and down to the cottages. There you will see not only the house where they lived, but also the garden that they cultivated for forty years. It still flourishes from the care given in those days, albeit now with docks and dandelions, rather than leeks and onions, cabbages and cauliflowers, broccoli, herbs and lettuce, shallots and spring onions, broad beans and runner beans, carrots and sweet turnips and of course, flowers in their season. There were dahlias here once, dahlias that every year, well, nearly every year, took first prize at Beanston Show. Look carefully and you will find one of Alice's brave marguerites still holding its own among its belligerent bedfellows.

Then, quite suddenly, it was over. The farm was gobbled up by BAI Farms and the contractors moved in. Now a field that had taken a day and half to turn over, took no more than three hours with a ten-share plough. Barley that had taken three days to gather in was now reaped, processed and reduced to clean grain within two hours by a combine harvester with a twenty-feet cutter.

'They'll never find a machine that can plant sprouts,' Alice assured Alistair.

She was wrong and their last slight hold on the old ways snapped. Contract engineers in their Diagnostic Facility Vehicle usurped Alistair's ability to fix things. Was it kindness to keep him on the books for those last two years, to pay him to drift around the farm and fields looking for something to do? In the end, he gave up and accepted a small redundancy cheque and a house in the Poplace scheme at Hecklescar provided by Borders Council. He was sixty-two.

Alistair did not take to retirement. He was a practical man, not one to sit and read or contemplate at leisure the great uncertainties of life. He would have been restless in a bungalow even though it had a front garden for flowers and a patch for vegetables round the back. They were given a doll's house in a terrace of doll's houses. The rooms: living/ dining, bedroom, kitchen, bathroom, were (what is the term?) compact. Outside, at the front, lay a patch of tired grass surrounded by a low broad-slatted brown fence. (In the many clauses of the tenant's agreement you will find one that informs you that this patch of grass is not be cultivated. Its function is architectural not agricultural. It is there to make the place look neat, not to feed the inhabitants)

There is a yard round the back, fenced from the other houses and from the back lane by a high wooden fence, dark stained. The yard is for drying clothes and a whirly clothes dryer is provided with the tenancy. There is also a patch of soil that could be persuaded to grow a few potatoes, a lettuce or two and perhaps a couple of dahlias or, as in most of the back yards, weeds.

These houses, no doubt, suit most people who want a place to sleep, eat and watch the telly. But Alistair hated his house. He contrived to make something of the handkerchief plot and grew a few vegetables. He had brought Dahlia roots from Fairnieside and he put them in pots but they too, did not like confinement. They grew, they flowered, but they never produced the blooms that had blessed the cottage garden up on the hill and won 'best in show' at Beanston.

Alice even persuaded him to invest his redundancy money in a tiny greenhouse, and for a couple of years, he produced a reasonable crop of tomatoes and courgettes. But it was all too small; he was playing at it, and he despised it. He felt shrivelled. In those early years the Lifeboat Committee persuaded him to make miniature lobster creels to be sold in the fish shop down the pier, but soon his output stripped demand and Dorothy the secretary suggested that he ease up a little. He then took to roaming the roads with Jess, the collie that had accompanied him in his life at Fairnieside, walking three or four miles morning and afternoon. But soon, what he saw in the ravished fields and butchered hedges sickened him and he gave up. He became irritable and frequently resorted to the cans he bought from the Co-op. The dog grew fat and unfit through rich feeding and lack of exercise.

Alice sympathised with him, lectured him, bullied him, dieted him, and in bed at night, in the old bed brought from Fairnieside, the bed they had saved up to buy at Fairbairns in Berwick when they first married; the bed which had given birth to Mary and David, and which now filled the tiny bedroom, in that same bed she now attempted to console him with her love. At first, he went along with it and that gave her some comfort but then he drew away and that made her feel cheap. His life and hers were wasting away. If you would feel what they felt, try living in your wardrobe for a week.

Then one day, quite suddenly she decided that it could not go on, that she must find a way out. She had come home and found him half-drunk, staring at his hands with tears in his eyes.

'Look at them, hen, look at them,' he blurted out, 'bloody white, bloody soft, bloody useless.'

She said nothing but took his hands in hers and held them up. They were neither white, nor soft, nor, she knew, useless. These were hands that had wrung utility from wood and metal, that had restored the ticking of a clock and the throb of an engine, that had lifted bale after bale to the top of the stack and wrestled bullocks to the ground; hands that had coaxed new life from dull tubers, that had wrung order, beauty and abundance from a wilderness, that had gently welcomed a new lamb from its dam's womb into a cold world; that had once, for entertainment of the bairn, bent the poker by the fireside; hands that had trembled with grief as they cradled their dead little girl; hands that had embraced and comforted her; hands she knew and loved. Something must be done.

Would you believe it was Olivia, Hercules' wife, that came to her aid?

It is true! Alice, once she had sorted the house in Poplace, found it almost as suffocating as her husband. (I would like to tell you what you do when you 'sort a house', but I have never been able to understand it. What I do know is that women of Alice's generation seemed to be either doing it or about to do it most of the time.) Without her work on the farm she found the days long and had decided that she could do a little cleaning to supplement the family income. (Alice would never admit that she found life hard. Nothing was hard after those searing months looking after little Mary.) She let it be known at the WRI that she could do with a little cleaning job to supplement the family income and provide a treat now and again for the grandbairn.

As it happened, just at that time Olivia had crossed MaggieB, her cleaning lady, once too often and MaggieB had walked out. Alice was recruited to do two mornings a week, and, if Olivia was entertaining, a Friday evening to wash the dishes and tidy up the kitchen.

Alice had been with Olivia for three years and living at Poplace for five when Hercules complained to Olivia that the house at Latchlaw was falling into disrepair and the wilderness around it was attracting the attention of the local authority. Olivia happened to mention it to Alice, and Alice instantly saw a way out for Alistair.

Five years after they had been confined to Poplace, they escaped to Latchly. On the day that Hercules stood on the golf course and contemplated *his* escape, Alistair and Alice had been happily settled at Latchly for seven years. So happily indeed, that Alice had given up working part-time for Olivia and now works full-time for Latchly and Alistair.

CHAPTER SIX

The days are long at the end of June and Hercules did not arrive home until well after his seven o'clock estimate. He found Olivia entertaining a couple of friends in the conservatory. She told him that he would find Sally in the gazebo in the back garden.

He greeted his daughter with a peck on the cheek and a cheerful, stock apology.

'Sorry I'm late. Things to do, people to see. How are you?'

Sally remained standing, but he settled himself into one of the wickerwork chairs and smiled up at her.

'Sit down, Sally, it's a nice night, warm too.'

Sally was in no mood for pleasantries. What she had to say lay well outside her emotional vocabulary. Words and phrases had simmered in her mind for days now but still had not settled into any sentence worth speaking. Her father's stock phrases, however, gave her an inroad.

'People to see?' she snapped, 'like at The Dome. In George Street. Last Friday night. People like that?'

This fusillade hit home instantly. He recognised the place, the time, the lady at once, but what are the honest questions of youth against the deceits of a seasoned cynic like Hercules?

'The Dome, last Friday?' he mused calmly. 'Was I at the Dome last Friday? Yes, I believe I was.'

'And who were you with?' demanded Sally.

'Why, Elvira of course. You've met Elvira, I think.'

'No, I have not met Elvira, and I don't know who she is. Who is she?'

Hercules surveyed Sally with a studied smile on his lips.

'Sally', he started calmly, 'I am not prepared to be interrogated. Nor have my movements and who I am with questioned by anyone. But I will tell you, Sally, because you are my daughter. I would not do that for anyone else. Elvira is a business colleague.' His voice rose to a snarl, 'and I am offended that you are insinuating that she is other than that.'

'I wasn't insinuating....'

Hercules stood up and glowered at her so intensely that she flinched.

'Of course, you were! What else could you mean? I can read you like a book, Sally. And I will tell you where all this is coming from. It's from that bitch up the hill. Watch her, my child, she will poison your mind.'

Sally made to protest, but her father gave her no opportunity. He strode out of the gazebo into the house.

As he walked those few yards, any doubt that he might have had about his decision to quit Hecklescar, house and home evaporated.

Sally, on the other hand, sat down and cried.

Who, we need to ask, is 'the bitch up the hill'?

We can do better than ask. We can meet her, accompanied by Olivia, for the bitch is Olivia's mother, Connie.

The meeting takes place on Monday, the morning after Sally's confrontation of her father. Sally has returned to her flat in Edinburgh feeling wretched. This morning she will return to Queen Margaret's College to continue to learn about nursing, but her studies will not cheer her for she does not like listening to lectures, reading up manuals or dissecting scenarios. She wants to look after people and, if she can, nurse them back to health. However, she will be prevented from doing so until she has a bit of paper in a scroll and a picture of her in her hood on graduation day. That she continues to slog on in pursuit of a useful life is down largely to the few weeks that she has spent at the Royal Infirmary, the Western and the Borders General Hospital in the company of those who know how it is done. Then, of course, there is Malcolm, whom, I'm afraid, you will not meet again in these pages. Let me assure you that he is a pleasant, easy-going young man she met at college. He is studying Physiotherapy, stacks shelves in Morrisons when he is not at college, avoids physical exertion if he can, and thinks the world of Sally.

For the moment, however, we need to meet the bitch.

Olivia does not often visit her mother. She sometimes goes months without popping into the council flat that shelters Connie up at Killies Court. Do not blame Olivia that her mother now finds herself at the mercy of public services. Olivia would have preferred that she stayed in the nice little bungalow in Upper Seafield, but Connie wanted out of the place after her husband died and found her own accommodation in the town. She pays full whack for her tenancy, refuses any financial help from Olivia and Hercules and rejects any suggestion that she cannot afford to live well.

Olivia has only come this morning because she has got wind of the flare up between Sally and Hercules and suspects, like Hercules, that Connie is fanning the flames.

'Has Sally been here in the last few days?' is Olivia's sighting shot.

'Yes, she came last weekend and said she wanted to see her father.'

'Did she say why?'

'Do you not know?'

'No.'

'Then she didn't tell you?'

'No.'

'Did you not ask?'

'Of course, I asked, but she wouldn't tell me. She said she wanted to see her father. She saw him last night.'

'I know.'

'So, she was here?'

'Is that a crime?'

'No, of course not. But did she tell you what she wanted with Harold?'

'She might have.'

'Did she?'

'What passes between me and Sally stays between me and Sally.'

'Would you please stop interfering.'

'Is it interfering to listen to a troubled young girl about something she cannot tell her mother? I always thought that that's what grannies were for.'

'Sally upset Harold.'

'That is not difficult. He is easily upset. I don't know how you put up with him – or why.'

Olivia did not respond. She never did when Connie attacked Harold. She simply stared straight ahead and waited for her mother to change the subject. Change it Connie did, dramatically.

'Did you know that Peter Munro is thinking of coming back to Hecklescar?'

Olivia swallowed.

'Is he? Where did you hear that?'

'From Ina.'

'Ina, Jakey's wife?'

'Yes, Ina.'

'She didn't mention it to me.'

'She wouldn't think you were interested.'

Olivia said nothing for a few moments. Then asked,

'How does Ina know what Peter Munro is doing. He's down south, isn't he?'

'He is. But apparently, he wrote to Cockburn Heath asking him to look out a property that might suit him here. Ina cleans there.'

'She gets around.'

'She has too; if her husband's boss would pay him what he is worth, she might not have to get around so much.'

Olivia snorted.

'If her husband didn't line his pockets at the expense of his boss, perhaps his boss could afford to pay him more.'

'Jakey's a good man, Harold would do badly without him.'

She broke off to haul Olivia back to the subject in hand.

'I'm surprised Harold doesn't know about Peter Munro. Everybody else in the town seems to know.'

'I'll ask him. Is Peter ... Munro coming back to stay?'

Connie noted that her daughter hesitated after the 'Peter', as if she needed to cushion herself against the name, the bare name, Peter.

'Looks like it. I thought you'd be interested.'

'Why would you think I should be interested?'

'Because I'm your mother. I know you. Do you think I have forgotten?'

If this exchange has not convinced you that Connie is a bitch, I am relieved. She is sour certainly, she may not like Hercules, she may even take some pleasure in needling her daughter, but before we stick labels on her we ought to consider who she is, what she has done, and what kind of hand life has dealt her. Connie has not had it easy.

For a start, she was not born and brought up in Hecklescar, and that, in this place, is a disadvantage. The grapevine winds round you rather than through you; you cannot avoid it or divert it; you must simply watch it pass by – or strangle you. If you compound your fault by growing your own, you will find yourself on your own, or worse, cultivated by equally isolated people who reckon to despise the gossip and tittle-tattle of the place. Connie, when she first came to the town, had made the mistake of joining such a group.

She had come as the Town Clerk's wife, in the days when towns had town clerks. Her husband, Fordyce, had been a solicitor in Edinburgh. One day he came home and announced that he had had enough of the chancers he worked for and the cynics he worked with. He was grasping the opportunity to break away from it all into a new career among honest fisherfolk by the seaside. That is what he told his wife of seven years, and she believed him. With their two children they moved lock, stock and barrel from Morningside to the said bungalow in Upper Seafield.

It was only after he was re-organised out of the Town Clerk's chair years later that the truth came out about his change of career. He had been eased out of his Edinburgh billet. He had led Cunningham, Goodwin & Scott into litigation once too often and they had asked him to move on. In his five years as Town Clerk of Hecklescar he did not do much better and would have done a lot worse had he not enjoyed the protection of Mrs. Somerville. Mrs. Somerville kept Cockburn Heath the Hecklescar solicitor out of trouble on Mondays, Wednesdays and Fridays, and Fordyce, the Town Clerk, on Tuesdays and Thursdays.

Nevertheless, his blunders mounted. He escaped a second sacking, however, by the extensive re-organisation of Scottish Local Authorities in 1975. This not only saved his bacon but also gave him fat to live on and a juicy lump sum on which to gorge. He was just over 50, and should have been able to provide for himself, his wife and family comfortably for many years. But that which had infected him in law and local administration plagued his retirement too.

The truth is that, mentally and temperamentally, he was not cut out for any work that demanded rationality, organisation and management. His mother was daughter of one of the founders of Fortingall, the department store on Princes Street, and his father a professor at the University. They could not accept that their little Fordyce lacked brainpower, so hired tutors to stuff enough knowledge into him to squeeze him into Loretto's, Edinburgh's prestigious school for the sons of those who could afford to pay the fees. His mother read Scott and Shakespeare to him, trailed him through art galleries and museums, took him along to orchestral concerts and the theatre and introduced him to respectable company. How he struggled through law school remains a mystery, but he came out of the academic wringer clutching a law degree and was shoehorned into a placement in Cunningham, Goodwin & Scott, the firm that handled Fortingall's legalities.

Fordyce thus acquired all the attributes of a civilised professional without any of the substance. I blame his parents and feel sorry for him. But I feel more pity for Connie, a clever, cultured woman, who deceived by appearances, found herself married with two children before she realised her mistake.

Fordyce's sophistication fed his weak will. He gambled;

horses mainly. When working he had little time for such a diversion, but once released from office by retirement, and from restraint by his lump sum, he sought out race meetings and attended them dressed as a country gentleman in regulation tweed jacket, cap, yellow tie and shooting stick.

He was not wicked. He did not intend to run through the family finances on the racecourse. But how could such a man with such a background, dressed in such clothes, not seek to impress his companions? He became a benefactor of bookies at Musselburgh, Perth, Newcastle and further afield.

Did Connie object to his absences? Not a lot; she preferred to be on her own. Although he behaved as a good husband and good father when at home; although he always asked permission to go; although he always brought her and the children a little present; although in many ways he acted as a thoughtful and assiduous partner, she despised him for his stupidity and posturing – and reviled herself for doing so. She also despised her callow acceptance of the impossibility of real happiness with him and the day-to-day pretence of being his wife and lover. She was forty-one, ten years younger than her husband. She had two children, Guy, 11, and Olivia, 9. How many more years of this could she stand?

Twelve is the answer, until she succumbed to ovarian cancer. Three weeks after she divulged the diagnosis to her husband, the day before she entered hospital for a hysterectomy and removal of diseased ovaries, she came home to find that Fordyce had gone. He had left a note.

The note was courteous, thoughtful and well-written; an honest note. He wrote that he was no good at tackling that sort of thing and would become a liability. The children were old enough to take care of her, and her mother could be called on, he was sure, so she would be alright. He did not, however, divulge that he had drained what little wealth they had accumulated and would take his pension with him wherever he was going.

I would like to say that that she heard no more of him. Indeed, after a short burst of resentment and some loss of face, she hoped that that might be the case. It was not to be. He re-entered her life as a seriously sick man six years later. Dying of bowel cancer, he said he couldn't face it on his own. The last woman who had accommodated him in health did not want to stay with him in sickness. The friends who had enjoyed his companionship in the happy days, no longer found his company congenial. His father was dead and his mother senile so he had come home.

Did she take him in? Yes. Why? Out of love? Of course not. Wifely, although detached wifely, obligation? A little. Guilt? Quite a bit. What had she to be guilty about? Peter Munro.

CHAPTER SEVEN

We ought to meet Peter Munro before you misjudge the man. The place to find him is a flat - no, an apartment, in Burleigh Square, in that part of Eastbourne that despises day trippers and caters for the quiet and elegant tastes of people who can afford such extravagance.

But we have left it too late. He has gone. This morning when Mrs. Flaherty arrived to clean his apartment, she found two envelopes on the book case, one for her, one addressed to a Mrs. Rostowski.

Mrs. Flaherty read hers:

'Bridie,

I am going away for a while and would be grateful if you would keep an eye on the apartment while I am away.

. Please give this note to Mrs. Rostowski when she comes. Give it only to Mrs. Rostowski. Mrs. Rostowski is a friend. I think you have met her, but make sure it is Mrs. Rostowski. Ask her for her identity. Please do not give the letter to anyone else.

Thank you

Peter Munro

'Thought it would come to this,' muttered Mrs. Flaherty, then busied herself in the flat until Mrs. Rostowski arrived.

'Thought it would come to this,' she said to Mrs. Rostowski as Mrs. Rostowski opened the letter.

Mrs. Rostowski did not reply but gave her attention to the letter. Mrs. Flaherty switched off the vacuum cleaner and studied the top of Mrs. Rostowski's head as she read. The letter ran to two pages. As Mrs. Rostowski turned to the second sheet, Mrs. Flaherty repeated.

'Thought it would come to this.'

Mrs. Rostowski ignored her and carried on reading.

Mrs. Flaherty watched her until she had finished.

'Well,' she enquired, 'what now?'

'Why did you think it would come to this?' asked Mrs. Rostowski.

'Depressed, not going out, brooding, lying in bed, switched all the lights off and listened to that music he likes. Well I think he liked it. Gloomy it was; never cheered him up; made him worse, I would say.'

'How long has he been like that?'

'You should know; you're his social worker.'

'I'm not a social worker. I'm a friend, just a friend.'

'Thought you were a social worker.'

'No, I am not a social worker. What I am is not important. When did this start, this ....?'

'Thought you were something official. He thought you were something official. Well that's what it sounded like to me, like a social worker. You came after he came out of hospital. You weren't his friend before that. He had no friends before that, as far as I could tell, not round here anyway. But then I only come on Tuesday afternoon and Friday morning.'

'How long have you been doing that?'

'Year and a bit. Started in the March. The agency sent

me. But he pays me now. A private arrangement. If you're not a social worker, are you from an agency?'

'No, I keep telling you, I'm a friend.'

'Know that, but you're something else, from the hospital or something.'

Mrs. Rostowski gave in.

'My official title is Health and Well-being Counsellor. But I regard myself as his friend.'

'Haven't seen you here before.'

'Mr. Munro and I normally meet elsewhere.'

'Why?'

'Why what?'

'Why didn't he want you here?'

'What makes you think he didn't want me here?'

'Never seen you before, and he never mentioned you were coming, and never any cups or anything. So, trying to keep it quiet, you and him.'

Mrs. Rostowski smiled.

'Ah, you think that we were up to more than counselling?'

'Not much to look at but he's worth a million or two. Often wondered that he was alone. I mean, nowadays nobody is alone that doesn't want to be. You can always find another one.'

'What about yourself?' asked Mrs. Rostowski smiling. 'Could you not have accommodated him?'

Mrs. Flaherty bridled, 'Me? Married with three children. Devoted to my husband - and good Catholic who knows what tarts are and what promises mean.'

'I am a Catholic too,' replied Mrs. Rostowski, 'and not a tart.'

Mrs. Flaherty grasped the handle of the Dyson but made no attempt to start it. Instead she went back to her previous pursuit.

'Why did you come today? If he didn't want you here, why today?

'He left me a message, asking me to come.'

'When's he coming back?'

'Not soon, he says he will be away for a while.'

'Thought it! Taken his clothes and stuff. Gone on holiday?'

'No, I wouldn't say that.'

'About his business, then?'

'Could be, but he doesn't say.'

'Where's he gone? Not abroad; his passport's still in the desk. He has family; could have gone to be with them. Or Scotland; he's from up there; that's where he'll be.'

'No; at least I think not. I don't know; he doesn't say.'

Mrs. Flaherty, frustrated by this lack of information, changed the subject.

'Who pays you – the council?'

'No, Peter does.'

'What about me? Anything in there about paying me?'

'Yes, he has asked me to make sure you are paid each week, but I could pay you monthly if that would be better?'

'Monthly? How long is he going to be away?'

'He doesn't say.'

'What does he say?'

'All I can tell you is that he says he is going to settle it.'

"Settle it'; what does that mean?'

'I don't know, and I don't need to know. I think it means

he wants to put things right.'

'With his missus, or ex-missus. Still married to her, is he?'

Mrs. Rostowski brought the interrogation to an end.

'I don't know and I'm afraid if I did, I wouldn't be able to tell you. What he says to me has to remain confidential.'

'Monthly's no use. I need paid once a week. If I waited a month the kids'd starve.'

'Then I'll come each week. What day would suit you best?'

'Friday morning.'

'Friday morning it is then.'

'Those letters. That's what's he's away to sort out. Knew it would come to this.'

'What letters?'

'Letters from her.'

'Ah, you know about those?'

'How not? Could tell as soon as I took the door that he'd got another one. Upset him for days. Got one last Thursday.'

'What makes you think the letters were from his wife?'

'Obvious. Signed the back: Mrs. Munro, or what was it? Dilys Munro. Dilys, that was it. Queer name, Dylis, doesn't get anywhere does it? Sort of fades away? Dylis. How did he come to get hitched to a Dylis? A nice man – and well-off; could have had a fair choice, so why pick a Dylis?'

'Because he liked her, perhaps.' replied Mrs. Rostowski gently.

Mrs. Flaherty considered this reply for a moment then dismissed it.

'Anyway, that's what she wrote on the back of the en-velope: Dilys Munro. A string of them: one a day, or every Friday. Then nothing for months, then start again. Whenever it came over her'.

'When what came over her?'

'Whatever. Don't know but something came over her - sending letters day after day. Hated him. Don't know what he'd done, but she hated him.'

'What on earth makes you think that?'

'On the back: 'I hate you' or 'pig' and worse, in thick red letters printed. Once it said 'I love you'. In green. But only once. If she wrote 'pig' on the outside, makes you wonder what was inside, eh?'

Mrs. Flaherty didn't expect an answer. She floated it in the off-chance Mrs. Rostowski might grab it and tell what she knew of Mrs. Munro.

'Yes,' replied Mrs. Rostowski, and in spite of Mrs. Flaherty's wheedling fell silent. Mrs. Rostowski knew what was in the letters, had read many of them - and they had chilled her, but she said nothing more. Mrs. Flaherty would have to go on guessing.

Go on she would. She screwed up her face and tightened her grip on the vacuum handle.

'That's where he's gone. Had enough. Gone to sort her out.'

'Perhaps,' muttered Mrs. Rostowski.

Mrs. Flaherty, satisfied that she had uncovered the truth at last, or at least enough of the truth to satisfy her, started up the Dyson, and was waltzing it round the room as Mrs. Rostowski left.

CHAPTER EIGHT

A t three in the morning, three weeks after we met Hercules on the golf course, just as the sun is clambering up over the cliffs at Hawk's Ness to start another day shift, Grubs from Corpach drives his 44ton truck along the quay at Hecklescar and stops outside the fishyard of Anthony Douglas & Son. He blasts a reveille on his horn to wake up Jakey. Grubs is well behind his appointed time and suspects that Jakey, waiting for him for over an hour now, is sitting dosing at his desk in the office up the stair at the back of the yard.

In any other organisation Jakey would have an office with '*Manager*' on the door. That could well be the designation on his contract of employment, stored in one of the filing cabinets in the office run by Fiona, Hercules secretary. Jakey has a desk in the outer office, and a chair, but is allowed to use them only if he takes off his plastic apron and boots and doesn't smell overmuch of fish. After he left, Fiona always sprayed the room with air freshener.

Whatever his official title, to his fellow employees, to the fishermen who deal with him, to the lorry drivers who deliver to him, to Angela and the girls that gut the fish and scrape out the carapaces, to the packers and processors, to Nudge, Wullie, Elaine, Eddie and Jennifer who ferry the produce far and wide he is known simply as Jakey. He has no need of implied authority for they all do what he wants them to do without the threats, bribes and deceits that pass for management in many organisations.

Ask Hercules why this is the case and he will cite culture, values and informed man management. Ask Jakey and he will say, provided they are not listening, that they are a bloody good bunch of workers. Ask them and they will state that Jakey is a bastard, but a bloody fair one - asks them what to do, doesn't tell them, and gives them time off when they need to go to the doctors or pick up the bairns.

(To be strictly accurate I must exempt Nudge from the above statement. Nudge attends the Free Baptists who frown on foul language. But he shares the sentiment. He knows that Jakey will not ask him to drive before midnight on The Lord's Day. A minute past and Nudge is available – and willing to go anywhere for Jakey and Anthony Douglas & Son. Why he is called Nudge is lost in the confusion of his teenage years, the most likely explanation being that he kept repeating the word when learning to drive - something to do with the gear stick.)

Having roused Jakey, Grubs drives to the end of the quay, turns and makes his way back to the yard, where Jakey is now standing to greet him. Grubs levers himself stiffly from the cab.

'Sheep on the road again?' gibes Jakey.

Grubs smiles.

'Can I try you with a jack-knifed lorry on Rannoch Moor?'

'It'll have to do. Let's get them inside.'

They swing back the doors of the trailer to reveal two rows of covered tanks. Each tank is filled with cold water; in the water are large boxes; inside the boxes in equally cold water are prawns caught in creels off Mallaig, away beyond Fort William late last night. The boxes are sectioned into rectangular tubes. In each tube there throbs a living prawn; tail, claws and all.

Jakey and Grubs with the aid of a fork-lift truck transfer the prawns to the processing yards. It takes just under half an hour. They then retreat to the little mess room to share a pot of tea and a chocolate biscuit.

As they drink, Grubs has a question for Jakey, a question that has been bothering Jakey himself for the past week or two.

'What's Hercules up to, then?'

'What do you mean?'

'He's selling the business.'

'Which business? Not this one?'

'Aye, this one. Has he no' told you?'

'No, and if it was up for sale, we would know. Who told you it was up for sale?'

'Donald, ye ken, The Clansman. He's on the Mallaig FC committee. He told me that Hercules had said that he was thinking of selling the business and would the Co-op think of taking it over.'

'When was this? '

'Last week sometime. He told me yesterday. A' body in Mallaig kens.'

'Naw,' asserted Jakey, 'Naw, naw, I ken about that. He's thinking of unloading the Mallaig end of the business; talkin' about it; about putting it into a shell - that's what he calls it, a shell company; a different name with a new plate under all the others on the door jamb. It has to do with corporation tax. He's up to all that sort of financial jiggery-pokery. Ye ken what he's like; aye shiftin' the chairs.'

'Why then would he ask dodgy Donald if the Co-op was interested? That doesn't sound like what ye're on about. Then there's the men from the Broch; they're sniffing around.'

'From Fraserburgh, whae? The Watts?'

'The very men. I saw one of their trucks just last week, loading from the Silver Way.'

'Loading what, prawns?'

'Naw, white fish, but they're trawlin'. It'll be prawns next.'

'They couldn't match us, could they? There's not the volume. Hercules has it sown up, I think you'll find.'

'So why does he want to sell up.'

Jakey laughed.

'Ye're awfy persistent. He's no selling up. It's rumours. We would know if he was - and we don't. Smoke and mirrors; gossip, that's all. Hercules kens what he's doin''

'I hope ye're right. It doesn't matter to me. I'll tak the truck anywhere the Co-op says – even to the Broch, so long as they pay me.'

'Ye're sittin' there drinking my tea and sayin' that?'

'Maybe they'll give me something stronger in Fraserburgh – and a better class of biscuit.'

'I wouldn't reckon on it. They're gey mean up on the Moray Firth; noted for it. Ye'd need to buy a thermos and a packet of digestives.'

Such back-handed pleasantries brought the exchange to an end.

(I should explain that Mallaig FC is not a football club but the Fishermen's Co-operative, an organisation launched by fishermen on the tide of socialism and optimism that swept in after the second world war. The fishermen hoped thus to cut out the buccaneers who seemed to make more money selling the fish than they, the fishermen, made catching them. Over the years, however, the Mallaig FC, like other co-operatives had floundered in the crosscurrents of declining fish stocks, EU regulations and the incompetence of their management committee. The tide had shifted back to buccaneers like Old Nero. and Anthony, who did not have to satisfy the other eleven on the committee before a decision could be made.)

Grubs drove the lorry to the end of the quay, parked it and settled down in his bunk for four hours' sleep. When he wakes, he will breakfast on a mug of runny porridge eaten cold. He doesn't have to eat it cold; Angela in the yard would heat it up for him, but he likes it cold, he says, with a banana sliced into it. After the porridge he will bite into a bacon roll, a cold bacon roll, washed down by a swig or two from his bottle of Irn-bru. But he will leave a little of the roll with a little of the cold bacon inside to feed to the seals in the harbour. He reckons that as seals regularly feed on podlies they will not object to eating meat. No need then to buy fish at £2 a time from the van to throw to the beasts. They will pop up just as readily for bacon.

At eight he will set out for Corpach, reaching there about midday. He will park the truck, go home for his lunch with his wife, then be ready to pick up a fresh load of prawns from the Mallaig boats as they land them after the sun has gone to bed for the night. He will repeat this on four days a week and sometimes on a Sunday.

While Grubs is settling down in his van, Jakey locks up the yard and goes home to Ina, a cup of tea and a snooze in the chair. He will report to the yard at 6.30 to despatch vans up into the Borders and down into North Northumberland to deliver fish to hotels, shops, cafes and paying customers at their doors. He will also commission Nudge to drive a 44-tonner to Spain with a trailer load of ice-filled polythene containers of still living langoustines.

But he will not inform any of these fellow-workers of his doubts about Dodgy Donald and the Mallaig Fisherman's

Co-op, or the dealings of the Watts of Fraserburgh with the Silver Way. He does, however, mention it to his wife Ina, and Ina will make it her business to find out what Olivia knows of her husband's manoeuvres. She's due there tomorrow for cleaning duties.

CHAPTER NINE

Y ou'll get nowhere,' said Janet when Duncan told her that to-day was the day he was going to see Hercules about letting him have the steading at Latchly for his joinery venture. He would also ask to withdraw his £10,000 from Golden Opportunities. He had an appointment he said: at the house, at half-past ten.

'Count your fingers after you've shaken hands,' sniped his wife.

'Oh, that's right, Janet, give me support, back me up!' Duncan snapped back.

Janet made no reply but, by way of encouragement, gave him a peck on the cheek as he left the house. He was back in ten minutes. He found Janet at the sink in the kitchen. He sat down behind her at the kitchen table.

'Well, that was quick,' said Janet, without turning round. 'What did he say'

'He wasn't there.'

Still Janet didn't turn. She had her hands in a dish of water and they were moving about but, as far as Duncan could see (and he was not brave enough to look), she wasn't actually washing anything; certainly, nothing emerged from the water. This was an ominous sign. He must expect interrogation.

He stood up, plucked the tea towel from the oven handle and moved beside Janet to dry the non-existent dishes

Janet wasn't washing. Janet drove on.

'He wasn't there!'

'Ina answered the door. She didn't think he was in the house but she took me into the room and went to look for him. She couldn't find him and couldn't find Olivia. They were both out.'

'I thought you said you had an appointment.'

'I did.'

'When for?'

'To-day.'

'You didn't tell me about it. When did you make it?'

'On Friday.'

'This past Friday?'

'Yes'

'You never said anything.'

The fact that Janet attended the dish and not him, and that he had the tea towel in his hands somehow emboldened him.

'I don't have to. I can arrange to see people on my own surely,' he said firmly but, he would claim, gently. 'I knew you'd go on about it. I told you this morning and look what happened.'

'You should have put it in the diary. Suppose somebody had rung up about a job and I'd told them you'd go and see them this morning, then you are not available, because you've flown off to see his majesty. That would look as if we didn't know what we were doing.'

'But it didn't, did it? Nobody rang up, did they?'

'Did you tell Ina about what you'd come for?'

At last he saw where Janet was headed.

'No, I did not.'

'Did she ask?

'Yes, but ... '

At last Janet pulled her hands out of the water and in one deft movement tipped the dish and poured the water down the plughole. She swept the tea towel from his hands, and as she vigorously dried her hands exclaimed,

'I knew it! She's a shovel looking for muck. You didn't say why you wanted to see Hercules?

'No ... '

'Because, if you did it'd be all around the town before dinnertime. What did you say?'

'Just that I had an appointment.'

'She'd think that was funny.'

Duncan, looking for a bolthole, retreated to his chair.

'She'd think I was chasing up the quote for the summer house.'

'That was months ago. After all your work you never heard anymore from him. At least I take it you didn't hear.'

Duncan ignored this thrust. She kept track of the quotes. She knew he had not heard.

'You shouldn't have got dressed up. That was the mistake. You should have gone in your overall. See what happens when you don't tell me about your appointments.'

'But nothing has happened.'

'Precisely. You didn't tie him down. Didn't remind him of the time and date. It would be just 'call round' sometime. Not fixed, nailed down. You have to nail people like that down. Send them a confirmation. You know the man. What were you thinking about?'

This little lecture arises from Janet's stint as secretary to the boss of Hutchinson's the builders' merchants in

Washington, the sprawling new town south of Newcastle. Janet lived there until she decided she'd much rather live in Hecklescar. This came after a dubious outing to the town over thirty years ago.

She was eighteen. One day her boss, Mr. Hutchinson, invited her to join him on a trip through Northumberland and the Borders to 'to meet the customers you write to and talk to on the phone. Oh, and by the way, call me Gus.' In retrospect she hated everything about the trip: the two-seater car, the lunch, the smirks of 'the customers' who wondered what she had come for; the proposition from 'Gus' to stay over somewhere seeing it was late; the long, dark, silent ride back home; the sleazy remarks of the men in the yard and the girls in the office; the shattered trust between her and her boss; the long uncomfortable weeks until she could find another job. Most searing of all, disgust at her own naivety.

In contrast and consolation Hecklescar metamorphosed into sort of Shangri-La: the beach, the cliffs, the little harbour with its bobbing boats, sleeping houses and gentle people strolling through quiet streets and stopping to chat to friends. Better, she thought, than the airless office, cluttered yard, frantic cars, concrete blocks, fractious shoppers and angry motorists she encountered every day.

Perhaps this rosy picture of Hecklescar would not have been so appealing had it not been for a diffident young apprentice she had met at Wood's. His name, he told her, was Duncan. When she had not heard from him before she left Hutchinson's she wrote to him c/o Woods, Builders. On October 22nd they will celebrate their Silver Wedding.

The accuracy of Janet's description of his arrangement with Hercules did nothing to sooth Duncan's irritation. It had been just that:

'Come to the house. What day would suit? Friday. That would be fine, morning's best.'

His immediate reaction to Janet's assault was to protest his human rights to do and say what he liked. He even loaded up the sentence to use: 'I don't have to answer to you for everything I do.'

Then he thought better of it. Their marriage is not built on the modern myth that the one partner ought not to crowd the other. It settled on a much more solid foundation. It is a co-operative; they must move together through life, hand in hand, shove by shove, each giving the other the benefit of their interference and unwanted advice. They hammer out decisions together, squabble over plans of action, fight over times and dates and possibilities, then face the world and its customers as a united front.

Duncan knew when he was cornered and opted for humility, albeit a rather stifled version of it.

'Don't think I don't appreciate it', he mumbled, with only enough conviction to persuade Janet he was sorry.

From the above interchange you may well have formed the view that Janet knows little or nothing about Duncan's plans to add Hector to his business and 'Joinery' to the side of his van. You could not be more wrong. Let me show you. One night, Duncan sat down with Beesknees and mapped out what he needs to fit out the steading at Latchlaw. Then Janet went to work, scouring the Internet for the best equipment at the best price. Then she laid it out and typed it up. It ran to four pages. Here is a summary:

Joinery Business: Start-up costs

Power tools: nail guns, battery screwdrivers, autofeed screwdrivers, circular saw, SOS drill, router and jigs: **£3082**

Hand tools: hammers, chisels, squares, levels, planers, sanders etc.: **£2200**

Workshop tools: table saw, radial arm saw, planer, mortice bench drill, grinder, chop/mitre saw stand: **£5524**

Opening stock of materials: *£1500*

Fitting out steading (materials): *£300*

Total (equipment and materials): *£12,606*

Additional costs:

Workshop: heating, lighting: *£2500*

Rent: *£2500*

Office expenses: *£500*

Total (costs): *£5500*

Grand Total: £18,106

Eighteen thousand pounds! A daunting amount, but Janet is no reluctant passenger. She will drive as hard as Duncan to see Latchlaw Steading fitted out and her daughter's man settled into his chosen vocation. Her concern is leverage. Seven or eight thousand she can scrape together without raiding the pension fund, but can see no way of laying hands on the rest except to retrieve the £10,000 Hercules filched from her husband when she was down looking after her mother before she died.

Why had Duncan done it? Why hadn't he talked it over with her? Duncan was too trusting. Look what happened with that house at Brisset. We never got our money back on that. That couple from down south took him for a soft touch. Well, they won't do it again so long as he's married to me.

That is what rankled - that Hercules had out-manoeuvred her. He is a snake. What possessed Duncan to put their hard-earned little pile into his greedy paws? (I know snakes don't have paws but when you're upset you don't worry about mixed metaphors.)

Now Duncan had tidied himself up to go cap in hand to beg for it back and the man had snubbed him. Made an appointment and didn't keep it. He's a rogue.

Janet thought the conversation was at an end. She had

made her point. Now she would take up the challenge and tie Hercules down to time and place.

Bur Duncan had more to tell.

'Do you not want to know what else Ina had to say?'

'I might have guessed. What was it?'

'She said that Hercules is selling up.'

'Selling up! What? The money fund bit; how can he sell that?'

'No, not that - the fish business.'

'What? You mean the yard and lorries and all that. You can't be serious!'

'It's not me. That's what she said: he's selling the fish business.'

'Where had she got that?'

'From Jakey. He'd been speaking to a driver from Mallaig this morning and he had told Jakey that the Mallaig Fishermen's Co-op are buying him out.'

Janet did not reply immediately. She stared at Duncan for a few minutes then turned, filled the kettle and switched it on. When it had boiled, she made two cups of coffee, then dived into a tin to pull out one chocolate biscuit, which she laid on a plate and set it down on the table. The she took up one of the cups and pushed the plate with the biscuit across to Duncan.

'I'm not having one,' she said.

Duncan did not need to ask why the sole biscuit was for him. He knew that whenever anyone overweight came into the conversation, Janet went on a diet.

This would be understandable if Janet were fat. But she is small and under nine stone; Ina is large and well over sixteen. What turns down the biscuit is fear of what might be rather than dissatisfaction with what is. Janet had seen many a woman her size and her age reduced or, should we say expanded, to the shape of a badly built snowman. She didn't want to move in that direction.

The purpose of the coffee and the biscuit was to encourage Duncan to tell more of what he knew about Hercules' plan to sell up – if that was what he intended. But Duncan didn't know any more. He hadn't asked Ina what else she knew and why she knew it. Had she mentioned it to Hercules, in which case what did he say? Or Olivia, what was she saying about it? But no, Duncan had just listened, and even now seemed more interested in the biscuit than the fish business. Surely there was more to it than what Ina had told him.

Any thoughts Janet had of digging further were interrupted by the arrival of her father-in-law, Alistair. A rap at the back door announced his arrival, followed by his face peering round the half-opened door.

'To what do we owe this honour?' asked Janet pleasantly, 'We're having coffee. Will you have a cup?'

Alistair stepped over the threshold and taking off his cap held it in front of him.

'Well. . .'

'No, you want tea?'

'Tea, please, if that's alright.'

Janet turned to the worktop to make the tea. Duncan stood up to let his father sit down. Alistair moved the chair a little way from the table and, still grasping his cap, sat down.

Duncan was surprised to see his father. Normally the only time they saw him was at Latchly and then only fleetingly as he was called in from the garden by Alice to welcome his visitors. If you could have persuaded Alistair to speak his mind (and that would not be easy), he would readily admit that he prefers ewes, dogs, or even vegetables, to humans. Certainly, he would rather be amongst his runner beans than visiting in Hecklescar, so both Duncan and Janet wondered what had brought him to them on this day.

'What brings you into town to-day, fither?'

Alistair looked at his son then glanced towards Janet.

'I've brought yer mither to the doctors. She had an appointment.'

'At the doctors?' asked Janet, putting down his tea in front of him. 'What's she at the doctors for?'

Alistair shot a glance at Duncan before replying.

'Something and nothing,' the old man replied.

'Is it her diabetes?' pressed Janet.

This information about his wife appeared to take Alistair by surprise.

'Is that what it is? She never said.'

'She did mention it,' said Janet, 'has it flared up again?'

'Aye, must have' said Alistair without conviction and picked up his tea.

Not long afterwards Alice opened the door and came in.

'Well, that's that,' she said.

'Cup of tea?' asked Janet.

Alice glanced at her husband and turned down the offer.

'We'll need to go. I've got the dinner in the oven.'

'Ye're all right, Mam?' asked Duncan, 'Nothing wrong?'

Again, Alice glanced at Alistair.

'No, no, just the usual, the usual,' she smiled. 'More tests and more pills!'

'There's something wrong with your mother,' pronounced Janet after the couple had left. 'We need to find out what it is.'

CHAPTER TEN

When Ina misinformed Duncan about Hercules selling up, she knew no more than what we know already about the deal. If there is a deal, that is.

We were there to hear what Grubs said to Jakey, but we don't know what Dodgy Donald said to Grubs, and we don't know precisely what Dodgy Donald heard at the committee meeting. He had had a week to process the dry words, ironing out any wrinkles of doubt and generally fluffing them up to make a better story of it. We also don't know what Jakey reported to Ina. Nor who else heard what Grubs had to say.

We tend to take out of a conversation what we want from it. What truth there is in Grubs' story about the Mallaig Fishermen taking over the Highland company, we have no way of discovering at present. We are, however, in good hands for Ina has an expertise, cultivated throughout her adult life, of uncovering the truth, or if not the truth, at least what *may* be the truth, in that it makes sense and confirms our suspicions.

As well as the veracity of the story, Ina has another interest: she wants to know how much Olivia knows about it. You don't go cleaning for a couple for several years without coming to your own conclusions about their connubiality. Although Ina didn't particularly like Olivia, she didn't mind having her as an employer. Olivia treated her fairly and paid her well. She didn't make a list of duties for Ina to carry out each day. (Mrs. Somerville at the Solicitors did that - and went around afterwards checking on the dusting and counting the pencils.) If Ina wanted time off, Olivia would come and go, and she had given her two months leave to visit her sister in Canada the year before last.

Ina had a pretty good idea of what held the partnership of Hercules and Olivia together, and suspected that sharing secrets was not part of the glue. She relished the prospect of telling Olivia something about her husband's activities that she did not know. She had learned over the years to read Olivia's reactions; she would be able to gauge if she knew anything about the Mallaig deal - if there was a deal.

Ina had come to work that morning and found Olivia not at home. This happened often, but Ina had a key and could let herself in and out of the house. Olivia sometimes left Ina a note but this morning she had not done so. Then Duncan Kerr had turned up. What did he want? Had it something to do with the business being sold? You can never tell with Duncan Kerr; the man's a big silence.

Ina's hours are ten to twelve but she dallied until half-past in the hope that Olivia might return. Then she contrived a return to the house at four, ostensibly to return a couple of towels she had been washing.

She hit the jackpot: Olivia was at home, in the lounge, on a chair in the lounge with a drink in her hand and a magazine in front of her. Ina spoke in to her as she passed with the towels. When she returned from the airing cupboard, she made to go into the lounge but heard, then saw, Hercules stepping into the house from the front door. He greeted Ina cheerfully,

'You still here?'

'No,' replied Ina, 'just popping in with the towels.'

Hercules joined Olivia in the lounge. What should Ina do? She must find out about the Mallaig deal. It would be something of a disgrace down the street if she did not know more than the general buzz. She must plump up what she knew this evening or it would be too late. She wanted to be able to laud it over Annie, Diedre, Gwen and the two Gracies tomorrow at their regular coffee gathering at McMaggie's in the High Street. They would crow over her if she had nothing to tell them. She decided to tackle both Olivia and Hercules. She entered the lounge. They both looked up.

'I thought you'd like to know that there's a story down the street that the fishyard's up for sale. I thought I'd tell you in case you hadn't heard.'

Although she addressed the question to Hercules, she kept Olivia in view. Olivia showed no sign of surprise.

'It's not!' replied Hercules bluntly, as if he had been expecting the question.

'And you can tell that to your friends,' put in Olivia mildly without putting down her drink or lifting her head.

Ina waited for one of them to say more, but neither did.

'See what I mean?' said Olivia to Hercules after Ina had left.

'I don't know where these things come from?'

'Don't you? I thought it came from something you said to someone in Mallaig. That's what's being said.'

'I told you before, I didn't say anything to anyone in Mallaig or anywhere else. There are no deals. I am not selling up. I don't know where Ina dredged it up, but she's mistaken. She's picked up something the wrong way.'

'What would that be?'

'What would *what* be?'

'The something that has been picked up the wrong way. What kind of something could it be?'

Throughout this exchange Olivia had not looked up. She wasn't reading the magazine in her hand, but she did not take her eyes off it – and Hercules had not looked at her.

Now he glanced in her direction then left his seat and went to the sideboard to pour himself a drink. He waved the bottle at Olivia to offer her a refill. She shook her head.

'Let me level with you, Olivia,' he said without taking his seat.

His use of her name alerted Olivia. He did not normally call her by her name; 'dear' or 'darling' was the common currency. He only called her Olivia when he was wanting something, or when he was up to something. What was this? What was coming?

'When I was at the Fish Producers Fed in Aberdeen last week, Hamish McBride from Mallaig was there. You know Hamish, I think we once had him for lunch.'

Olivia rebuffed this effort to fold her into the story. She had put down the magazine, but now took it up again and flicked over the pages. He recognised the signal and ploughed on.

'After the meeting he invited me for a drink in the bar. We were at the Grosvenor, you know, in Union Street. We've been there a couple of times; I think you'll remember. He had been asked by the West Highland Fisherman's Co-op to sound me out about them taking over their end of the business. They want to set up a processing plant in Mallaig.'

He stopped and glowered at Olivia. Her feigned lack of interest irritated him. But he knew the game: three pitches comprised the usual play. One more should do it.

'It's not a deal; it's not even a proposal, just an approach.'

'What did you reply?' asked Olivia, at last looking up from the page.

'My immediate reaction was to knock it back, squash it.

Then another thought struck me and I said I'd think about it.'

'And have you?'

'Have I what?'

'Thought about it?'

'Yes, and I can see merit in it. That end of the business is stretched. God knows what's going on up there, but it's not delivering the return it did – or should. It needs sorting out. They're almost certainly selling stuff on the side. The trucks from Fraserburgh are never away, and I'd like to know what they're doing with whom for what. But I really don't have the time –or the inclination– to go charging up there to sort it all out. There could be a strategic advantage in offloading it.'

'I do wish you'd stop trying to impress me with business jargon. It's tedious. What you are saying is that there is something in it for you.'

He sat down over against her and took her hand. She made no attempt to snatch it away it, but let it lie in his grasp as if it did not belong to her.

'Not for me, Olivia - for us,' he purred. 'There could be something in it for us.'

'Us', Olivia thought, 'there is no us! That flame went out many years ago. There is no hearth at which we warm ourselves. I am content with the central heating that allows us to live in the same house without any need for cosying up to a common fire.'

'What on earth can be in it for me?' she asked distantly, deliberately changing the pronoun. Her voice sounded flat and uninviting, but had no apparent effect on Hercules. It was as if he had not heard her, as if the 'us' did not signify me and you, but merely provided a convenient peg on which to hang his words.

'Latchlaw, that's what I mean. With what I get from Mallaig we can at last develop Latchlaw.'

Olivia finally looked at him.

'Latchlaw,' she said, 'you are wanting to build a house at Latchlaw?'

'Yes.'

'Why?'

'It is what we have always wanted. Now it's within our grasp.'

'I thought you had given up the idea.'

'Of course not. It's been on the back burner, but not off the stove. The time has come to look to our future, Olivia. Up on the golf course a couple of weeks ago, I looked out over Hecklescar and, to be honest, I felt trapped; in a rut. What with the demands of the business, every day plodding through the same mundane routine, staff coming through the door with the same bloody tedious issues.'

He paused. He did not normally swear, not with Olivia anyway. Down in the yard it was different. He could foul-mouth with the best of them, but it did not fit the soft furnishing of Avignon somehow, so he normally left it outside the door. Now he used it for impact. Olivia's blank face, however, showed no sign of it hitting home. Nevertheless, he expressed regret.

'Apologies. Sorry for swearing, Olivia, but it gets to you – the same miserable grind. I remember that day, that day when all this dawned on me. Jakey, you know Jakey, Ina's husband, comes in and reports that one of the vans needs a new set of tyres. 'Is it in the budget?' I ask. 'No', he says. 'Why not?' I ask. He mumbles something about it just happening. I ask him how old the van is. He says he thinks it's three years' old. I ask, how many miles does it do a year? He says, about 30,000. I do the math and calculate that the van has done 90,000 miles since it was new. '85, I think,' he replied. So, I say, 'when we sit down in February to set the budget, do we not ask ourselves the question whether that van or any of the others will need new tyres so we can factor it in?' Do you know what he said? (Listen, Olivia, this is what I have to put up with!) 'I didn't think that was my job; I just get the fish delivered.' I asked him, 'So whose job is it to think about tyres? Mine?' He just shrugged his shoulders and repeated that the van needed tyres otherwise it wouldn't pass its MOT.'

'That's what my life consists of. Well, I've carried them long enough. It's time to move on, out and up, I say; and a deal at Mallaig and a house at Latchlaw sounds a good place to start. There now, that's it in a nutshell. The opportunity has presented itself. I say, let's go for it.'

As you may have guessed, this speech was neither sincere nor spontaneous. He had been rehearsing it for a week at least. He had thought of concluding with *There is a tide in the affairs of men, which taken at the flood, etc.*, but the look of indifference on Olivia's face, and the thought that she had not had the benefit of a classical education persuaded him to leave it out.

Like Hercules' speech, Olivia's indifference was studied. She sat through the performance, hearing the torrent of words, but not listening to them. Instead she sought to draw out, not what Hercules was saying, but what he meant – and, of greater significance, - why he was telling her. By the time he had finished she had not fathomed it, so she fell back on her usual tactic, withdrew her hand, and picked up her own pursuit where she had left off.

'So, there *is* something in it. You *are* thinking of selling the business.'

Hercules stood up, walked to the sideboard and put down his glass.

'Not all of it, just the West Highland end,' he said casually.

'Alright,' said Olivia patiently, 'some of it, the West

Highland end.'

'Well, yes...'

'When Sheila mentioned it, I denied it. Now you tell me it's true, so what do I tell her now?'

'Nothing! You tell her nothing, nor anyone else. You tell them nothing. Particularly that bitch that came sniffing round here to-night. This is between us. You tell them I am not selling the business.'

'You want me to lie to my friend?'

'It's not lying. There is no plan, no proposal and what there is, is 'commercial in confidence'. It is demanded by the regulator. It's called 'privileged information.''

'Now here's a change. Privileged information, and I am to be privileged with it. I ask myself why? Why are you telling me? I can't remember, Harold, you taking me into your confidence much over the past, what, ten years, so why now?'

Hercules ignored the question.

'I am not selling the business, not Anthony Douglas and Son; not that, just the Western Highland firm; it's a separate company.'

'It's a separate company?'

'Of course, you know that: A Douglas (West Highland) Ltd'

'I know that, do I?'

'You should; you're a director.'

For a few silent moments Olivia digested this morsel of information and found food for thought.

'Ah,' she said, at last looking at Hercules. 'Now I get it. You can't sell the business without the directors' say-so, and I am a director. That is why you're telling me. Who else needs to agree? Who else is a director?'

'Just Alexander.'

'Does our son know you are selling....?'

'I have not said I am selling...'

'Sorry, does our son know that you are thinking of selling? (Will that do, '*thinking*'?)'

Hercules ignored the gibe.

'Not yet, but when the deal is to be closed, if it is to be closed, he'll go along with it. He takes no part in the fish business; he just looks after Golden Opportunities. He'll do what I tell him to do.'

'So, I am the stumbling block. I alone stand between you and this scheme of yours. Good, I like that. Now then, tell this director, persuade this director why I should agree to this deal. What's in it for us? No, what's in it for me?'

Until now the exchange had been in the normal currency between them: thrust and counter thrust, distant and unemotional, ordered and even-tempered. With her 'me', Olivia had left the game; that needled him. Hercules changed the mood. He became aggressive.

'Two reasons,' he stated as if reading from a prospectus. 'For a start, you do nothing for the business; it means nothing to you. It only turns a profit because I manage it. If I stop managing it, it will go belly up. If it goes bust you will be liable for its debts because your name is on the articles. There is more to being a director than shares and picking up the dividends.'

Olivia gave no sign of being intimidated. Hercules had been standing, hovering over her almost. Now he sat down next to her. For a while he said nothing and Olivia wondered what he was cooking up. Then he spoke softly.

'And you don't want to go on living in this crummy little house for the rest of your life, do you? Latchlaw has been on the postponed list far too long. With this deal – if I can screw enough out of them - we can build the house we've always wanted – the house we deserve. That would be nice, wouldn't it?'

You do not live with someone for over twenty years without recognising wheedling when you spot it. This had all the signs of a wheedle. Yet Olivia, who had stared Hercules down when he was expounding the duties of directors, dropped her head back into her magazine when he sat down beside her.

At the end of his little warming speech he leaned forward, gently laid his hand on the magazine and pulled it down as he repeated,

'Latchlaw would be nice would it not, Olivia?'

Olivia felt her heart lift a beat or two, felt the after-breath of long dead excitement, found again in the dusty attic of her dreams what she had once felt for this man and the house he had promised her. But did she want Latchlaw now? Did she want the man?

'Would it?' she said flatly.

CHAPTER ELEVEN

Hercules was content with his handling of the conversation with Olivia. She had not scotched his plan to sell West Highlands and had nibbled at the bait of Latchlaw.

That's what Harold concluded, but not Olivia. She had reached a conclusion of her own.

You may live in a house for years, sit in the same chair, sleep in the same bed, eat off the same table, cook on the same stove. You do not notice that it is growing old and looking grubby. Paint flakes, handles fall off, taps drip and fabrics fade. But it does not register; it is familiar and ordinary. Then, one day, you wake up and see the house not as it feels but as it is. What rouses you? Rarely anything clear cut: a stain on the carpet, a blocked sink, a scuttling spider, crumbs down the side of a chair, a friend who compliments you on a 'lived-in-look'. Then you must change it; urgently.

Harold's proposal, his lie about Latchlaw, had precisely this effect on Olivia. Not about the house; not about Latchlaw. But about 'us'. It was over. There was no 'us'. It had died and decayed. It must be buried.

This conclusion startled Olivia. What is she to do? Where is she to go? How can she afford to do anything, or to go anywhere, different?

While such thoughts troubled Olivia, Hercules that

evening dined with Elvira well pleased with his deception.

'I can work on the Latchlaw thing; it's just a strategic staging post. No need to push it. I have time.'

But has he? A complication is on its way in the person and plans of Duncan Kerr. Ina had informed Hercules that Duncan had come last Saturday claiming he had an appointment. Hercules had forgotten the appointment, forgotten that Ina had told him and forgotten that Duncan wanted to see him. Executives like Hercules often come equipped with a memory that screens out unwelcome interruptions to their own plans. Indeed, I believe there is a business term for it; it is called *prioritising;* concentrate on the important issues, relegate the trivial to the pending file or the bin. To Hercules, Duncan is trivial.

Duncan, however, would persist. He is dogged by nature, and had he thought of giving up, he has a wife in his corner who will sponge him down, straighten him up and send him back into the ring to fight until he succeeds.

Janet may think that Ina is a shovel looking for muck but when she needs a shovel, she knows where to find one. She won't seek Ina out, doesn't go to her door or turn up at McMaggie's for the daily gathering of the Hecklescar Information Exchange, that some insensitive folk call a gang of gossips.

Certainly, the ladies at McMaggie's indulge in gossip - and they are all ladies apart from Des. He is a retired haberdasher who used to run a shop in the High Street, a business that faded away thirty years ago, leaving Des at leisure to make applique cushions for anyone who wanted one, and to join some of his old customers for coffee when he has no cushions to make. Des takes no part in the exchanges except to confirm the family history of the person under discussion, and to drink the coffee the ladies buy him. No-one can recall him ever having paid for coffee for himself or anyone else.

'His breeks hev nae pockets,' Ina comments when he's

not there.

Yes, the ladies talk about their neighbours, friends and others they know nothing about, but who does not, and is not such talk the oil that allows us to rub along together? Does it not show a decent concern for each other, that someone is interested in us enough to talk about us? Is that not better than sitting unnoticed in our own kitchen staring at the clock? And is it not a truth universally acknowledged that while we are never quite sure what to do with our own lives, we have no difficulty in prescribing for others precisely what they should do with theirs?

Janet did not attend the meetings in McMaggie's. She was after all, a stranger, having only lived in the place twenty-five years. Not that being a stranger is a bar to membership. Dierdre is an incomer but knows her place. She is there to there to learn, to listen carefully when Ina or Des is chasing down MaggieB's ancestors, descendants, and relatives and their doings and misdoings over the past half-century.

Janet has no interest in such matters and is too wrapped up in her family, her home and the affairs of the business to concern herself with tittle-tattle. Besides, she doesn't like Ina. Janet will not seek out Ina; she will wait until Ina contacts her.

She knows that an experienced hand like Ina would not be content until she has discovered what Duncan in his best suit wanted from Hercules. Within the week Ina stopped Janet in the Market Place to remark on the weather and half-suggest that sometime, but not just yet, she might need a builder to fix the wooden fence at the back and put a gate in it; and would that be the sort of thing that Duncan might tackle now that Hector was working for him? And how is Christine?

Janet agreed that Duncan and Hector could tackle the fence if and when she and Jakey wanted it done. In the meantime, could Ina tell her when the best time would be to find Hercules at home, for Duncan needed to see him about the job that Hercules had asked him to quote for – for the business, that is.

'It's not up for sale, then?' asked Ina.

'What is?' replied Janet.

'The business, the fish business down the pier.'

'Up for sale? Is that the story?'

'Yes, Grubs from Mallaig....'

Janet cut her off and descended to flattery.

'Don't know anything about that. But when Duncan said he needed to see Hercules, I said to him that Ina would be the one to tell us. When would be best?'

'He'd catch him on Thursday just before twelve,' replied Ina. 'His majesty'll be going to the Rotary Lunch. He's the President. He comes back to the house to change and pick up his chain.'

This was not quite what Janet wanted; Hercules would be in a hurry, but it would have to do. Consequently, when Hercules arrived home on the Thursday just before twelve Duncan was waiting for him. He had been shown into the reception room by Ina.

Duncan quickly stated his business. I don't suppose Janet had ever heard of marketing hooks, whereby retailers seek to hook the interest of customers, but she knew how to use them. She knew Hercules well enough to suspect that he would not be the least interested in Duncan's plans for the business. Accordingly, she had primed Duncan to talk about Hector, Hercules son. She didn't exactly script what Duncan should say, or rehearse him in it, but as he waited for Hercules he kept repeating: 'your son Hector; workshop; and £10,000 from Golden Opportunities, please, to fund it for the boy.'

There would be no problem, Hercules said. If you can use the steading by all means fit it out for the lad. I'll put the process in hand to release your investment. That may take a little time; the market's slack at the moment and I wouldn't want to short-change you for the sake of a couple of weeks.

'How much can I expect?' asked Duncan.

'What's your holding?'

'Ten thousand.'

'Good. We haven't had it for too long but we should be able to add a few hundred to that. But as I say, no need to rush, we need to pick our opportunity. Jot down the number of your holding and let me have it. I'll get back to you with an amount and a release date.'

Duncan came away from Avignon well-pleased with his meeting and sat down to his cup of tea feeling he had accomplished something.

'He gave you plenty of time, anyway,' Janet said as he tucked into a crab sandwich at the kitchen table. 'I was wondering what on earth you could be talking about.'

'Oh no,' said Duncan, 'I just nipped along to Latchly to tell the auld yins the good news. When I told ma mither the other day that I was going to see Hercules about the steading, she asked me to let them know how I got on.'

'What did you tell her?'

'It's not that,' said Duncan answering a question Janet hadn't asked. 'It's ma mither, Alice; she's behaving strange.'

'What do you mean strange?'

'Well, fither wasn't in – as usual. Mither was in the kitchen, boiling up some soup and making him a bacon roll. She asked me if I wanted soup but I said no and then she asked if I wanted a cup of tea. I said yes.'

He stopped and glanced at the tea that Janet had just given him.

'I mean, just to please her. Anyway, she put a mug in front of me on the table, then went back to watching the soup.'

'So?'

'Well, she didn't put the kettle on. She just went back to stirring the soup.'

'Well it had to be done, it wouldn't stir itself.'

'No, it's not that. She didn't say anything. You know how she is. She always talks – even when she's cooking. She's always full of news. Well, she didn't say anything. She just went on with the soup and the bacon. There's something wrong. There's something wrong with her. There's something on her mind.'

'Did you not ask her?'

'Yes, I did.'

'What did she say?'

'She said she was fine.'

'And you accepted that.'

'Well, yes. . . .'

'But she's not, is she?'

Duncan did not reply for he understood the look that Janet gave him. She had not asked a question. She had stated a fact.

'This is what your father mentioned the other day. When he came in here after they had been to the doctors. I told you to find out what it was. Did you speak to your father?'

'Yes, he said that mum had fallen. I told you that. But you were dashing out at the time.'

Janet ignored Duncan's wriggle

'Why did she fall? Did he tell you that?'

'He doesn't know. She'd been doing the ironing and he found her fallen over at the ironing table. She'd been taking the plug out of the iron and toppled over.'

Janet considered this diagnosis for a minute or two,

then said, 'Now she's acting strange. I'll need to find out what it is.'

'Dad thinks it was just an accident.'

'Does he? He would. He's a man. Now tell me. Did you get your tea?'

'No,' mumbled Duncan.

'We'll need to go and see her. Find out what it is with her.'

Janet re-filled Duncan's cup and sat down with a cup of her own across from him at the kitchen table. Duncan immediately suspected he was about to be interrogated.

'Now then', she said, 'tell me how you got on with His Excellency.'

Duncan gave his report on his meeting with Hercules and expressed satisfaction with its outcome.

Not so Janet. She had expected Hercules to be difficult, particularly about the money. What did, 'picking an opportunity' mean? When precisely would it crop up? Is he just putting us off?

'I'm suspicious,' she concluded

'You're always suspicious,' said Duncan.

'Concerning him, yes,' she replied, then added. 'I'm going to talk to John Hendry about it. He'll know what it means.'

John Hendry, you may remember, was one of the old men knocking a ball about on the golf course when we first met Hercules. He had been a bank manager before he retired and had invested nothing at all in Hercules Golden Opportunities Life Fund.

'He'll be up to his neck and eyes in the Hecklescar Queen this next couple of weeks. He's the treasurer. But I'll mention it to him and see what he says.'

'By then we might have the money,' said Duncan.

'Don't hold your hand out just yet,' replied Janet.

CHAPTER TWELVE

Mrs Rostowski didn't tell her Care Co-ordinator that Peter Munro had abandoned his care plan and disappeared. If you had asked Mrs. Rostowski why she kept it quiet she may have blocked your query with a client confidentiality clause. She could have claimed that, seeing as Peter Munro paid her privately, no-one else had the right to know where he had gone. But if you pressed her, she would confess that these were just excuses.

If you were knowledgeable enough you could remind her of the provisions of The Care Act. They would lead you to ask about the Care Plan that had been carefully drawn up to chart Peter's route back to robust mental health. If you did, she could argue that she was following the 5-point official guidance:

1. that care and support ought to help the client to live independently;

2. that the client should have as much control over their own lives as possible;

3. that they should participate in society on an equal level;

4. that they should have the best possible quality of life; and

5. that they should keep as much dignity and respect as possible.

But none of these clauses and opinions would let you into her mind, or should we say her heart, for she had come to love Peter Munro.

Here I must scotch the suspicion that we are about to embark on some sort of clandestine sexual liaison between client and counsellor. It's not that kind of book. Anyway, in the apartment at Burleigh Square we heard Mrs. R deny any involvement with him and we ought to take her word for it.

If we were ancient Greeks, we'd have three decent words for 'love' that would keep us out of trouble. We have the feelings but not the symbols. We would have a word for like (philia, as in philately, the love of stamps), a word for erotic attraction (eros, as you might expect) and a word for caring (agape). This last you will have heard if you have been to a decent old-fashioned wedding and heard 1 Corinthians 13 read in the Authorised Version: *'Though I speak with the tongues of men and angels and have not charity...* you know how it goes.

Think of 'charity' not as a rattling tin on the High Street, but as the love that signs off a birthday card from your devoted elderly aunt; that is expressed by a young child with a cuddle and a kiss; that visits a neighbour from whom we expect nothing; that warms the heart at the sight of an old friend coming through the door. Charity is that which provides the common life of a good home: food, shelter, day to day companionship, while philia is choosing the furniture and eros is larking about in the bedroom. This love is a choice – to care for another human being; to see them happy and at peace with themselves.

That is the kind of love that Mrs. Rostowski has for Peter Munro. She will keep his wanderings secret because, as his friend, that is what she feels she ought to do. She'll take the risk. This is no part of a Care Plan; it is simply care. She does not know why he has taken off, does not know whether it is in his best interests that he has done so, does not know whether it will make his life better or worse. When they had talked (and they had talked and talked, hour after intense hour), occasionally she thought he glimpsed light at the end of the tunnel; more often he stumbled back into suffocating darkness. But never in all his ramblings and reasoning, his angst and agonising, had he ever suggested cutting loose in search for answers to his tormenting questions. Although he had mentioned vaguely and wearily going back to where he came from, he had always been too afraid of the world beyond his four walls to venture into it.

What were these questions? We could label them regret, but that doesn't tell you what's in the tin; no one word could do that. Mrs. Rostowski had tried to explain Peter's condition to Mr. Pander, the Clinical Psychologist, but he said she had become too involved with the client and insisted on talking to Peter himself. Peter agreed to meet him but only once. After that meeting, he refused to talk with anyone except Mrs. Rostowski. When she asked him why he would not see the psychologist again, he showed her the notebook in which she had encouraged him to write down his thoughts. He half-smiled as she read out loud what he had taken down: *You may wish to view your depression as the result of diminished self-worth, stemming from either actual or perceived self-schema role disruptions. Your vulnerability to depression may be manifested in your propensity to evaluate your life performance according to excessively rigid and perfectionist criteria.*

She also imagined the discomfort of Mr. Pander when Peter had asked him to speak slowly so he could write down his statement. (Mr. Pander is a recent graduate, keen, richly furnished with the latest psychological techniques and sure of his ability to help the afflicted. But had he not come across anyone like Peter Munro who had an intensity of listening that made you suspect he could read your thoughts before you'd tidied them up). She had half-laughed at the convoluted phrases and said that she wondered what they meant. Peter had replied instantly that he knew precisely what they meant.

'Mr. Pander is keen to shift the blame from my shoulders to my upbringing and is offering to help me dig it up and rake it over. But the blame is mine; I must deal with it.'

That was months ago. Not then and not since had he ever talked of leaving the security of his apartment. Indeed, she had often encouraged him to set aside his solitary existence and go out amongst people but he had not shown any enthusiasm for her counsel. She had tried to persuade him to visit his children, Daniel and Dolinda, both now settled in their own homes but, although he always half-promised that he would do so, he had never followed it up. Nor did he invite them to visit him. It seemed to her that he had withdrawn from a world that caused him pain, to sit in a chair and brood on questions to which he had no answers.

Why then had he taken off now? Had the letters finally got to him; those malign, abusive, hateful, letters from Dilys, his wife? Was that it? Was it as simple as that? That he had decided, as Mrs. Flaherty had concluded, to sort her out once and for all? Finish with her completely, perhaps? Mrs. Rostowski contemplated, but only for a second, contacting Mr. Pander, then held to her course. Peter had sworn her to secrecy. Perhaps this was the break she had been hoping for. She would keep faith.

CHAPTER THIRTEEN

Although the Hecklescar Queen festival does not lie immediately inside our story, we ought to step aside and take from it what enjoyment we can. The committee have worked hard and require only that we join in the activities and throw a few coins in the bucket.

The Hecklescar Queen is crowned every year in a week in July. Who is to be queen is determined by the votes of the two senior classes of the High School and always results in controversy, claims of favouritism and complaints about gerrymandering (for details of which see Ina, Jakey's wife).

Which week in July is determined by the tide. The festival starts with the arrival of the Queen on the lifeboat. She embarks at The Shore two miles up the coast and sails down the bay to disembark at Hecklescar harbour. Nowadays boats can enter the harbour at all states of the tide, but before the harbour was deepened in the final years of the last century, they could land only for a few hours either side of high tide. This set the pattern that is still observed: The Queen comes in on the high tide. Besides, the rise and fall of water in Hecklescar harbour can be as much as six meters, which means that, if she arrived at low tide, she and her maids in their full frocks and fancy regalia would have to clamber up a rung ladder to the pier. This would not be conducive to her dignity. She therefore sails in at high tide, so a convenient high tide early in the afternoon on a Saturday sets the day for the start of the festival.

Incidentally, the Queen used to be called the Herring Queen, but the herring and the boats that caught them have long since departed. To add insult to injury, Charlie in the fish shop recently told me that even if a Hecklescar boat caught a herring or two, under EU Fishery Regulations they would not be allowed to land them in the port.

But that will not stop the townsfolk enjoying what the HQ Committee has arranged for them. On Saturday the Queen will arrive in a flotilla of boats, large and small and will then ride along the High Street in a stretch limo to the Co-op Car Park. There, on a stage specially erected for the purpose, she will be crowned before a company of invited guests and a large, colourful crowd of onlookers. At night she will attend a ceilidh in the old High School Hall and on Sunday, the Parish Church for her 'kirking'. In the afternoon musicians of various combinations and ability will perform in a marquee erected in the square outside the Auld Kirk, to be followed at six by Songs of Praise led by the Parish Minister who plays the guitar, and the Episcopal Priest who accompanies him on the harmonica when she knows the tune.

Monday will see the Sand Castle Competition on the beach for the bairns who, on Tuesday, will turn out in weird and wonderful outfits for the Fancy Dress Competition. Later that day their mothers, fathers, aunts, uncles and other adults who should know better will join a team of four for the Dry Boat Race. They will dress up in ridiculous outfits and, surrounded by a wood and cardboard 'boat', will tour all the pubs in the place, calling in at each establishment to refresh their thirst. Not many finish the race. So far nobody has fallen in the harbour and not been fished out.

Wednesday is the day for games. Novelty Races on the beach in the morning, Raft Race round the bay in the afternoon and, in the evening, darts, bowls, Bingo, and for the more intellectually inclined, Countdown in Gelatinos and a Quiz in The Old Flotilla.

On Thursday there's a Regatta in the bay, and Zumba at the Swimming Pool (or the Community Leisure Amenity as we are now required to call it). In the afternoon (outside in the Co-op carpark if it's dry; if not, inside the old fish market), the Guidance Teacher from the High School will host 'Hecklescar's Got Talent', and all contestants, in the interests of diversity and equality, will be awarded prizes. Anyone over 70 who is daft enough to join the audience is advised to bring earplugs and sit at the back.

I should have mentioned that there's a Pet Show in Kirk Square in the morning, to be judged by Gwendola out of the pet shop. She has let it be known that she will not allow her distaste for fancy crossbreeds to rule out, for the first prize, a Labradoodle, Jack-a-Pooh or Shih-Apso. This statement of intent comes after the better class of local dog-owners threatened a boycott over her decision last year to choose a mongrel for the top award.

The committee are praying for fine evening on Friday when they intend to turn the whole of the High Street into an old-fashioned Open-Air Street Market. They have rented out twenty-three stalls, hired thirty-seven Victorian Street Outfits, bought ten cases each of Dandelion & Burdock and Sarsaparilla, and invited the Shilbottle Colliery Brass Band to play marches by Von Suppé and excerpts of Gilbert & Sullivan in Kirk square.

The week closes with the Torchlight Procession on Saturday evening. If last year is anything to go by you ought not to miss it. The policeman on duty at the Free Kirk corner remarked to spectators there that he had not seen such a procession anywhere in the Borders at any time during his fifteen years supervising such events.

That is where we ought to stand to see the wonder of

this parade: the Free Kirk Corner. It is close to ten o'clock in the evening. The light is fading fast and a stillness has settled on the road, the kirk, the houses and the little huddle of men and women who have gathered to see the procession. The stewards arrive in their luminous yellow waistcoats and place themselves officiously on the roads at the junction to keep the traffic away from the procession route. One of the stewards carries a bucket of water to dowse any torch that gets out of hand.

The spectators comment on the nice night, the queen and her maids, the week's activities, festivals past, it being late for the bairns, last year's shambles; 'did you know that they've taken Jacob into hospital again'; and 'd'ye think that steward there, the tubby one, knows what he is doing with that bucket - where's he from anyway? I haven't seen him before.' But the quiet night subdues their conversation to a loud whisper until MaggieB, who is standing a little apart from the huddle announces:

'That's them on their way'.

Far off they hear the strains of 'Blue Bonnets over the Border' played by the Hecklescar Pipe Band. (They are not always the Hecklescar Pipe Band. When they play at Langton's Wynsome Maid, they are the Langton Pipe Band, and when they step over the Border into England at Gainslaw they become The Berwickshire Pipes and Drums. In each case you will see the same people in different kilts and tartans. But wherever they go and whatever they are called, the sound stirs the blood!).

The band and the bairns have gathered in the Co-op car park and are now in the High Street. From there they will make their way through the Market Place along Church Street, up the Smiddy Brae and round the corner to emerge into the view of the huddle at the Free Kirk corner.

The pipes fall silent as pipers save their breath for the

Bryan Webster

brae. They march to the clack of a single drum. As the band appears round the corner, the huddle laughs then cheers. The band, pipers and drummers, all, me   n and women both, are decked out in their pyjamas, and what a flamboyant spectacle they make. If you can translate their pyjamas into their usual clothes you will recognise Duncan as one of the pipers and Christine, his daughter, as the exuberant drummer in the back row. After them march the Hecklescar Queen and her maids, then last year's Queen and her maids all in like colourful out-fits and carrying flaming torches.

But these sights are mere foretastes of the main feast. For after them comes a stream of light, colour, movement and sheer delight as bairns of all ages, shapes and sizes strag-gle round the corner poking their torches into the night air. Oh, the wonder of it! You can read it in their faces: excited, subdued, half-frightened, bewildered, yet overjoyed - and you know that they will remember this night for the rest of their lives; that when they are far away from Hecklescar; when they are corralled into bleak classrooms, confined to dull jobs in concrete blocks, are braving blaring highways, or setting their foot on an urban road, they will see a light, or hear a sound, and the inexplicable and accumulated joy of this night will sweep over them and they will smile. Then they will bore their chil-dren with their conclusion that 'we had it good then, not like now with your face aye buried in an iPhone.'

The dazzling, dancing snake wriggles its way round the corner and sets out on the long climb up Priory Road. More and more torches, more and more children, more and more adults emerge. Mothers arrive pushing buggies, and older women, clutching the hands of their bewildered grandchil-dren, huff and puff up the brae. Even some of these grand dames have donned their night attire. A man or two has been brave enough to join the procession, but we see none that have turned out in anything other than scruffy casuals. The strains of the pipes and the faint rattle of the drums grow fainter as the band, the bairns and the Queens pass the old school and march past the Police Station and Cemetery to the brow of the hill.

Suddenly a shriek splits the air. We look and see a child waving an empty stick. The top of the torch he is carrying has fallen, blazing, to the ground. Where is the stout steward with the bucket? Having a discussion with a fellow member of Rotary across the road. Where's the bucket? He can't re-member where he left it, and runs around in a sort of agitated wobble searching for it. In the meantime, one of the mothers treads on torch and puts out the fire. He has found the bucket but the fire is out. Undeterred, he paces to the site of the blaze and pours water over the ashes. The spectators cheer and he carries away his injured authority with his empty bucket.

Will the pageant never end? Just when we think that we have seen the last, another group straggles into view and heads up the hill. We look up the hill in the gathering darkness and there see a ribbon of flickering lights running up into the darkening sky.

'It's like that thing they do in Shetland,' says someone and we all agree that it is spectacular.

'Awe-inspiring and atavistic,' pronounces Edward. We seldom see Edward out on the street. He retired from teaching English a few years ago to write impenetrable poems and gloomy novels. We look at him, see his sad face, and profess agreement.

But we must hurry. This night there is more to see. A quick cup of tea then, when it is thoroughly dark, out to see the lighting of the bonfire and firework display on the beach.

CHAPTER FOURTEEN

We have allowed the festival to distract us and take us ahead of our story. We need to go back to Sunday afternoon, to the marquee that has been erected in Kirk Square. Playing as we enter are the Codlings, a group of local men growing old musically, singing sentimental songs about the sea to the accompaniment of two guitars, a concertina and, occasionally, a tambourine.

There, listening to them, sits John Hendry, the man that Janet needs to see. John, a retired bank manager, is a canny man. If you hail from Tyneside you have probably misunderstood me, for 'canny' there means decent, straight up, can be trusted, nice to know. John is all of these but he is something more; he is astute, not easily taken in, cautious: canny. But not suspicious, at least not until he has tripped over something to be suspicious about – or someone – like Hercules.

He is not a wealthy man. He made his living from money but has never made money his life. Independence is what he sought and what he has gained. Ask him about today's top bankers, those that ran us into debt and the banks to bankruptcy in two thousand and eight and he will label them 'financially obese'. Ask him about his own finances and he will say he has enough; enough, that is, to meet his immediate needs; to provide a fortnight in the Caribbean in February, and, every year or so, to fund a visit to his brother in Perth, Australia. No doubt when John dies his brother's family will inherit a little pile of savings and investments and the 3-bedroom house in Hallyknowe Terrace.

John did not pursue ambition. Though he had the ability 'to go further' he did not wish to undertake the journey. His elevation to bank manager from accountant came by way of luck and geography. He happened to be on the spot when Old Shylock succumbed to a heart attack. Having attained the local pinnacle, he had no desire to push on to higher and remoter peaks. With his wife Lizzie, he settled into the life of Hecklescar and let it provide the raw material from which he had manufactured his own interesting and productive life.

Nothing seemed off limits: he devoured The Times daily, and each weekend digested The Economist. He knew about the fishing, about the fragility of running a small business in Hecklescar, the geology of the coastline, about birds, molluscs, and butterflies; about the French Fort up on the point and the old Smeaton Wall at the harbour entrance.

Although he had no garden, he grew vegetables in a raised bed in his backyard and brightened it all summer long with a dazzling array of begonias. These he reared in pots that he had thrown himself on the wheel at St Ebba's Pottery, an enterprise that he propped up financially for many years until he persuaded Gladys the potter that she would find a better outlet for her talents, and a steadier income, teaching ceramics at Border College. The pottery probably still belongs to him.

John Hendry's chief interest and concern is the folk of the town. He is not a local, but married Lizzie, a local lass, after he met her in the bank when he was sent from the Glasgow office sixty odd years ago to cover for staff holidays. We might be tempted to call him a pillar of society but he would firmly reject such a title. He regarded himself more as a pavement; someone down to earth who took you to where you wanted to go. He knew how the system worked, knew who did what in the government or council, knew who to persuade to take up a cause and who to frighten with a stinging letter to their boss or the East Borders Gazette. He could be called on to straighten out a grant for loft insulation, direct a school leaver to the appropriate college and course, and transport an old biddy to the Health Centre or the Borders General Hospital. He had enough street knowledge of the weaknesses of youth to help their parents steer them clear of the pitfalls of alcohol, drugs and petty crime or, when they tripped up, to stand by with emergency rescue and life-repair kits. He often procured a mobility scooter for those whose legs had given up supporting them and could point sufferers of all ages to the right packet or bottle in the chemists. Ina will tell you that if it hadn't been for him little Josh Grant would have died from the croup. Mind you, she might also add that had he realised what was really wrong with his wife, 'she would be with us yet'.

Had John Hendry heard what Ina says about his wife he would have agreed with her. He accuses himself of neglect and suffers the agony of it every day. He listens with good grace to any comfort anyone gives him; who tells him that he and Lizzie were blessed to have such a long life together, that they were close, that they shared so many interests, that they loved each other. He accepts it all, but when their voices fall silent, he speaks to himself and says, 'I was not kind enough. I could have eased her way, walked close with her those last few steps, but I did not. I could have held her hand, I could have kissed her and hugged her and told her that I loved her, but I did not. All my life I took her for granted. Now I know what I should have done – and what I would do now, but it is too late. It is too late.

John and Lizzie did not have children. He is eighty-three and lives alone.

Being a financial man, he is called on the 'do the books' of a variety of the town's firms and institutions. Many of the tradesmen: plumbers, electricians, builders and others depend on him, as do two or three of the shops. He calculates

Duncan's exposure to VAT and taxes and is able to re-assure Alistair that HM Customs and Revenue are not in the least interested in what he is paid for his onions and leeks.

Although his religious beliefs are eccentric, and his appearances at church erratic, John had been recruited by the Parish Church to be its treasurer, and keeps an eye on the incomings and outgoings of the Common Good Fund, the British Legion and, as we have heard, the Hecklescar Queen.

But John Hendry is not sitting listening to the Codlings out of duty. He is there because on this damp Sunday afternoon he felt his house empty and lonely without his companion wife of fifty-seven years. Two years ago, although she was not well enough to be out of the house, she had accompanied him to the Codlings because he said he wanted to go. The thought of what it cost her torments him. So much so that last year he stayed away from the marquee. This year he has braved it. Sitting there on his own, where they had sat together, gives him a disturbing, yet reassuring consolation.

Enjoyment too. He appreciates music; his tastes running from Country & Western through Runrig and Scots songs, to the more popular classics. At the moment he is trying to master Saint-Saën's organ concerto on an orchestral organ that he had installed in his back room just over a year ago.

Ina will tell you that his wife Lizzie would never have allowed him to have such an expensive organ and that he used his wife's insurance policy to meet the £2,500 he had to pay for it. Like most of Ina's stories this has some truth in content but little in substance. Certainly, the money came from the insurance pay-out, but truth to tell, Lizzie had an ambition to buy her husband the organ to replace the keyboard that had accompanied their songs for thirty years. His purchase of the organ therefore constitutes an act of love and the keeping of a promise. If you could persuade him to speak about it (which you coiuldn't), he would tell you that when he played the

organ, he felt just a little closer to her. He always started his re-
cital with her favourite, the old Everly Brothers' classic: 'Let it
be me.' Later the Codlings will sing it, not knowing how much
it means to him, and he will pretend to wipe his nose to brush
away a tear.

As we join him the Codlings mark his presence by strik-
ing up *'John Henry was a steel driving man'*. We now need to confess that his name is not John at all, but James Norman. The J
and the N collapsed into John when the song about the steel-
driving man came along and James Norman has been John ever
since.

John acknowledges the compliment with a wave of the
hand and the band nods back. John, however, is not to remain on his own for long. An old friend has spotted him and
is pushing along the row to reach him. His name is George
and, although born and brought up in Hecklescar, he has, for
many years now, lived away beyond Glasgow in Helensburgh,
a small town not far from the Faslane Base where nuclear
submarines are serviced and maintained. The base gave him
a good livelihood for many years and, now he is comfortably
retired, he will not desert the place. But on high days and
holidays and certainly for the Hecklescar Queen, he arrives in
Hecklescar to meet friends and hoover up gossip about old ac-
quaintances. He has laid hold of a story and is determined to
tell it to anyone who will sit still long enough to listen. Seeing
John Hendry sitting on his own makes him a target.

John welcomes George to his side but we do not need to
listen to all they have to say for, whilst our own memories are
lively and exciting, the remembrances of others tend to be tedious. George, however, soon moves from the abstract to the
particular: does John know Peter Munro? John confirms that
he does, he knows him well; Peter's a decent man.

'He's a millionaire, a multi-millionaire.' continues
George. 'He went to London just as the property boom took

off. Made a fortune, buying, doing up and selling on.'

'So I believe.'

'Have you heard he's thinking of coming back to Hecklescar to bide?'

'Yes, that's the story down the pier.'

'And have you heard that Hercules is selling up?'

'Yes, I've heard that too.'

'Now then,' says George warming to his task, 'What's the connection?'

John had been sitting facing the platform, giving his attention to the singers and the songs, now he turned and looked into the excited face of his companion.

'No, tell me.'

'Olivia!'

'Olivia, Hercules' missus?'

'Yes, Olivia'

'How is Olivia the connection?'

'Well, didn't Peter leave town when Olivia ditched him for Hercules. They were an item, you know, her and Peter, then Hercules came back from Edinburgh and swept her off her feet. Whirlwind. Three weeks. Then off up north somewhere and they came back married. Peter hung around for a month or two, then left. There was talk about Olivia's mother giving him comfort, eh? - and she old enough to be his mother. It was the talk of the town. What was her name?'

'Connie, and not was, is'

'Is she alive?'

'A spring chicken from where I stand.'

'And here?'

'And here.'

'So what's she saying about Peter Munro coming back?'

'I don't know. I haven't asked her.'

'That'll be why Hercules is selling up.'

'You'll need to explain that to me. I don't see the connection.'

'Well, they say they don't get on, him and Olivia. Ina, ye ken, Jakey's wife, cleans for them. She says they have separate bedrooms and he's always away, in Edinburgh or sailing that muckle yacht of his. He brought it over to Rhu last year. I saw it. It was there most of the summer. For entertaining, eh? The ladies, eh? They say Olivia thinks he has a fancy woman up in Edinburgh.'

'But they have a family, don't they?'

'Aye, but they're all up. They wouldn't be in the way.'

'In the way of what?'

'Olivia ditching Hercules and taking up with Peter again.'

'Or her mother?'

'What?'

'Or her mother, Connie. Peter taking up with Connie. That's what you said, wasn't it?'

George made to answer then studied John's face. The hint of a smile played on the old banker's lips. The penny dropped. John was having him on.

'You no' believe it, d'ye?' smiled George.

'Tell me this, George,' said John pleasantly, 'Peter Munro, is he married? Perhaps he is, and intends bringing his wife with him. If he's coming, that is - and if Hercules is selling up - and if Olivia is going to ditch him, and if Connie is. . . I don't know what about Connie. Ina, as usual, is making half of it up.'

He then asked after George's family, and George told him that his son had landed a job in Aberdeen. Then they sat in silence and paid proper attention to the sea songs.

After the Codlings, a scruffy woman in a long skirt mounted the stage and, to the accompaniment of a guitar and a sad face, wailed out long litanies of false lovers and unrequited love. Since John and George had no experience of either they abandoned their seats and left the marquee.

CHAPTER FIFTEEN

Duncan goes to the Parish Church every Sunday with his mother Alice. Janet attends often but not always. Songs of the Sea is a special service so Janet will be there. The songs are sung in the Methodist Church on Sunday at 6 o'clock to mark the end of Hecklescar Queen week. The Queen and her Maids parade in down one aisle and last year's Queen and Maids down the other to their reserved seats at the front of the church.

The singing is not what it used to be when almost everyone in the town knew the Sankey sea songs and could sing 'Eternal Father Strong to Save' in harmony without looking at their books. It is still, however, a happy, busy occasion with The Queen reading the lesson about Jesus stilling the storm and the Mission Man reciting the fisherman's version of the Twenty-Third Psalm with a Pilot doing for fishermen what a Shepherd does for sheep.

This year Janet has an additional motive for attending. She knows that John Hendry will be there and we know that she wants to see him about Duncan's investment in Golden Opportunities. But before she arrives at the church, she will go to pick up her mother-in-law Alice at Latchly. Alistair won't be going. It is no use asking him. He has never been in a church since he was married and even then, he had to be reinforced with a tot or two before braving the congregation.

When Janet arrived at Latchly she saw Alistair away

down at the bottom of the garden, hoeing. She shouted to him and he raised his hand in acknowledgement, then went back to work. Janet entered the kitchen expecting to see Alice sitting there, coat on her back and hat on her head ready for the service. But she wasn't in the kitchen. Janet went through to the sitting room but Alice was not there. Janet shouted and heard a faint reply from upstairs. Entering the bedroom, she found Alice sitting on the side of the bed dressed only in her petticoat.

Alice greeted her cheerfully.

'What are you doing here?' she said.

'I'm here to take you to the church; it's the Songs of the Sea.'

'Now?'

'Yes,'

'Is it Sunday? I lose track of the days.'

'Why haven't you got your dress on?'

Alice looked down at her petticoat.

'I came to get changed. That's it. I came to get changed. To go to the church. Yes, that's it. Am I too late?'

'Of course not,' said Janet. 'Here, I'll help you, what frock do you want?'

She chose the turquoise one with the check and Janet helped her into it; then her coat, the pale green, and her straw hat. Together they set out for the Songs of the Sea. Alistair waved to them as they left.

After the service, Janet left Alice drinking a cup of tea in the hall with Duncan and sought out John Hendry.

'Oh dear,' he said when she told him about Duncan's plans and that he needed to lay his hands on the money in Hercules' Golden Opportunities Life Fund.

'How much does he have tied up?'

'Ten thousand pounds.'

'How much does he need?'

'All of it.'

'How long has Hercules had it?'

'About four years.'

'Oh dear,' repeated John.

'Why 'oh dear'?' nipped Janet,

'Sorry,' said John, 'It's just that I have doubts about this fund of Hercules.'

'But Hercules said it would be no problem to take the money out.'

'Did he? Was that all he said?' asked John and Janet remembered that it was not all that he had said and tried to recall what Duncan had told her. John listened to her patiently then said he would come to see them tomorrow night.

Sitting at the kitchen table on Monday evening, John opened his laptop computer and said,

'Let me explain what this Golden Opportunities Life Fund is, and what it is for. Suppose you have more money than you know what to do with' (Here Janet glowered at Duncan and Duncan dropped his head.) 'Or you don't like the interest you are receiving on your ISA. You may decide to buy shares in a limited company or buy government bonds or other bonds in order to increase your return. But buying shares is a messy, risky business and normally bonds can only be bought with big bucks – tens or hundreds of thousands of pounds, millions, even. The little man (that's you and me) can't afford to buy these, but investment managers have thought of a wheeze to help us over our difficulty. The manager buys shares and bonds then chops them up into units and sells them to you; like you'd buy a packet of sweets out of a jar. You now have a stake in a range of businesses as well as having a share in the interest on the bonds. Your units are then traded in financial markets. If the price of the units goes up you gain a better return on your little nest eggs than sticking them in a savings account with your high street bank or stashing them in a biscuit tin under the bed.'

'So that's what Golden Opportunities is: a fund?' asked Janet

'Yes.'

'And you can sell these units, (is that what you call them?)' John nodded. 'at any time?'

'Yes, that's guaranteed.'

'So, we can sell ours?'

'Yes.'

'That's that then,' said Duncan, leaning back in his chair.

'Not quite,' replied John. 'You can sell them but you have to accept what you can get for them. That's the bad news. I've looked up the Golden Opportunities Units. They're trading at £2.12 per unit. What did you pay for them?'

He looked at Janet. Janet looked at Duncan. Duncan looked guilty.

'I don't know,' he mumbled. 'I gave him £10,000. The Basildon bandits had paid up for the Brisset house. Well, not all they owed, nothing like. I lost a lot on that job. The house with the overhanging gable, ye ken, halfway down the brae. I lost a lot. But Cockburn wrote them a letter and I got £15,000 out of them. That was ten years after the job. Janet was away looking after her mother, so I asked Cockburn what I should do with the money. He said he wasn't allowed to give financial advice but thought I should talk to Hercules. Hercules said I'd be better investing it rather than putting it in the bank. That's how he got the ten thousand.'

'So, Hercules is one of these investment managers?'

asked Janet

'No.'

'No? But he sold it to Duncan.'

'And to many others. But he is not an investment manager; he's an agent. The Golden Opportunities Life Fund was his idea, but he doesn't manage it. It is run by M&S Investments.'

'Marks and Spencer's,' exclaimed Janet, 'them that sell clothes.'

'Not Marks and Spencer,' said John, smiling, 'Methuen and Sinclair, offices in George Street, Edinburgh, Renfrew Street in Glasgow, and Wick'.

'Wick? Up north?' put in Duncan out of interest. Janet tutted and brought him back to Hecklescar.

'You're saying Hercules doesn't run it. I thought he was training up his son, Alexander, to take it over.'

'No, Alexander works in Hercules' Edinburgh office. He's a sort of Office Manager.'

Duncan had become alarmed at the drift of the interchange.

'These M&S people. Are they reliable?'

'Very. An old established sensible firm. I have units with them myself.

Duncan smiled in relief.

But not Janet.

'But it is Hercules that sells these Golden Opportunities things. We have the certificate he gave us. He signed it.'

'Did he now? Show me.'

Janet went to the filing cabinet and pulled out a mock leather folder and handed it to John. John studied the folder before he opened it. Janet searched his face for a reaction. All she detected was a slight flick of John's head as if he were saying, 'now fancy that'. What prompted this response was not the title of the folder. *'Golden Opportunities'*, it announced in block gold letters. Nothing wrong with that. But immediately underneath the title ran the legend: *'a bespoke portfolio for the astute investor'*. What did that mean? Then there was the name of the provider in the bottom right hand corner: *'HD Investments'*. John looked up, saw the concern in Janet's eyes and said, 'that stands for Harold Douglas, I expect.'

'Who's Harold Douglas?' asked Janet.

'Hercules,' put in Duncan, anxious not to be ignored.

John opened the folder and rummaged through leaflets and other material until he came to a letter, which he drew out. An impressive document, on top quality Conqueror paper with embossed letter heading, it proclaimed the 'Golden Opportunities Life Fund'. But even before it was in John's hands Janet saw what John would see. It was not from Methuen & Sinclair, Fund Managers. It was from Harold Douglas, Investment Advisor.

'Is this what he gave you?' John asked Duncan.

'He let me read it, then put it in the folder and handed the folder to me.'

John again riffled through the papers in the folder.

'There's nothing else?'

'No.'

'He didn't give you anything after this?'

'No – that's the certificate, isn't it?'

'Yes and no. Yes, it's a certificate, but it is not *the* certificate. It simply confirms that you have given Harold Douglas £10,000 to be invested in Golden Opportunities. The question is, which Golden Opportunities? The units issued by M&S or in a bespoke portfolio chosen by HD Investments?'

'I knew it' exploded Janet; 'He's robbed us!'

'Wheesht,' John muttered irritably. 'Let me think about it. Give me a couple of days and I'll get back to you. Can I take the folder away?'

They agreed and John carefully wrote a receipt confirming that they had given the folder to him.

'It is valuable,' he said, 'It may be worth £10,000.'

They were not reassured, however, when he added,

'Or rather, might be.'

John is not normally an irritable man and, once he had left Janet and Duncan, he felt badly about being sharp with Janet. He knew Janet well and liked her. For a few years she had served with him on the Hecklescar Queen Committee, until she tired of the intrigue, the in-fighting and, particularly, of Ina. When she handed in her resignation, John Hendry had tried to dissuade her. She was one of the few on the committee who said what she thought and did what she promised. He had crossed swords with her himself on one or two occasions but had never before found himself irritated by her persistence. So, why this time? He picked over the conversation and realised that what rattled him was not Janet's doggedness, but his own clumsiness.

He wasn't a vain man and he did not, as professional people are inclined to believe, think of himself as the answer to the world's problems. He had always prided himself on his ability to think on his feet; to anticipate, to grasp, to respond to the problem thrown at him. But sitting at that kitchen table, with Janet and Duncan hanging on his words, looking for his counsel, he had not been able to lay hold on the right words to express what he wanted to say. He had found himself staring at a blank page.

But calling in his scattering thoughts, he determined what he must do with this document that Hercules had given to Duncan. Before he settled to it, he called in to the news-agents, to pick up his daily copy of The Times. *His* copy, for before he collected it Mrs. Mussen had cut out the answers to yesterday's crossword. He insisted on this every day. If he could not complete the puzzle using his own ability, he would rather suffer the rebuke of not having done so, than the humiliation of having to look up the solution.

Before you give him too much credit for self-discipline, let me add that Mrs. Mussen kept the answers in an envelope under the counter and let him have them each Saturday. He could then, having admitted defeat after days of trying, look them up and decide which he should have solved and were therefore his failure, and which were over-contrived and therefore the fault of the setter.

Let me add that, similarly, when he picked up a detective story, Iain Rankin or James Patterson, he shut his eyes and clipped a paper clip over the last ten pages of the book. He would not then be tempted to look at the last chapter to see how it all worked out.

I told you he is a canny man.

CHAPTER SIXTEEN

W hen do the prawns change into langoustines?' asked Grubs of Corpach. He sat drinking coffee with Jakey one Tuesday in late August and had run out of other sticks with which to poke him.

'I keep my eye on them all the way down but I never see them change.'

'You should keep your eyes on the road,' replied Jakey solemnly, 'a driver can easily turn into a casualty.'

'Very clever,' conceded Grubs, 'but answer the question. When the boats land them, they're prawns; when we load them into the wagon at Mallaig they're prawns. When you and me take them off the wagon and put them in the yard they're prawns. But when they come out in your dinky little polystyrene boxes the label says langoustines. When do they change?'

Jakey tapped the side of his nose, leaned towards his listener and spoke in a loud whisper.

'It's a trade secret. Hercules learned about it at Business School. It's called brand marketing. You take something common and give it a fancy name and put it on the menu. It creates a different ambience, and you can charge more.'

'Ambience!' scoffed Grubs, 'what on earth is - what d'ye call it?'

'Ambience.'

'Ambience. What is it?'

'It's like a smell,' replied Jakey.

'A smell?'

'Yes, like a smell or taste. See, suppose you have something with a common name . . . like. . .. Grubs. You know nobody would buy anything with a name like that so you change it. Now, what would we call you if we wanted to project a positive ambience?'

Jakey studied Grubs from head to foot, from his scrubby weather-beaten face topped with a battered baseball cap, down past his dirty off-red tee shirt and scruffy breeks to his salt-stained trainers.

'What's your real name?' he asked.

'Reginald.'

'Yer mither called you Reginald in Corpach?'

'Naw, we lived in Portsoy then.'

'Portsoy. She called you Reginald in Portsoy, did she? I take it she's English.'

'Naw, she belongs Buckie.'

'Buckie! It gets worse. Reginald! Naw, that's no use. You look nothing like a Reginald.'

Jakey fell silent as he continued his examination of the man from Corpach – and Portsoy. Then he shook his head.

'No, it can't be done. We can do nothing with Grubs. It's a fair description. That's the brand. We'll just have to put it in a bin by the till and knock something off.'

Grubs laughed, but would not be put off the scent.

'Let's get back to prawns. What's the matter with calling them prawns and putting them on the menu as prawns?'

'Because nobody would eat them.'

'I'd eat them. I do eat them. When we were in Lanzarote

last summer I asked for prawns and chips. Laura didn't want me to. She said it made us look common. But I ordered them – and I got them.'

'I'm with Laura. I'm surprised she still puts up with you. How long have you been married?'

'It'll be seventeen years come October.'

'She's a brave woman.'

'How do you mean brave?'

'Never mind! Tell me this, Grubs, what's the buzz in Mallaig about Hercules selling up? It's gone quiet here.'

'And there. No-body's talking. Not even Dodgy Donald.'

'That's a surprise. He's not usually stuck for something to say.'

'That's what's suspicious. He's walking round with a grin like the cat that came in from the cold. Something is definately going on.'

This gave no comfort to Jakey. For the past two months, ever since Grubs infected his mind with the thought that Hercules might be selling up, Jakey had expected something to happen either to confirm or deny the rumour. But life in the yard, in the town, and on the lorries in and out of the place, had trundled on down old familiar roads.

Such trundling, however, is not a matter of course. It would not happen unless someone drove it. Hercules thought he did; but he only waved the map about in the back seat; Jakey sat in the driver's seat and took the business where it needed to go. If Dodgy Donald in Mallaig, or Mack in Fraserburgh, or Wisley in Ballantrae needed a lorry off-schedule, they would say, 'I'll give Jakey a ring'. If Diane asked Angela if she could have three weeks off to visit her son in Canada, Angela would reply, 'I'll speak to Jakey'. If Manuel in the Algarve was facing the weekend without enough langoustines, he texted Jakey.

Working hours? Jakey had none; he had them all. Job Description? Do what is needed to keep the firm rolling and the people paid. No-one can remember him ever taking a week off. Ina remembers two days in Manchester for their son's wedding three years back in February. Remuneration: salary: £25,000 a year paid monthly; a bonus, occasionally, from Hercules, when he remembered; every Friday, four lemon sole fillets, and half-a-dozen monk fish tails, if he could lay his hands on them. Why did he do it? He enjoyed it - and it gave him a position in the town and in the industry. *'It's him that runs it, you know.'* will be a fitting epitaph when he comes to need one.

For the last two months, all of this had been under threat. Jakey took his responsibilities seriously and took the threat of the sale of Anthony Douglas and Son Ltd in the same spirit. Outwardly he went about his job with the same diligence and commitment: he hustled, bustled and badgered. He batted away any tittle-tattle about the future of the business. He reassured Angela and the girls in the yard and Nudge, Little Dod, Elaine, and the other drivers, and all the others that their jobs were safe and that the company had a bright future. Of a night, however, as he lay awake beside (the now, thankfully, silent) Ina, he wondered what Hercules was up to. No matter how many weeks flowed on without any developments and no matter how often he reassured himself that it was all smoke and mirrors, he went to work each day expecting Hercules to call him into the office to give him the bad news.

Then a straw in the wind. Not from Hercules or Grubs but from his wife, Ina. One of her unspecified duties was to lift any mail she found on Olivia's doormat and lay it on the small side table in the hall. This was no hardship. With experience and imagination (and she had plenty of both) you can learn a lot from envelopes that you find behind someone else's door.

She found, however, not a letter lying on the mat, but one sitting on the side table already. It was addressed to Mr.

H Douglas but when she picked it up, she noticed a note on it: *'Olivia, For your info. H.'*

Ina saw that the envelope had already been opened and persuaded herself that it would be no infringement of her contract to take a little peek inside. The letter had been sent by Aitken, Buchanan and Carmichael, Solicitors & Notaries Public, 143 Renfield Street, Glasgow G14 5DA.

The Subject, underlined and in bold type above the body of the letter didn't give much away. It read: **A Douglas & Son (Highland) Ltd.**

The body was a single sentence: 'We thank you for yours of the 14th inst. and have forwarded the documents you attached to Mallaig Fishermen's Co-operative for their perusal and consideration.'

An hour later, Jakey, in for his lunch, was told by his wife that Hercules was selling the business, the whole business, and was using Solicitors in Glasgow to do it. He snapped at her and told her not to breathe a word to anyone about it until he had confronted Hercules. Ina agreed and, in street and coffee bar, restricted herself to knowing smiles and obscure hints. That made things worse and by the morning of the second day Jakey found himself the focus of gripes from the people who worked with him. No matter how often he protested that nothing was 'going on' and that he would tell them when he knew anything, he felt the sand shifting under his feet. No longer could he wait until Hercules turned up at the yard; he would go to see him at the house.

Hercules was not at home; he'd be back about twelve. In the meantime, Olivia, seeing Jakey's agitation, brought him into the lounge and asked him if she could help. At first, he demurred but when she asked again, told her what was on his mind.

He could not mention the letter Ina had opened so he called in Grubs and the Mallaig men to help him out. Jakey is a plain man. He used words to convey what he meant and what he felt. He had not been schooled in the art of using them to conceal the truth or cover his sentiments. His explanation therefore rambled on about rumours that the Highland end of the business was being sold off to the Mallaig Fishermen's Co-op.

Olivia understood immediately what Jakey meant - and felt for him. But what could she do? She had been told of the sale of the Highland business, knew that it wasn't a done deal, but that Hercules was determined to sell it. She also knew, or at least, thought she knew, that only the Highland business was up for sale and that the Hecklescar company was safe. But she had been sworn to secrecy. What should she say?

Jakey had finished his spiel and sat on the edge of his chair, waiting for a response. For a brief moment Olivia thought of telling him what she knew. She found herself weighing the merits of this decent man with his anxious face, against her settled suspicion of the man who shared her house but never looked her in the eye. She suspected that she did not know the truth; that she had been told only what Harold wanted her to believe. Did she believe him? No! But what could she do? She had been sworn to secrecy – and, who knows, if Highland were sold, there might be something in it for her. Something that would help her, perhaps, to throw off her dependence on a man she increasingly distrusted.

Such cowardice and self-interest eclipsed her concern for Jakey. She must answer him.

'I see,' she heard herself saying, 'I'm sure there is little or nothing in this, but it really is remiss of Harold not to let you know if anything is moving. You must forgive him,' she added, 'he is having to spend quite a lot of time in Edinburgh these days on his financial interests. As soon as he comes in, I will tell him you are anxious to see him.'

'Yes, thanks,' muttered Jakey. 'If you would. I need to

keep the lid on it. The natives are getting restless,' he added with a forced smile.

After he left, Olivia felt wretched. The unintended yet inevitable freezing of her heart over the last ten or perhaps twenty, years thawed a little. That she had chosen to side with a man she mistrusted against a man she respected; that she had chosen to put her own grubby interests before the concerns of the folk in the yard disgusted her.

And why, after all these years, just at this time, in this moment, here in her own house, should the memory of dumpy Peter Munro step through the door?

CHAPTER
SEVENTEEN

Olivia vented her unease on Hercules. She had persuaded herself that the fault lay, not with her deception, but with him for not being at home to answer Jakey's questions. When Hercules came home, she would not let him rest until he had arranged to see Jakey.

Jakey duly arrived at Avignon after work on the evening of the day after he had met Olivia. Olivia answered his bell and ushered him into Hercules' den. He had not been inside this room before; he had always been lodged informally in the lounge or conservatory.

The den, as you might expect, exuded opulence without elegance. From its panelled walls and beetling book shelves, to its sulking Axminister and brooding curtains it reeked of that surly superiority from which the self-important look down on their inferiors.

Hercules sat enthroned in a buttoned, burgundy leather chair behind a desk that spread before him like a banqueting table. Fashioned in mock mahogany it boasted a red leather inlay on the top and a spacious kneehole beneath, around which clustered bowed drawers with bright brass handles. On the desk sat a brass table lamp with a long green shade, two large wooden correspondence trays, a grotesque Victorian pen and ink stand, a little pile of papers and an expensive leather writing case, closed as if to protect some vital and highly important document.

Hercules motioned Jakey to the chair in front of the desk and told him not to be overawed by being shown into the Holy of Holies.

'Not many people have seen the inside of this room,' he confided. 'This is the command centre. This is where the big decisions are formulated. I want to take you into my confidence, Jakey. I am planning...' (he paused, for the word 'escape' had popped into his mouth. He quickly swallowed it.) 'I am planning a directional shift in strategy.'

He stared at Jakey willing him to hear but not to understand. Jakey obliged and said nothing. His blank face encouraged Hercules to move on.

'Olivia tells me that you have heard rumours that I am selling the Highland end of the business. Is that right?'

'That's what's being said, and the troops are getting edgy. Grubs from Corpach...'

Hercules cut him off.

'What do you say when they talk like that?'

'I have told the yard that if you were selling the business, you'd make sure we'd know first.'

Hercules smiled.

'Of course. You would say that. I have great faith in you, Jakey. You're a good man; loyal, dependable. I like that in a lieutenant - and you're right. When the time comes our people down the yard will hear it from me personally. I won't shirk that. You can be sure I will tell them when I have something to say.'

'You mean there isn't anything at the moment?' muttered Jakey. The sentence came out more like a statement than a question.

Hercules studied Jakey for a moment. He stood up, strode to the door, opened it, looked out, then closed it. Then he sat down behind the desk and leaned forward towards his manager.

'This is difficult,' he said. 'and complex. I had not wanted to show my hand quite yet. On the other hand, I want to keep faith with you. I owe that to you - so I will tell you the state of play. That is, if you want me to. You may decide that ignorance is best, then you can go on denying the rumours with a clear conscience.'

He stared at Jakey again. Jakey glanced back, not sure whether he should speak; not sure whether Hercules expected an answer. Had he asked a question?

Hercules saved his embarrassment.

'With your agreement, then,' he murmured. 'I'm repositioning the company. It has been clear to me for a while that the cost to profit ratio of the production arm of the business is poor; hardly worth the effort we put into it. The money is being made at the front end; with the boats. We do all the hard work – logistics, processing, marketing, packaging and shipping. All they do is stick a net or a few craves in the sea then pull them out and fish the pound notes out of them, eh? Our pound notes! Isn't that the way of it?'

Hercules laughed at his own wit. Jakey smiled nervously.

'It could be sorted out with tighter controls and closer supervision. But is it worth it? Do I want to go traipsing off to Mallaig twice a week? Do you? Would you want to? And what for? Peanuts! No! So, when they came looking for a slice of the action, I grabbed their hand off. They don't know what the business is worth. There are no assets to speak of. What is there? A yard, a van, a clapped out 44 tonner, a couple of fork lifts and a few hundred fish boxes; that's about it! What's it worth? What? Written down say, £50,000; no more. Most of the worth is in intangibles: contracts, contacts, knowhow, and especially the Douglas brand. But they don't know that. They see me in the Merc and think I'm coining it at their expense - so they want to buy it to lay their hands on the big money, the phantom big money, the big money that doesn't exist.'

'Because,' Hercules added, tapping the desk in front of him, 'because the intangibles stay here, with me, with us.'

How much of this did Jakey follow? Not much. To him Anthony Douglas & Son is the name on the big board at the gate and on the side of the lorries. The firm is down there, in the yard, in the shops and on the vans, in prawns and fish from West, North and in Nudge's truck on the way to England and the Continent. Anthony Douglas & Son had no substance beyond that, except perhaps that it paid the wages. Of course, he was aware that Hercules owned it and, imagined rather than knew, that Hercules made money out of it. But of profit and loss, returns, and capital to sales ratios – and intangibles, he knew nothing.

What did he make of Hercules' assessment of Anthony Douglas (Highland) Ltd.? Only this. That Hercules is selling the Mallaig business to invest his efforts and money on the Hecklescar operation.

Which is precisely what Hercules wants him to believe. Just as he wants Olivia to think that he is selling up in the Highlands to build the house at Latchlaw. He has also made another calculation: that Jakey will not keep quiet about the deal with the Mallaig men. That the man's loyalty to the folk he works with will trump his loyalty to his boss, and the story will leak out. For is he not married to the News of the World, to Ina? The workforce will then be reassured that their jobs are safe and will not withdraw the goodwill on which all such enterprises rely.

He needs to keep the business in good health, for he has

'repositioning strategies' for Hecklescar too.

CHAPTER EIGHTEEN

August, and two months since Peter Munro walked out of his flat, yet not a day had passed but that he crept into Mrs. Rostowski's attention. Where is he? What is he doing? Is he all right? He hasn't...? No, no, not that, I'm sure. I would have heard. Or, perhaps, he is with his family; with Dolinda or Daniel.

Then Daniel rang looking for his father. Had she seen him? When she said she had not, Daniel seemed to lose interest and more or less hung up on her.

After the call she went about preparing the evening meal for her young son and husband. But riled, frustrated and experiencing a guilt that she considered irrational yet insistent, she burned the potatoes. Her son, as usual, complained and, as usual, she dismissed his complaints as excuses for not eating what she had plonked in front of him. He did not believe in meals; food could be consumed at the play station, taken off a plate on the floor beside the cat or chewed while waiting for the school bus. Greg, her husband, expressed greater sympathy for the potatoes and offered to run down to the take-away for chips. However, she salvaged enough to produce a plate of mince and mash, bulked up with more carrots than she had originally intended.

After her son had escaped, Greg asked what was wrong and she realised that she had failed in her resolve to keep client and home separate. Instinctively she hated that word 'client'. That is Peter Munro's label on the schedule and on the front of his file - and that is what the Trainers had emphasised he must remain. *'You will render your contribution useless, if you turn client into friend and intervention into interference,'* they had warned on the Induction and Familiarisation Course.

At first, Mrs. Rostowski protested her innocence, but her husband would not be put off and she eventually confessed that Peter Munro had wormed his way into her anxiety. Greg listened attentively as she laid out her concerns and considerations.

'What do you make of it?' she said when she had run out of words.

'Who else have you talked to about him?' he asked.

'Well, Nikolai, the Clinical Psychologist, but that wasn't a lot of help. He specialises in sexually obsessive behaviour. As soon as I told him that Peter had made no improper advances and that his dilemma was more spiritual than sexual, he more or less lost interest.'

'The man has no taste,' said Greg, smiling, then went on, 'No, I meant have you talked to anyone who can inform you as to the status quo?'

'What do you mean?'

'Well, what's he's usually like. The status quo.'

'That's not what status quo means.'

'It does to me. What's he like, this Peter, usually? You don't know. Maybe the man just feels bad all the time about everything.'

'That's very profound for a van driver,' she clipped then wished she had not.

'Excuse me! Logistics' said Greg pleasantly.

'Logistics?'

'Yes, logistics. That's what it says on the van door: 'Logistics Solutions'. That's what I am; I'm not a van driver; I'm a solution.'

He chuckled and his wife found herself smiling.

She depended on Greg. Life did not faze him. When she first met him fifteen years ago, she could not believe he was just 'a van driver' and said so. He seemed then and seemed now to be capable of more. But he liked what he did and had no ambition to do anything else. A few years back he came home and announced that he had been promoted to Assistant Traffic Supervisor, but within a month, he'd resigned and was back on the road.

To him life is an insoluble riddle, insoluble but not unliveable. You did what you could when you could. When you couldn't you just got on with it and slogged through it. Before she got to know Greg Mrs. Rostowski had imagined that, with a Polish name, his stoicism had grown from family experiences in a ghetto or in a labour camp in the forests of Poland during the German occupation. She then discovered that his grandfather had been left behind drunk when his merchant ship left port without him sometime in the nineteen-twenties. He had found a job in an oil depot in Folkstone – driving a lorry.

Greg expanded his philosophy.

'When you go around every day, delivering, say, 150 parcels a day, you come across people. They're all different. I told you about him up at Hurst Green: he's never satisfied. If you're late he complains; if you're early, he complains. If it's in a box he wanted it in a bag; if it's in a bag he wanted it wrapped up; if it's too heavy he can't lift it, if it is light, he thinks something's missing. But it's none of that - it's him. I understand the man, but if you met him, you'd take him as kosher, and try to sort things out. But you couldn't. He doesn't want sorting out. He's happy the way he is. Well, not happy, satisfied. Well, not satisfied, settled, sort of, addicted. He's got himself down as one of life's victims. That keeps him going, gives him a purpose. Maybe your man's the same. It's not her; it's him. He doesn't want it solved. It makes him feel good to feel bad about it. You could be making things worse - encouraging the man to think he's heard done by. His wife left him years ago.'

'Or he left his wife.'

'No, not him; not your man - him at Hurst Green - *his* wife. Which just proved to him that nothing ever goes right. But it wasn't her. It was him.'

Although Mrs. Rostowski loved Greg for his constancy and contentment, occasionally it grated. Like now. This was always his solution. 'He/she needs to get on with it. Nothing can be done. That's life.' That is easily said, but it is not the answer for Peter Munro. He is not like the man at Hurst Green. His guilt is genuine. He feels deeply and it gives him no settled feeling about himself. His guilt disturbs him. He cannot be left to just strangle himself with his own tortured feelings. Surely, he was not always like that.

Or was he? Something Greg had said had sneaked past her protestations. What was he like before? She didn't know. She and Peter Munro had talked about his life before he came to Eastbourne but not often and not for long. For wherever they started they quickly ended up in that wasteland of a marriage and the arid track to pain and separation.

For her own satisfaction, with the bonus of proving her complacent life companion wrong, she determined to find out what was going on in Peter Munro's life before she met him.

CHAPTER NINETEEN

L ater that evening, Mrs. Rostowski left husband Greg sprawled in front of the television and drove to Peter Munro's apartment. What did she hope to find? She didn't know. Something; something to account for him taking off. Where had he gone and why? Could Greg be right? Had he always been gloomy? She had knocked back his suggestion but how well did she know Peter Munro? A year ago, she didn't know him at all and what she knew now came from what he had told her. What was he like before? Who could tell her? His children, surely.

The filing cabinet beside Peter's desk was locked, as was the bureau in the corner; but a key had been left in the top drawer of his desk. She opened the drawer and found a file with a one-word title: *Personal*.

Would it be professional to open and read a file with such a title? *'You are not investigating a crime'*, they had been lectured, *'respect client privacy.'* But there again the Care Co-ordinator, a seasoned veteran, had remarked that *'rules are for the guidance of the wise not the slavish obedience of fools.'*

She opened the file and found a list of names, addresses and phone numbers, her own amongst them. She was about to copy the phone number of Daniel, Peter's son, into her day book, when she changed her mind and stuffed the whole file into her briefcase. To ease her twittering conscience, she left a note in the drawer registering that she had taken it.

Daniel did not want to speak to her. Would he meet her?

'Can it not be done over the phone?'

'No, I need to see you. I'll come to you.'

'If you must!'

Daniel lived in the better part of Guildford and, two days after his brusque phone call, he showed Mrs. Rostowski into his lounge at the squeezed-in time of 6.30. Earlier, he would be at the office, later, they would be having their evening meal.

'Who are you?' he enquired when he had seated Mrs. Rostowski in an armchair. He himself perched on a dining chair at an angle from his visitor, not settled, making it clear that the meeting would not last long. Mrs. Rostowski handed him her ID card. He studied for a moment, then handed it back.

'You are a social worker?'

'No, my official title is Health and Well-being Counsellor, but I regard myself as your father's friend.'

This latter title clearly irritated him.

'A friend! Are you paid for what you do?'

'Yes.'

'Who pays you, the NHS or the local authority?'

'Your father.'

'My father pays you. It is a private arrangement. So, you are not an official at all. You are, to use your term, a friend. Is that it? My father's paid friend.'

Mrs. Rostowski ignored the gibe.

'I am appointed by the local council to help your father in any way I can. I can give you the name of the Care Co-ordinator to whom I am responsible, if that would help.'

'What would help,' stated Daniel, 'is that you stopped

interfering in our family affairs.'

This assault was unexpected. From her phone conversation Mrs. Rostowski had expected some preliminary suspicion from Daniel but believed that once they were face to face Daniel would thaw and answer her questions. She wanted to help his father. He would respond to that, surely.

She wanted to know if Peter had always been prone to depression and guilt; that's all. That, and where he might have gone. It hit her now that she had not prepared for the meeting. Had she not been warned always to prepare; not to take anything, anyone, for granted? She had allowed the notion she had of Peter's children, of Daniel (and Dolinda, for that matter) to lodge unopened in her mind. Nice children, affable, open and only too willing to help their troubled father.

Not so. Daniel sounded distant, assertive, superior. Her interest clearly offended him. What should she do? Then a thump in her stomach informed her that she ought not to be sitting there at all. She had not cleared it with her Care Co-ordinator because, as she well knew, the Care Co-ordinator would have raised doubts about the wisdom of it. It rose not from the Care Plan - not from a careful consideration of all the issues; but a hunch instigated by her van driver husband.

She frantically tried to remember what tone of voice her mentor had advised for use with uncooperative clients. She decided conciliatory would be best.

'Forgive me,' she replied quietly, 'I do not mean to interfere. If you would rather that I leave, I will do so.'

'Yes, that would be a good idea. There is nothing much wrong with dad. He should never have got tangled up with you lot in the first place. We could have sorted all this out without involving anyone else.'

'Does your sister think the same?'

'God, you people never give up, do you? Yes, Dolly

thinks the same. In fact, for your information, she told me not to meet you.'

He stood up to make it clear that the conversation was at an end.

'Thank you,' said Mrs. Rostowski, walking to the door. 'I will leave it to you whether you tell your father that I contacted you.'

'Tell him if you want,' said Daniel at the door, 'when you find him!'

When Greg came home that evening, he did not need to ask his wife how the interview had gone. Mrs. Rostowski confessed her humiliation almost before he closed the door.

'He's hiding something,' replied Greg.

'What do you mean?'

'What did he say about the mother?'

'Nothing! I didn't mention her. I didn't dare.'

'There y'are then. That could be it. They're embarrassed. A skeleton in the cupboard,' pronounced Greg; 'something they don't want you to find out.'

'No! What makes you think that?'

'Well, it figures, doesn't it? Why wouldn't Daniel want to help you? You're trying to help his father. Maybe he doesn't like the idea of his father needing help; not being able to cope with the mother and those letters. That might bug him and his sister.'

Mrs. Rostowski gave in.

'You could be right,' she agreed somewhat wearily. 'He was very blunt, aggressive even.'

'Ignorant bugger,' said Greg, then added, 'but you got what you went for, didn't you? Well half of it.'

Mrs. Rostowski was in no mood for riddles.

'By which you mean?' she clipped

'Well, his son said there was nothing wrong with him.'

'Nothing *much* wrong!'

'OK, nothing *much* wrong! That means that your man likely has always been on the dark side.'

'What do you mean, 'on the dark side''?

'Some people are born on the dark side.'

'Who told you that?'

'Gwyneth, in the office. She's into all that sort of thing. It all depends on the day you were born, who your mother is and which sign lay in the house of the sun on her birthday, or is it in the moon, or is it the sun in the house of the sign, I'm not sure, but Gwyneth has a chart that shows you.'

'What a lot of rubbish!'

'You can say that, but Gwyneth comes from Cornwall and they know all about the other side down there. She was right about me – and the man at Hurst Green. If you could find out what Peter Munro's birthday is and when his mother was born, she could look it up for you.'

'I am certainly not going to dabble in that sort of thing.'

'What are you going to do, then?'

'I'm going to find someone else who knows him. Not family. Peter talked about a good friend called Oliver. I'll track him down. He lives up in the Midlands somewhere.

'That's a big somewhere. Do you know who he works for? If you could find out I could look him up on the system.'

'Applegarth, I think. He mentioned them anyway. I think it was Applegarth.'

'What do they do; can you remember that?

'Property, I think.'

'Right, when I go in tomorrow, I'll see if I can find an Oliver at an Applegarth's in the Midlands somewhere.'

Then he added, 'and I'll speak to Gwyneth.'

'No, you will not!'

'Gotcha!' said Greg, laughing.

His laughter lifted his wife's mood enough for her to ask, by way of retaliation,

'What does Gwyneth say about you, then?'

'She says I am 75% light.'

'Did she? What about the other 25%?'

'Nobody's all light,' said her husband, sounding vaguely hurt. 'The deficiency comes from my father, she says. He was born in November when Saturn lay in the wrong house, in Watford.'

'What was Saturn doing in a house in Watford.'

'Not Saturn - the old man; he was born in Watford.'

'And that makes a difference?'

'So Gwyneth says.'

'Is he serious?' thought Mrs. Rostowski, but decided, from the little smirk on her husband's face, to let it lie.

CHAPTER TWENTY

I n Hecklescar, Jakey bottled up the confidence of Hercules and no matter how often tempted to uncork the truth, kept quiet. To some people, to his wife Ina, for instance, the thought of knowing something others didn't, was a delicacy to be savoured, but Jakey found Hercules' confession unappetising so he slid it to the side of his plate and picked the bones out of his life's main course.

At four in the morning Grubs from Corpach arrives to report that he thinks the cooling system for the prawn tanks is kaput and the water is too warm. It's not too bad but Angela and some of the girls are drafted in early to deal with the fish before they deteriorate.

Later Jakey has to decide who is going to cover for Superman? Eddie has called off again. What is it this time? A bad back. Of course. Yet had not Mick seen him playing golf on Friday? Eddie is called Superman by the other drivers because once, in a meeting about late deliveries, he accused Jakey of expecting his drivers to travel at superman speeds to deliver the fish. A retired Sanitary Engineer from Sunderland, well into his sixties, he is relatively well off and looks upon his job as helping out a fellow Rotarian. That, along with his enthusiasm for explaining his spinal problems to anyone who has an hour to spare, frequently made him late with deliveries so Jakey found himself almost welcoming the news that Eddie would once again not be able to undertake his round.

Eddie is one of Jakey's drivers, well, not his, they drive for Anthony Douglas & Son. Along with Elaine, Wullie, Jen, Mick and Little Dod, he takes fish from the yard at the crack of dawn each morning and brings it to the kitchen doors of hotels, cafés, pubs and restaurants throughout the Borders.

Once again Jen stands in for Eddie. She'll be glad of the money. It will go to provide for her son's three bairns. He cannot provide for them himself for he is now, and has been for the past ten weeks, in the Borders Mental Health Unit; there locked in for his own safety. Jen will visit him on Sunday. He may or may not consent to see her. She will then take some of what she has earned to Keira, his partner, on the Poplace Estate, to help her feed the bairns. Keira may or may not allow Jen to play with her grandchildren.

You must not think that Jakey knows nothing about this. He knows Jen, and he knows Callum, her son; knows about his attempted suicide, knows about Keira and the bairns, and how awkward she can be. And, although he has no qualification in psychology or social science, he knows that were Jen to lose her job she would also lose her hold on life; for did not her life consist largely of the bustle of the yard, the companionship of her fellow drivers and customers, and her ability to work long hours and boast of the distances she travelled?

What would she and the others do if the business folded? Is that what Hercules intended? Or, hopefully, it's just the Mallaig end. He wouldn't lead me on, would he?

At seven he receives a call from Little Dod. He's been given the wrong order. Edrom House needs monk fish tails and there are none in the box, and no crevettes, and the chef doesn't want hot smoked salmon, so whose order is this he'd been given? Check with Angela.

'Little Dod picked up his own orders this morning,' she reported. 'Didn't have time to wait for us. Serve him right. The order from Edrom House is still here. What ye're going to do?'

'Somebody'll have to take it. I'll ask Nudge.'

'He's just back from Barcelona. Got back late last night.'

'I'll ask him.'

'But what about the order for The Kitchen at Lauder?'

'The Kitchen at Lauder? What's that got to do with it?'

'That's the one that Little Dod has; he's taken it to Kelso.'

The phone rings. It is Elaine. She's in Lauder and doesn't have the order for The Kitchen.

'It's been taken to Kelso. You'll need to pick it up from there. See Karen at the shop.'

'What? I need to trail to Kelso? Who's to blame for this cock-up? It'll be Eddie again.'

'No, these things happen. But you'll do it for me, won't you, Elaine.'

'Yes, I'll do it. But if it's Eddie fouled up again....'

'It's not Eddie. He's not in.'

'Bad back again?'

'Yes, bad back – again!'

Shortly afterwards, Hercules arrives and wants a report of the day's events.

'Nothing we couldn't handle,' reports Jakey, for he thinks it is important that Hercules believes that the business is sailing along nicely and avoiding the shoals and reefs that may sink it.

Two streets away, a little later, at the Health Centre, Janet is sitting with Alice and Alistair waiting to see Dr Ross. Alistair does not want to be there; thinks there is no need for him to be there; thinks there is no need for Alice to be there. She had a fall, that's all. Janet thinks differently.

Dr Ross, one of the old school, pulled out of retirement to cover for the two doctors off on maternity leave, knows the onset of dementia when he sees it, but is required by guidance and checklists to humiliate Alice with the stipulated questions:

'Forty-two Hope Street. I want you to remember that.'

'Forty-two Hope Street.'

'No, not now,' says the doctor gently, 'I will ask you later.'

Alice smiles at the doctor and nods her head. She wants to please him.

'Where do you live?' 'Latchly Farm House.'

'How old are you?'

She looks at Alistair, then at Janet and speaks to them. 'I'm seventy-seven, no seventy-eight, aren't I?'

Janet assures her that she is seventy-eight next month.

'What year were you born?' 'Nineteen thirty-two.'

'Who is the current ruler or governor?' 'The Queen.'

'What is her name?' 'Elizabeth'.

'When did the First World War start?'

'Nineteen thirty-nine. I remember because we were all taken to the church by the headmaster.'

'No. that was the Second World War. When did the First World War start?'

Alice turns to Janet and mumbles, 'the First World War, in the trenches'

'Nineteen eighteen'.

'That's when it finished,' whispered Janet.

'Let her answer,' murmured the doctor and when Alice kept quiet ticked a box.

Alice stumbled her way through more questions; some she answered crisply, others with hesitation, a few baffled her completely. Then the doctor asked,

'Now let me hear you count backwards from 20 to 1?

'Twenty,' Alice started, 'nineteen, eighteen, seventeen,' she paused, 'seven….no sixteen, thirteen,' she stopped. 'Is that enough?'

'Yes,' replied Doctor Ross kindly, 'that's enough.'

'Now then, what was the address I asked you to remember?'

'It was….. Home Street, something Home Street.'

Home Street is a street in Hecklescar.

'We will need to refer your wife for assessment,' said the doctor to Alistair. Alistair didn't reply. But as they came out, he muttered to Janet.

'That was a bloody waste of time.'

They went back to Latchly. There they met Duncan and Hector clearing out the old steading and Alice made them all scrambled egg. Alistair did not stay with them long. He went out to hoe up his tatties.

That same evening, John Hendry, retired banker and friend of Duncan and Janet, walked up the path of Avignon to keep his appointment with Hercules. In his document case he carried the letter that Hercules had given to Duncan in exchange for his £10,000.

Hercules did not keep John waiting and John did not beat about the bush. After the briefest of pleasantries, he produced the letter. As he handed it over, he studied Hercules' reaction.

'Duncan Kerr is asking me about this letter,' said John, 'he thinks it is an investment certificate.'

Hercules did no more than glance at the letter. Then, in a studied gesture, he turned it over as if looking for a second page – or another document.

'Where is the certificate that goes with it?' asked Hercules.

'He doesn't have it,' replied John. 'In fact, he says he has never had a certificate.'

'Never had a certificate. Are you sure?'

'That's what he says, and so does Janet, his wife. She keeps the family's documents and she says there is nothing but the letter.'

'That's strange,' murmured Hercules, 'I'm sure one would be issued.'

'Not according to M&S,' said John, pleasantly, 'I spoke to Stephen yesterday morning (you know Stephen - GI Manager). He couldn't track it down. Thought it may have been an oversight, or that it's not one of theirs.'

'There will be a certificate,' asserted Hercules. 'It's just a matter of where. You'll need to leave it with me. I'm up in Edinburgh tomorrow. I'll track it down. We are meticulous about these things. . . . '

'. . . as you are required to be' put in John.

Hercules bridled.

'Of course. I'm at the office tomorrow, I'll check then.'

'And you'll bring me the certificate,' said John.

Hercules glowered at the banker.

'No,' he said bluntly, 'not to you. When I have the certificate, I will give it to the investor - Duncan Kerr, and to him alone.'

'Forgive me, of course,' answered John calmly, 'to Duncan; that's right. It is his money you have.'

Hercules stood up to bring the conversation to an end.

John also stood up, then said,

'If you cannot find a certificate because it has not been issued – due to an oversight, for instance - no doubt you will raise a new one.'

As he said this he stared steadily at Hercules. Hercules did not flinch. John had not expected him to flinch, but John detected more than a hint of animosity in his suppressed smile.

'Of course,' muttered Hercules.

'By the end of the week?' stated- John pleasantly but firmly.

From Avignon, John walked seaward along the harbour to where it met the sea wall, then he turned along The Bantry. (In more upmarket resorts The Bantry would be called a Promenade, but in Hecklescar the walkway behind the sea-wall is named The Bantry in honour of the Irishmen who built the wall in the early nineteen fifties). Neither the harbour nor The Bantry lay on the way home for John. But the bright evening persuaded John that it was too early to go back to his own house. In the winter, the curtains could be closed at seven and he could settle down in front of his log fire to read a book or watch television. But summer evenings brought no comfort to his home, so he decided to do what he and Lizzie often did on such evenings. He would buy an ice-cream cone and sit on a seat on The Bantry and watch the sea.

Of course, he would not sit there undisturbed; it is no place for brooding. Locals, alone, in pairs or with dogs, like him seeking solace from the pleasant evening, strolled along and greeted him as they passed. Some stopped and accused him of posing as a tourist, sitting there licking an ice cream. He responded in kind protesting that 'can't a man eat his cone in peace without someone wanting a lick.' Truth to tell he is glad of the banter, the company, the quiet interchange, the opportunity to talk.

'It is good to be here', he told himself as he took in the sea, the beach, the sky, the quiet town. The sun felt warm, he breathed in the clear air and attended the waves as they hurried up the beach in a hubbub of foam. Gulls had settled on the water and, for enjoyment, purely for enjoyment, surely, rode up the gathering wave as it reared towards the beach. Sometimes it seemed to John that the breaking wave must engulf the bird, but the gull would slide over the wave inches before it broke and surf gracefully down the other side. Now and again they delayed until the wave loured over them, ready to dash down and engulf them, but they took flight just in time and soared over the wave as it crashed down into the empty sea. Surely, thought John, one of them is bound to miscalculate and be swallowed up in the breaking wave. But none did. At least none in the hour and a half he sat there.

If only that last dread wave had spared my Lizzie.

CHAPTER TWENTY-ONE

Three days later, on Friday, Janet was able to report to John Hendry that Hercules had delivered the certificate by hand to Duncan the evening before. John, sitting at Janet's kitchen table, inspected the certificate and pronounced it satisfactory.

'What did Hercules say when he handed this over?' John asked Janet.

'I wasn't there, but Duncan said he told him that the certificate had been in preparation in the file in Edinburgh. An oversight, he said.'

'Did he now?' said John then wished he had not when Janet glared at him across the table and asked him what he meant.

He immediately apologised.

'Sorry,' John blustered, 'I am being overly suspicious'

Janet snatched back the certificate and inspected it.

'What's wrong with it?' she demanded.

'Nothing, not at all. It is perfectly valid. It entitles Duncan to ten thousand pounds worth of Golden Opportunities Units. It is issued by M&S. You could put it up as security tomorrow. No, it is fine. Rock solid. Sorry. I didn't mean to alarm you. It's okay.'

That is what John said, but what John had noticed, and what disturbed him was the fact that the units had only just been purchased. His suspicion had been justified. Duncan had handed over the £10,000 four years ago. Clearly, Hercules had not invested it in the M&S fund then, so where had it been? And why?

John has no means of determining the answer to his questions, but we are not similarly restrained for we can accompany Hercules the morning after he met John at Avignon.

He left Hecklescar early and arrived in India Street in Edinburgh shortly after nine o'clock, at the offices of HD Investments. Or, not so much offices, as office, one large Georgian room that housed two desks with an executive chair behind each, three filing cabinets and a low cupboard. To one side, close to the large window and hedged behind two or three Swiss Cheese Plants, there lay a small conference table with four chairs, a fresh water dispenser, a small fridge, an electric kettle surrounded by mugs, and a tin for biscuits. This is where Harold Douglas, Investment Advisor, entertained his clients.

In one of the chairs, behind one of the desks sits Alexander, Hercules' eldest son and Assistant. How people navigate their way through life fascinates me, but I already have far too many characters in this story, so I must resist the temptation to tell you about Alexander. Suffice to say that he takes after his father in sophistication but lacks his interest in business – any business.

He is behind his desk but he is not working; he is fiddling about with his mobile phone. He greets his father cheerfully and suggests that seeing that the office is now staffed without him he will go out for a little while; he's been stuck in the office all week.

'What about M&S? Have you not been there?'

'Oh, yes, every day.'

'You must go today to pick up a GO certificate. They know you're coming to collect it.'

Had Alexander been more interested in the business he would have enquired whether this was a new customer, but he had not that interest and did not ask. New customers were in short supply; had been since the start of the downturn two years ago. This lack of trade did not trouble Alexander. He knew about it, but did not regard it as any concern of his. As long as his salary appeared his bank account each month and as long as he got to live in Edinburgh, he was content.

However much this lack of ambition had grated on Hercules in the past, now it suited his purposes. Had Alexander been more assiduous he would have enquired, like John Hendry, where Duncan's money had been if it was not invested in M&S's Golden Opportunities Units. With a bit of probing he would have uncovered the mess that tangled the affairs of H D Investments.

Hercules had set up the business in good faith. Encouraged by his father and dazzled by the MBA certificate on his study wall, he had decided that more money lay in pound notes than fish - and they weren't so smelly. Almost as a side-line he had set himself up as a sort of financial adviser. Hecklescar and the villages around accommodated not a few retired people. Such people, like the four old men we saw on the golf course, had money to spare, to save and to invest. They had comfortable pensions, savings, and often had sold a substantial house in places where substantial houses sold for substantial prices. When they heard that the son of respected local businessman Anthony Douglas had trained in financial management they turned to Harold for advice, and HD Investments was born.

At first Hercules restricted himself to giving advice for a modest fee, but as more and more money bypassed him into other firms' coffers, Hercules decided to divert some of it into his own hands. He did not want to have to jump all the hurdles that regulators throw up in the path of those who want to set up Unit or Investments Trusts so he did a deal with M&S to set up the Golden Opportunities Life Fund. They took the business; he took a slice of the investments. The scheme took off; not spectacularly, but well enough for Hercules to set up the office in India Street. He was twenty-seven and looked forward to harvesting a small fortune before he was forty. He could then leave fish and fishworkers stranded in Hecklescar.

At first, he employed an experienced assistant to run the office, a Mrs. Taggart; a woman of maturer years with a grasp of the investment trade, and a stickler for financial propriety. Hercules put up with her until son Alexander left college at eighteen without much resembling qualifications.

He was, however, in Hercules estimation, qualified to sit in a chair, answer the phone, speak respectfully to clients and administer anything that needed administering. Alexander had sat in his chair for seven years when Hercules asked him to leave it to collect the certificate for Duncan.

The promised golden day of Golden Opportunities never dawned. Hercules' goal to be rich and out of fish by forty came and went but his self-delusion did not depart with it. The cause of his relative failure, he concluded, lay in the process whereby the money he so assiduously collected from his clients ended up, not with him, but in the pockets of the brokers at M&S. Certainly they threw him a share, but it wasn't much of a share, and as the years went by Hercules convinced himself that it did not reward him sufficiently his contribution. He did all the work; why should he not have more of the wealth.

Something else irked. Lately, Golden Opportunities Units had underperformed the market. Put another way, clients would have been better off putting their money into Post

Office savings. The promises that Hercules had made to them when they trusted him with their money began to sour. A sceptical few even traded in their Golden Opportunities thus depressing the price even further. Hercules had his work cut out persuading the more savvy of his clients to leave their money with him. Investments, he assured them, are for long-term growth. They would eventually come good.

The long-term stretched longer. The units grew, certainly, but not a lot. Eventually Golden Opportunities Units took on a tarnish, not least in the eyes of Hercules. After years of frustration, not aided by snide remarks from sceptics like John Hendry, Hercules convinced himself that he could surely do better than those jobsworths at M&S.

If ever you consider buying investment units you will find yourself accused of delinquency for leaving your hard-earned cash in a savings account or in a tin under the bed. 'Give it to us', the experts say, 'we will make it work for you.'

If, however, you are tempted by such allurements, you will find yourself bombarded with warnings, not once, not twice, not occasionally, but often and repeatedly, that *income from investments cannot be guaranteed*' and that *'the value of your investment may go down as well as up.'*

Investment managers do not tell you this because they want you know, but because they want to be able to say 'we told you so' when your little pile begins to dwindle. What they do want you to believe is that, in your case, with these particular investments, such warnings are unnecessary.

Hercules dissatisfaction with his lack of progress towards wealth led him to take the next, and fateful, step. He started investing clients' money not in M&S's Golden Opportunities Units but in what he called '*a bespoke investment portfolio*'; a collection of Hercules' own choice of investments '*tailor-made for you*'. You could have investments for income rather than capital growth, Asian, European or US, small companies or large, ethical or aggressive, innovative or pedestrian, nimble entrepreneurs or plodding corporations, coming stars or cash cows.

The name on the literature remained the same: Golden Opportunities - and Hercules would argue that the destination stayed unchanged. The money would eventually end up in a certificate like the one that Duncan now has. But in the meantime, in the two or three, or five, or ten years before that, it was in the care of HD Investments where it would be put to work in investments suited to the client. Investors would receive the mock leather folder with gold lettering, enclosing publicity bumf, glowing tributes to the financial genius of Harold Douglas, and an impressive letter, such as were found in the folder that Janet fished out of the filing cabinet in her kitchen.

Hercules' decision to go it alone coincided with Alexander's arrival in the firm. Indeed, it would scarcely have been wise for Hercules to venture on it had Mrs. Taggart still been keeping the books. Alexander, however, not only had no objection to his father's plan; he was blissfully unaware of it - and has remained in innocence ever since.

Hercules had designed another strand to his strategy (and he regarded it as a strategy, for he believed that strategies - dynamic, risk-taking strategies - are what separate the men from the boys, leaders from serfs, winners from losers).

Something had to be done to make 'brand Golden Opportunities' more attractive. He could produce new literature and 'more aggressively market' the firm, but he knew that word of mouth matters more than brochures. He had many opportunities to spread the word, not only amongst the retired well-off in Hecklescar, not only in the various towns and ports he reached through his trade, but also to those who could be found in the clubhouse at Gullane and at other prestigious golf courses throughout Scotland and beyond.

The word he spread sealed his fate for he promised a fixed percentage return on any money entrusted to him. He did not precisely *'guarantee'* any particular return on capital but, when he chatted to potential clients, (and that was how he went about winning business - person to person with a glass in the hand), he told them confidentially and confidently that he *'envisaged'* that a typical Golden Opportunities portfolio would return at least 10% year on year.

In the heady days before the financial crash in 2008, such a promise was reckless; after the crash it was suicidal.

CHAPTER TWENTY-TWO

At first, Hercules' strategy to go it alone with Golden Opportunities seemed to pay off. There were buyers a-plenty for his new portfolios. He kept clear of seasoned investors who, immunised by past offers that were too good to be true, kept their hands in their pockets. Instead he courted gullible amateurs - people with savings and lump sums from their pension fund; those with unexpected windfalls like Duncan Kerr, skippers with ideas above their station and old men playing golf. People, that is, that he could bamboozle with financial gobbledegook.

He convinced himself that, as a successful businessman, he had a deeper understanding of trade and commerce than the office-bound stock-pickers of firms such as M&S. He could see what they could not: he lived and operated in the real mercantile world so he had inside knowledge of what was going on, where the trends were leading, who was going places. He could pick winners.

Money rolled in, ostensibly into Golden Opportunities Life Fund Units, actually into Hercules' own portfolio of stocks and trusts and government bonds. He was on his way out of the fish business.

In the very first year he missed his 10% target by a

couple of percentage points. Such a warning shot should have sent him running for cover, but he put it down to teething troubles and pressed on. He paid out the promised return using money that had just come in from new investors. It would be replaced, he assured himself, once the investments ripened: 'you can't judge a portfolio on one year's returns.'

In the second and third years he fared little better and thus became entangled in something close to a Ponzi scheme, where earlier investors are paid dividends out of money paid into the fund by those just joining. He found himself in a bind. On one hand he could not afford to pay out what he had promised; on the other he could not stop promising it, otherwise he would not attract the new money he needed to meet his commitments.

When we see him on the golf course contemplating disappearance, he has been juggling this impossibility for six years. The last two have been hellish as the world-wide financial crisis throttles the banks. In turn they choke off the loans that companies rely on to keep them breathing. Many go to the wall. Some of those take the investments of HD Investments with them.

As the storm rolls in Hercules finally admits defeat and shuts down his home-made fund to new investors and cuts the 'envisaged' return. This creates a run on his portfolio; investors want out. He finds himself having to buy out those wanting to quit and reassuring those that remain that his investments are sound and that under his leadership 'we can weather the storm.'

I have bored you long enough with financial wordery. Let us cut to the chase. Where does Hercules get the £10,000 to buy Golden Opportunities Units from M&S to give to Duncan? From the coffers of Anthony Douglas & Son Ltd, that's where; from the fish business he despises. Can the firm afford to lose such sums of money? Of course not! Having been milked in similar ways over the past four years it is teetering on the brink of bankruptcy.

Now you know why Hercules plans to disappear. Like a man whose roof is leaking in a thunderstorm he has run out of buckets. The damage cannot be repaired. He must leave the house before it falls in on him.

It is not only his troubles that afflict him. He has reached fifty and the years have soured him. Time was when he was flattered to be introduced as Chief Executive of his own company. 'You're young for that,' was the response he expected and often received. Now, at Gullane, in the club at Edinburgh and elsewhere he often heard, 'still slogging away at the fish?'

That is bad enough. What is worse is his estimation of his achievements. His businesses are faltering. He is not prospering. He is not wealthy. Not wealthy, and he ought to be. He could have done so much better had he not been tied to Anthony Douglas and Son. 'I have wasted the best years of my life creating and sustaining a piddling little peripheral business!'

At first when these convictions grumbled, he consoled himself that he had done the right thing by the old man. He had lent the business his time and expertise. He also envisaged Jakey, Angela, the girls in the fishyard and the drivers on the road as lost sheep in need of a shepherd. Fishermen too, of Hecklescar, Mallaig, the Moray Firth and the South-West were hapless sailors in a sea of uncertainty in need of his helmsmanship.

These consolations, never deep-rooted, had withered with the years. His father was long gone and for Jakey and the others he now felt no obligation. 'Is 20 years not enough? What have I got to show for the millions of pounds I have put into their pay packets? How many of them are ripping me off? Do I have to nurse them until I drop? Am I really condemned to spend the rest of my days paddling about in this backwater?'

Such perceived shackles reassured him. He is not to blame for his misfortunes; they have been forced on him. Two years ago, before the financial crash, cold reality had tapped at the door of his arrogance. A troubling voice suggested that his misfortunes might be self-inflicted. The collapse of the financial markets had silenced the still small voice. It was not his fault - but that of the markets and the bungling financial institutions. He had been on the path to recovery and onward to riches; in it for the long term, but fickle circumstance, the perversity of markets, the incompetence of global institutions, the loss of nerve of his investors had cost him his future. So be it, *'when the going gets tough, the tough get going.'* He must create for himself another future; must re-invent himself. For that he needed a clean break - and as much money as he could lay his hands on. He must sell up lock, stock and barrel. That includes not only the Highland company, but also Anthony Douglas & Son and Latchlaw.

Hang on, you say, has he not promised Jakey that he has no intention of selling the Hecklescar business? You are correct: he has made such a promise, but Hercules understands how Hecklescar works. He must create a diversion. No-one must know what he has in mind until it is too late for them to prevent it. Anthony Douglas & Son is not a company; it is an institution; it is to Hecklescar what Harrods is to London or Princes Street to Edinburgh. The rumour of its sale would send a shiver through the town and undermine morale, just at the very time he would be trying to persuade buyers that it is a thriving, well-loved company. Any future owner must be assured of the goodwill and enthusiasm of a committed workforce.

He needs Jakey to believe that the Hecklescar business is safe, and through him he wants Ina and other news spreaders to scotch any rumour that the yard is on the block. So that when 'sale of business' comes up in conversations and queries on the streets, homes, pubs and cafes of Hecklescar those in the know will be able to say,

'No, it is only the Mallaig end.'

If he has calculated aright, hearers will then say, 'It's an awfu' place this, folk aye get the wrong end of the stick.'

Hercules has another reason for caution: Peter Munro. 'He must not know what I am about until it is too late for him to do anything about it – and Cockburn Heath says Peter is thinking about re-settling in Hecklescar.'

Peter Munro tormented Hercules. When he recalled Peter Munro, searing questions ripped through his mind. Who the hell does he think he is? Where was he educated? Hecklescar High! What are his qualifications? City & Guilds, eh? What's his profession? A bricklayer! Son of a builder! What has he done to deserve his millions? What's the number? Thirty-five million! How the hell did he make that kind of money? He didn't make it! It landed in his lap! Luck, that's all! Not ability, not shrewd business management, not long-term strategy, not slogging it out in a fish business! None of those! Just a bit of property your father left you, and being in the right place at the right time!

On such burning questions he could dab but one cooling consolation.

'Ah, but who got the woman, eh? Quit the field, eh? Couldn't compete! Wouldn't compete! Slunk off, eh? See what I mean - the man has no guts - and no quality.'

CHAPTER TWENTY-THREE

Greg, terrier-like, sniffed out Applegarth's, a builders' merchant, with sites spread over the Midlands and East Anglia. He rang the head office, but they didn't have an Oliver. They used to have an Oliver but he left about ten years ago after his accident.

'Do you have his address?

'Yes. Who's asking?'

'Social Services, East Sussex,' says Greg, assuredly.

'He's not in trouble, is he?'

'Far from it,' replies Greg, 'but it's confidential, you understand.'

'Of course. It's Oliver Twist, 35, Frobisher Drive, Long Eaton.'

'Oliver Twist?'

'Yes, that's not his real name, but that's what he goes by. D'ye want his phone number?'

'If you have it.'

'Tell him Doris is asking after him, and hopes he's making out OK.'

When Mrs. Rostowski rang, the voice at the other end answered, 'Oliver Twist'.

Mrs. Rostowski introduced herself and, conscious of her frosty reception by Daniel, Peter's son, cautiously explained why she wanted to speak to him. Oliver's reaction could not have been more different.

'Peter, of course, where is the old bugger? I've been trying to lay hold on him, but he's never in.'

'No, I'm afraid not. He's left home and nobody seems to know where he is.'

'Ah,' replied Oliver, 'So he's done it'

'Done what?'

'Look, where are you?'

'Eastbourne.'

'That's quite a way. Could you come here?

'Where's here?'

'Long Eaton.'

'Of course. Yes, I could make that. When would suit you?'

'Any time except Fridays. I'll not be going anywhere any other time. Better in the afternoons.'

On a bright Saturday in the early days of August, Greg Rostowski drove slowly along the beetling bungalows of Frobisher Drive until he arrived at number 35. There he dropped off his wife and told her he would come back in an hour. Mrs. Rostowski rang the doorbell and prepared to meet Oliver Twist.

Let me guess. When I first introduced Oliver, a picture formed in your mind. Certainly, that is what had happened to Mrs. Rostowski. When she spoke to Oliver on the phone, a dumpy, bright, active man in his sixties materialised in her imagination. How close is that to your picture of Oliver? She expected someone answering that description to open the door in Frobisher Drive, and usher her cheerfully into the house.

However, a woman opened the door, a woman perhaps in her late fifties, a neat, pleasant, gracious woman.

'You'll be Mrs. Rostowski?'

'Yes.'

'I am Moira Twiss,' she smiled, 'without the 't'.'

'Ah, I wondered,' started Mrs. Rostowski.

'Blame his mother,' replied Moira, 'for calling him Oliver. He's in here.'

They had reached the door of a room. Mrs. Rostowski entered, expecting a lounge, but found herself in a bedroom. Immediately in front of her lay a bedstead, and lying on it, lying flat on his back, fully dressed, with only his head raised, was the man she had come to see.

'Come in, come in,' he shouted in the voice she had heard on the phone.

'He's not up yet; we're having a slow morning this morning,' explained Moira, then seeing the surprise of Mrs. Rostowski, said,

'Oh dear, has no-one mentioned to you. Oliver is paralysed from the neck down.'

'But it doesn't stop me from being an awkward bugger,' exclaimed the man on the bed.

'Forgive him, he's cantankerous until we stick him in his chair,' Moira smiled and picked up a hand-held control from the bedside rail.

As Mrs. Rostowski watched, the pair, in a series of swift, choreographed movements, conveyed him from flat on the bed to sitting comfortably in the wheelchair beside it.

Moira, using the control raised the head of the bed lifting Oliver into a position where he could loop an arm into a sling that hung over him. As he took the weight of his inert body Moira slid out a draw sheet from under him. (Moira explained later that this draw sheet could be pulled from one side or the other to turn him over onto his left or right side. This was particularly useful during the night when he had to be turned every three of four hours to stop bedsores developing). Moira pulled a strong bright blue sling under his body and he lowered himself onto it. She then brought into position a hoist that ran along a rail mounted under the ceiling. She lowered the hoist, and having strapped Oliver's legs together to stop them spreading and flopping about, she attached the straps of the sling onto the metal frame of the hoist and lifted Oliver bodily into the air.

Mrs. Rostowski, disconcerted by the matter-of-fact way the pair went about the routine, blurted out,

'I'm sorry, I didn't know, I wouldn't have....'

'Stop right there,' put in Oliver, dangling in mid-air. 'I might not be able to walk, and I can only move one arm, but I can talk and I can tell you about Peter Munro if that's what you want. He's a good man. Have you found him yet?'

'No.'

'Well, I can't help you with that. He's not here. Unless the missus is hiding him in a cupboard.'

'It's not that; I'm sure he'll turn up when it suits him.'

By the end of this exchange Oliver was sitting comfortably in his wheelchair and had dispatched Moira to the kitchen to make tea.

Now that he was settled Mrs. Rostowski told him what she knew of Peter Munro, of his breakdown and of his troubled recovery. The tea came and Moira asked Mrs. Rostowski,

'Has he told you why he is like this?'

Oliver made to object. His wife cut him off.

'He won't tell you, so let me. It was an accident at work. He was working at Applegarth's. They were loading roof beams,' She glanced at her husband, 'is that it?' Oliver nodded, 'roof beams onto a lorry when the sling slipped and the load swung out and hit Oliver. They say he dropped like a stone. That was it; he has never moved since. They took him to hospital, then to the Spinal Injuries Unit at Sheffield, but nothing could be done. He has a little movement in his left arm and some movement in his hand, but that's all.'

Then she added,

'Unfortunately, it had no effect on his mouth or vocal cords.'

Oliver had heard this little description with a faint smile on his lips. Now he laughed out loud.

'How do you cope?' Mrs. Rostowski heard herself saying.

'I am a nurse and I have help. Carers come twice a day every day and, two nights a week, one of them sleeps here and does for Oliver what needs to be done during the night.'

'A piss; that's what she means,' put in Oliver.

'There's a lot more to it than that,' she said, and would have given further details had Oliver not cut her off.

'Are you finished? She hasn't come to hear about me.'

'Another advantage,' said Moira from the door, 'is that if he goes too far, I can always run away and leave him. He couldn't catch me.'

Then she left the room.

Mrs. Rostowski turned back to Oliver and caught a tightening of his smile. That made her wonder if the banter and bravado were a mask put on for strangers, or defence against a life hemmed in by impotence and uncertainty? Or love, perhaps; love applied to impossibility.

'Sorry about that interruption,' he said pleasantly, 'Now what do you want to know about Peter Munro?'

'What do you know about him? How long have you known him?'

'I met Peter, what, twenty years ago; a bit more perhaps. He hadn't been here long. He came from up North somewhere - Scotland. I was working for Applegarth's, the builders' merchants, managing the larger contracts, when he turned up looking for advice. He hadn't been down here long but he'd come with a bit of cash and had bought up a few older properties that he was thinking of developing. We hit it off straight away. He was a straight guy; innocent, almost. I kept him shy of some of the hucksters. He rode the housing boom, buying up old council houses and doing them up. Then he moved to London and did even better. He hit the jackpot with the Docklands development. He bought up a few properties there for a song and sold them for a fortune. He asked me to join him when he moved down there. He offered me a partnership. If I'd taken him up on it, I'd be a rich man now. But Moira didn't want to leave her folks.'

Oliver stopped.

'That's not fair,' he added. 'It wasn't just Moira. I didn't want to go. At the time, it looked a bit iffy, and I had a lot to lose if it went pear-shaped. We'd the family to bring up and we'd just bought our house - and I liked what I was doing at Applegarth's. To be honest I thought he'd be eaten alive down there. But he was shrewder than I gave him credit for. He's no pushover.'

'So, you lost touch with him?'

'No, Peter Munro's not like that. We stayed in touch. He would come on the phone for hours, asking about prices and materials, and costings - and he paid me for it. I didn't want it, but he kept sticking a thousand pound now and then into our bank account. Still does. This house is his. He bought it - and paid for all the equipment. Eventually I had to tell him to bugger off. What with what I get from Applegarth's (they've been very good), the compensation and the disability we're better off now than when I was working.'

He smiled, then added, 'but I wouldn't recommend it.'

'What do you know about his wife?'

Oliver did not answer immediately and Mrs. Rostowski could almost hear him re-arranging his thoughts

'A sad case that. She could cope up here but went to pieces down there.'

'She belonged here? I thought she was a Londoner.'

'No, she worked in our Dereham depot, in Norfolk. But she belonged out in the sticks, a little village called Tittleshall, I think.' He paused. 'That was the trouble. Like Moira a bit, only worse. She should never have gone to London. She thought Dereham too big and noisy, God help us, and he took her to London! It almost destroyed her. She just couldn't settle. He thought about bringing her back here. I believe at one time he bought a house in Norwich, but Canary Wharf took off so he felt he had to stay. He offered to move her back up here with the kids but she wouldn't have it. She was old-fashioned, you know, 'a wife should be by her husband's side.' So, she stayed, and it cost her. When the kids reached their teens and no longer needed her, she tried going back to work but hated it. She was a looker and attracted the wrong sort of attention. She gave up her job and then had a bad nervous breakdown. She would sulk for days; at other times she would shout and scream at him. Then she would say sorry and try to make it up to him. Sometimes she would lie in bed all day; at other times she would prowl round the house at night. One night he found her in the front street, in her nightie, crying in the pouring rain. Peter couldn't cope with that so booked her into a rest home for a few months (a private place), where I think, she was treated for what - anxiety, depression, I don't know.'

He stopped and asked Mrs. Rostowski to give him a drink. He pointed out a beaker with a lid pierced by a straw. She picked it up and put it up to his mouth. He took the straw between his lips and sucked it strongly and steadily for a few seconds. As Mrs. Rostowski held the beaker to his lips, it occurred to her that she had forgotten that Oliver was paralysed. His narrative had flowed so freely and clearly that she had forgotten that he could move hardly anything other than his mouth. He withdrew his mouth from the beaker and thanked Mrs. Rostowski. Then he carried on with his story.

'Peter tried to look after the kids on his own, then packed them of to Dylis' mother in Tittleshall. When Dylis came out of the home, she seemed better. He bought a house in Dereham and they moved there. At least that was the plan. He'd work from Dereham. But he made the mistake of keeping the house in London to use as a base when he worked there. I told him it wouldn't work – and it didn't. He was up to his neck and eyes in contracts in London and began staying away longer and longer.

'Then, of course, he never knew what kind of reception he'd get when he went home. He used to come to our place. We lived in Peterborough then, and he would come and bend my ear about it all. In the end he persuaded himself that he was the problem and that the children would be better off without him - not so much disruption. He reckoned she looked after the kids well. I couldn't see it. But he convinced himself that they were better off left with their mother.'

Ever since her first conversations with Peter Munro, a suspicion had bothered Mrs. Rostowski. She had suppressed it, but as Oliver talked it surfaced again. She interrupted Oliver.

'He hadn't been seeing anyone else, had he?' she asked.

Oliver paused as if considering the question; as if the question might have more than one answer. Then he said firmly,

'For him? No, I don't think so. Peter's not like that.'

'Sure?'

This time there was no pause.

'Sure enough! He would have told me. He talked about some woman up north that had knocked him back, I think. In fact, I think that's why he came down here. But I'm pretty sure he wouldn't go off with another woman with her in the state she was in – and with the kids. No. Peter Munro wouldn't do that. He's a decent man.'

He continued, 'they divorced in the end, didn't they?'

'No,' replied Mrs. Rostowski, 'Peter wouldn't think of it.'

'Figures. Now he's taken off?'

'Yes,'

'When?'

'About two months ago.'

'He has family – in Guildford, I think. A son and daughter, I believe. Maybe he's gone there.'

'No, he's not there. I spoke to the son, Daniel, but he wasn't very helpful; seemed to resent my interest. He asked me not to interfere in the family affairs.'

'That doesn't surprise me. Peter didn't see much of them. There is something sour there. I'm not sure what. I asked Peter what had gone wrong, but he wouldn't tell me. I think it must have been something to do with Dilys. But I'm not sure what.'

'Are the son and daughter in touch with their mother?' asked Mrs. Rostowski.

'I don't know. Maybe that's what it is. If he was away a lot and left her with them, they might resent that. They might even blame him for what happened to their mother, for her depression. But I don't know. I really don't know. Peter would never talk about it. He would just shrug and say, 'these things happen."

'Yes, I found that when I started on the family. I always thought that he didn't want anyone criticising his son and daughter. I tried to tell him not to take all the burden on himself but he would just go quiet on me.'

'I've had that often enough,' stated Oliver. 'Now he's taken off and you don't know where he's gone?'

'I don't. But he did write me a long letter telling me he was going: 'to settle it' he wrote. He told me he would keep in touch, but I haven't heard from him. I really don't know what he's up to. The more I hear about him, the less I understand. That's why I am here. What do you make of it? You know him better than I do.'

'I'm not sure of that. But let me take a guess. I would say it started with big money he made from those deals down at Canary Wharf. It became an obsession with him. He thought some of them were dodgy. He kept on about putting right what he'd done wrong. I told him that he had acted no worse than the rest of us, and better than most, but he wouldn't listen. He just felt guilty. Or is it just about Dilys - not being fair to her, taking her away from her family, taking her to London, leaving her with the children? Who knows? But he'll have told you about that. Let's have another cup of tea.'

Mrs. Rostowski hesitated, half-expecting him to rise and make it. Then she said hurriedly,

'Do you want me....?

'No, I have Possum,' said Oliver cheerfully. 'With Possum I can switch the lights on and off, put on the telly or the radio, and change the channels. It's the number of clicks that counts.'

He turned his head sideways and took between his lips the mouthpiece of a tube that extended from behind the bedside cabinet. He sucked it. A small screen on the cabinet clicked. He counted to five then stopped sucking. Mrs. Rostowski heard a buzzer sound from somewhere in the house.

'Five. That'll summon the servant girl,' he said with a short smile, 'if she hasn't skived off.'

After a couple of minutes, Moira arrived.

'A cup of tea for the lady, love,' he said.

'And, no doubt, for the gentleman,' she replied, then turned to Mrs. Rostowski.

'Your husband is in the kitchen.'

'What?' protested Oliver, 'entertaining strange men behind your husband's back!'

'Not half as strange as my husband,' riposted Moira and went to make the tea. When she came back Greg came with her and shared the tea.

Greg and Oliver hit it off immediately, finding in vans, pallets and building materials, enough interest to please them both.

Shortly afterwards Mrs. Rostowski and her husband left to make their way back home.

'Did you find what you came for?' asked Greg as they drove back to Eastbourne.

'I've forgotten what I came for.' replied his wife gruffly.

'To find out if he's always been on the dark side.'

'Would you stop going on about the dark side? It seems he regretted what he had done to his wife - and maybe to other people, and now can't put it right. But, by all accounts he comes over as a decent man. The more I know about Peter Munro, the less I understand.'

She sounded agitated and looked displeased. Greg shut up. He liked to talk and didn't like his wife not talking to him. Had she fallen out with him? Had he said something? About the dark side, perhaps? Had she stopped speaking to him?

After ten long minutes, he tried his hand.

'Grace,' he asked gently, 'if I was like him, like Oliver, would you look after me?'

Her expression softened.

'Of course,' she said quietly. Then added,

'And would you do it for me?'

Greg did not hesitate. He spoke as a man who had considered his position.

'Emphatically' he announced.

CHAPTER TWENTY-FOUR

After Mrs. Rostowski had relieved her sister-in-law of her son and fed him, she left him in the care of his father and retreated to the kitchen to write up her notes. She did so in that irritable state of mind that had settled on her since she'd left Oliver's house in Long Eaton.

Her conversation with Oliver had solved nothing. Could Greg be right? Was Peter Munro, if not a clinical depressive, simply someone who preferred black clouds to silver linings? She had not thought so when, over the months, she had talked with him. Certainly, doubts and anxieties plagued him, but she believed that their cause lay in something he had run into rather than something that welled up from within; a circumstantial storm, not inner turmoil.

Oliver clearly knew Peter well and his account of the man reinforced her opinion that Peter Munro, generally, was a pleasant, open, decent sort of man, driven to distraction by a depressive wife and to despair by self-condemnation.

Whatever detail Oliver had added, the problem remained the same: regret. Regret about what he'd done to his wife by taking her away from her family and community? That's it, isn't it? Or is it? Mrs. Rostowski felt back where she had started. This is the cause of her agitation. Not only is she not getting anywhere, she doesn't know where she wants to be.

She had taken rough notes as she spoke to Oliver and had now typed them into her laptop. She would print them out and put them in the file: *Case Notes: Peter Munro;* it said on the label – a troubled life reduced to scratches on a piece of paper. What help is that?

As the printer rattled off the pages, Mrs. Rostowski, as a matter of habit, glanced through her notes to make sure she had not missed anything. At the very end of the interchange she noticed a scribble that, in her irritation and in her desire to finish the chore of typing, she had not bothered to decipher: *'deals CW'*. She knew what that meant. CW for Canary Wharf and the lucrative deals that Peter Munro pulled off in East London that had set him on his feet. No need to scratch around; she knew about that, didn't she? As she went to close her notebook a doubt crept into her mind: Oliver had told her about the deals at the beginning of their conversation,

'so why did I write that note at the end? It was just before Oliver ordered the tea. It's amazing how he did that, with the tube.'

Which thought now replicated what she had thought at the time, the thought that had distracted her. What was Oliver saying when she scribbled *'deals CW'*?

Suddenly, vividly, it stepped forward. She heard Oliver speaking. *'I would say that is when it started'.* When what started? Peter's overwhelming sense of regret, that's what. Why did Oliver think it started at the time of the deals? What had happened then to trigger it? Why hadn't she followed it up? The tea and the tube, that's why. They had distracted her - and the unexpected appearance of Greg.

She must contact Oliver again. On her ToDo list she scribbled *'contact Oliver about 'deals CW''*. Instantly she felt her irritation ease. She had something to do next.

When she returned to the lounge, Greg found, to his relief, that he had a much less agitated wife.

CHAPTER TWENTY-FIVE

'Who is Peter Munro?' asked Sally of her grandmother one day in early September. Sally, you remember, is the daughter of Olivia and Hercules, training to be a nurse in Edinburgh, but now in Hecklescar on four days' rest after three twelve-hour night shifts at the Royal Infirmary.

She is sitting with Connie, her mother Olivia's mother, in the little conservatory at the back of Connie's house in Killie's Court. She is helping her grandmother stitch small patches of cloth into a patchwork quilt.

'How have you heard of Peter Munro?' responded Connie with a little smile.

'Christine mentioned him when I was out with Hector and her last night.'

(Hector, you recall, is Sally's brother, boyfriend of Christine, Duncan and Janet's daughter.)

'Do you like Christine?'

'I do, she's not. . ..' Sally paused as she searched for the right word.

Connie supplied it.

'Stuck-up?'

'Yes, I mean no. She's not stuck-up, she's down to earth. She's just what our Hector needs.'

Connie sensed Sally's frustration with her parents' practised superiority. She knew that, given encouragement, Sally would once again launch into a complaint about what her mother expected of her; how she didn't want to be a doctor; wanted to be a nurse; that is what she intended; she didn't want to earn a lot of money; didn't care what other people (the snobby people her mother and father mixed with), didn't care what they thought of her. She would make her own choices. In spite of what her mother and father wanted; if they didn't like it, they could stuff it. Connie prevented the fusillade by returning to the original question.

'What did Christine say about Peter Munro?'

'We were just chatting and his name came up. Something about him coming back to live in Hecklescar. She seemed to think I should know about it. When I said I had never heard of him, she went all secretive and said I should talk to mum, or you. Who is he?'

'Well, let's put it this way,' Connie said, leaning forward towards Sally as if she were letting her into a secret, 'if your mother had listened to me, Peter Munro would be your father.'

'What? He and mum were lovers!'

'No, not that. At least I don't think so, but they were close and courting. Then Harold Douglas arrived in a sharp suit and a flashy car and swept her off her feet, as they say.'

'Who? Mum?' exclaimed Sally. 'Swept off her feet! That doesn't sound like her. She's always been so ..... hard, so unsentimental. I can't see her being swept away by anything.'

'Yes, it does sound strange, doesn't it? But she was younger then; not that much older than you are now. Harold Douglas seemed quite a catch. At least that's what most of the town thought – and your grandfather. He was flattered when the Douglas heir, as he called him, started paying attention to his daughter, and encouraged him – and her.'

'But you didn't?'

Until now Sally and Connie had been sitting along alongside each other at a small table stitching the quilt. Now Connie put down her work and took hold of Sally's hand.

'I am becoming a bitter old woman, Sally. You mustn't listen to me.'

'You're not bitter,' protested Sally, and would have continued to protest had Connie not intervened.

'Let me be the judge of that. Life makes us what we are, and my life....'

She stopped, looked at Sally intensely then released her hand. She made to go back to her stitching. But Sally grabbed back her hand and said firmly,

'Don't treat me as a child. What were you going to say?'

Sally felt her grandmother's grip tighten and saw that her eyes had filled with tears. She rose from her chair and hugged the old woman. Then whispered,

'Tell me, gran, what is it?'

For a while neither woman moved or spoke. Then Sally released her grandmother and Connie, with her needle busy in her hand, related to Sally for the first time, something of her life with Fordyce. Of her discovery that she had married an empty shell; that his slight abilities, interests and affections clattered around in him like a baby's rattle. He was, she had soon discovered, incapable of the love she had anticipated and hoped for in her life's companion. She poured out to Sally the whole weary story of her life fettered to Fordyce, including, almost in passing, that after Olivia was born, they never made love again, never slept together in the same bed. She talked about making a life for herself, bringing up her children, mixing with other mothers, serving on committees, gathering around her a circle of goodish friends, learning new skills, like quilt making and making marmalade, of playing bowls and joining the walking group.

She told Sally too, of her struggle with cancer, and the guilty relief she felt when Fordyce left her. She recounted the quiet pleasure she gained from welcoming Olivia's boys, Alexander and Hector, into her life. She closed her story with an account of what she called 'a redeeming miracle'- the love and company of a precious granddaughter.

Sally listened intently to all Connie recounted and half-blushed when she herself stepped into it. But for a while she stitched on and said nothing. Then she said,

'I don't remember grandad, but mum said he came back and you nursed him till he died. That's true isn't it?'

'Yes, that is true,' said Connie flatly.

'That was very, very understanding. Not the action of a bitter old woman.'

'I wasn't old then,' replied Connie brightly, trying to make light of it.

'But it shows you are not bitter – and you have every right to be.'

'Do I? Do you not think that perhaps, as well as Fordyce not being the husband I wanted, that I was not the faithful wife he needed?'

Connie had not intended using the word 'faithful'. She had meant to say 'loyal': going along with what he had to offer; taking him as he was. That is what she had meant to say. But the word 'faithful' popped into her mind and out of her mouth before she could catch it. Sally noticed.

'You mean that there was someone....'

She got no further.

'That is not a question you should ask your grandmother,' said Connie, bluntly, then continued, 'but since I have led you into it. No, there never was anyone else. I was 'faithful'. And I hope when you find a good man you will be faithful too.'

'How do you know a good man when he comes up?' said Sally philosophically, 'neither you nor mum seem to have found one.'

'I did find one, but it was too late by then,' said Connie.

'Did you?' exclaimed Sally, 'Who was he?'

'His name,' said Connie blandly, 'was Peter Munro.'

'The same Peter Munro?' exclaimed Sally.

'Yes'

'The one mum jilted.'

'The very same,' replied Connie, then added, 'but I don't know why I am telling you this. I have never told anyone else.'

'Because he is coming back?' suggested Sally, sounding like one of those Life Counsellors that are springing up everywhere.

'Now, now, Sally' Connie scolded, but pleasantly for, truth to tell, the intimacy warmed her.

'Good heavens, Sally, I was old enough to be his mother.'

'How old were you? You couldn't have been that old.'

'I was fifty. I remember that because Peter Munro bought me flowers for my fiftieth birthday.'

Sally pressed on in pursuit of a love story.

'And how old was he?'

'I'm not sure. He was older than Olivia by, what, six years. Olivia would be 24 then so he must have been about thirty.'

(Do not be fooled by all of this, *'not sure. . .. Olivia was . . . .so he must be. . .. about thirty.'* She knows his age precisely, almost to the day: he was thirty, twenty years younger than she.)

In her naivete Sally saw through it all. She did not shift her gaze from the quilt but asked quietly,

'Were you in love with him?'

Connie erected a wall to keep out the question.

'I was a married woman.'

'But you said you and grandfather didn't love each other. The fact that you were married to him makes no difference to your feelings. Either you love someone or you don't and you didn't love grandfather. You said that.'

'That certainly is the modern way. All based on feelings. But then it was different; it depended on......what? What did it depend on? It's not right to say 'legalities' – though to be respectable you had to have a bit a paper that said you were married. But not only that. You didn't keep looking at the certificate. So, what was it based on? Promises. Yes, I suppose that was it. You promised and you stuck to your promise.'

'Even if it made you miserable?'

'Especially then.'

'But it couldn't stop you loving someone else – even if from a distance.'

'Loving from a distance! You really should stop watching soap operas.'

'I don't watch soap operas. I don't like soap operas. I don't have time. Stop wriggling, gran. Did you or did you not love Peter Munro?

Connie laid down her needle, sat back into her chair, and instead of looking at Sally looked up out of the conservatory into the cloud blown blue sky.

'I suppose I did.'

'And do you think he loved you?'

'I suppose so.'

'Gran, what's all this 'suppose'? Did the pair of you not talk about it?

'No, of course not,' declared Connie flatly, then added as if it had just occurred to her, 'we didn't dare.'

'So, you were...'

'Enough,' said Connie, 'that's enough! He went away and that was best for both of us. Before long I heard he had married – and I can honestly say that I wished him well. Shortly afterwards other problems occupied my mind.'

'Your cancer?

'Yes.'

'So, when he comes back....'

'He has been back many times.'

'And you've met him?'

'Of course. I was a good friend of his mother. Peter came regularly to see her after his father died. They didn't get on; Peter and his father. He thought Peter should have stayed and kept the business going. Peter's father, (Raymond, I think they called him) started as a builder but had gone into property development when I knew him. I believe he had properties all over Hecklescar and in the country. But Peter seemed to lose interest once he lost Olivia. He moved away then and stayed away for a couple years. Then his father died quite suddenly; collapsed on the golf course. Afterwards, Peter came quite regularly to see his mother and when he did, he often called on me. Since his mother died, he is not here so much. But he does come and when he's here he normally calls round for a cup of coffee.'

'And mum - does he go to see mum?'

'I don't think so. I'm not sure he would be welcome at Avignon'.

'So....'

'So, nothing, Sally. Leave it. If he comes to live among us, he will be welcome, both he and his wife – and children. I hope the gossips and tittle-tattlers will leave him alone. Peter Munro is a good man. He deserves a good life - and we have a quilt to finish.'

CHAPTER TWENTY-SIX

T he folk of Hecklescar are not wealthy but they are generous.

When fishermen were earning big money at the Seine net the place prospered. The skippers built bigger boats, bought flashy cars, built new houses and refurbished and re-furnished old ones. Their crews, share-fishermen, enjoyed bumper pay packets that flowed into shops and tradesmen in the town. Fish cadgers in their vans, too, made money, carrying fish from the nets into the frying pans of the Borders within twenty-four hours of landing. Jobs were a-plenty and incomes high.

Those days are long gone. Jakey, who ponders these things while pretending to listen to Ina, has come to the conclusion that there is only fifteen thousand pounds in the town. It circulates, passing from one business to another, with none able to hold onto it for long. He doesn't include his own business in this (which is not his business but Hercules') for he believes that, but for Anthony Douglas & Son, the town would be flat broke and everyone would have to leave. He also suspects (with some justification and considerable support from Ina) that were it not for him the business would fold.

Recently however, he has amended his economic theory to take into account what he calls 'the auld fat cats'. By this he means pensioners, like the four old men we met on the golf course a while back. Such folk did not trawl their living from the sea, prise it from crabs and lobsters or hawk it round the country. They had gathered it from the honey pots of Edinburgh, Glasgow, Aberdeen, and south of the Border in Newcastle, Manchester, London and elsewhere. Some of the most affluent are natives coming back home with pockets filled in the Gulf, the States, or further afield. I know one who made his pile in Mongolia and another in Argentina.

These comfortably retired are the exception. For the rest, jobs are few and pay poor. In spite of this, they are generous. Christine, for instance, Duncan and Janet's daughter, is organising a sponsored swim. Hecklescar Co-op where she works has a policy of supporting local charities and Christine has been appointed unofficially by the manager to respond to any requests for such support.

Christine goes beyond the call of policy and is forever implementing schemes of her own. When she heard that little Louise Swanson could come home from hospital if her house was adapted, Christine set out to raise the £26,000 the family needed. (Little Louise fell off the pier into the harbour and was pulled out half-an-hour later brain-damaged and half-paralysed.)

Christine is well on her way to the target but has proposed to the manager that they sponsor a swim in the sea to give the fund a boost. The manager agreed but immediately ruled himself out of participation due to a previously undisclosed lung condition. Christine forgives him for this cowardice for is he not an old man? He must be nearly fifty, almost as old as her father Duncan, whom she could not imagine swimming in the sea at Hecklescar - or her mother Janet. In this she is absolutely correct. They fear not only the cold, but also the ridicule.

If you would like to sponsor someone else, say Nudge, Wullie, Elaine or Angela from the fishyard, all of whom have signed up, you can pick up a form at the Coffee Morning that Janet is arranging to support the cause of Little Louise.

Hecklescar Coffee Mornings are an institution. So much so that if regulars turn up at the Mason's Hall on a Saturday and find that there isn't one, they hang about the High Street complaining to anyone who will listen that somebody should have a coffee morning every week. The somebody is anybody that wants to raise a bit of money.: The Scouts hold one, as do the Guides and the Brownies. Christians host them: Church of Scotland, Episcopalians, Methodists, and Catholics all turn up from time to time and all support each other. Nudge's Baptists, however, turn up their noses at using the Mason's Hall and have coffee in the much more theologically sound surroundings of their own hall. They also disdain the raffles that play an important part in the fundraising of their less scrupulous church-goers. Rotary host a coffee morning with an emblazoned gazebo outside, around which their members stand trying to look distinguished whilst their wives and partners sweat it out in the kitchen. Outside too, when the Fisherman's Mission host the morning, you will find books for sale, and occasionally a tombola stall where you buy a ticket from a bucket which, if you're lucky, matches a ticket on the neck of a bottle or the lid of a box of chocolates.

The Heart Foundation is generally credited with running the best coffee mornings, the volunteers turning out in bright red tee-shirts advertising their charity. (I recommend the peanut butter flapjack made by Jean to a recipe that has been handed down in her family for generations and will not be shared with you no matter how often you ask). Friends of the Health Centre take their turn, as do the Friends of the Museum. Other organisations muscle in, some with torturous titles, others with obscure objectives. All are supported. I suspect that if you held one for The Poor Children's Fathers' Beer

Fund, you would not come away empty-handed. Hecklescar is a charitable place.

For her coffee morning Janet ropes in John Henry to take the money at the door: £2 this time, for which you are given a cup of tea or coffee with a buttered scone, either cheese, plain or fruit. If she catches any of the regulars complaining that they only paid £1.50 last Saturday, she will silence them with: 'It's for little Louise. You walked here, she can't. Be thankful.'

For weeks Janet has badgered businesses for donations, collected prizes for the raffle, and told her friends what baking she expects from them for the cake stall.

One of her most faithful bakers is Alice, her mother-in-law. Alice's sultana loaves and lemon drizzle cakes always sell well. She normally hands in five of each, but this year, by nine o'clock none have turned up. Maybe she hasn't been able to carry them down, thought Janet and dispatched husband Duncan to Latchly to collect them before the doors open at half-past.

Since his mother stumbled through the dementia test at the doctors, Duncan had approached Latchly with a sense of foreboding. What would he find? What could he expect? Would he see a change? So far, his mother had always seemed to be perfectly normal and firing on all cylinders. Perhaps the doctor is over-cautious. Perhaps it's just the loss of memory that comes with age. Perhaps it's not dementia at all. Alistair hasn't noticed any change and he lives with her all the time.

Until now he had always been pleased to find his mother bright and well. The fact that she had not delivered her cakes troubled him.

Duncan parked his car at the back of the house and shouted a greeting to his mother as he pushed open the door. He was relieved to hear his mother call out that she was in the kitchen. Her voice reassured him. She must be packing up the cakes! That was what he expected. But when he entered, he found his mother sitting at the table shelling peas. His heart sank.

'Yer fither brought these in and I'm awa' to freeze them,' she said pleasantly. 'What brings you here sae early in the mornin'?'

'I've come for the cakes. It's Janet's coffee morning.'

Alice studied him for a moment, then said,

'It's the day, is it? They're in the tins.'

She got up and made her way to the cupboard. She took out three large tins.

Duncan breathed a sigh of relief. She hadn't forgotten. She opened the tins and produced six sultana loafs.

'There y'are. I pit labels on them. Janet'll know what to charge.'

Duncan expected her to return to the cupboard to bring out the drizzle cakes but she sat down at the table again.

'That's it then,' Duncan said.

'Aye, that's it, son. I hope it goes well.'

Duncan didn't know what to do. He thought about asking for the cakes then changed his mind. He picked up the loaves and left.

He reached the car, then hesitated. Had she not made the cakes? Or had she forgotten that she had made them? What would be worse for her? To know that she had not done what she had promised to do, or that she had made the cakes and would find them later when it was too late for the coffee morning?

He went back into the kitchen. She had gone back to the peas.

'Mam,' he said quietly, 'Janet said there might be lemon drizzle cakes.'

Alice looked at him and he could see confusion trouble

his mother's eyes.

'Aye,' she said vaguely, 'I no' got them finished.'

* * * * *

"She didn't get them finished.' Is that what she said?' demanded Janet of Duncan when he returned to the coffee morning. 'What did your father say?'

'He wasn't there.'

'Where was he?'

'He must have been in the garden.'

'Is he ever anywhere else? We'll need to go and find out what's going on.'

When they called the following day, Janet found Alice in her pinnie preparing the Sunday meal. She informed the old woman that all her sultana loaves had sold, then asked her about the lemon drizzle cakes. Alice repeated what she had said to Duncan. She had started the cakes but hadn't finished them. Just that; that is all she would say.

Janet wasn't satisfied. She had bought her mother-in-law the ingredients and now went searching for them. They were not where she had put them, and she couldn't find them anywhere in the cupboards or in the kitchen. All the while Alice stood quietly at the kitchen table preparing the vegetables for the meal. She had collected a little pile of them: carrots, broccoli, potatoes and was now slicing them and loading them into a steamer. Janet turned to her to ask her again what had happened to the cakes and noticed that the old woman's eyes had filled with tears.

Janet took her in her arms and sat her down at the table. Then she called Duncan from the Sunday papers in the front room and ordered him to sit with his mother.

She went to find Alistair and found him clearing out runner beans. He straightened his back and grunted a greeting.

Janet was in no mood for small talk.

'Tell me about the cakes that Alice was making,' she ordered.

'I know nothing about that,' muttered Alistair.

'Oh, yes you do, Alistair Kerr, and it's time you woke up to what is happening to your wife. What happened to the cakes? Where are they?'

'What cakes? I don't know what ye're on about,' muttered the old man.

'Alright,' said Janet, 'let me try you with this. She dumped the cakes, didn't she? She made a mess of them and dumped them.'

'Aye, they were in the bin. When I came in for ma tea they were in the bin. I saw the flour and butter and that.'

'She'd thrown them out.'

'Must have.'

'Did you ask her?'

'Naw, she'd made a mess of it. She's done that afore.'

When?'

'Last week, or it might have been the week afore that.'

'What was it that time?'

'I canna' mind. It was a cake. Something like that. I came in the door and smelt burning. She'd gone away upstairs. Aye, it was one of those round cakes she makes.'

'Did you ask her then what had happened?'

'Naw, she said she'd gone upstairs and forgotten about it. That's all it was.'

'You didn't think tell us?'

'Naw, why should I? She just forgot. That was all.'

'What was it this time, Alistair?'

'I no' ken, I was in the garden.'

'And as long as you can go to the garden, it doesn't matter what happens to Alice, is that it? As long as she's there when you come in to coddle you? Alice isn't well! Has that not sunk in yet? She's not well! You don't care, do you? As long as she puts your porridge on the table in the morning and your dinner at dinnertime you don't care, do you?'

Alistair's face reddened and he gripped his spade and for a fleeting moment Janet thought he was going to lift it. To strike her? Surely not. Yet he was clearly angry.

'Look, get out of here! We don't need you and you're not welcome. There's nothing wrong wi' Alice. She's a bit forgetful. Auld folk are like that. That's it. Now go away and leave us alone.'

'I'm going,' said Janet. 'But I'll be back.'

When she entered the house, Duncan sat talking to Alice while she stood at the stove watching a pan.

'Did ye see Alistair?' she asked.

'Yes, I saw him,' snapped Janet, choking back her frustration, but not enough to deceive Alice.

'No' be hard on him,' she said quietly, 'he canna' cope wi' trouble, ye ken.'

'What is it I'm supposed 'to ken'?' she asked Duncan on the way home, mimicking Alice's dialect.

'They lost a bairn afore I was born,' answered Duncan. 'Mam said he's never got over it.'

'Well, he needs to get over it now,' declared Janet. 'He's had long enough. He's not a child. Your mother is going to need him.'

CHAPTER TWENTY-SEVEN

On the 13th of September, the Monday after the coffee morning, Duncan left a message on John Hendry's voice mail asking to see him. He wanted to talk to him about the steading at Latchlaw.

For over a month now, whenever other work permitted, in evenings and at weekends, he and Hector had been renovating the steading. They had made it wind and water tight, broken up and re-laid the stone floor, re-dressed the walls and marked out on the new floor where each piece of equipment would stand.

The more Duncan accomplished the more uneasy he became. He had reached the point where he would have to spend scarce money on machinery and tools. But he had no right to the building, did he? What agreement did he have apart from Hercules' casual remark: '*if you can use the steading by all means fit it out for lad.*' The more Duncan thought about the phrase the more it bugged him. What did it mean? What did Hercules mean by it? Did he mean that, once fitted out, it belonged 'to the lad'- to Hector; not to me? Or perhaps it 'belonged to neither of them; not to me, not to 'the lad'. All Hercules had said was that they could use it. 'Use it!' Did Hercules mean, 'it's mine, but you can have the use of it, borrow it, in fact - until I take it back!?'

Duncan had nothing in writing. No-one was present in Hercules' front room when he and Hercules did the deal - if it was a deal. There were no witnesses. 'If it came to it, it would be my word against his - and there would only be one winner in that contest.' Of course, Hercules could have forgotten all about it. He hadn't talked to him since – and neither had Hector.

The more Duncan thought about it, the more anxious he became. When he confessed his fears to Janet, his doubts became obstacles. He should go no further, spend no more time and money until they had something in writing giving them at least, what? - ten year's use of the building.

'Go and talk to John Hendry,' she instructed.

John Hendry, sitting in his yard, listened carefully to all Duncan had to say and noted the details in the small notebook he always carried with him. When they had finished, he pronounced his verdict: it would be unsafe for Duncan to go any further with the renovation without some sort of formal agreement. The steading belonged to Hercules no matter how much work Duncan had put into it, and yes, he could put them out at any time without so much as a letter through the door. Then, detecting the rising dismay in Duncan's mind, the old banker suggested that he would accompany Duncan to Cockburn Heath, the solicitor, to see what he had to say before they tackled Hercules.

When Duncan stood up to leave, John Hendry asked him to sit down again. John had something else to say, and clearly it troubled the old man. Duncan sat down and wondered what was coming. Something financial, something legal, something about Hercules. None of these.

'It's about your wife. About Janet,' began John Hendry softly, and Duncan wondered what was coming. He knew that some folk thought Janet bossy; that she took too much on herself. Was John Hendry about to warn him not to tell Janet too much; that this was delicate work; that she didn't like Hercules and might rattle him and make an agreement more difficult?

John Hendry hesitated, looked steadily at Duncan and spoke softly, 'Cherish her, Duncan, cherish her. I wish I had cherished my Lizzie more than I did. Like Janet, she was a good wife; loved me, served me, fed me, looked after me, kept me straight. She traded in her own life to buy me mine. I realise that now, now that it is too late to make a new bargain. All she asked was that I loved her. I did, but not enough, not anything like enough to company her through those last dread days when one by one those little loving tasks that were her life were wrenched from her.'

John Hendry stopped. Clearly there was more to say, two years' worth of grief and regret composed into a daily litany of painful recollection. His voice broke and he could go no further. Never before had he spoken thus to anyone and he would not do so again. He became aware of Duncan's embarrassment at such frank confession, then of his own. He stood up, gripped Duncan's hand and muttered,

'Sorry, Duncan. Thanks. Cherish her, cherish her!'

Duncan returned home and gave Janet a kiss when she came into the kitchen to greet him - and she wondered what she had done to deserve it, or what he had done to think it necessary. She then asked him to tell her what he and John Hendry had agreed about the steading. Duncan did so with the assurance of a man with reinforcements at his back. It wasn't to last.

'That's good,' pronounced Janet, then added the words that, over the years, had taught Duncan to duck, 'and I've been thinking'.

What she had been considering (or rather whom), were Alistair and Alice. As far as she knew, his father and mother had no formal agreement with Hercules. They were just allowed to stay there. For the moment this suited Hercules; the house and the land around it were kept in good order. But what would happen if he changed his mind? Could he just put them out? If the steading needed a firmer legal footing, so did the house.

Janet's thinking went beyond the problem to a solution. The time is coming, she explained to her husband, when Alice would no longer be able to care for Alistair; not long after that she would not be able to care for herself. What then? Before Duncan could think of an answer, Janet supplied it.

'What if we bought Latchly?' she asked, 'then we could keep eye on your mother and father and you and Hector could work in the steading?'

Stunned, Duncan sat and said nothing as he sought to absorb what Janet had proposed. Then he protested,

'We couldn't afford to buy Latchly. It must be worth millions.'

'Not the whole thing, not all the land,' exclaimed Janet with more than a hint of exasperation, 'just the house and steading, and a little bit of garden for your father. That wouldn't cost all that much, you'd think. The house is in a poor way anyway. It's no use to Hercules the way it is. He would probably just pull it down. We could maybe buy it cheap and you could do it up once we're in there.'

'You mean move from here?' muttered Duncan apprehensively.

'Yes. We'd have to sell this place to buy the house there.'

'Hold on, Janet,' he protested, when he'd recovered his breath. 'You come up with some hare-....'he stopped, looked at his wife and detecting her determination, diverted.

'Nah, no way, Janet, we couldn't take that on.'

'Right then,' replied Janet, 'what's your solution? What

kind of deal do you think you'll get from Hercules? It'll be full of ifs and buts – all in his favour. And what will you have then? Not your own workshop, like you've always said you wanted, but a place that you've rebuilt and fitted out that you pay rent for – to him. He's done nothing, but you have to pay him! That's what you'll have - and when it suits his majesty, he'll give you notice and turf you out. Where will you go then?'

'Let me tell you something else. For years there's been talk in the town that Hercules wants to build a mansion at Latchly. He has a picture of it on his wall, they say. Now, if he decides to go ahead, what happens to your workshop? He won't want you turning up every morning to work in his back-yard, will he? So, he'll pull the plug.'

'But,' Duncan objected, 'if he is going to build a house, he wouldn't sell it to us any way.'

'Oh, yes he would,' expounded Janet, who had been cooking up her plan ever since she found Alice bereft in her kitchen. 'That house is no use to him. He'd pull it down, and build his own house somewhere else, further up the hill away from the road. If you offered to buy the farmhouse and do it up, it might suit him. He wouldn't have the expense of pulling it down, and he'd have something to put towards the cost of his mansion. It makes sense. It would all belong to us: house, workshop, garden and all. We wouldn't have to pay rent – or kowtow to anybody - and we'd be able to keep an eye on Alice and your father. In the end we'd have something to pass on to Christine – and Hector.'

Duncan retired hurt; well, winded. Janet had thought it all out. Apart from the sheer audacity of it, Duncan could find no argument against it, provided, and it was a very big pro-viso, that the sums added up: that the sale of their house in Priory Road would come close to the cost of buying house and steading at Latchly.

Although he ceased to protest, he did not say that he

accepted the plan. It was too much to swallow in one gulp. He did, however, say that he would think about it and promise to go back to John Hendry and talk it over with him. For that he got a peck on the cheek and a pat on the back of his hand.

CHAPTER TWENTY-EIGHT

Y ou need to find Marney Wegg,' said Oliver when Mrs.
Rostowski rang him the day after she had met him. She
was following up what she had missed in their conversation. Oliver had suggested that Peter Munro felt badly
about a deal down in East London just as the Canary Wharf development started.

'Almost every time we talked, he mentioned it,' said
Oliver, 'it seemed to bug him. I kept trying to reassure him.
'A deal's a deal,' I told him; 'you win some you lose some'. He
had nothing to reproach himself for. He would agree with me.
Then, the next time, it would come up again. It hung around
him like a bad smell. You know how it is; you can't track it
down; you think it's gone - then back it comes.'

Oliver went on to explain to Mrs. Rostowski that he,
Oliver, being in the trade, occasionally came across what
would be called in the business ads, 'a commercial opportunity'. Peter had money from selling up in Scotland and had
asked Oliver to tip him the wink if he got wind of such an
opportunity.

One turned up in the shape of a rundown warehouse in
East London. Oliver stored materials in it from time to time.
The owner, Marney Wegg, seemed something of a wide boy, a

chancer with lots of fingers in lots of pies. He had mentioned to Oliver that the council was breathing down his neck about fire regulations and asbestos. They had issued him with a fifteen-point improvement plan to bring the building up to a safe standard - or else. Marney had told Oliver that it would cost him an arm and leg to do what they wanted him to do; money that, at the moment, because of other leads, he did not have. Oliver mentioned it to Peter in passing and forgot about it.

Almost a year later, Oliver paid another visit to the warehouse and found Marney packing up. He had sold the warehouse to a bloke from up north called Munro.

Oliver had felt guilty about leading Peter into a bad deal, so he rang him up to apologise. Peter then told him that no apology was required. He'd done a bit of digging and turned up the stirrings of a plan to develop the area, so he'd taken a punt.

'It paid off,' concluded Oliver. 'The plan firmed up and Peter was made an offer for the warehouse he couldn't refuse. What was it? Eight times, something like that, eight times what he had paid. It set him up in the property business.'

'Why should he feel badly about that? He was lucky,' replied Mrs. Rostowski

'I told him that. But there is more to it. Peter confessed that he had known about interest in the site or rather, had had an inkling, before he did the deal. But he hadn't told Marney. That, I think lies at the bottom of all the agonising. Peter always played straight. I could imagine that he felt he'd conned Marney.'

Until now Mrs. Rostowski had been an interested spectator, now her vocation as a Health and Well-Being Counsellor cut in.

'Do you know if he ever tried to contact this Marney, what was it?'

'Wegg.'

'Wegg. That's a strange name.'

'Not if you come from Norfolk. There's a good scattering of Weggs in Norfolk.'

'Did Peter Munro try to put things right with Mr. Wegg?' asked Mrs. Rostowski.

'I don't think so. Not at the time anyway. Peter was chuffed. He'd put a foot in the door - and Marney Wegg is not the man to brood over bad deals. The only deal that figures with him is the next one. He wouldn't hold it against Peter, I'm sure. He would have done the same, if he'd known what Peter knew. I mean, look what he said to me after he'd sold the warehouse to Peter. He said he'd 'unloaded it onto some mutt with more money than sense'; that's how he put it to me. So, no, I don't know if Peter tried to make amends, and secondly, I can't see why he should have tried.'

As far as I know, it is not a requirement that Health and Well-Being Counsellors should be married to van drivers, but it ought to be. Greg, Mrs. Rostowski's husband, lived by a principle that cannot be taught in university, and is not included in health and social work manuals: *destination is delivery*. There is no point in setting out unless you intend to arrive - and there's no point in arriving unless you deliver.

A fortnight after Oliver mentioned Marney Wegg to Mrs. Rostowski, a fortnight during which she had not done so because she couldn't find him in any of the directories and information banks she could consult, Greg came home and reported to his wife that he had tracked down Marney Wegg, or rather that he hadn't; Marney had disappeared.

We have seen Greg at work tracking down suspects so we do not have to go into it again. He told his wife that he had happened to be in Crawley and, on one of those industrial sites that persuade local authorities that they have a grip on economic development, he had come across a storage facility (*Secure Indoor Heated Storage, Commercial/Domestic. Easy Access*) that advertised its owners as M & Y Wegg. 'No harm in chasing it up,' he confessed, 'seeing I was there.'

Mrs. Rostowski smiled, knowing what was to come. When Greg had a tale to tell; she would listen. Such give-and-take stitched together that hard-wearing fabric that wrapped them in the same bundle of life. After the children were put to bed at night, Greg would make a cup of tea and they would sit down and each tell the other the story of their day. Greg's accounts were always entertaining, even if, on occasion, Mrs. Rostowski suspected that some of it strayed into romantic fiction.

Greg had parked the van in the car park of M & Y Wegg, and entered a door marked 'Reception'. There he had found himself in a poky room fitted out with three or four tired wooden-armed, black leather armchairs and a forlorn glass coffee table; on which lay a litter of dog-eared magazines. The walls were bare apart from a large board festooned with fading notices. Greg felt reassured at this general air of neglect. He had expected no less of Marney Wegg.

At the rear of the room, he saw the familiar solid wood hatch (there to protect the staff from intimidation) – and a bell push. Greg rang the bell and after a minute or two the hatch opened and framed the head and shoulders of a furtive, scruffy middle-aged man.

Greg asked if he could speak to Marney. The man mumbled a reply that Greg did not catch and closed the hatch. He knew a lot about hatches and what went on behind them. This time he suspected his request to see Marney had created more interest than 'just a van driver.'

Greg waited. After a few minutes a young man, much younger than the man at the hatch, a smart, pleasant young man, opened the outside door and stepped into the room.

'Hi,' he said, 'Marney is not available at the moment. Can I help?'

'I'm afraid not,' replied Greg pleasantly, 'it's personal.'

'Ah well,' said the young man, 'I'm afraid he's not here.'

'So, he's not just not available, he's not here.'

'No, I'm afraid not.'

'Will he be here tomorrow?'

'No, not tomorrow.'

'On Wednesday?'

'No.'

'Next week?'

'No, I'm afraid not.' The young man sounded irritated.

'When will he be back? Is he on holiday?'

'No, he's not on holiday,' replied the young man tersely, 'We're not sure when he'll be back.'

'Where is he then?'

'I am not at liberty to tell you.'

*****

'Marney's in jail,' reported Greg to his wife, 'Or he's done a runner; South America, somewhere like that. Or further afield - beyond this mortal pale.'

'What makes you think that?' asked Mrs. Rostowski.

'Call it instinct – or experience. It has all the signs of someone trying to disappear.'

'So, who was the young man?'

'His nephew, he's the Y in M & Y. Yaris! He must have been conceived in a Toyota.'

Mrs. Rostowski laughed. But Greg had not finished. He had kept the best till last. He lowered his voice and leaned across towards her as if to tell a secret.

'Something else,' he said softly, 'when he wouldn't tell me where Marney was, I told him to tell Marney that Peter Munro had been asking after him.'

'And,' whispered Greg to his wife, edging even closer to her, 'Yaris said, 'I know that; Peter Munro came last week looking for him."

CHAPTER TWENTY-NINE

Although Janet smiled when she presented to her husband her plan to buy Latchly, you must not think that Janet has reached her decision lightly. I know a woman in Hecklescar who moves house every three or four years; she has lived in seven houses since she married thirty years ago; it's a sort of career. But Janet is not like that. She is essentially a homesteader: sensible, orderly, never quite satisfied with the status quo, but working on it, not throwing it over to start again. The table at which she made her dramatic proposal is as old as their marriage, though I grant you that the chairs are somewhat younger.

The thought of giving up her home troubled her; the thought of all the work to make Latchly fit for them to move into; of negotiating with Alice and, particularly, Alistair about how the house would be shared, and, after that, of how to live together in it. She must preserve Alice's independence for as long as it served the old woman. Alice's remaining happiness depended on such sensitivity. But how would she know when to intervene and when back off, when to speak and when to keep silent? She supposed that there would be no sudden shift, no capability on Monday that had gone by Tuesday. Alice's last Sunday dinner could not be predicted or planned, and she may well make simple teas long after she had given up making meals. Janet must take every day as it comes, reading signs and circumstances; supporting, cajoling, caring.

The process of selling the house and buying Latchly she would leave to Duncan and John Hendry, but there were practical tasks that she must accomplish: packing up the accumulation of twenty-five years' living; things belonging to her, to Duncan and to Christine, sorting them out - what to keep, what to leave, what to throw out. (Surely Christine will help me with that). Then start all over again at Latchly, creating from a rambling, ramshackle farmhouse a home for herself, her husband and her daughter.

Through all of these activities ran the turbulence of leaving the street, the neighbours and the town for, as she saw it, the back-of-beyond.

Janet had never lived in a house without a house next door, had never had far to walk to a shop and had always had a street lamp to light her there and back. Now she would have to look out at fields, hedges, a smelly cabbage patch perhaps, and cows – perhaps there would be cows. Cows frightened her.

Latchlaw is scarcely a kilometre from the centre of Hecklescar. In the winter, when the trees are bare, you can see the roofs of the houses in Millerfield, the executive estate that twenty years ago set out to climb the hill on the outskirts of the town. Nevertheless, to Janet, Latchly lay 'in the country'. The only consolations she could find for the isolation were that Christine would be in the house with them and Duncan and Hector working out the back whenever they were in the workshop.

One thing more concerned her, or not so much concerned than grated: what would Ina and Co say about the move when they heard of it? For they would hear; you can't blow your nose in Hecklescar without being under the doctor for flu or pneumonia.

The gossip rattled around in her mind: 'my, my, have

you heard, Janet and her man are moving out of town – to Latchly. She's come up in the world, hasn't she? The streets of Hecklescar aren't good enough for her. They're taking over Latchly; they're going to rebuild it; quite a little mansion, I hear. Of course, he'll be doing the work on trade. How else could they afford it? Duncan wanted to stay put but she's intent on it. Of course, that was always the plan when they moved his mither and fither into it. They always had their eye on it. That's why he took Hercules' boy on, so they would get a foot in the door. Mind you, I think Hercules might put a spoke in their wheel. He has plans for Latchly hissel. I say, 'watch this space'; there could be a nasty fall out. Then what is poor old Alice going to do – and auld Alistair? Hercules'll put them out - and she's got dementia, you know. You would have thought madam would have thought a bit more about her guid mither afore she got ideas above her station. I feel sorry for Duncan. He didn't want to go but she's talked him into it.'

This is a monstrous calumny but Janet will bear it and forge ahead, provided, of course, that the numbers add up. That calculation will be made by Duncan with the help and advice of John Hendry.

These two gentlemen are, as we speak, closeted with Cockburn Heath, the solicitor, on a bright Friday morning in the middle of September. Cockburn Heath, named by his father after Lord Cockburn, the Lord Advocate at the beginning of the nineteenth century, had disappointed his ambitious father, by showing more interest in sailing than in law. True, he qualified as a lawyer and true, he paid his annual registration to maintain his status. But that exhausted his interest and the practice had slowly sunk until was taken over by McIntyre & McKinley, a bustling Edinburgh firm who kept Cockburn on as a sort of local mascot.

Cockburn was tall, thin and stiff and looked as though a decent breeze would snap him at the waist. Now in his fifties, his hair, still long and black, drooped over his eyes when he bent forward at his desk. And bend forward he did, to within a few inches of the desk top, for he could only read documents in comfort if he were uncomfortably close to the page. A genial man, he liked nothing better than to chat to his clients most of whom, like John Hendry, were personal friends.

He now met his customers in, for him, the hopelessly cramped conditions of the converted front shop of the old bakery just across the Market Place from his old offices. These had been housed in the rambling, crumbling building that once belonged to the Commercial Bank. It galled Cockburn to arrive of a morning, pass the grand doorway of the old bank building, and crawl into a poky little shop through a flimsy wood and glass door.

In his spacious Victorian office in the old place, Cockburn had surrounded himself with the clutter of 50 years of requests, records, requisitions, responses, and the wrangling and mangling of Hecklescar's legal affairs. Now he had two filing cabinets - and the continuing organisational services of Mrs. Somerville. He had half-hoped that, offsetting the move, he might leave Mrs. Somerville behind in the old building, but his new employers had correctly assumed that Cockburn without Mrs. Somerville would be a liability and moved her with him.

He greeted John Hendry and Duncan warmly and asked them if they thought the weather might hold to let him take the boat up the Forth for the weekend. They agreed it might do so, then outlined their thoughts on the purchase of Latchlaw and the sale of Duncan and Janet's house in Priory Road.

Cockburn listened carefully and scribbled his thoughts onto a loose sheet of paper that Cockburn believed would find its own way into a file labelled Duncan Kerr, but would almost certainly end up in the miscellaneous pile now growing on top of the filing cabinet. When Cockburn finished, John Hendry found himself impressed at the solicitor's grasp of the essentials. It was as if he already had had time to think about it.

'Do you have any idea what Latchlaw is worth?' he asked them. 'Hercules has planning permission for a house on that site.'

'Then he's going to build his mansion, is he? It's not just gossip?' murmured John Hendry.

'Oh, come on John,' chaffed Cockburn, 'you know better than that. It is in the public domain. It was advertised at the time. That was over twenty years ago and is likely time-barred, but he'd have no difficulty renewing it.' He paused, 'Let me put something else to you. This is between us. Okay?'

He stared at them until they both nodded.

'You know as well as I do that Hercules is in financial difficulty.'

This came as news to Duncan but he noticed that it did not take John Hendry by surprise.

'Supposing Hercules, instead of building one house on the site, decided to sell it to a house builder. Let me run through the numbers. The site measures five acres. You can put ten decent houses on one acre, so there is room for fifty houses. A house site with planning permission would cost you £35,000, plus £30,000 for services. Fifty plots at £65,000 a time. I make that three and a quarter million. That's what Latchlaw is worth to a house builder. Now if you were Hercules and you were in trouble, what would you do?'

Cockburn sat back with all the satisfaction of a stand-up comic at the end of a good joke. He expected applause – and got it; from John Hendry, but not from Duncan.

Cockburn had shot down Janet's little plan, hadn't he?

CHAPTER THIRTY

When Duncan reported that Cockburn Heath half-expected Hercules to sell off Latchly to a builder, it took Janet only a day and a half to bend her plan to accommodate it. The old farmhouse, the steading and a little bit of land, she argued, was worth more than site value and could be comfortably settled in amongst other houses. She even tried to persuade Duncan that any builder, hoping to sell new houses, would welcome the inclusion of a traditional farmhouse to lend the estate character.

What had started out in Janet's mind as an accommodation to circumstance had now taken on the exhilaration of a campaign. Cockburn's suggestion that, into the bargain, she might have neighbours increased rather than diminished her enthusiasm. If Hercules were really short of ready money would he not jump at the chance to top up his coffers quickly?

John Henry did not share her enthusiasm and gently tried to dissuade Janet from pursuing it. When he saw that she wouldn't be shifted he agreed to accompany Duncan to try it out on Hercules.

We have all been at meetings where the minutes bear no resemblance to our recollections. That is not necessarily the fault of the minutes. We filter the words that are spoken, accepting much that is promoted by people we like and throwing away almost everything said by people we don't. In addition, if we are searching for answers, we will find them even when they are heavily disguised as tentative suggestions.

The three men at the meeting at Avignon on Thursday 23rd Sept: Duncan, John Hendry and Hercules are no exceptions. They all took away different conclusions from the same meeting.

Duncan reported to Janet that Hercules would very likely accept their offer. Hercules hadn't knocked it back the way Hercules does when he doesn't like something. He had listened carefully to their plan to buy the farmhouse and steading, said he was sorry to hear about Alice and that he respected their desire to move in beside the old couple. He had jotted down the details and promised to give them a decision by the end of the month. When Janet pressed him, Duncan did confess that Hercules had admitted that he had plans of his own for Latchly - but had said that he didn't see why the farmhouse and the steading shouldn't be put to use rather than being knocked down. Janet felt inclined to accept what Duncan said that Hercules had said, not because she had changed her mind about Hercules but because what Duncan reported matched what she wanted.

John Hendry sat on his garden bench among the plant pots in his back yard, sipped real coffee and considered the meeting. In his estimation, it had raised more questions than answers. Hercules had not knocked back Janet's offer to buy Latchlaw farmhouse and the steading. Nor had he accepted it. He had, in John's estimation, put it on the side of his plate: to be swallowed later – or, perhaps, to be thrown away when no-one was looking! What were Hercules' own plans for Latchlaw? He had not mentioned the mini mansion that had been, as far as John knew, the original intention. Although Hercules had referred to his plans, no hint of the grand house had passed his lips. If the house no longer featured, what had taken its place? What did he intend to do with the site? Had Cockburn Heath put his finger on it? That Hercules was thinking of selling the whole site to a house builder, pocketing three and a quarter million, and saving his financial skin? Cockburn's theory stacked up.

If Cockburn were correct, how could Hercules accommodate Janet's plan? Would he actually sell the farmhouse and steading to Duncan before he did a deal with a builder? What did such a scheme offer Hercules? True, the farmhouse lay on the edge of the site and wouldn't block any layout a builder might intend. But could they expect Hercules to be considerate? John Hendry dismissed out of hand Hercules' professed concern for Alice, and his smarmy assurance that, if he were to agree to sell, any transaction would include a little plot for Alistair to cultivate. In John Hendry's estimation, Hercules remained concerned about only one person – himself.

No price had been discussed. Maybe Hercules thought that the Kerrs would pay more for the farmhouse and steading than he could raise bundling it with the clear ground around. Any builder would have to factor in the cost of clearing the farmhouse and that might depress the price. Was that it? Perhaps Janet is right; it might be easier to sell it to them than to have to demolish it or lump it into a deal with a builder at a discount.

'What do you think, Lizzie?' he muttered and glanced at the empty bench beside him; then smiled sadly at his sentimentality. Sentimental or not, it reinforced his determination to clear up his suspicions about Hercules.

Then another thought occurred to him: a recollection. In the meeting, Hercules seemed more concerned with 'when' than 'what'. He had asked more than once how quickly they wanted to move in. When John Hendry asked how long he would take to come to a decision, Hercules had taken out his diary and had agreed to come back with answers by the end of the month, a mere week away. Why the urgency?

When Hercules considered the meeting with Duncan and John Henry, he felt it had gone well. Why does that old banker keep poking his nose into my affairs? It has nothing to do with him. I thought I had made that clear the last time we crossed swords. No matter, he didn't get in the way.

By 'gone well' Hercules does not mean that he was pleased with the outcome. Nothing much pleased him nowadays; he tossed about in a growling sea of apprehension and irritation. After the meeting he retired to his study at Avignon, unlocked the filing cabinet and took out a flowchart. A flowchart resembles the maps you see of London Underground, and serves a similar purpose - of shifting you from one place to another. Hercules' plan was to be clear of Hecklescar by the end of October.

On the left-hand side of the chart were headings for the Key Areas of his Strategic Withdrawal (remember Napoleon on the golf course way back in June?). He had listed these Key Areas as:

1. Liquidate Golden Opportunities;

2. Divest A Douglas (West Highland) Ltd;

3. Divest Anthony Douglas & Son;

4. Divest Latchlaw;

5. Consolidate assets and investments

6. Determine and carry through future career/life plan.

When, three months ago, back in June, he had first scribbled these headings into a notepad, they had excited him. Not only that, but the exercise had given him a sense of release and purpose. He felt back in control. He had let things slide; had let fickle circumstance – and the unreliability of other people deflect him, but now he knew where he was going. He did not mean by this that he had settled on Bermuda or Argentina or some obscure corner of the Far East. Just that he now had a compass bearing out of the shoals and narrows that hemmed him in.

I am sorry to inflict this marine metaphor on you, but I do it to draw your attention to something you may think that Hercules has overlooked. Under none of the headings comes the sale of his yacht Olympian. Certainly under *'Consolidate Assets and Investments'*; he intends to sell Avignon, his house. That is why he is trying to convince Olivia that he is planning to start work on their house at Latchlaw. However, you would think that almost the first asset a cash-strapped man like Hercules would offload would be the luxury of an ocean-going yacht. Particularly as, in the last ten years, it has never wet its keel in any ocean. (Unless you count, as an Atlantic voyage, cruising to Coll and Tiree out of Oban for three days five years ago.)

The yacht is worth in the region of half-a-million pounds. It was built by McConaghy of Sydney, and Hercules will tell you that he brought it from Australia. If you take this to mean that he sailed the yacht from Australia, then you believe what Hercules would like you to believe. If you question him closely, however, he will admit, with some irritation, that he *had it brought* from Australia after he had bought it from the owner of a near bankrupt fish processing firm down under. This owner had been anxious to make off with what he made on the yacht before his creditors discovered that he had left his office. Hercules, in the market for a yacht, and in the fish processing business himself had done his sums and discovered that he could afford to buy it and ship it to the UK. It was bought by the firm, Anthony Douglas & Son Ltd, not by him, ostensibly for the sound commercial purpose of entertaining prospective customers. That has long been forgotten; Hercules regarded the yacht as his own. He has no intention of selling it. You may wonder why. Could it be that when he sees it lying at its mooring in the harbour it allows him to dream like nothing else in his life permitted; that its tall mast, taller than any other in the port, pointed a way out of a life cramped by circumstance?

Back to the flow chart. *Divesting the Highland business* to the Mallaig Fishermen lay on track and he had been surprised that they had offered the £1.5 million he had asked - surprised but not pleasantly. Had he underestimated what the worth of the business? How much more would they have been prepared to pay? What did they know that he didn't? What did they do that he wasn't aware of?

He has bigger fish to fry, however, and one of them keeps jumping out of the pan. He has acquired the discreet services of CoCarvers, a London agency, to track down a buyer for the Hecklescar business without advertising it; a discreet private sale, it is called.

His intention is that Jakey & the troops would hear nothing of the takeover until the new man turned up with a new sign for the door. By then Hercules would be somewhere else, well away from the disgust that would inevitably descend. He would claim, of course, (Hercules never did anything without gauging how it would be portrayed) that commercial confidence demanded such secrecy. In truth he no longer cared what Hecklescar folk thought. He had so shaken off his kinship with the town that had nurtured him; had so thrown off his obligation to the men and women that laboured for him, that he took a grim satisfaction in the clamour that would follow his disappearance. 'Stuff them - I've carried them long enough!'

The agency, however, had turned up nothing. No matter how discreetly it went about its business, no matter how many clandestine private clients of integrity with deep pockets they contacted, they found no-one prepared to take Anthony Douglas & Son Ltd off his hands.

This should not have surprised him. The company lay seriously sick, terminally, perhaps. The day-to-day business remained sound: suppliers still supplied the firm and buyers still bought its fish and prawns. But Hercules had bled the company dry propping up Golden Opportunities. Starved of cashflow and investment, owing millions to the bank, it now relied wholly on the goodwill of creditors, workers, suppliers and customers. It any one of these switched off life support the company would be pitched into a coma – and no-one with any business sense would commit to resuscitating it.

He could do no better than walk away from it - literally, one morning, drive out of Hecklescar and not come back. Factor that into the plan. On the flowchart on Line *3*: *Divest Anthony Douglas & Son,* at the end of the trail of activities: (*appointment of agency, sifting of offers, negotiations, closing etc.*) that were meant to conclude in *'divested'* by the beginning of October, he now scribbled *'walk away'*

CHAPTER THIRTY-ONE

What Hercules had done with the business he had also done with Latchlaw. He had entrusted it to an agent; this time to Proctor and Porteous, an Edinburgh Law firm with a reputation for handling delicate matters delicately. The leading partner, Dominic, played off ten at Muirfield and was known to Hercules as 'The Doc'. Hercules wanted a buyer who would keep quiet about the sale until he was well clear of Hecklescar. The Doc had had no difficulty attracting such buyers. Several nibbled at the bait. The Doc had whittled the list down to three, all of whom were prepared to bid for the land.

Cockburn's calculations were not far out. Proctor and Porteous would start the bidding at £3 million whenever Hercules gave them the nod. Hercules had this information in his head when Duncan, an hour ago, made his pitch to buy the farmhouse and steading, and now had it in his hand as he considered what he should do next. When he had spoken to The Doc last Friday, he had not been aware of Duncan's interest. He knew, of course, that Alistair and Alice lived in the farmhouse, and had been vaguely aware that Duncan wanted to do some work in the steading for Hector. But these were details, to be dealt with once the property had been sold. Selling the land would not mean that the old couple would have to move out immediately and, whilst they were there, there was no reason why Duncan and Hector should not use the steading. The builder who bought Latchlaw may be simply banking the land against a future project or, if not, would not be able to start work for a year or two as he sought planning permission and met other regulatory provisions. By then, Hercules had concluded, the old couple would no longer be his problem.

Now, following the meeting with Duncan and John Hendry, he had a new proposition. His first reaction had been to dismiss it out of hand, but when Duncan suggested that the house and steading might be worth more than the plot, he had played for time. Surely, no builder would want to retain such a dilapidated building. It could well be that Duncan would offer more for the house than any builder would for the site, encumbered as it was with buildings they would have to clear. If he could make a few thousand selling to Duncan, he'd be better off, wouldn't he? And sooner!

It all depended on how much detail Proctor and Porteous had given prospective buyers. Something to talk over with The Doc.

But where did the house and steading stand on the site? He took out the Latchlaw file from the cabinet, withdrew the site map and laid it on the desk. As the farmhouse and steading bear witness Latchlaw had originally been a large farm, 300 acres or so. As surrounding farms expanded, almost all the fields had been sold off, leaving just 5 acres at the back and side of the house. These had been converted into a market garden on a small portion of which Alistair now cultivated his vegetables.

The site map confirmed what Hercules thought he knew. The house lay at the side of the site, towards the front edge of it, not far off the road. Perhaps it could be sold off without compromising the attractiveness of the site to a builder. Hercules could see this on the map but could not bring to mind what it looked like on the ground.

A few years back, he would have been able to call up a vivid picture of the site, down to every brick, tussock, bush and branch. Then it lived comfortably in the back of his mind as the site of his new residence. He would often stop the car on the road to view it and dream of what it would become. But since he had abandoned his plans the place frowned at him. For the past five years or more, he had seldom glanced at Latchlaw as he drove past.

Now that he could make use of the ground, now that it provided a way out of his predicament, now that its value heralded a new dawn, he found himself drawn again to it. He closed the file and locked it in the filing cabinet. Then taking the map, he made to go out. At the door he stopped, went back into the house and called to Olivia. She emerged from the back of the house into the hall.

'Olivia, darling,' he said, 'I am just taking a walk up to have a look at Latchlaw. Would you like to come?'

Olivia studied him for a moment.

'No,' she said, 'I am expecting Rachel.'

He smiled. He had the answer he had anticipated: that she would not accompany him. He did not want her company. He simply wanted to keep alive in her mind the fantasy of their new house at Latchlaw.

When he reached Latchlaw he found himself reassured as he viewed the quiet lane leading from the corner where the Beanston road bridged the old railway line. The lane dipped then rose to climb the hill, bordered on either side by hawthorn hedges, now bright with red berries. Just as the lane lifted a short track led past the cultivated garden to the farmhouse and, behind the house, the steading. Further up the lane, away from the house, the site stretched almost to the belt of trees that breasted the top of the hill. Below the trees and to the side of the house away from the lane lay the old market garden, weed-covered now but bright with the flowering weeds that thrived in the still rich soil.

As he cut off into the lane, no longer did he envisage the grand house that would have lauded it from the brow of the hill. Now he populated the site with imaginary executive houses and estimated that any builder could easily fit in forty or fifty prestigious properties.

Did the farmhouse and steading take away from the site? If they were not included, would that diminish its value to a builder? The house didn't dominate the site. It lay in a corner not far from the road, yet close to where the main access to the housing estate would be. Site preparation and building work would have to find their way round it. That might be awkward.

On the other hand, it occupied one of the less attractive sites. The most sought-after plots would be higher up the hill where a house would command a view of the valley. The farmhouse lay lower down, and stared blankly into the trees lining the road.

Would it be worth his while to sell the house and steading to Duncan? Depends. Depends on what? On how much Duncan is prepared to pay and whether it would diminish the value of the whole site. Maybe it's not a good idea. It's a complication, and life is complicated enough, keeping all the balls in the air and under wraps. Keep it simple.

As he turned to leave, he heard a voice calling to him from the farmhouse. He moved from behind the hedge and spotted Alice. She toddled forward out of the gate; neat, tidy and wearing an all-enveloping floral overall. He had never seen her wearing anything else. The sight of her suddenly enveloped Hercules in disquieting memories of her cleaning days at Avignon; days warm then, now grown cold.

'Oh, it's you, Mr....'

'Douglas.'

Yes, Mr. Douglas. I can't always remember names, but I know who you are. How are you?'

'I'm fine, how are you?'

'Y'see it all,' she said, '. ... and how is Mrs. Douglas.'

'She's fine too, thank you.'

Alice stopped and Hercules could see the old woman scrabbling around for what to say next. Suddenly the words burst out.

'We like it here.' She hesitated. 'The man - Alistair, has his bit of garden; I do what I can in the hoose. It's good. It was guid of you to let us have it. We were miserable in the other place. D'ye like beans? Alistair has beans, ye ken thae long stringy anes; he has some ready; I'll give him a shout.'

'No, no,' began Hercules, but Alice had scurried away and he heard her calling for Alistair. In a short while she came back with her hands cradling runner beans. She handed them to Hercules, he took them from her and noticed that her hand trembled.

'I'll nip in the hoose and fetch a bag,' she said, then added, 'would ye no come in a tak' a cup of tea.'

'No, no,' mumbled Hercules, 'must get back. Things to do, decisions to make.' Familiar words, useful words, words he often turned to. Here, they sounded cheap and empty.

Alice scurried away to fetch a bag. She was gone scarcely three minutes, yet standing in the quiet lane beside the red-berried hawthorns, in the warm sunshine, in sight of the house whose destiny lay in his hands, for the first time for many years Harold Douglas felt the impact of his decisions on someone other than himself. The innocent warmth of this old woman's affection, her simple acts of kindness in giving him beans and offering him tea, flashed a light into a heart shuttered by years of calculation and self-interest. For a fleeting moment, strategies, plans, schemes, and flowcharts fled from his mind displaced by an overwhelming concern for this old woman. Here, in sharp clarity, he saw someone who had nothing to aim at or plan for, for whom the road led inexorably downwards, who faced a slow trudge into frightening confusion and loss, who had no money, no position, no influence; nothing with which to bargain; no options left; except one – hope, hope that someone would be kind to her; that *he* would be kind to her. Throughout his walk home these thoughts clung to him and disturbed him.

When he reached home, he rang The Doc at Proctor and Porteous to ask him to factor into his calculations the independent sale of Latchlaw farmhouse and steading. He told The Doc that he had not decided to sell it to Duncan, he just wanted to see the figures. Once he'd seen them, he would make his decision.

THIRTY-TWO

On the twentieth of September in McMaggie's, Ina addressed her coffee companions:

'The auld fishermen used to say that when the sun crosses the line, we aye get a gale o' wind.'

Ina took her authority for such a forecast from her father, a fisherman, and the son of a fisherman. During the next day, September 21st, the autumnal equinox, the sun crossed the equator on its tour of duty to our cousins in the South. In spite of Ina and her father, the day dawned fine and calm and set the weather for the week. But on the twenty-ninth, as if roused by sudden recollection of auld fishermen, a near hurricane smacked into Hecklescar and rampaged through the town.

Grubs had had a hazardous run from Mallaig when he turned, with a sense of relief, into Harbour Road. But of relief there was none. He had arrived at more or less the same time as high tide. Harbour Road was awash.

The harbour at Hecklescar lies at the mouth of the river Ale. When torrential rain falls up country and on the flanks of the Lammermuir Hills the river quickly swells and seeks an outfall at Hecklescar. Early Hecklescar folk, however, ignored this fact of nature and built the harbour and most of the town on the flood plain. Consequently, although the river is now diverted into its own channel away from the harbour, occasionally, when rain, tide and an onshore wind conspire, the river reclaims its own and floods into Harbour Road, the fish yards and, Harry will tell you, into the surrounding streets. Harry, who sandbags his front door in Church Street whenever it rains, believes that it is time the Regional Council stopped blaming forces of nature and did something about it.)

Jakey had saved the yard of Anthony Douglas & Son from the worst of the flood by building a low wall of sandbags across its access to the pier. Other properties along Harbour Road were not so fortunate. Most were flooded. The architect, a few doors down, had had the foresight to erect a neat flood board in front of his door and Tom and his missus in Shingle Shore had sandbagged their front door and moved upstairs when they saw the waters rising. However, when Jodi battled her way to her Harbourside Café to open up she found a foot of water sloshing around the tables, so went home to await low tide.

John Hendry set out that morning for the Bantry. He is an old man, over eighty. He does not need to go; there is nothing that he needs from the Co-op, the bakers or the paper shop that cannot wait until the wind eases. Nevertheless, he set out in his waterproofs and tie-down hat to fight his way along School Street, down through the pend into Cockle Aw and along the High Street to the seafront. When going along High Street it required all his strength to press forward against the gale. At times he had to stop, at others, between strides he was thrust back. Yet he pressed on. Why?

Because he loved the sea, and the sea on this morning rejoiced. He reached the Bantry and standing in the lea of the Amusement Arcade watched the wild, uninhibited jubilation of wind and water. The rollicking waters ran riotously into the bay, leaping over the rocks, flinging streamers twenty, thirty feet into the air. Waves dancing with each other rushed in roistering ranks to the beach, there to crash and foam and rejoice in their power and magnificence, and to dash in their bombastic majesty up and over the seawall, showering it in torrents of dancing, shimmering white water.

John Hendry came for another reason: to see whether the Regional Council had had the effrontery once again to fence off the folk of Hecklescar from their Bantry using ugly aluminium barriers and jargonised notices ordering: '*Wave overtopping of Sea Wall forecast, no entry to Promenade*.'

'What right have you to tell us that we cannot walk along our Bantry? It is not a promenade; it is our Bantry. We are not children. We do not need a nanny telling us what we cannot do. We are adults who can make our own decisions. We do not need protection from the sea; it is an old acquaintance; we know it well – in all its moods.'

The barriers were in place so John Hendry ventured from his shelter, lifted a barrier out of the way and, battered by wind and rain, stepped onto the Bantry. He staggered a few breathless yards. The sea, anxious to greet him, leapt over the sea wall, fell on his shoulders and drenched him. He smiled then went home to dry out and have his breakfast.

'He's an old fool,' said Ina to her husband as she served him his porridge. 'Shifting the council's barrier like that; ye think he'd ken that it's been put there for safety. Lizzie would never have let him away with that.'

Jakey did not think John Hendry a fool. He understood instinctively why John Hendry defied the notices. But he didn't contradict Ina; he had no time for a discussion, he had to get back to the yard. The roof of the fish processing room was leaking like a sieve and Hercules sulked in another of his vile moods.

The gale had also ripped through Latchlaw, and at six o'clock in the morning the phone rang in Duncan's house. When he answered it, he heard his distressed mother crying that a window had blown in, the kitchen was flooded and the roof had been ripped off the steading. Duncan battled his way to the farm to give them what aid he could and, at Janet's bidding, brought the old couple back to Priory Road until the storm subsided.

By evening of the following day, the wind had eased, the waters had abated and the folk of Hecklescar had started to tidy up the mess and to repair the damage.

Duncan and Hector were much in demand, patching and making wind and water-tight houses, shops, fish yards, cafes, offices and even the Session Room of the Parish Kirk.

They also found time to inspect the damage at Latch-law. They soon concluded that, although they could patch up the roof of the steading, the best solution would be a new one. The kitchen roof of the farmhouse, however, a flat roof, could not be patched and made up. The felting came off in sodden lumps when Hector tried to peel it away. The beams and planking under it were rotten. The only solution was to replace the whole roof; beams, planks and all.

'Who'll have to pay for that?' asked Janet anxiously when Duncan reported what they had discovered.

'It all depends, doesn't it,' replied Duncan tensely, 'on whether Hercules is going to sell it to us. If he is, then we will have to do it, won't we?'

'And if he doesn't sell it to us?'

'Then we walk away.'

For a few minutes, Janet considered this answer. Then she issued an order.

'You must go and ask Hercules whether he is going to let us have Latchly. He promised to give you an answer by the end of the month. Well, this is the thirtieth, this is the last day. You'll need to go and see him.'

'I'll do that,' said Duncan, trying to sound decisive.

'Now,' put in Janet. 'You'll need to go now. We need to know. Your mother is all at sea. She doesn't know where she is.

She wanders about the house all day in her pinnie looking for something to do. Your father is worse; he sits in the chair and growls. We have to move them back to Latchly quickly, before your mother loses the place completely. You need to go now; Hercules will be coming up for his lunch at half-past twelve. On your way take your father to Latchly and put him in the garden. Otherwise I'll crown him for grumbling all the time.'

'Should I take John Hendry with me?'

'If you can raise him. Certainly. That would be a good idea. But go!'

Janet's persistence rankled. Duncan thought about objecting to being lectured. But as he formed his response, John Hendry's words echoed in his ear: 'Cherish her.' He looked steadily at his wife and asked softly,

'Janet, do you still think we should take on Latchly? It'll be a lot of work and it'll not be easy with mam the way she is - and dad the way he's always been. They're mine, you know, not yours. Are you sure?'

'I am,' said Janet, sitting down beside him and taking his hand in hers. 'Whither you go I will go, whither you lodge, I will lodge, and your people will be my people.'

'Where did that come from?' laughed Duncan in embarrassment.

'Ruth, in the Bible,' replied Janet smugly, then added seriously, 'We can do it, love, can't we?'

Duncan looked at her, smiled and said,

'Nae doot! Eh, ma lass?'

CHAPTER THIRTY-THREE

I don't believe Harold has any intention of building the house at Latchlaw,' said Olivia to her mother Connie, a few days after the storm. She had surprised her mother by inviting herself for afternoon tea.

'Welcome to the real world, dear,' replied her mother. 'Did he ever?'

Olivia ignored the thrust.

'I think he's in serious trouble,' she pronounced, then added quickly, 'financially, I mean.'

'Is he now? There's a surprise.'

'Mother, I'm trying to talk to you about me and Harold. It has taken me a long time to bring myself to do it.'

'I make it twenty-five years.'

'Mother would you stop nipping. I'm serious. I need someone to talk to. Is that not what mothers are for?'

Connie studied her daughter. She detected the same distant woman that had dropped in occasionally over the past twenty years. Olivia had assumed that elegant aloofness worn by women who have, in their own estimation, risen above the common through their own success or that of their husbands. Of course, she had had a flying start - witness the Earl Grey tea she now sipped from the bone china cup supplied by her own mother.

As we have learnt, Connie too was once (and to some extent, still is) a sophisticate. Soon after her own marriage to Fordyce, however, Connie had found that sophistication does not make up for a sensible life companion. Fordyce had all the appearance of a cultured man without any of the substance. More and more she found his presence in her life irritating. Soon she was welcoming his absence.

But women do not live by men alone; she had formed other interests. Then there were the children, Bruce and Olivia. At his father's insistence Bruce left home when he was eleven to attend Lorretto School and never really came home again. After school, university; after university, a traineeship with an Edinburgh law firm; after three years, marriage to a fellow lawyer; after marriage, a move down south, then to Strasbourg for a career with the European Commission; no children; seldom seen - mutual cards on birthdays and a flower arrangement for his mother at Christmas. Four years ago, he called into Hecklescar to visit his mother. He was en-route to a conference in Gleneagles.

Olivia stayed at home and garnered her mother's love and hopes. After High School in Hecklescar she took a Social Science degree at Glasgow University, then returned home to work for Borders Council as a Social Worker; a job she hated. Throughout all of this she remained close to her mother and her mother to her. When she was at school her mother helped her with her homework and projects and with course work and dissertations at university.

Connie pushed the boat out when Olivia graduated, turning up at the ceremony in a stunning pale blue outfit and a wide brimmed ribbon-festooned hat. Whilst Fordyce showed her off as a sort of exhibit, ('haven't I got myself a splendid wife'), Olivia rejoiced to see her mother in such an array.

For however carefully Connie had played the part of the contented wife, Olivia knew instinctively the poverty of their relationship. The outfit, the hat, her mother's whole demeanour she saw, quite accurately, as an act of defiance, an assertion of independence. They never discussed it, not then, not ever. But Olivia and Connie both knew that the relationship that mattered in her life was not wife and husband, but mother and daughter, close companions.

Even when Peter Munro crept into their lives, he caused no breach in their easy affection. How did Olivia meet Peter Munro? Not at the school - he had left school well before she started. In the street, or at a function of some sort, a dance, or dinner party? Connected with her work; something to do with one of his father's properties? Neither Olivia nor Connie could remember how they had met. He somehow just appeared in their lives and made himself at home. He and Olivia started going out. Connie welcomed him, finding his openness, simple tastes and untutored manners more to her liking than the hollow refinement of her husband.

When Fordyce was away or busy, the three of them often gathered for a congenial meal with Peter always reluctant to leave and Connie and Olivia always loth to see him go. Slowly, and it seemed inevitably, they each began to assume that he and Olivia would make their lives together.

Then Harold Douglas blazed in in a smart suit, flashy car and a seemingly limitless supply of cash. The delicate sphere of their mutual affection shattered. Peter and Connie found themselves alone wondering where Olivia had gone – and why.

That was twenty-five years ago. Shortly afterwards Peter Munro left Hecklescar. Two years later Connie went down with ovarian cancer and, deserted by her husband, had to face it on her own.

She discovered (as do we all sooner or later) that life is

as unpredictable as the weather and our plans as unreliable as the forecasts. She patched together an interesting sort of life and would say, if you pressed her, that she had enjoyed it. But deep down she knew that the loss of her daughter's love had frozen something inside her. Certainly, granddaughter Sally's unqualified affection had warmed her more than a little, but Sally was not her daughter; not Olivia, and Olivia, her daughter lived on, inhabiting in the same place, yet not at home and not in the heart.

Now, on this day, as she studied her daughter sitting in the chair beside her, and glimpsing her discomfort, she felt drawn to her. As one human being to another in distress? As a mother to her child? As a parent seeing the prodigal afar off? Or, perhaps understandably, a troubling satisfaction, that after all this time, her daughter saw what she had always seen, from that first introduction, seen with near horror that her daughter should be taken in by such a charlatan; that her mother's counsel to her daughter had been brushed aside; that her warnings had been ignored; that her denunciation of the man had been rejected with contempt. She had recalled and relived over and over again that horrible moment when Olivia flounced out of the house into Hercules' waiting BMW, followed by the defiant roar of the engine as he snatched her daughter from her grasp.

As year built on year, these settled memories had bricked up the wall between herself and Olivia. Could she now hear her daughter's voice calling to her through the wall? For a split second, as in a lightning flash, she saw her own life mirrored in that of her daughter.

Not until this sudden insight had Connie understood that her confident, elegant, yes, arrogant, daughter was unhappy. Although Connie had never understood how it could be so, Olivia and Harold seemed to live comfortable, fulfilled, satisfying lives. They had the house, the furnishings, the treasured artefacts, the company of cultured people, dinner parties, theatre, trips abroad – and their position in the town. Why, they were almost the laird and his wife in the place. Looked up to, admired, consulted, envied.

Yet what is this that Olivia is saying? What does she mean? That she is unhappy as I was unhappy? That she despises Harold the way I despised Fordyce?

This conclusion had no sooner formed than Connie rejected it. This signified no prodigal repentance. Olivia had not come seeking motherliness but money. That's what she had said. She, they, were in a spot of bother and needed her help out of it. Harold is in financial trouble! Money! That is at the bottom of it! That is where this started; that is where it has arrived. They are running out of money and Olivia can't bear the thought of not having it. Her own job at the council doesn't pay enough for the lifestyle she enjoys. She can't face the prospect of anything less affluent so she has crossed the street and sidled up to her mother with a begging bowl. What is it she wants? A loan or a handout? What makes her think that I have anything to give?

'I cannot help you,' said Connie bleakly.

'But he is going to sell Avignon,' pleaded Olivia.

'What makes you think that?' exclaimed Connie

'That bitch that cleans for me, Ina, made a point of throwing it my face this morning.'

'How on earth would she know? She's just tittle-tattling.'

'She might be. But she cleans at the solicitors and reckons to have seen a letter on Cockburn Heath's desk.'

'From Harold?'

'No, from some firm in Edinburgh.'

'Why would they be writing to Cockburn Heath?'

'Ina said they were asking for location details and price

guidelines. The letter was marked 'In Strict Confidence.'

'And Ina read it! The woman should be jailed.'

'I've sacked her.'

'Oh, that'll look good down the street. Your name will be mud before the day is out.'

'I don't care. If Harold is trying to sell the house over my head, I am going to shout as loud as I can.'

Connie studied her daughter and thought she saw a tear glistening in the corner of her eye. Connie softened. 'Is that not what mothers are for?' her daughter had said.

'Look,' said Connie quietly, 'It sticks in my craw to defend Harold, but think straight, Olivia. Don't get carried away by emotion. Before you start shouting, consider that, if he is thinking about building at Latchlaw, he would put Avignon up for sale to pay for it, wouldn't he?'

'That's where I came in,' snapped Olivia. 'He has no intention of building at Latchlaw. He is going to sell the land to a builder – and, if he runs true to form, run away with the money.'

'How do you know that? When did that happen?'

'Never mind how I know. I know. He's selling up, lock, stock and barrel. The lot: the business, Latchlaw and the house. He thinks I don't know, but I have made it my business to find out.'

'So, what are you going to do?'

Up to this point Olivia had been strident, assertive, confident. Now her whole demeanour changed. She leaned forward and took her mother's hand in hers. Connie stiffened at the touch but let her hand be held.

'That's why I came, mother. I'm afraid. I don't know what to do.'

Connie looked at her daughter and felt the rekindling

of what? Love? No, not that, not even of affection; those were much too deeply buried to be resurrected so easily. She felt – pity – and sympathy. Her daughter was distressed, afraid she would lose her house, her livelihood, her position in the community. The pedestal she had constructed over the years was crumbling beneath her. What could she say; what help could a mother give?

'Whatever,' said Connie gently and, she hoped, reassuringly, 'Olivia, remember, whatever he does he cannot leave you penniless. You have a wife's rights; he cannot take those away.'

'I am not his wife,' replied Olivia bluntly. 'We were never married.'

CHAPTER THIRTY-FOUR

D id he say why Peter Munro had come to see them?' asked Mrs. Rostowski of her husband. He had reported that Peter Munro had visited the offices and warehouse of M&Y Wegg just over a week ago.

'He did,' replied Greg, 'but I didn't believe him.'

'What did he say? What was his name again?'

'Yaris – like the car. He said that Peter had enquired about storing furniture. Yaris said that Peter had a flat in Eastbourne but was giving it up and moving back to Scotland. He needed somewhere to store his furniture until he found a place up there.'

'That sounds reasonable,' said Mrs. Rostowski, 'He has never been happy here.'

'Has he been happy anywhere?' interjected Greg.

'That's not what I mean, I mean he's . . .'. She scratched around for the right words.

Greg supplied some: 'not where he should be.'

'What do you mean by that?' asked his wife.

'Everyone has a place where they should be,' he pronounced with the satisfaction of a teacher that has a copy of the answers. 'No other place is the right place. There is just one place that has been allocated to us. We have no choice. It is predestined where we should be, and happy is he who finds it.'

'This is not Gwyneth again, I hope,' cut in Mrs. Rostowski.

Greg sounded miffed.

'It is not! I thought it out myself. It's true, isn't it?'

'Not really. You're talking about home. Everyone wants to go home - back to where they came from.'

'No, it isn't. Would you like to go back to Horsham and that High Rise? I thought I saved you from all that.'

Mrs. Rostowski had to admit she did not want to go back to Horsham.

'That's different.'

'No, it's not. You are happy here, aren't you?'

Mrs. Rostowski looked at the earnest face of her husband and did not dare deny it. She was happy; she loved him, loved her son, loved their home; she loved their life together. She was happy.

'Of course!'

'Then this is your place; this is the place where you should be.'

'And you, my husband and philosopher, are you where you should be?'

'If you are, I am.'

Mrs. Rostowski thought about pointing out that this answer undermined his theory but decided to let it lie.

'You could be right about Peter Munro. Quite apart from all this trouble with Dilys, he never struck me as a man who belonged here. In fact, I don't know why he came to Eastbourne. It's not particularly close to his son or his daughter – and they don't seem to bother much with him, anyway. There's nothing holding him here. I suppose he doesn't feel that he is where he should be.'

'There you are,' said Greg smugly accepting his wife's supposition as proof of his theory. But he had not finished.

'He might be going back to where he should be,' he said, 'but he didn't go to Crawley just to enquire about furniture. There is something else.'

'What makes you think that?'

'Well,' replied Greg, 'if Peter Munro wants to store furniture, he could go to Woodhouse's or Bennet's, here in Eastbourne; why trail out to Crawley?'

He stared at his wife much as you would expect Poirot or Rebus to intimidate suspects. When his wife shrugged her shoulders, he continued,

'You know what I think?'

'Go on then,' said Mrs. Rostowski with a little smile, 'tell me.'

'I think Peter Munro has shares in the place. He might even own it outright. A sort of sleeping partner.'

'What on earth is a sleeping partner?'

'It's a partner that sits at home. He has money in the business but takes no part in running it. I think that's what Peter Munro is in M&Y Wegg. I think we should go back and talk to Mr. Toyota and....'

'Look, Greg,' cut in his wife, 'We are not the Board of Trade. We have no right to ask these questions. I couldn't care less whether Peter Munro has shares in or sleeps at Marney Wegg or whatever they call the firm. All I am interested in is finding Peter Munro. Did the Yaris man say where he had come from, or where he was going?'

'Not that I can remember. No, I don't think so. He was very cagey. I think he is hiding something.'

'Greg!' cried Mrs. Rostowski, 'that's enough. Give me this

man's phone number and I'll talk to him and see if he knows where Peter Munro has gone.'

That brought the conversation to an end. Greg gave his wife the phone number of Yaris Wegg, and Mrs. Rostowski rang him.

No, he didn't know where Peter Munro came from, or where he had gone. He had just arrived one day then gone away when he couldn't see Marney.

Did he have a contact address or number? No.

The trail had gone cold - again. Put the file away. Get on with other cases. Peter'll contact me again when he's ready.

Put the file away! - in a box file where she stored the bits and pieces she had collected on Peter Munro. As she put away her notes, she turned up the address book that she had found in Peter's flat. She wondered: are M&Y Wegg in the book? Look under W: Wegg, Yes! Marney, M&Y, Yaris, all in the book, all with the same address – in Crawley. But then next down the page: Wegg, Florence! Her first address crossed out: 14, Mill Lane, Dereham, then another, 39 St Luke's Road, Isleworth, also crossed out, then another: 4/3, Oakshot Close, Eastbourne. Oakshot Close! Just round the corner from Peter Munro's apartment in Burleigh Court. Who on earth was, is, Florence Wegg – and what is she doing in Peter Munro's address book?

'Chasez la fam,' said Greg when she reported her surprise to him.

'Don't jump to conclusions, love. Florence could be any-one – She might be Marney's mother, or his daughter.'

'Whoever she is,' said Greg, still chasing la fam, 'she's fol-lowed Peter Munro round. He was in Norfolk, she was in Nor-folk; he moves to London, she moves to London; he comes to live in Eastbourne, so does she.'

'Greg!' Mrs. Rostowski shouted, 'Stop looking for sleaze.

He's a decent man. I've spoken to him – and Oliver is quite sure that there is no other woman.'

'He would, wouldn't he? He's his mate, isn't he?' explained Greg, and if he had been aware where he was and to whom he was speaking, he would have stopped. But, oblivious to all but the chasez, he ran on.

'There is always another woman', he pronounced as if presenting a Social Science report to a Select Committee. 'There are three types: tarts, nymphos and ice maidens'.

Then he glanced at his wife and woke up. Before he could retreat, Mrs. Rostowski, a menacing smile playing on her lips, aimed a question at him,

'And which one am I?'

'Oh no, not you, it's not for you; it's not for wives, just for other women, the other woman, that's what I meant, the sort of women who would be the other woman.' The sentence died in his mouth.

'And you don't think I could be 'the other woman' to some other man.'

'No.....'

'If I were, which one would I be? What was it? Ice maiden, tart or nympho? That was it, I think. I'd like to be an ice maiden. But I have a pair of suspenders in the drawer I could look out.'

'I didn't mean.... 'spluttered Greg.

'And what's your other woman like, my good husband?' harried Mrs. Rostowski now enjoying Greg's discomfort, 'she'll be a nympho, I would think. I don't think an ice maiden would have you and you're not rich enough for a tart.'

'I don't have one,' mumbled Greg.

'Don't have one what? You mean you have more than one? Perhaps one of each?'

'I don't have any and I don't want any. I'm happy with my wife.'

'That's good to know but soft soap won't get you anywhere'.

'There is no other woman,' mumbled Greg, now sounding miserable.

'You would say that wouldn't you?' needled Mrs. Rostowski, 'but what do you say to your mates.'

'Come off it, Grace. I give in.'

He got up from his chair walked over to his wife and kissed her.

'Apology – and kiss, accepted,' pronounced Mrs. Rostowski. 'Now I will go round to 4/3 Oakshot Close, and I will not expect to find a nympho, a tart or an ice maiden. I hope to find a woman who can help me understand Peter Munro.'

Mrs. Rostowski could have rung Florence Wegg but decided to visit her in person. She was curious to see how the woman lived, what sort of house she lived in, what sort of furniture and effects she owned. You can tell a lot about someone from the stuff with which they surround themselves.

3, Oakshot Close is a low modern demure apartment block, the sort that houses in comfort better-off single people and older couples who have downsized or let their children have the big house in the suburbs. It sits contentedly in a leafy street surrounded by a neatly kept lawn punctuated with neat rose beds. The door into the block is controlled and can only be opened from inside. To enter, you press the number on the panel at the side of the door; the person inside will then talk to you on the intercom, check out your bona fides and, if they accept you, will admit you by opening the door.

Mrs. Rostowski often ran into such systems and rebuked herself for not realising that an address like 4/3 would be in a controlled apartment block. She should have rung Florence to alert her of her visit. Nevertheless, she punched '4' into the keypad, and waited to be summoned. No answer. Mrs. Rostowski keyed the number in again. Again, no reply. As she made to leave, she caught sight of a middle-aged sari-clad woman approaching the door from the inside. When the woman opened the door Mrs. Rostowski asked her,

'Could you tell me if a Florence Wegg lives in this block?'

'Florence, certainly,' replied the woman, 'but she is away at the moment.'

'I see,' said Mrs. Rostowski, 'do you have any idea when she might be back?'

'I don't. I take her post in and that sort of thing. She's been away a while; she said she'd ring me when she's coming back. But I haven't heard.'

Then, spotting Mrs. Rostowski's ID badge added, 'Is it something I can help you with?'

'No, thank you,' said Mrs. Rostowski, 'it's nothing important.' She turned away then turned back and asked the woman,

'How long did you say she'd been away?'

'I know exactly. It was the day after my daughter gave birth and Flo handed in a lovely little baby sleepsuit for her. When she handed it in, she told me she was going away.'

'When would that be?'

'The second week in July.'

'Thank you - and the baby is doing well?'

'Yes, thank you, very well.'

'I wonder,' asked Mrs. Rostowski, 'would you give her my card and ask her to ring me when you next see her? Would you mind?'

'Not at all.' She glanced at the card. 'Mrs. Rostowski?'

'Yes, and you are?

'Mrs. Raschid. Mrs. Aneisha Raschid'

* * * *

'She's been away twelve weeks,' reported Mrs. Rostowski to Greg when he came in that evening.

'Isn't that when Peter Munro left home?' asked Greg innocently.

'Do you not think I have worked that out,' replied his wife in a tone that Greg recognised immediately as a command not to re-start the chasez for la fam.

CHAPTER THIRTY-FIVE

John Hendry had escaped the day and was sitting, or should we say hiding, in his front room, in front of his log fire, trying to finish his crossword, trying not to think of Latchlaw, Anthony Douglas & Son Ltd, Golden Opportunities, or anything else that would put him off his sleep. Then the phone rang. For a while he let it ring. He hoped it might be a call about a PPI he did not have or a new boiler he didn't want, but suspected it might be from Jakey. asking him what he could do to save the yard. What could he say to him?

The phone rang on. Whoever it was seemed determined to send him to bed in no frame of mind to sleep. Eventually he picked up the phone. Jakey? No. Duncan Kerr.

'John,' he said, 'I've been onto Hercules. I've been trying to get him all week. He's just off the phone. He said he can see me tomorrow night. Ye'll come wi' me?'

'Who do these people think I am?' flashed into John's mind, immediately followed by Lizzie's tongue-in-cheek rebuke: 'To whom much is given....'

'Aye,' he said to Duncan, 'I'll be round. What time's he seeing you?'

'Half past six.'

'I'll be with you at five to put our ducks in a row. It's not going to be easy.'

* * * * *

'Are you sure you want to go ahead with this', asked John Hendry when he met Duncan and Janet in their kitchen in Priory Road.

'Sure,' stated Janet before Duncan could speak. John Hendry glanced at Duncan. Duncan nodded nervously.

'Let's run through it again,' said the old banker. 'You will sell this house in Priory Road and buy Latchlaw outright. You will not consider leasing it?'

'No,' said Janet firmly. 'We buy it. It must be ours – and the steading, and a little bit of ground for Alistair.'

'And you will move in beside Duncan's mother and father?'

'Yes.'

'How is Alice, anyway?'

'Much the same. She does very well. She still makes all their own meals and cleans the house. I go up there on a Thursday night and work out a menu for the week. It's what she has always done. Then we list the messages she needs and Duncan takes her to the shops on a Saturday morning, or if Duncan can't do it, Christine takes her. Most of the time she knows what she is doing, though Christine did say she had to stop her buying more bread; I'd put two loaves in her freezer already. But she wanted to buy more. Duncan's there early every day, at the steading with Hector, and Christine goes up regularly to see her gran. She's always been close to Alice.'

'And Alistair?'

Duncan cut in to prevent Janet speaking.

'He's surprised us,' he said. 'He's doing a lot more in the

house. He's still in the garden most of the time, but he pops in from time to time, and does bits and pieces. Every time I go, he tells me how well Alice is, and what she's able to do, and how he can't see much wrong with her, now that she's got over that dizzy spell. He's still got his head in the sand - but he's trying. I found him putting away the hoover for mam the other day.

Looking for assent, he glanced at Janet. Janet smiled,

'He certainly is trying,' she said, letting the ambiguity hang.

'Right then, numbers,' said John Hendry. 'This house will sell for what? Say, £200,000. Then, by the time Cockburn takes his cut. . ... You'll go through Cockburn, right?'

Janet and Duncan both nodded.

. . .and other expenses, say a hundred and eighty, to be cautious. Then you've got to bring Latchly up to standard. It's in a poor way, isn't it?'

'It is,' confirmed Duncan.

'It will take, what, to put it right?'

'I'm not sure, could be £50,000 or. ...'

'What?' exclaimed Janet, 'Fifty thousand pounds!'

Duncan stared at his wife and for a moment John Hendry thought he was going to back off, but he recovered and repeated the figure.

'I don't know 'til we have a good look, but it'll be a fair whack. Could be lower, but no, I'll stick to £50,000 to be on the safe side.'

'Does that include the ten thousand we drew out Hercules' fund to pay for fitting out the steading?' Janet demanded.

Duncan hesitated.

'Well, yes.' he conceded.

'So that £10,000 doesn't come out of what we get for this house?'

'No.'

'That's forty thousand then. That's better – but not much.'

Janet slumped back into her chair.

John Hendry comforted her.

''Now Janet,' he said softly, 'I'm sure it can be done. You will have over a hundred thousand pounds to offer. Cockburn Heath says that Hercules can expect to make about £30 to £35,000 on each site, but that is, I would think, for open ground. For the farmhouse and the steading, I don't think he'd make that. A builder would have to take it down and that would cost him.'

'Unless they wanted to do it up,' put in Janet bluntly. 'Like we do.'

'Different business, I think, Janet. Builders are interested in building houses, not doing them up; not a house on its own, anyway. No, the best deal for Hercules will be a private deal. I think if we make him an offer of £90,000 – three times what he'd make for one site - he'd take it.'

He looked at Duncan for agreement, Duncan looked at Janet, Janet sat expressionless for a while then smiled and said doubtfully,

'So be it. We can but try.'

John Hendry had one final question.

'The mortgage on this house is cleared, isn't it?'

'No,' stated Janet, and waited for John Hendry to react before she went on. 'But it will be a fortnight come Friday, twenty-second of October! Our Silver Wedding anniversary. Twenty-five years to the day – and the day we pay off the mortgage!'

John Hendry laughed.

'I am invited?'

'We'll be offended if you don't come. Just quiet – in the house, just the family and a few friends.'

* * * * *

'Nothing like what I had in mind,' said Hercules when he heard of the ninety thousand that Duncan was prepared to offer for the Latchlaw Farmhouse and Steading.

They were sitting in the lounge at Avignon, John and Duncan both sunk into a low white leather sofa; Hercules lording it from a higher easy chair with papers laid out neatly in front of him on a low coffee table.

'Selling off the house is something of a distraction. I'm not sure how well it will go down with contractors. There's a lot of interest in the site. Building land is in short supply at the moment, and I've had some very attractive offers for Latchlaw.'

'What? About two million? Eh?' said John Hendry pleasantly, 'It must be worth all of that.'

Hercules studied the old banker for a moment, wondering what he was up to. His estimate was not far out; he'd done his homework, but why was John Hendry talking up the price? What was £90,000 against £2 million?'

'Of that order,' replied Hercules, 'so you can see that your offer falls well below my aspirations for the site. As I say, selling the house separately is, to be honest, a bit of a nuisance.'

'Ninety Thousand looks quite attractive,' replied John Hendry, 'if you reckon that the farmhouse and steading take up less than three sites, and each site is worth, what? £25-30,000? The farmhouse and steading spoil the site the way they are now. They're an eyesore. I would think any contractor looking at it will see it as a problem. Either he has to pull it down and clear the site. That's costly. Or do it up, which, as you say, is a distraction – and even more costly. Duncan here is prepared to put the farmhouse and steading into a presentable state. I tell you what, as part of the deal, I'm sure he would agree to put it into a presentable state now, in the next two weeks, before the builders start viewing it. Better than that. It'll give the place a character it won't have if it is just a rundown farmhouse or a pile of rubble. That's what people want nowadays; a bit of character, a sense of history, of being connected with the place and the past. The fact that an old Hecklescar family is in residence is a plus, and then the residents will be able to pop along to buy a few vegetables from the market garden on the estate. You don't get that in the big smoke. A taste of country living, that's what they're looking for when they come out here. A smart farmhouse and steading will convince them they've arrived.'

Hercules showed no sign of being impressed by this sales pitch. He made no reply. He had a thought-out proposition of his own.

'I want to help you, Duncan. You've been good to the lad - and I'd like to help the old lady. I met her the other day along at Latchlaw. What I'll do is this. Let's say £175,000 for the farmhouse, the steading and the extended garden.'

He then glanced at John Hendry.

'If you do what John here says. Tidy it up before the contractors arrive to view. OK?

He looked at Duncan. Duncan looked at John Henry.

'That's steep,' said the old banker. 'Say £150,000.'

Duncan looked alarmed.

''fraid not,' said Hercules gathering up his documents to signal that his offer was final and the meeting was at an end,

'One, seven, five. . . .' he started, then dramatically suspended his paper-shuffling, and smiled, 'No, I tell you what, one, six, five. If you get it to me within a couple of weeks. OK?'

He looked at Duncan again. Duncan glanced at John

Henry. John Hendry nodded his head.

'I'll take it,' said Duncan abruptly.

Hercules put out his hand to Duncan, Duncan took it and shook hands. John Henry then put out his hand to Hercules. With some hesitation Hercules took it. The hand that John Henry grasped surprised him. I felt limp, hot and sticky. John Henry glanced into Hercules' eyes and saw in them what he had detected in the hand: that this, all of this, was costing Hercules more than his bluster could cover.

As they separated John Hendry added, 'We'll put in a formal letter of offer in the next couple of days. Cockburn Heath will handle our end of it. Addressed to you, or to your solicitors?'

'To me.' said Hercules.

'Who is going to tell Janet?' asked Duncan anxiously as they walked down the front path of Avignon on their way home.

.

CHAPTER THIRTY-SIX

The day after his meeting with John Hendry and Duncan, Hercules tackled Olivia about the house. Unlike Golden Opportunities, Latchlaw and the businesses, this would be plain sailing. After all, it was *his* house. It had been his father's house; now it was his. He could sell it if he wanted to. He acknowledged that Olivia had not bought his deceit of a move to Latchlaw. That, like their relationship, had terminated years ago.

'It's over; put it out of its misery. I'll do a deal. Olivia will not be much worse off. She can go and live with her mother until she finds a place of her own. Avignon can be sorted.'

When they met however, Hercules found Olivia more prepared than he had anticipated. He had reckoned that he would take her by surprise, but almost immediately found himself on the back foot.

He had designed the narrative to be tough but conciliatory. The prize lay in the money tied up in Avignon, so must be relegated to a sub plot, incidental to the inevitability of their separation, brought in at the end almost as an afterthought, as something he had not really considered, something they would have to think about and re-visit. 'What should we do with the house when we no longer need it? We both know it was always a stopgap on our way to – well, we know where - so we need to be shot of it.'

'Brutally bored and honest' labelled the jacket he had put on for their meeting: he was tired of the unrewarding slog and tired of the mediocrity of this place. In particular, he was tired of pretending that they had mutual interests. Had he not attempted to revive their relationship with his Latchlaw proposal? And had she not poured contempt on it? He accepted that it was futile – and finished. He wanted out; must get out - whatever it took. He'd spent all of his life accommodating others now he would accommodate only himself. If that upsets you and anyone else, so be it.

Yes, and he'd be frank about Elvira because he suspected that Olivia already knew about his affairs - this one anyway. No doubt daughter Sarah had bleated to her mother. Magnanimously, he would shrug off her indiscretions. He had little evidence of these - a few unexplained missing nights, an enigmatic phone call or two, a gift that appeared out of the blue. He would accuse her and forgive her in the same breath; put her on the defensive; concentrate her mind on protesting her innocence, and under that smokescreen ride in the sale of the house. He'd give her, (what?), quarter of what he made on it - £100,000, say?

This formed his plan of attack. But before he could open up, she spiked his guns.

In fading light with rain pattering on the roof and spattering the windows, they sat in the conservatory facing each other across a coffee table. On the table in front of them lay china cups and saucers. Beside each china cup and saucer lay a china plate, and close to them, a larger china plate holding four delicately buttered scones. Olivia had poured milk from a china jug into the cups and filled them with tea from a fluted china teapot. As she put down the teapot and before Hercules could launch his broadside, she spoke.

'I'm staying at Avignon,' she stated. 'I am entitled to half of it and I will buy out the other half. You are asking for £450,000 for it. You'll not get that. I will pay £200,000 for your share. A scone?'

Startled, Hercules instinctively lifted a scone from the proffered plate. How did she know he had put the house up for sale? How did she know that he wanted £450,000 for it?

He stared at Olivia; that stare he had cultivated to intimidate and subdue. This time it produced no reaction. Olivia held his gaze. He fell back on bluster.

'You must be joking,' he said. 'How will you lay your hands on that kind of money? Besides, four hundred and fifty grand is just the asking price; it's worth a lot more than that; they're hot in Edinburgh.'

'Could be,' said Olivia softly, 'but it's not in Edinburgh and I am told you can't sell without my say-so. Is that right?'

'Who's feeding you this rubbish?'

'That is for me to know and for you to guess. It is true, is it not? You can't sell without me – and I will make sure you don't. I am staying in Avignon. You can go off with your floozy if you like; sail round the world with her if that is what you intend. But I am not shifting from Avignon.'

'It's that interfering mother of yours that has put you up to this, isn't it?'

'Harold, as you have often lectured me, 'if you are in a hole, stop digging.' You want money out of the house; I am prepared to give you it.'

Hercules sat silent for a while. Olivia had routed his arguments. He must regroup and respond.

As he sat considering his next move, he discovered what many a general before him has discovered: that the heat of the battle exposes not only the enemy's weaknesses, but your own.

Hercules had prepared his exit strategy with great care; had, he thought, covered all the angles. He would walk away from Golden Opportunities and sell up everything else: the businesses, Latchlaw, Avignon. He would take the money and run before Peter Munro or anyone else, could stop him. The sale of the Mallaig business was proceeding as planned and Latchlaw would make him a mint whether or not he accommodated Duncan Kerr. With these deals he had anticipated some obstacles and had laid out tactics to overcome them. But with Avignon he had made no elaborate plans because he could foresee no serious difficulties. The house was his to sell: put it up for sale, accept the first reasonable offer and pay off Olivia.

He had not anticipated she would want to stay in Avignon, for he had never regarded the house as *her* house. It had been his father's house; now it was *his* house. In it *he* had accommodated Olivia and had brought up *his* family. Certainly, we have heard him talk about *our* dream house at Latchlaw, and it may well be that at the beginning, twenty-five years ago, he did think of Latchlaw as *our* house, but of Avignon never.

Olivia stay in Avignon after he had gone? No! That must not be! The thought of it vexed him. But Olivia was waiting for an answer. Deceit came to his rescue.

'That needs thinking about,' he spat out, hoping she did not pick up the tremor in his voice. 'I'll get back to you.'

He stretched out to lift the cup of cold tea from the coffee table in front of him.

'When?' demanded Olivia, 'I need to know if I have a home!'

A voice inside Hercules screamed, 'It is not your home. You live here on my sufferance'. Had he not been in the act of swallowing cold tea the words would have shot out of his mouth. But he swallowed them with the tea.

'It will not take long. A day or two,' he growled. 'In the meantime, you can tell your bloody mother to keep her nose out of my business. She is not getting her hands on my house.'

Olivia picked up her cup and stood up.

'Let me give you something else to consider,' she said; 'I seem to remember that you need my agreement to sell the Highland business; I'm a director I believe. Well, I'll be generous. You agree with me about Avignon and I will agree with you on Mallaig.'

Then she left. She will go to her mother's. There she will break down - and Connie will melt a little and put an arm round her shoulder. But we will not intrude. We must go back to Avignon and Hercules.

Hercules sat on in the conservatory after Olivia had gone and sought to call in his rampaging emotions. What Olivia had offered was eminently reasonable. Like the rain battering the windows, that conclusion hammered at the door of his reason but he would not let it in. He knew full well that he would make nothing like the £450,000 the estate agent had slapped on the house. Hercules' fellow golfers at Gullane, had reckoned he would be lucky to make £400,000; £350,000 sounded more likely. Olivia's £200,000 constituted a good offer.

Not only that; it would avoid a wrangle. He knew Olivia well enough, and behind her, that bitch of a mother of hers, to know that they would make life difficult for him if he tried to sell the house over her head. That would take time; time he did not have.

Again, the house might not sell quickly. The last one in Alexandra Drive took two years to sell; he had two months. He did not want to give Olivia half; a quarter was what he had in mind. But if he could walk away with £200,000 in the next few weeks, was that not much better than gaining nothing at all?

Then there was the Highland business. He didn't want any delay there either. She couldn't block the deal, but she could hamper it.

Hercules recognised all this. But the thought of Olivia continuing to live in the house sickened him. Why?

All of life's whys are rag-bags of reasons, fears, hunches, ambitions and bloody-mindedness. Hercules' bags are no different, but we have no time to rummage through them and check for moths. What we can say with reasonable certainty is that two causes lie close to the frustration he feels when he imagines Olivia living on in Avignon. Arrogance drives one, sentiment the other.

He is infuriated at Olivia's command of the position in which they find themselves. He had a plan, but her plan trumps his plan. The fact that it meets, or almost meets, the objective he has set himself grates. Emotionally he does not want to give her, and through her, her mother, the satisfaction of having outflanked him.

Then there is sentiment. Sentiment! What? Hercules? Sentiment? Yes, sentiment! About Olivia, about the end of their life together, regret for a dead love? No, not that; sentiment for the house!

But he's thinking of trading it in for cash! He is, but that he can accept. He's a desperate man in need of money, so the hundreds of thousands of pounds will warm his heart much more thoroughly than any nostalgia for the house. No, it is not the selling of the house that troubles him; it is the thought that Olivia will continue to live there.

Without Olivia, Avignon is a pile of stone with a roof, realisable in cash. As Olivia's house, it displaces his home, the home of his mother and father, his family, his people, his memories. His father had bought it as Selkirk House. Hercules had re-named it Avignon when he and Olivia moved into it. Unplanned and uninvited the house had lodged deep within an enclave of his mind, an area he had not visited for many years. Had he been able to continue to think of the house as a realisable asset, or as an empty building to be furnished by some anonymous buyer with new curtains and new memories, he would not have opened up what lay in the cellar of his mind.

But Olivia's insistence that she would stay in Avignon had prized open the hatch and allowed his vulnerability to escape. It poured out with an energy that frightened him. Suddenly, as he sat in the rain-spattered conservatory, Hercules felt the rising storm. What was he doing? Where was he going? What was he leaving behind?

So strongly did the emotion sweep over him that he could no longer sit still. He jerked to his feet, knocking over his teacup. Tea splurged onto the floor. He bent down to soak it up, then ran to the kitchen to fetch a paper towel. Having dabbed furiously but ineffectively at the spillage, he abandoned it and ran into the study and slammed the door.

Frantically, he scrabbled for his keys and opened the drawer in his desk. He pulled out his 'exit folder' and out of it snatched the control chart. He must regain control. He must force the plan back onto the written page, must confine it again in words and numbers, must bring it under management.

He found the line on the chart that contained 'Avignon' and, taking a black pen scratched out the name, overwrote it again and again until the name could no longer be deciphered. Then he wrote in 'Real Estate'. But went no further. His hand trembled over 'Progress'. He must enter something; he must decide – rationally! He had a firm offer of two hundred thousand pounds. But from Olivia! For the house! So she can take it over! Go on living in it! Make it hers! He felt as if he had been kicked in the stomach.

He let out a howl of exasperation, slammed down the

pen and left the box blank.

CHAPTER THIRTY-SEVEN

Hercules was learning the hard way that life does not easily bend to strategies, particularly where other people are concerned and certainly, when the other people included Olivia, and behind her, her mother, Connie. Olivia's proposal to buy Avignon had sickened him, but three days tossed in crosscurrents of resentment and opportunity persuaded him to steer for compromise.

For the fishyard at Hecklescar, however, no such way forward had opened up. CoCarvers, the agency, had drawn a blank. No wonder! The debts of Anthony Douglas & Son Ltd towered over its assets. Even if someone bought it for the proverbial £1, they would be liable for its liabilities and be well out of pocket. As the agency eventually (and irritably) informed Hercules: no-one with any business sense would touch it with a barge pole.

'A coffin case; bury it,' Claudette at CoCarvers had said; 'bury it and walk away'.

It would be cheaper, she concluded, for any interested party to let the company go broke, then rummage through the debris to see if there were anything worth picking up. The order book, for instance, might be worth buying from the liquidator.

Hercules bridled at such advice but could not counter it. What was he to do? For weeks he had brooded on it. The more he brooded the more it rankled. Liquidation, bankruptcy, 'Recovery Administrators' stripping out its guts, picking over its bones; himself vilified, disgraced: the incompetent son who lost his father's firm.

Then the night after his confrontation with Olivia, a sleepless night when he had quit his unquiet bed to make tea, he picked up The Times and read that some female fashion entrepreneur had handed over her company to its employees 'so she could pursue other opportunities'. Of course! Hand it over to the employees – no, better - sell it to them! For what I can get. That would be better than losing the lot.

Bright ideas in the night often fade in the light of the day, but this one did not. The more he considered it, the more it appealed. What probably clinched it was the consoling conclusion that if, in the future, the firm went broke, it would not be his fault but that of the employees.

Having come to his decision and decided his tactics, he walked down to the pier, strolled around the yard, chatted to Angela, hailed Little Dod, then retired to the office to look through a mountain of neglected post with Fiona. All just to show that he was still around, still the boss; still the owner. He then instructed Jakey to attend him that evening at Avignon. He had an interesting proposal to put to him. 'About the firm,' Jakey asked. 'Indeed,' replied Hercules.

Hercules knew, or rather had been taught to believe, that a strategy is no use without a narrative. The narrative need not be true, it need not be fiction, it just has to cast the best possible light on what you are trying to achieve. Passing the business on to the employees lent value to the strategy. It could be presented as philanthropy, or rather, as philanthropic business management. It could be reckoned as generosity; hopefully it would go down well with the locals. This script he had worked up and written down. Now he would re-hearse it with Jakey.

Lately, Jakey's days have been full of anxiety, and many of his nights sleepless. While Hercules has been planning to ditch the business, Jakey has sweated to keep it afloat. He had worked with Hercules long enough to know that the man could be economical with the truth, but he acknowledged Hercules as the boss. The skipper might be a rogue and liar on shore, but once afloat, the boat and the crew were in his hands. What else could he do but to translate what Hercules commanded into what lay in the best interests of the ship.

'You can't have more than one hand on the tiller,' he always replied when Nudge, Little Dod, Angela, or any of the others complained about Hercules' latest deceit.

Jakey epitomised the loyal lieutenant, but lately, more and more often, being loyal to Hercules had meant being disloyal to the people who worked with him. He was a plain man with simple principles, unskilled in rationalisation and sub-terfuge. Having to straddle the ever-increasing gap between what he knew to be true and what he believed he had to say, stretched his integrity to breaking point. It sickened him.

Daily one or another brought him reports of the news on the street, on the pier, by the customers, by the fishermen up on the Firth. All sang the same song.

'Hercules is pulling out of Mallaig, He is going to do the same at Hecklescar, isn't he?'

'No, that's just a rumour. The yard here is okay.'

'You might believe that, Jakey, but no-one else does. Hercules has lost interest. How often is he in at the yard these days? The business is going down the pan. Nudge says that agents in France and customers in Spain are complaining they can never reach the man; he is always unavailable. Watt's from Fraserburgh are hoovering up the lobster and langoustine discontents on the Continent and Little Dod brings back reports almost every day of Border chefs defecting to bandits and con merchants from Granton and North Shields.'

'He'd tell me if he was thinking of selling up. He told me we'd be the first to know. He hasn't said anything yet, so let's keep going, eh? That's what we're paid for.'

'But our jobs depend on it.'

'D'ye not think I ken that? But I'm seeing him th'night. I'll ask him. There now, will you get in that van and get up to Kelsae with the fish? And you - go back into the yard and sort thae prawns.'

They go back to work this day as they have gone other days. They go because Jakey had asked them to, and Jakey wouldn't lie to us; he'd tell us what is going on, if it is going on. We'll see what he says tomorrow after he's seen Hercules th'night.

Such is the fragile expectation that Jakey carries to collide with the cold pillars of Hercules' strategy and narrative. What can be expected of a meeting where the protagonists bring such different aspirations? What can we expect Hercules to gain, or Jakey to take away from such an encounter?

'Help yourself to another scone, Jakey.'

Hercules heaved himself out of his chair and offered the plate to Jakey. Jakey, surprised, lifted a scone from the plate. Hercules returned wearily to his chair.

'I want to share with you Jakey. I'm tired! I've been running this business now for twenty years, and it takes its toll. I've taken it from a bit player in the Scottish market to a major player in Europe. When I took it over it was in a poor way. Yes, I know the old man was a grafter, and for someone from his generation he did well and achieved great things. But, as you know, Jakey, the company was badly managed. It had no strategy, no clear objectives, no controls. That happens when a company grows wild. You know what I mean. When he saw an opportunity, he went for it. Sometimes it worked out, sometimes it didn't - as you know well. We had to untangle ourselves from some of the deals that were costing us. You remember that Polish deal, Jakey, and what it cost us; that gave us serious pain as you well knew. You remember that?'

At first Jakey did not recognise the question for Hercules rarely asked his opinion on anything beyond prawns and lorries. When Hercules repeated it, Jakey was forced to answer.

'Aye, I remember that. But we aye thought it was you that brought the idea back when you went with that delegation to Berlin. I mind a' the excitement of trading behind the Iron Curtain.'

'That's true - an idea, but it needed research and strategic planning. When I started to strip it down, I knew it wouldn't fly and advised the old man to back off. But he forged ahead – you know what he was like; when he had the bit between his teeth he wouldn't let go. But once I sat in the chair, I killed it off and switched resources to the Mallaig business - and that paid off in the end.'

'Is it sold?'

'More or less, and I did a good deal. Whether they'll do as well as we did with it is another matter.'

By now Jakey had begun to sniff the scent Hercules was laying, so he asked the question that, for weeks now, had lain on his mind like a suffocating blanket.

'You were saying you were tired. Does that mean you're selling up here as well?

Inwardly Hercules smiled; *lead them to the well* flickered in his mind.

'Have some more tea,' he said amiably. Jakey felt his pulse quicken. He turned the offer down.

'Am I thinking of selling up here? Yes and no,' Hercules

continued. 'Yes, I am thinking of retiring. I turned fifty this year'

He stopped suddenly and stared at Jakey.

'Let me confide in you, Jakey.' (*Attach them to the narrative.*) 'A couple of months ago, I was standing on the first tee up on the golf course. I'd gone up there to clear my head after that snarl up at the Channel Port; you'll remember that; we lost the load. You remember that?'

Jakey nodded. What was he up to now?

'Up there, I ran into the Strolling Minstrels,' he gave a short laugh, 'you know Michael, Maxwell, and that John Hendry – and the other one, you know who I mean. I looked at them, and I thought, is that what I want to do? Is that what lies ahead? They were still on the green so I looked out over the town and saw two things. One was the yard. I could read the nameboard: Anthony Douglas & Son; the other was the mast of Olympian.'

Hercules detected Jakey's confusion and added, 'my yacht'. Jakey nodded nervously.

'Proud of both! Then I asked myself, 'Harold, in five years, where do you want to be? Down in that yard or out on the ocean?' (You don't mind me opening up to you like this, do you Jakey? You are perhaps one of the few people who might understand.)' (*Stitch them into the narrative; tie them tight*).

Jakey nodded and could now see clearly where Hercules was steering.

Hercules continued.

'Then I checked myself and said, 'No, Harold, where do you want to be NOW?' The answer hit me, Jakey - strongly. 'You've done enough, Hercules. You've carried the business for twenty years; you have given it the best years of your life. Now you must do what you need to do. You want to set out on a new venture? Go for it! - before you are too old, while you are still able."

Jakey had heard enough. He didn't need the conclusion. Fears and doubts battened down all summer burst out. With a trembling hand, he put down his cup and stood up.

'You're selling up,' he growled, 'that's what all this about. You're selling up! That's it, isn't it? I've been denying it. But that's what you're telling me. You're going to sell the business. That's it, isn't it?'

A boss more sympathetic to his employee, more committed to a faithful servant; a man more concerned for his neighbour, would have backed off at such a response, but Hercules did not. He saw immediately that Jakey's outburst could be used to advantage.

Instead of backing off, he stood up, stared at the red-faced Jakey, and said bluntly,

'Yes, Jakey, I'm selling up. That is precisely what I intend.'

He paused long enough for the dreaded words to rebut Jakey's anger. Then he added,

'If that is what you want. I told you there was a Yes to my selling up. But I also said there was a No. Yes, I'm getting out. You can't deny me that. But no, I don't want to sell up. I want you and your colleagues to take over the company in an employee buyout.'

'What?'

'I plan to hand the company over to you and the employees. You can run it, Jakey. You virtually do that now. We'll agree a decent price, far below what I'd get on the open market and you and your colleagues will own the company.'

'Buy it?' cried Jakey, 'You're joking! We can't buy it! Where the hell would we get that kind of money?'

'Sit down, Jakey,' Hercules purred, 'I've put it badly. We'll arrange to transfer the business to you and your colleagues. There are well-established procedures for this. A price will be agreed that will allow the bank to release funds to me and allow you to pay it up over time from the profits. There will be practically nothing to pay up front, a few administrative expenses and fees but that's all.'

'Look, this is not the time to discuss the detail. I've hit you cold with it. Forgive me! Go away and think about it; talk it over with a few trusted friends.'

Jakey had returned to his chair. He stared at Hercules, his mind heaving. He said nothing; he could think of nothing to say. Hercules stood up to indicate the interview was over. Jakey stood up. Hercules grasped his hand.

'Let's make a go of this, Jakey. It could be the best thing that's happened in this town for a long time. The best thing for you - your own boss. Talk it over and come back, when? When would you say? What, a week today? Would that give you time?'

'I don't know,' mumbled Jakey. 'I'll need to think about it. It's a big ask. I'll need to see.'

'And you'll get back to me?'

'Yes, I'll need to talk to them down the yard. But, no, I don't see it.'

'Do that, talk to them - but this is between you and me. Let's keep it simple. We don't want a lot of hassle. You know and I know that there are one or two in this town who negativize any proposal. Keep clear of them. You know who I mean?'

Jakey looked blank so Hercules explained,

'Well, for instance, there's a certain old banker that pokes his nose into other people's affairs. You know who I mean. Keep clear of him. He'll throw all sorts of shit in the way. My advice would be to take your own counsel – and those you trust in the yard. They know what is best for the firm – and their jobs.'

Hercules led Jakey to the door. There he shook him by the hand again, then staring into his face, quietly and firmly added,

'Jakey, if you don't take it on, I'll need to sell it. You understand that. And whoever buys it will likely shut it down? You see that, don't you?' (*Lock all the doors but the one you want them to open*).

CHAPTER THIRTY-EIGHT

J ohn Hendry walked through Hecklescar the day after Hercules' declaration to Jakey and heard many different versions of what had taken place.

In the Co-op, Gwen of the coffee crew told him that Ina had announced that Hercules and Olivia were splitting up. She told them that she had held her peace for years about what went on in that house but seeing as she no longer worked there, she now felt no 'obligement' to keep confidences. This declaration had surprised the congregation because daily she had reported the comings and goings, the ins and outs, the ups and downs of the pair. She had told them about the separate bedrooms, about Hercules' 'bits on the side'; about Olivia's mysterious absences, about the flowers she once took in for Olivia and the message on the card that happened fall out of its envelope when she was carrying them into the kitchen to find a vase.

Coming out of the bakers with a barley loaf and a custard slice, John Hendry was hailed by Alan, one of the Codlings, to ask if he'd heard that Hercules had put the fishyard up for sale. His daughter worked there but was on holiday in Salou so he hadn't heard anything about it before he'd met Nudge just back from France. Nudge had told him that Jakey has called a meeting in the yard th'night at 7 o'clock, to tell them what's what. Nudge also reported that Grubs, the driver from Mallaig, reckoned that this had been on the cards for months, that Hercules never intended to sell just the Mallaig bit but all along wanted shot of the lot. He's run it into the ground.

Alan, a retired Maths teacher and amateur economist, calculated that anyone wanting to buy the business would have to shell out, what, one and a half million? More, perhaps. But from what his daughter says - and Nudge and the others, the place is falling apart, and would need a lot spent on it. It has been starved of investment. The lorries too, are clapped out and would need to be replaced, at say, £200,000 a time, so do you discount that, or would someone buy it for the order book and the staff? The people that work there have stored experience, which must be worth something, and Jakey seems capable of running it day to day. But could he manage it? Doubtful; he's hands-on, not a planner and has no grasp of the economics. But there are people who might help him with that.

While they were talking, Maxwell, the retired Director of Social Work whom we met on the golf course three months ago, came up and stood fidgeting, waiting for Alan to move on. Once Alan had gone, he invited John Henry to Porto on the Pier for coffee; there was something he wanted to discuss.

John Hendry agreed reluctantly. He had promised himself a quiet cup and a custard slice in his own backyard amongst his begonias but could see that his friend was agitated and he had a pretty good idea of what pestered him. He wasn't wrong. They had scarcely settled themselves into the armchairs up the stair at Porto before Maxwell blurted out his concern for the money he had given to Hercules to invest in Golden Opportunities. He had heard that Hercules had run into financial trouble and was selling up. How did that affect his holding?

'That depends,' said John Hendry, 'who holds your money. If it is with Methuen and Sinclair it is safe; if it is with HD Investments, I'd withdraw it before the day is out.'

'How will I know?'

'You'll have a certificate or a letter.'

'I have, I looked it out this morning.'

'And which is it: M&S or HDI?'

'Hercules signed the letter.'

'He would in any case. You'll need to look at the certificate. Who issued it? That's what you need to know. When did you invest? How long ago?'

'It would be in 1990, the year I retired; I took a lump sum from my pension.'

'That's early. It's likely you'll be all right, He didn't start up on his own until later. But you'd better check. Make sure the certificate is a certificate, not a letter and make sure it's from Methuen and Sinclair, or sometimes it is called M&S.'

'That's a relief,' said Maxwell, sitting back in his chair. 'The wife said at the time that it was a lot of money to hand over to Hercules.'

'If it's not confidential, how much did you give him?'

'£50,000'

'That *is* a lot of money! Has it done well?'

'What do you mean?'

'I mean, have you made a decent return on it?'

'I didn't need income; I've got a decent pension. I went for growth.'

'And has it grown?'

'Oh yes, it's worth over £200,000 now.'

'So, you didn't panic and take it all out when the banks

crashed?'

'No, I thought about it, but Hercules told me to hang on.'

'He was right. The stock market picked up quickly. Which is more than you can say for the banks. Your little pile wouldn't be earning much interest now in a savings account in the Royal.'

'So, what do I do now?'

'As I say, check your paperwork. If the money is with M&S I would leave it where it is. But if it's with Hercules you may well have lost the lot.'

'But you think it'll be all right. George and Michael were on the phone this morning asking. They've got money with Hercules. I said I'd see you and let them know. They'll be relieved you think our money's safe.'

'No, no, Maxwell, I didn't say that! I don't know. You will all need to check your certificates.'

(When they did, Maxwell and George had M&S certificates. Michael, ex of Hecklescar Boatyard and the White Fish Authority held an elegant letter with embossed heading from HD Investments signed by Harold Douglas for his £20,000. John Hendry has offered to try to help him retrieve it but is not holding out much hope.)

When John Hendry called to collect his paper from Mrs. Mussen, he found a group of locals taking Hercules apart. 'He is selling up and buying a villa in the South of France.' 'He has this woman in Edinburgh and is throwing Olivia out of the house. She is going back to live with her mother.' 'He has offered the yard to Jakey and Ina for three million pounds. If they can't find the money, he'll sell it to a firm from Holland.' 'He has sold Latchlaw to a builder who is going to build 100 luxury houses on it - and who is going to buy them all?' 'He has diddled hundreds of people out of their savings. The police are chasing for him for fraud if they can find him.' 'Mind you, his yacht is still in the harbour and his Mercedes is still outside the house, so they'll be able to seize those.'

When Mrs. Mussen asked John Henry what he thought of Hercules, he said that Hercules had done a lot for the town and given a lot of people jobs for a long time. It isn't easy running a business, he told them. And we ought not to speculate until we know the truth. The group fell silent, but no doubt knitted John Henry into their harangue once he had left the shop.

John Hendry cut down Manse Road and along the harbour heading for home. Passing the fishyard, he came across Angela with her 'girls' and some of the men from the yard squatting on the baulks that line the harbour wall. They had emerged from the fishyard into the bright light of the first day in October to drink their tea and devour their sandwiches.

'Here's a man that'll save the yard for us,' Angela shouted as he came up, and the girls cheered.

John Henry laughed and waved back. But he felt sick. Why did they shout that? What could he do? 'Save the yard for us!' The words stung. Why should they want the yard saved? For us! Us who stand all day at a fish bench; work that teachers use to frighten their pupils: 'that's where you'll end up if you don't stick in.' Some of the 'girls' who sat on the baulk had started in the yard 20 or 30 years ago; some were still hoping something better would turn up. More than one had started in the last six months. Save the yard for us! They want it saved!

John Hendry did not know many of them but knew enough about them to understand why they wanted to go on turning out on the freezing mornings of winter or the stinking ones of summer: they had no choice. For all the fine talk of economic development, for all the waffle about high-end technical jobs, for all the airy promises of tourism, the yard offered a job every week, all week, and a wage at the end of it - for as long as you could stand it.

Many of these women had set up homes on the pay

they took home on a Friday. Many houses bought, many sticks of furniture moved in and carpets laid, many 40" TVs and mobile phones for the bairns, many fortnights in Turkey or Lanzarote, had been coaxed by these women out of wet fish, squirming prawns and crawling crabs and lobsters.

He also had heard that one or two of them had been able, when their hands were clean, to pass around proud photographs of their children in their academic gowns holding graduate parchments from Edinburgh, Herriot Watt, or Queen Margaret's University. Several had become teachers; a couple, doctors; one, he knew, managed Commercial Lending at the Bank of Scotland and another researched particle physics at CERN, the European Organisation for Nuclear Research. All bought by their mother's or father's grind in the yard.

Some of the women, John Hendry knew, turned out day after day, week after week, year after year to stand at a bleak bench, in a cold, damp, dingy room, to put a meal on the table for a thankless partner, fractious bairns, or whingeing teenagers. More than one came with a heart near broken by infidelity, crushed by indifference, or tormented by a son or daughter whose devotion had been usurped by cocaine or heroin.

A few said they liked it. How, I don't understand, but then I've never understood why some men like golf.

Like it or not, they just got on with it. The pay wasn't up to much – a pound above the minimum rate, but it was a job, it paid the rent, you got a laugh with the girls, and Jakey was a decent man. He gave you the hours, (not like the council who were always cutting them) and would give you time off if you really needed it. It's a job; what else is there here?

John Hendry brooded on all this as he made his way home. What could he do? Why did they think he could do anything? If Mick had still been a councillor, he could have bent his ear. He was a local man; his father had been a fisherman; he understood what fish meant to this place. It wasn't just an industry; in it lay a way of life. It is what made Hecklescar Hecklescar. But Mick had retired and his seat had been taken by Nicola, a party placewoman with a degree in political science, on her way up to Holyrood; a woman of words, reports, reviews, grand plans and empty rhetoric. If John contacted her, he would hear sympathy and vague promises, but would detect a low cheer. For hasn't the Border Council plans for the pier - and they do not include boisterous women in yellow waterproofs embarrassing passers-by with ribaldry.

The Economic Development Committee at Borders Council would be delighted if Hercules did do what they had been afraid to accomplish for years: shut down the yards, and move all the fish workers, the lorries and the vans, the fork lift trucks with their pallets and boxes to a tree-screened Fish Technology Park on the outskirts of the town – downwind, of course. The yard stood in the way of their Tourist Strategy, the which, the Committee had concluded, was the future.

They had plans to prettify the pier, (or as they liked to call it, Harbour Quay) with painted houses, fancy pavements, hanging baskets, flower planters, tea-rooms, and trinket shops.

What about the workers? 'We have plans for them too: they can be re-deployed. Not by us (we don't have the money or the jobs). The National Government has plans for revitalising Scotland's fishing ports and would offer investment in re-training and redeployment. Angela, for instance, could be trained to give tourist advice in the Information Centre. Provided, that is, she could be taught quaint Scots instead of that unintelligible local gabble they call Heckla. We'd take her out of those ugly yellow waterproofs and wellies and dress her in a smart suit with a tartan scarf and a name badge in Scots and Gaelic. The job would be part time, four days a week, for the whole of the summer. Surely, she'd rather do that than turn in at seven in all weathers to pack prawns and gut fish in a smelly fishyard? Less hours, of course, but pro-rata the pay would be roughly the same. She'd lose the company of the other women and there'd be no fish fillets or a bit of crabmeat to take home at the weekend. But you can't have everything; these are hard times. Any other business?'

John Hendry trudged home feeling old, weary and helpless. He did not have the wealth, the time, or the energy to save the yard. Why should they call out to him like that? What could he do? He reached home, made himself a cup of tea, retreated to the yard amongst his flowers and attempted to distance himself from the women and men down the pier. But their cry still reached him: 'John Hendry will save the yard for us!'

'There's nothing I can do, Lizzie; nothing.'

CHAPTER THIRTY-NINE

Mrs Rostowski had put off so much time trying to track down Peter Munro that she had neglected her other clients. She had spent the last three weeks catching up. Her search for Peter Munro had gone cold so she had put him on the back burner, if you catch my meaning.

Then, on the Wednesday of the first week in October, while trying to persuade her son to come to the table to eat his chicken nuggets properly, Peter Munro reappeared on the menu. The phone rang and a woman's quiet voice introduced its owner as Florence Wegg. She had returned to her apartment in Oakshot Close and Mrs. Raschid had told her that a Mrs. Rostowski would like to speak to her.

'Yes, hello, I'm Mrs. Rostowski. I am Peter Munro's Health and Well-being Counsellor – and his friend. Could I come and speak to you?'

'Yes,' said the quiet voice, and agreed to see Mrs. Rostowski the following evening.

'She sounds younger than I thought she'd be,' she said to Greg, and, give the man credit, whatever speculation galloped about in his head, he said nothing and looked blank.

It was a small slip of a woman, hardly more than a girl, that met Mrs. Rostowski at the door of 3 Oakshot Close. She opened the door for her visitor, but not very wide, as if she were reluctant to let anyone in. Similarly, she crept into her apartment through a half-opened door and invited Mrs. Rostowski to follow her.

Mrs. Rostowski found herself in a sparsely furnished room; minimalist, I believe they call it: two armchairs, a small coffee table, a side table with a table lamp on it, and a wooden shelf over a gas fire that did its best to look like coal. On the wooden shelf were one small bright vase that Mrs. Rostowski recognised as Moorcroft, and a framed photo that she recognised as Peter Munro.

Florence sat down in one of the chairs but made no attempt to start the conversation. Mrs. Rostowski found herself pouring out in too many words that she was Peter Munro's Health and Well-Being Counsellor which is not the same as a Social Worker, that she wasn't prying into his affairs, and that he had written her a note saying that he would be going away; but that was three months ago and she hadn't heard from him; she wasn't hunting him down; far from it, but she was concerned about him; wanted to help him and when she had looked through his address book, which she was sure he would not mind her doing, she had found her name and address, and seeing it was just round the corner from Peter's and not far from where she lived with her husband Greg and her son, 'I thought that I may as well look you up.'

(I should add that this, apparently, is not what you should do if you are trying to encourage someone of a quiet disposition to speak to you. I am told you should ask short leading questions, be prepared to stay silent, look at them, and yes, embarrass them into speaking. But Mrs. Rostowski hadn't been a Counsellor long and, with Greg as a husband, had little experience of her hearer having nothing to say.)

'I hope you don't mind,' she concluded.

'No,' said Florence quietly.

'Are you in touch with Peter regularly?' Mrs. Rostowski pressed.

'Yes,'

'And you've seen him recently?'

'Yes,'

'May I ask when you last saw him?'

'Yesterday.'

'Yesterday?'

'Yes'

'Where? Here?'

'No, in Dereham.'

'That's in Norfolk, isn't it?'

'Yes.'

'Is that where you come from?'

This question clearly troubled Florence. She shrugged her shoulders and said nothing. Mrs. Rostowski tried humour.

'With a name like Wegg, it is difficult to believe you come from anywhere else?'

That sank the conversation. Florence stared at her, then stood up and moved to the door and opened it. Clearly, she expected Mrs. Rostowski to leave and Mrs. Rostowski soon found herself back home grumbling to Greg in frustration.

Her husband brushed aside her complaint.

'You wear her down,' he advised, 'she has something you want, so you keep at it.'

'And what is it I want?' she asked wearily, as if she didn't know the answer.

'She knows where Peter is and what he's up to.'

It is not easy to keep at it with someone who is not keeping at it with you, and after two more short monosyllabic contests she left 4/3 Oakshot Close determined not to submit to such treatment any longer. She had managed, just, to keep her cool but she seethed inside; seethed not only at Florence's refusal to talk to her, but also at her own inability to prise open Florence's locked mind and find a way into her thoughts and feelings.

'That's enough' she muttered to herself as she stepped down the stairs. She was so absorbed in her own frustration that she did not notice Mrs. Raschid until she ran into her as she pushed open the door leading into the street.

'I am glad I meet you,' said Mrs. Raschid. 'Let me encourage you. Flo needs your help. Persist and you will win her confidence. She has been let down by many people. She is a good woman and she had been very kind to me. She has a soft heart but it is dying. She has been greatly hurt. She wants to talk to you. She always lets you in, does she not? Would she do that if she did not want to see you? Do not give up on her. She will shrivel if you do not save her. I have told her to trust you.'

It wasn't until she talked it over with Greg that Mrs. Rostowski realised how crucial this interjection might be. 'Keep at it,' he repeated. She would, she would try - once more.

She left it a week, partly to calm down, partly to try to understand what Mrs. Raschid meant, but mostly to try to work out how she should go about approaching Florence again. She had no appetite for it. The thought that Mrs. Raschid believed that she could help this woman, could *save* this surly, uncooperative woman, sickened her. Any early sympathy she had had for Florence had been drained by Florence's seeming determination to dislike her.

Did Florence show just a little less reluctance when she let her into the apartment? Mrs. Rostowski thought so. She had determined her approach. She sat down in one of the armchairs but before Florence could sit down, she said.

'Florence you couldn't give me a cup of tea, could you?

I'm awfully dry.'

Florence stared at her intensely for a second or two, weighing her up, Mrs. Rostowski thought. She held Florence's stare and smiled gently. Then, without speaking, Florence turned and walked into her kitchen.

'What is it?' thought Mrs. Rostowski. 'Is she angry? Frightened? Depressed? Hurt? Sitting in a bunker waiting for the next shell to explode? Waiting for rejection? Again? Is that it? Scared that any new person she meets, like the others, will not like her?'

After what seemed an age, Florence re-appeared. She brought the tea in on a tray. There were two cups and a plate with two buttered scones. Mrs. Rostowski looked at the scones and for a moment choked. Florence had buttered a scone for her! She had taken a risk. That this new person might be trusted; might like a scone, might like a scone that I have taken out of the freezer, thawed out and buttered.

'A scone,' Mrs. Rostowski murmured, 'it's a long time since I had a buttered scone.'

Florence smiled and sat down.

'Now then, Florence,' said Mrs. Rostowski comfortably, 'what can you tell me about Peter Munro?'

'What right do you have to ask these questions?' Florence asked.

The question was blunt but lacked sting. It was asked, Mrs. Rostowski thought, more in exploration than examination.

'None at all. I'm just trying to help Peter. He's in a poor place and I want to help him out of it. When I saw your name in the address book, and that you had moved around with him, I thought perhaps, you might be able to help me.'

'I was his secretary when he was in business,' said Florence tersely. 'When he sold up, he asked me to stay on and help him with his own administration. I agreed. He provided me with this flat, but... '

She stopped and swallowed hard as if the words tasted sour. Clearly what she had been about to say troubled her. Mrs. Rostowski took a shot at what it might be: that there had been those who doubted that she was just a secretary to Peter, and that the provision of the flat was more than a friendly gesture. After all, thought Mrs. Rostowski, even her own husband Greg had suggested something of the sort. She could have asked Florence to explain but to save her she assumed she knew already.

'Evil people think evil thoughts,' Florence said and quickly moved on.

'You said the other day that you had seen Peter Munro recently; in Dereham, I believe'

'Yes.'

'Do you feel you can tell me what he is doing there? Do not worry, I have no desire to hunt him down. He will contact me when he is ready. That's what we have agreed.'

'He is trying to put things right with Dilys, but he is wasting his time.'

'Why do you say that, Florence?'

'Friends call me Flo,' she said, then continued with a question of her own. 'You know about Dilys?'

'And I am Grace. Yes, I know about Dilys, but only by report. I haven't met her. She sounds a troubled woman.'

'That's one way of putting to it. Do you know that Dilys is my mother?'

Why had she not guessed that? Of course! It lit up corners of Peter Munro's life that she had conjectured but had never seen. In her confusion, she set out on a sentence she soon found she could not finish.

'No, I didn't. I know about Dolinda and . . . '

Florence, well used to such surprise, cut in.

'She is my mother - and I am her disgrace. She had me out of wedlock as they say and has never forgiven me.'

'But. . . . '

'Yes, I know what you want to say: I am not to blame. But that is not the way she sees it. I should have done the proper thing and not been conceived, or the decent thing and not been born. Apparently to add to my faults I was a weakly baby - only one and a half pounds, and should have let myself die, to save her the embarrassment of having to explain me and bring me up.'

This torrent of words gushed out from Florence and almost bowled Mrs. Rostowski over. They were not pitiable, nor touching, but raw, ugly and contemptuous; meant to offend, to repel, to pierce and disengage any defence; stated not as an opinion, but as a fact; not a plea for understanding but a conclusion; not a search for sympathy, but a declaration of defiance: 'this is what I am; do not dare to contradict me!'

The assault rocked back Mrs. Rostowski, yet she thought she detected a lack of conviction. It came over more like an old rehearsed speech than a spontaneous outpouring. But dare she risk her hunch. Should she respond to it, sympathise, expose the sore, diagnose, search out causes and remedies, seek to dress, cool and heal the hurt. Or barge through it as the last door to be opened to let her in; a door to be opened and closed behind her. She surged forward.

'Florence, Flo, when I asked you if you came from Dereham I thought it troubled you. Was that where you were born?'

'Yes.'

'I know of a Marney Wegg. `Is he any relation?'

'No, and I know what you are thinking.' Flo snapped, and

for a moment Mrs. Rostowski feared that the door might slam shut again. But Florence continued, 'Marney Wegg is not my father! He is no relation. Wegg is my mother's maiden name.'

'I see,' said Mrs. Rostowski as softly as she could manage.

'My name is not Wegg,' continued Florence, defiantly. 'Not now. It is Munro. Peter Munro has at last defied Dilys and acknowledged that he is my father.'

CHAPTER FORTY

J anet had set her heart on a Silver Wedding much more extravagant than 'just the family and a few friends in the house'. For the past three years she had put away a little every month against an all-expenses-paid trip to Fuerteventura for the whole family. Her plan to buy Latchlaw now grounded it.

When her husband and John Hendry had come home from Avignon after their meeting with Hercules, she had met them at the door with eyes wide in expectation. John Hendry asked her for a cup of tea and refused to tell her what had transpired until she fetched it. Then with Duncan hiding behind his cup he broke the news. They had offered as agreed, £90,000. Hercules wanted £200,000; they had settled for £165,000.

'What!' she exclaimed, 'one hundred and sixty-five thousand! We can't afford that! That's seventy-five thousand more than we have. Seventy-five thousand! Where are we going to get seventy-five thousand pounds – no - a hundred and sixty-five thousand!'

Duncan pushed his face further into his cup and wondered how John Hendry would react.

John Hendry let her run, then said quietly.

'Janet, we've got a deal. Hercules will hand Latchly, the steading and the garden to you. To be honest I did not think he would do it. But he has agreed. We have shaken hands on it. It will be yours. The house, the steading, the land. That is what you want.'

'But a hundred and sixty-five thousand!'

'That's the price. That's what it will take,'

'But we haven't got that. Have we? Duncan, we haven't got that kind of money?'

Duncan took his face out of the cup, smiled nervously and agreed with his wife. John Hendry found them both staring at him, and he thought he saw the beginning of a tear glisten in the corner of Janet's eye. Duncan looked at her then mumbled,

'We can't do it, John. It's too much.'

John Hendry glanced at Duncan then turned his attention to Janet.

'You can do it if you want to. It'll cost but it can be done. I could arrange a loan.'

'But we have....'

'Yes, you have just cleared the mortgage on this house. I know. It's sickening. But think of Alice and Alistair. What is your plan if they have to move out to make way for a contractor? What effect would that have on Alice – and Alistair?'

''There are places,' put in Duncan coming to Janet's aid, claiming Alice and Alistair as his responsibility not hers. 'There's two or three places in Gainslaw. That one just across the bridge is quite nice. I went to see old Jock in there. They might even get into Harbourside just down the pier....'

'They'd be separated,' said John Hendry bluntly

'Separated?' asked Duncan.

'Yes' said Janet, 'separated. They don't cater for couples.'

'That's wrong...,'began Duncan, but got no further.

'It has to be, Duncan,' stated Janet, 'We have to go ahead.'

She swallowed hard and turned to John Hendry.

'You can arrange a loan, you think?'

'Yes.' replied John Hendry, 'I'll put that in hand. But I want to tie it up with Hercules before he changes his mind.'

If, from this, you assume that Janet handles the finances of the family you are paying attention. Duncan does the work; Janet does the books. Computer literate, she has bought an app that allows her to book out the money for wages, materials and expenses and book it in from invoices and cash in hand. She settles the bills, pays the wages, calculates the VAT, meets all regulatory and business commitments, satisfies the council, the government and HM Revenue and at the end of the year reckons within a few pounds how much profit they have made. The household finances are handled with similar skill and precision. She is, what is called in larger concerns, the Chief Financial Officer. Duncan calls her Janet and knows in heart and head that he could not do without her.

The Silver Wedding, then, must be a quiet affair. No printed invitations; just a printed note and a short notice on the Co-op Local Community Notice Board (sneaked on there by Christine who, as you know, works at the Co-op).

Duncan & Janet Kerr invite you to drop into The Old

Manse, Priory Road on Friday 22nd October from 1 o'clock, to celebrate their Silver Wedding with a drink, or coffee, or tea, and a light buffet. No presents please.

Christine, her daughter, however, has a surprise for her parents. Well, two surprises but we'll take the slightest first.

Christine has negotiated a cake out of Lucy who works alongside her in the Co-op and who, when she is not working or looking after her two daughters, bakes and decorates cakes for special occasions. The one she made for old Mr. Turner, the retired science teacher, four years ago is still talked about. He loved astronomy and had caught many a cold sitting outside with his telescope on winter nights. His niece commissioned a cake from Lucy and she iced one in the shape of the sun, then, on wires reaching out from the sun, a series of marzipan planets: Earth, Venus, Mars, Jupiter, Saturn and the rest, and the moon, all in the correct sequence from the centre. The cake has long gone but if you ask Mr. Turner (he is in Kittiwake Court now, the sheltered housing down by the harbour) he will show you the sun and planets that he stripped from the cake and preserves in his bottom kitchen cupboard.

For Duncan and Janet, Lucy has come up with a builder's yard, including ladders, wheelbarrows, a pile of bricks and one of sand, a cement mixer and at the centre a bridegroom dressed as a builder and a bride in dungarees – with a veil and flowers, of course. The legend reads: *'In business for 25 years and still going strong.'*

Christine brought the cake to her mother on the Wednesday before the Friday, to prevent Janet making something of her own. When she handed it over mother and daughter hugged each other until they cried. Why they cried, I don't know, but some women do that when they are happy and these two were happy when they hugged.

John Hendry has a surprise for the couple too. He has asked a couple of the Codlings that we heard singing in the rain on Hecklescar Queen Sunday to stand in the hall and play some auld Scots songs interspersed with one or two Geordie ballads to keep Janet happy.

I could introduce you to the people who drop into the Old Manse, (I know most of them personally, and others by repute; not the Tyneside contingent, except Janet's uncle, who gathered a little notoriety a while back for subsidising the landlord of The Whale to such an extent that he couldn't find his way back to his niece's house. Gossip has it that Janet refuses to have him back. But he is invited for the Silver Wedding day provided he's on the train back to Newcastle before seven o'clock.)

As I was saying, I could introduce you to virtually everybody that comes in the door, but I already have far too many people crowded into this story, so I will limit myself to a few of those you have met previously: Angela, Elaine, and Jennifer from the yard come almost as soon as it starts and stay almost as long as it lasts. They are good friends of Janet. Wullie, Little Dod and Eddie drop in for a dram with Duncan. Nudge won't be coming, Duncan knows, because he doesn't approve of parties where there's free drink and may therefore tend to debauchery. He will, however, make a point of dropping in on a sober afternoon to wish his friends well. Jakey comes in with Ina, whose antennae are tuned to the little group of her coffee cousins who have collected on a sofa in a corner to keep the party under observation. She will later circulate to hoover up any information she can suck out of anyone who is prepared for speak to her. Hercules looks in for a few minutes, as does Olivia, but not together. Olivia does not stay long when she sees that Ina has turned up. Connie won't be there, but Sally, Olivia's daughter has travelled from Edinburgh after a long night shift at the Royal Infirmary to help her friend Christine with her mother and father's happy day.

At four o'clock the last of the drop-ins drop out and the three of them, Duncan, Janet and Christine clear up, wash up and put away, then sit at the kitchen table with a cup of tea and a slice of the cake. There they talk over a satisfactory afternoon and reflect on the blessing of having so many caring friends

It is now that Christine springs her other surprise, or should we say, 'drops her bombshell'. She and Hector have agreed to set up house together. A bomb, certainly! Janet reacts immediately and violently.

'What! Move in with Hector, like the other trollops in the town? A daughter of mine - and your father's, 'moving in'. I thought you were above that, Christine.'

'Mam, listen. . . .'

'No, I will not listen. I know what you are going to say. You are going to tell me you love him so it's all right. You are going to tell me everybody does it. You are going to tell me there is no need to wait until you are married. Well, I've heard it all before and I don't accept any of it. We don't accept any of it.'

She glanced at Duncan, Duncan nodded. Janet drove on.

'What have we been celebrating today? Our silver wedding! We married twenty-five years ago. After knowing each other for three years. Up and down to Newcastle and back, for a day, or a weekend. Do you think that was easy? Do you think we didn't want to be together – all the time? We could have moved in together, but we waited. Do you not think we loved each other? We did, but we did more than that. Yes, there is something more than love – honour and respect, respect for the other person and their reputation, their dignity, if you like. I can just see Ina drooling over our disgrace...'

'It wouldn't be disgrace . . ., 'protested Christine, but Janet wouldn't be silenced.

'I thought about what other people thought about your father and his family. That they looked up to him and I wouldn't pull him down. Oh, there were plenty couples moving in with each other then. That's when it all started. It was all about love then, but what kind of love was it? Not love, just lust tarted up as love; that's what it was; that's all it was. Then it went downhill, until nobody knew what it was. We were laughed at for waiting. Cousin Audrey laughed at us, called us straight-laced, inhibited - that was another of her words, 'inhibited'. She's had three 'partners'; supposed to be permanent. Three! - and dozens of men in between. She's still looking for the right one, and thinks she'll find one by making herself available. Do you want that - selling yourself cheap? Did it last with her? Or any of them? Are the permanent partnerships permanent? No. Why? No respect, that's what. He doesn't respect her, she doesn't respect him. Knows them about three months then moves on, him or her; whoever comes along. It's all flutter then sputter, then out. Then he's off after some other easy touch, some excitement. You saw her to-day. All done up. Is she happy? Is that what you want, Christine?'

She finally ran out of words.

'No,' replied Christine quietly, 'that is not what I want. I want to give Hector a home. Hercules is selling their house and his mother is trying to hang on to it. But it is not his home anymore. Hector doesn't have a home. It's not about me and him sleeping together. I do respect Hector and he respects me. But if we don't get a place of our own, he'll be on his own somewhere in digs or in a flat. I don't want him to have to do that. I want to give him a home. Is that so bad?'

Janet cut her off.

'Then marry him,' she said, and walked out.

CHAPTER FORTY-ONE

J anet's response to Christine is not a proposal of marriage. Yes, I know that's what she said, that if her daughter wanted to provide a home for boyfriend Hector, she should marry him. That's what she said, but you must remember that she was high on indignation at the time. It aptly countered Christine's proposal. Janet didn't need to manufacture her response; it came readymade into her mouth. It followed logically from her polemic, but she hadn't thought seriously about it. She knew how friendly Christine and Hector were, and for how long they had been a pair. They had met at the school and had been an item ever since. She expected that eventually, in due time, they would marry and settle down together. Indeed, you heard her saying that if they bought Latchly it would be something to leave to Christine, then she had added 'and Hector'. She liked Hector. He was sensible, quiet, industrious; rather like her own Duncan. Yes, Christine would do very well with Hector, and Hector would be lucky to have our Christine.

Nor had she thought much about what they got up to when she wasn't around. She chose not to think over much about what young folk did nowadays when their parents weren't looking – or, for that matter, what the parents got up to, when they weren't lecturing their children on what they ought not to get up to. But moving in; living openly with someone not your husband offended her.

In this you may wonder at her being so out of touch with modern mores but we all have our own take on life, and most of it we have adopted without examination. We believe what we believe without being able to give chapter and verse of where we received it. Nor do we always live what we believe. Wherever it has come from, Janet's belief about what her daughter should do is firmly and emotionally held. What Christine is proposing touched a nerve, crossed a line, offended a principle, so she had blurted out the only answer that came into her head. But she had not intended to propose marriage.

She had not waited to hear what Christine had to say. She had walked out. Christine found herself feeling angry, frustrated; feeling disgraced, dirty almost, and glaring at her father.

'That might be a good idea,' he said almost to himself.

'What? Me moving in with Hector?' spat out Christine.

Duncan didn't speak for a while. He couldn't speak. His thoughts had scattered, blown about by both Christine's proposal and Janet's. He had no skill at this. This could not be measured, cut and fitted until it looked right. He leaned across the table and patted his daughter on the hand. She made to withdraw it, then allowed it.

'Who does she think I am?' she exclaimed. 'Who does she think Hector is? We're not like that. It's so unfair. I'm not like Cousin Audrey. She shouldn't have said that. That's not what I meant. I love Hector. He needs a home. I'll make a home for him. What's wrong with that?'

Duncan found his voice.

'Give your mother time; she'll see what you mean. You sprang it on her. I'll have a word with her. Remember Christine, she's your mother, she wants the best for you. She doesn't want to see you throwing your life away.'

'You think I'd be throwing my life away by living with Hector, do you?'

'No, I didn't mean that. I wasn't thinking about you. I was thinking about your mother. She's very sensitive about what they say down the street. They love a bit of scandal; they'd be delighted to pin something on your mother. Janet's always fiercely defended her reputation – and yours. She came from decent people; church people; Methodists down on Tyneside. Her father was a Lay Preacher, or something. That's what this is all about. Think of what the gossips would say; you know what they're like. They'd crow all over her. She'd hate that. You are the apple of her eye; she brags about 'our Christine' when they are slagging someone off.'

Duncan stopped. There was more he wanted say and the words came barging into his mouth. But they had long been banned by Janet, so he swallowed them and just repeated,

'Give your mother time. I'll talk to her.'

'When you do,' stated Christine, 'tell her I'm determined.'

With that she rose and stormed out of the door.

Duncan sat for a while staring at the table, feeling inadequate; not knowing what to do. The two people he treasured most in the world had walked out on him. It wasn't true what they said about Janet back then. I loved her and she loved me. We didn't do it until we were married. Mind you we didn't wait long. The first night at Perth; but we waited. I daren't say that down the pier; they'd mock me, but we did. Janet's right: we respected each other; we did. I don't suppose it matters all that much, when. I can see what Christine means. Her and Hector, well, they're a couple. They don't have a piece of paper but they're a couple; everybody knows that. Better, a lot better than some people who do have the certificate, a lot better. I suppose her and Hector have been in bed together already. Does that bother me? No, I can't say it does. It doesn't seem to count nowadays. But then couples don't stay together like they used to. How many of today's couples will celebrate their Silver Wedding. Christine's gone and spoiled Janet's – and mine, I suppose. I know how Janet feels. She has a lot on her mind, with the move and Alice and Alistair. Then Christine throws in this grenade. But I can see what Christine means. If Hector needs a home. I wouldn't like to be on my own in digs or a flat. If Hercules is throwing him out and making things hard for the lad, I can understand Christine wanting to do something.

'Has she gone?' Janet's voice pierced his attention.

'Aye, she's gone,' replied Duncan sounding weary.

'What is she thinking about?' demanded Janet plonking herself down opposite to him at the kitchen table.

'I'll make us a fresh cup, love' said Duncan gently, 'and we'll see if we can sort it.'

Over the tea Janet poured out her wrath at her daughter for half-an-hour. Duncan listened, agreed and supported all the way When her reel had run out, Janet started to cry.

Duncan rose, knelt beside her and took her hand in his.

'Come on, lass,' he whispered, 'You've a lot on your mind. Christine caught you on the hop. Let's think about what we should do.'

'She'll dig her heels in, I know it,' she said. 'She'll defy us. – and then what?'

'That depends' replied Duncan softly, 'whether you defy her.'

'Don't you start!'

'Shush, shush, I don't mean you have to give in. You're right, we don't want her shacking up with Hector.'

He had not intended to use the word 'shacking' but it leapt into his mouth and he let it out to show that he understood what Janet feared from Ina and the gossips.

'But you need to hear her out. You cut her off. She's worried about Hector. He's going to be on his own. We need to deal with that. This is our Christine we're talking about. It can be sorted. When she comes back, we'll see what can be done. If you say sorry for going over the score, we can talk it over.'

'That's typical of you,' snapped Janet, 'anything for peace. She is not going to move in with Hector. That's it. I am determined.'

Duncan raised his voice and interrupted.

'That was her last word as well: 'determined' - and I know you both well enough to know what it means. It means a standoff – and a lot of hurt. You said a lot of unkind things to Christine, Janet. She's not a trollop, and she is no way like Audrey. That was unfair - and you need to say sorry. When she comes in, do that, will you?'

'I'll think about it,' Janet replied sharply, 'but it makes no difference. I won't have it. If she goes off with Hector, that's it. She goes. But she mustn't expect any help from me. It's her bed, she'll lie on it. I'll tell her what I think – and I'll let her know how much she's hurt her mother.'

'We'll talk it over,' said Duncan encouragingly.

'There's no point in talking it over. If she's determined to move in with Hector, I don't see what can be done. What's the point of talking if nothing can be done?'

Duncan half-expected his wife to stalk out of the room again. But she didn't. Duncan thought, or rather hoped, that he saw Janet softening, just a little, so he ventured,

'What about suggesting that Hector moves his stuff into Latchly; we'll give him a room there – and a home – until him and Christine decide what to do. In the meantime, Christine will go on living here. That'll give us all some time to sort something out, eh? How about that?'

He smiled and from his knees stretched and kissed his wife on the cheek.

Janet smiled in return. It wasn't much of a smile, more a flick of the lips, but it encouraged Duncan. All he could do now was to hope – and pray.

CHAPTER FORTY-TWO

Jakey found it a long week, the week that Hercules had given him to think over an employee buy-out for Anthony Douglas & Son. Had Jakey talked it over with anyone? Was there anyone he had not talked it over with? They had all come back with solutions that were obstacles.

The Morning Meeting, the morning after Jakey had met Hercules, the meeting that should have been about what work must be done that week, quickly became an inquest into the death of the company. None of them, not Fiona and Angela, not Nudge, Wullie, Elaine, Eddie, Little Dod, or Jennifer, at first believed that Jakey could be serious. Although they ran the company and ran it successfully, this little group of experts did not believe that it could or should belong to them. There had to be a big boss.

The belief in the indispensability of the big boss is lodged firmly in the culture of our time. Perhaps its roots stretch back to the hunter-gatherers, when the man (and it could only be a man) who knew how to bring down a mammoth earned the respect and obedience of the others. Perhaps it was bred in us during long centuries of feudalism where the king sat on top of the pile and doled out favours to those who pleased him. I once heard it argued that when industry moved out of cottage into factory, owners looked to the only large organisations around - army and the church, and they both rely on a big boss: a general or God.

Or it could be that most bosses, like Hercules, insist that they have been appointed by Providence to manage the serfs. Seeing that they own the place and pay the wages, what worker is going to contradict them?

There had to be a big boss. Fiona, Angela, and the others all agreed; the fishyard could not do without a Hercules. They disliked the man, called him arrogant, blamed him for paying them sink wages, complained about the cold and dilapidated work rooms he expected them to work in, put him down as insensitive and unfeeling (like getting Moira sacked for taking a couple of aprons home; we all do it; Jakey knows we do it; he does it; but Hercules copped Moira coming out the door with her carrier bag). They hardly see Hercules anyway. 'His faither was aye in the yard. He was a hard driver, but at least he was here. The son we never see; he's lost interest in the place.'

But he was still 'the boss'. If he wasn't in the chair, who would sit in it? Jakey? No way! Jakey's . . . .. well, Jakey's one of us!

The local MSP listened to Jakey and assured him she would contact the relevant agencies to see what might be done, but that would take time. Nicola, the Regional Councillor met Jakey, accompanied by a bright young graduate, who banged away on her laptop taking notes, a transcript of which Jakey received three weeks later. The councillor listened carefully to what Jakey had to say, expressed support, then burdened him with her own concerns about budget restraint, government cutbacks and the difficulty of helping one business when there were so many that would look for the same assistance. However, she assured Jakey, because of the vital part Fish Technology played in the life of the Community, that she would raise it with the Executive Member for Business Development. Would Jakey keep her informed of developments, please?

Jakey also talked it over with Ina, or rather, mentioned it to Ina then listened to what she had to say. What she said was all about Hercules: what was wrong with him, what everybody thought of him, how she knew all along that it would come to this. When she had finished verbally assassinating Hercules, she turned her guns on Olivia and polished her off. None of which in the least raised the burden bearing down on her husband. She did add, however, that she thought he could be the boss, and that there were one or two whom she could name that he should get rid of straightaway.

Jakey discussed Hercules' proposal with one or two of his friends who ran little businesses of their own: Collin was an electrician, Martin a plumber, Eck a painter and decorator. They all told him of the joys of being your own boss, then piled up the drawbacks – the responsibility and the buck stops here, and all the hours you had to work. Then they admitted that they wouldn't like to take on anything the size of the yard. But they were sure, they all said, sure, that he could do it – with a bit of help. You'd need help. Why not talk to John Hendry?

Wasn't John Hendry, however, the nosy negative old banker that Hercules had ruled off limits. Nevertheless, as decision day approached, Jakey's anxiety trumped Hercules' warning. Late on the evening before he was to give his decision to Hercules, he banged on the door of John Hendry's house in Hallyknowe Terrace. John Hendry feigned surprise but, truth to tell, he had been expecting Jakey all week; not only expecting, but dreading.

He wanted to help; help lay in his nature, and many in Hecklescar had reason to be grateful to him. But this was different. First of all, it loomed larger than anything he had tackled before, and he could not see what help he could give.

Secondly, he felt old, or not so much old, as weary – and half-frightened.

When he first lost Lizzie he fell, as many before him have fallen, into a dismal void where nothing is worth doing since life has lost its purpose. Slowly over the following year he had clambered out of the pit and had found, in the help he could give to others, an aid to his own recovery. Certainly, to those he met day by day, he had recovered; had retrieved his old wit and drive - someone with whom you could swap banter when you met him down the pier or in the Co-op. But like many a recovering addict, activity stimulated dependence and now, increasingly, he found it hard to relax. He wanted to be out doing, or in working, or at the plants in the yard, tinkering. At the same time, he felt his strength ebbing and his mental agility faltering. He wanted to rest, he wanted to relax, he wanted to enjoy his home and his flowers and the simple joys of the seaside on golden days, but he found that he could not. Often, he came to to find his teeth clenched and his fist closed.

Of course, he wanted to help Jakey and the folk down the yard - but he felt that it would be well beyond him; that he did not have the stamina or the knowledge to do what they expected of him. Felt it, not only in his imagination, but, when he saw Jakey standing at his door, in his stomach.

John Henry had never seen Jakey, had never seen anybody, in such a state. He made him a cup of coffee, gave him a biscuit to take with it and told Jakey to tell him slowly what Hercules had said.

It surged out of Jakey in a torrent of recollection, commentary and confusion. Figures poured out of him in a surfeit of staccato sentences. 'Seven million, that's what Fiona says, seven million in the year, thirty-seven staff, not all fish workers, drivers, office, mostly part time, some full time, she says, that's one and half million a year. Expenses double that: tax, VAT, National Insurance, then fish and prawns and boxes, and ice, and packing, pallets and fork lift trucks and lorries, freezers. They cost a fortune to run day in-day out, you need them. There's maintenance; the roof leaks, there a quote in for £24,000, twenty-four thousand, and business rates, Fiona says. Nudge reckons two of the artics are knackered, that's fifty thousand each, or more, and that's second hand - and boxes, waterproofs. And new freezer units. God knows what they cost. Fiona is trying to find out.'

John Hendry did not know Jakey well, but had always considered him as a quiet, laid-back individual; a solid sort that let the vagaries and misfortunes of life wash over him. He now saw in front of him a man scared out of his wits. Like a ball on a pin table he no longer sought solutions but ricocheted helplessly round the questions.

John Henry brought the headlong rush to a halt. He ordered Jakey to keep quiet and poured him another cup of coffee. After a few moments, he asked quietly,

'Hercules has given you till when to think about it?'

'Till tomorrow,' blurted out Jakey. 'What am I going to say? They're all saying I should take it on. All them down the yard, and Collin and them. But where will the one and half million come from? Nobody tells me that. It's too big. I can run the yard, but there's a lot more to it than that. Fiona says she can show me. But I don't know anything about accounts or investment. Where do you get the money to pay the wages, and what about the bank?'

John Hendry saw that Jakey was back diving down rabbit holes so stopped him in his tracks.

'Jakey, I'll come with you to see Hercules. What time?'

Jakey glared at John Hendry for a few moments then, in frustration, he wrapped his hands round his face and rubbed it two or three times.

'He told me he didn't want you in on it.'

John Hendry feared the man was about to break down altogether.

'I can believe that,' said the old banker, gently, then he added, 'you must not go to see him. You will pick up the phone here, now, and tell Hercules that you won't be coming tomorrow. Then you will tell him that you are not taking over the yard.'

'But... 'began Jakey.

'Here's the phone, ring him.'

Jakey hesitated, grabbed the phone then put it down again. John Hendry lifted it, dialled Hercules' number then handed it back to Jakey. His hand shook as he took hold of it.

Hercules was not at home. A recording invited him to leave a message.

'Do it,' instructed John. 'Say you are not coming and that you are not prepared to take over the company.'

Jakey did as he was told. Then sat back into his chair and sobbed.

John Hendry let him weep for a few minutes, then topped up his cup and made him drink it.

'What'll I tell them down the yard?'

'Tell them to work on, until we find a way forward. It is not over yet.'

That is what John Hendry said. It comforted Jakey. It would comfort the workers down the yard in the morning: 'John Hendry says, 'It is not over yet."

But what does it mean? John Hendry doesn't know.

CHAPTER FORTY-THREE

John Hendry had told Jakey: 'It is not over yet'. The phrase comforted Jakey; it troubled John Hendry. After Jakey had left, John asked himself why he had said it. He had not intended to say it. He had thought about the yard; had heard the women calling to him as he walked along the pier; had expected Jakey to call, but he had not planned how he would respond. Why? It is not like him. He is a methodical man; you have to be if you are responsible for looking after other people's money. But he had not planned his response to Jakey.

Why not? Because the task scared him. When he was younger; not much younger; in fact, up to a couple of years ago, he relished a challenge - the more difficult the better. He had had to take on the might of the Scottish Football Association over Hecklescar United's accounts and dues, had fought them to a standstill and saved the club thousands of pounds. Now he was frightened. What had changed? Old age? Could be. Often, lately, he had felt like an old fox chased remorselessly by circumstance and human weakness. He had holed up, out of the way, to let life pass him by. He had almost given up reading The Times for the trouble it might bring to his door, and frequently now skimmed through it and gave only the crossword his full attention. Yes, old age and weariness had robbed him of drive. But oppressing age did not weigh as heavily as a crushing sense of inadequacy.

Where is my Lizzie? Over the two searing years before she died, he had witnessed his resourceful, accomplished, energetic wife reduced to frailty, uselessness, and tears - and there was nothing he could do for her. None of the consultations, care, arrangements or aids, the diligence of nurses and carers, the twelve tablets meticulously taken three times a day, his own cajoling and encouraging, none of it was any use. Days drove over her inexorably, each day crushing out a little more life. Until the inevitable, the only possible result: the still body in the lifeless bed. What is the point of life if that is how it ends? What is the point of trying? What is the point of anything?

He did not want to think about the fishyard. He had stood by Duncan and Janet with Latchlaw. Was that not enough? Do not ask me to do more. I am too old to tackle anything as complicated as a fully blown commercial company. What do I know about the financing of fish processing? Nothing! I am too tired!

He had sent Jakey away reassured, at least in part, with a phrase that meant nothing. He must now honour a commitment he had not meant to make, to negotiate a way forward between a man he did not trust, and a crowd of people who trusted him too much. He went to bed and did not sleep until 3 o'clock.

His sleep did not improve his mood and the burden that weighed on him last night pinned him to his bed this morning. But the call of a life's long discipline and the still small voice of his wife's long love had not been silenced. He knew what he must do to fit him for the task ahead.

He rose at half-past seven, before the sun had risen. By eight he was walking along the Bantry. The northerly wind had subsided but the seas it had whipped up rolled into the bay in majestic crests to sputter among the rocks and crash on the beach in a riot of sound and sight. They rolled into his heart too, flaunting their casual beauty in his gloomy face and flinging their fleeting power to the air in glorious indifference to time, purpose and result. Many times, had he seen it; many times, it had convinced him that although nothing is for ever, it remains that nothing is ever finished; there is always more to come. 'Convinced' is not the right word, if by that word you mean knock-you-down proof. It is not from the mind or reason that John Hendry seeks answers. What he craves from sea, wave, and shore is a deep-down assurance that the song is still on air. From the little town and its bustling streets too; to it also he looked for comfort. With the loss of his life with Lizzie, the vigour of all these had been drained, the colour had faded; everything looked grey and felt cold. On this walk he is trying to revive the dying embers of his life. 'Is it possible for a man as old as me to live again? Will the wave run through me once more? Will the wind blow, and fill my sails for the task ahead?'

He turned into the pier and stood and watched the Bright Morn, a Blyth boat, unloading prawns. Using the on-board derrick, a weary fisherman, clad in yellow waterproof breeks, a checked shirt and a ludicrous teddy bear hat, hoisted ice-littered boxes of prawns from hold to a waiting pallet. When six boxes had been stacked on the pallet, a fork lift truck came bustling down the pier to pick up the pallet and boxes. The fork lift truck driver nodded to John Hendry, and John Hendry nodded in return. He thought he recognised him as one of the Polish workers employed by Jakey.

'What is he thinking,' thought the old banker. 'Is he one of those who thinks that 'It is not over yet' means something? Means something more than an old man's rambling? That John Hendry has a plan to keep the yard going? He is a banker, isn't he? He knows about these things. John Hendry turned away from the boat, the forklift and, eventually, the pier and headed for home. He met no-one else, although he could tell that yard was in full swing. Coming up the brae from the pier, he found his path overshadowed by the moving, looming bulk of the Highland Laddie, the tartaned 44 tonne articulated lorry that every day ferried fish from the ports of the Moray Firth to the yard of Anthony Douglas at Hecklescar.

Once home John Hendry ate his porridge, buttered his toast and drank his tea, then in an act of courage, resolution and defiance he closeted himself in his back room to thrash out what might be done to save the yard. He entered the room at quarter past nine and did not emerge from it until five o'clock. By then he had the makings of a plan.

If you think that, because the outline plan took so long to compile it must be a clever, complicated affair, covering all the arguments and counter arguments, then I must disappoint you. You will find most of the work in the wastepaper basket, and most of the rest in the trash bucket on the computer. Of course, being a meticulous man, he has done his research, has considered the aspirations, demands and motives of all the players - of the directors, of the workers, of the customers and suppliers, of the banks and creditors, and particularly of Harold Douglas, the principal. He has put up solutions and shot them down; has tested options; imagined the consequences of various outcomes; tallied up the costs and calculations, and thought long and deeply about the cash needed to put the business on a sound financial footing.

At a quarter past five, he walked down to the Chinese Take-away, bought himself lemon chicken to heat up and eat for his dinner, then watched a recording he had made of Wild China. After that he went to bed.

Over the next few days, he refined and tested his assumptions, making phone calls, contacting old friends, talking to people his friends recommended, picking their brains, learning from their experience, waiting until they could reach him with more accurate information and wiser opinions.

He searched the records of institutions, tested and re-tested his data, and checked and double-checked his calculations. Whenever Jakey rang - and he rang every day - John told him that he was working on it and that he must be patient.

'John Hendry is stringing you along,' said Ina when Jakey complained, 'I told you he would. You shouldn't have listened to him. You should have kept your appointment. Better the devil you know.'

By the fifth day John Hendry was ready. He rang Hercules and, when he found that he was not at home, left a message on his answer machine saying he would like to arrange an appointment with him. He had a proposition to put to him on the sale of Anthony Douglas & Son Ltd.

CHAPTER FORTY-FOUR

Every Friday morning, Mrs. Rostowski went to Peter Munro's apartment to pay Mrs. Flaherty. One morning in early October, she arrived to be assaulted by the news that Peter Munro had been at the flat, had stayed two days, had collected his dark suit, and had gone away. Peter Munro had come back, Mrs. Flaherty reported, had spoken to her, Mrs. Flaherty, but had not contacted his Health and Well-Being Counsellor – deliberately had not contacted her. Mrs. Flaherty had gone out of her way to ask Peter Munro if he had seen Mrs. Rostowski, and he had said, 'Not this time.'

The early skirmish over, Mrs. Flaherty reported more news: Peter had granted the apartment to a woman called Florence, who would call round soon. But she hadn't called round yet. She then interrogated Mrs. Rostowski as to who this Florence might be. Mrs. Rostowski balked at telling Mrs. Flaherty what she knew, and salved her conscience with a claim of client confidentiality.

'He's paid me till the end of the year, but he wants me to leave at the end of the week,' Mrs. Flaherty reported.

'The end of which week?'

'This week.'

'This week?'

'Yes,'

'To-day, that is.'

'That's right. He doesn't want me here after today. But he's paid me 'til the end of the year – and then some. He's given me a cheque. That's alright with me. If that's what he wants.'

'If that's what he wants,' thought Mrs. Rostowski. He wants Mrs. Flaherty out of the way. Knowing Florence's fragility, Mrs. Rostowski could well understand that Peter would not want Florence to run into Mrs. Flaherty and her innuendoes.

'This is me clearing up,' said Mrs. Flaherty, then added, almost as an afterthought, 'he left a letter for you.'

She handed over the letter and stood over Mrs. Rostowski as she opened it. Mrs. Rostowski briefly glanced at the first few sentences then, in the glare of Mrs. Flaherty's attention, closed the letter and put it back in the envelope. She then deposited it in her bag carefully, or perhaps it would be clearer to say, audaciously. As she snapped her bag shut, she glanced at Mrs. Flaherty and smiled.

'Well,' asked Mrs. Flaherty, 'What does it say?'

'It says, 'Confidential''.

'Does he not say why he's giving up the flat?'

'I don't know, I haven't read the letter.'

'Does it not say where he's going?'

'I don't know.'

'What about his things? Is he leaving them for this Florence, whoever she is? If you ask me it all sounds very fishy.'

'Well, I won't ask you,' said Mrs. Rostowski and made to leave.

'He looks awful,' added Mrs. Flaherty. 'Haggard, I would say, haggard. It's that woman. That's where he's been, hasn't he? Trying to bring her back, but she doesn't want him. Mind you, since he went away there's been no more of those nasty letters. That's where he must've been. Trying to make the peace. But it's no good. She's off, off. He looks awful; worn out I would say.'

Then, having delivered her diagnosis, she picked up her duster and turned her back on Mrs. Rostowski.

* * * * *

Mrs. Rostowski went straight home. She had intended calling on that silly girl with the three kids all to different fathers, but that would have to wait. The few words of Peter Munro she had glimpsed had called out to her to read the rest.

'Dylis has died,' Peter wrote. 'She passed away last Thursday, in circumstances I will explain when I see you. I will be attending the funeral in Dereham on Tuesday but am not at all sure what the reaction of Dolinda and Daniel will be. I have invited Florence but I do not think she will come – and perhaps that is just as well. You have met and spoken to Florence, I believe. Could I ask that you continue to do so? We will come to some financial arrangement to take that into the future. She needs you and trusts you. I assured her that she would find you worthy of her confidence.'

'That's what was happening between my visits,' Mrs. Rostowski muttered to herself. 'That's why Florence kept letting me in. She was talking to Pet. . . . her father - and I almost backed off. Thank you, Mrs. Raschid. But for you I may have given up.'

Peter's letter continued:

'As you know, I have thought for a while about going back to Hecklescar. Now there is nothing holding me here. There is nothing more I can do for Dilys, and Florence wants to try it on her own. I have made up my mind to be back in Hecklescar by the end of next month. Florence will take over the apartment. I have paid Mrs. Flaherty off. I will arrange to have my stuff packed up and sent to my new address when I have one.'

'You must forgive me for not talking to you in person. You have been very patient and helpful, but I'm afraid I have been using you as a prop and I know that, as long as I depend on a prop, I won't learn to stand on my own feet. Once I am clear about what I am doing I will ask you to meet me and we can wrap things up.'

She set the letter down and closed her eyes. Wrap things up! What did that mean? This is the end, is it? In which case it signified a messy, unsatisfactory end – with no finish, no completion; it had just run down, run out, faded away.

She had been taught to anticipate this, or rather, if the tutors were to be believed, to welcome it. She had been told that, if the counselling process were successful, the client would go on their way if not rejoicing then, certainly, stable and able to cope. She had also been told – and had experienced at least once – that, as the client walked away from the suffering, they also walked away from the counsellor. When you are well you stop going to see the doctor. She had been advised to spot the early signs of closure and quietly withdraw. 'Don't hang onto the client no matter how fond you have become of them. Your best and final service is to let go. It may be hard but it is wise.'

She remained unconvinced that she had helped Peter Munro. He had often expressed his gratitude, had often apologised for burdening her but, hand on heart, she couldn't say, didn't believe, that she had done much for him. She had spent most of the time trailing behind, trying to keep up, hanging onto whatever scraps of hopes he threw her way, most often suspecting that she might be making things worse rather than better.

Should she see in his long absence the early signs of recovery, and now, in this letter, a desire to step out on his own – and away from her? Perhaps, and if so, she should be content, shouldn't she? But she did not feel content; she felt confused, inadequate, and, at heart, resentful. She had tried her best; now he was walking away. Thank you and goodbye!

'What's that then? A letter from the boyfriend?'

Mrs. Rostowski jumped in surprise. Greg had come into the house, entered the room and now stood at her elbow. She started and, as if to confirm his suspicions, stuffed the letter back into the envelope.

'What are you doing here?' she demanded.

He explained that he has been on his way with a delivery but had taken a slight detour to change into his thicker trousers.

'I told you it's too cold for shorts, even in that overheated cab of yours.'

'Right', he said offhandedly, 'now who's the letter from?'

'Peter Munro,' she replied, 'you can read it.'

She handed him the letter.

Greg read the letter slowly and deliberately.

'When did he write this?'

'He called in on Monday and Tuesday.'

'He says the funeral's on Thursday.' Greg said. 'Does that mean next Thursday? Or yesterday? It could have been yesterday, if he'd come for his suit on Monday.'

Greg had guessed correctly, as Mrs. Rostowski discovered later in the day. That evening, with her son in bed, or at least in his room with his X-Box switched off, and her husband absorbed in a tv programme on sharks, Mrs. Rostowski picked up the ringing phone to find Peter Munro on the other end of it.

The call instantly drove out any hopes she entertained about Peter Munro's recovery. In a voice high with emotion, he told her that he had attended the funeral of Dilys, his wife, and had met Daniel and Dolinda, his children. They had made him welcome, had asked him to sit with them at the front. He also had gone to the short reception held afterwards.

All of which could have encouraged Mrs. Rostowski to think that Peter, aided by his family, had started to clamber his way out of the pit into which he had fallen. But as Peter spoke, she could sense, could almost hear, the uproar in his mind. She did not know what to say; whether to stop him in full flood or to let him run. She had no choice; a torrent of words silenced her. Not that the words flowed; he spat them out in short bursts, between each burst a long pause in which she pictured that familiar face of his, that taut unhappy smile and sad eyes.

Then, abruptly, he stopped. Surely, he must have taken some encouragement, no matter how slight, from meeting his children. But she dared not make such enquiry. Something neutral would have to do.

'And what do you make of all of this?' she said quietly after a short silence

'They continue to blame me for what has happened to their mother,' he said sharply.

Mrs. Rostowski noted that he did not call her his wife, or Dylis, but 'their mother'. Was that significant? Could she see some light in it? Had his wife's death been cathartic ('is that the word they used on the course?')? No longer blaming himself for it? Isn't that what must be achieved? Would that not be progress?

She had tried often enough to soften his self-disgust by arguing that, in any separation, the blame could not be laid exclusively at one door. Dylis, he had claimed, may have been insecure and sensitive but she was a good wife – and, he would always add, 'immensely brave'. Mrs. Rostowski had not been able to explore this last phrase for Peter usually choked as he said it. It always brought the exchange to an end.

'Is that what they said?' Mrs. Rostowski now asked gently. 'Did they say they held you responsible?'

Peter ignored the question.

'Daniel found her in that disgusting flat. Lying on the bathroom floor. She'd committed suicide. She'd washed all her pills down with a bottle of vodka.'

The staccato sentences hit Mrs. Rostowski like bullets.

'My God,' she started, 'Are you sure…?'

She got no further.

Peter exclaimed, 'She left a note. Do you know what she said?' His voice broke. He fell silent, but she could hear him struggling to overcome his emotion.

Then in a voice so strangled Mrs. Rostowski could scarcely hear it, 'Do you know what she wrote? Do you? She said…. It was not to me, the note, not to me. It was addressed to the children. Do you know what she said? To them. She said, 'Do not blame your father'. That's it. That's all she said: 'Do not blame your father."

'Listen, Peter, surely….'.

The line went dead. Peter Munro no longer listened. He had put down the phone.

CHAPTER FORTY-FIVE

Hercules did not respond to John Hendry's phone call. Late in the afternoon of the following day, he walked down to the yard and, entering his office, asked Fiona, who shared it, to leave. Then he called Jakey. Jakey came in smelling of fish, dressed in his gutting gear of yellow waterproof trousers and apron, and peeling off his tight rubber gloves.

Hercules asked his manager the usual questions about workload, deliveries, staffing and shipments.   The questions were blunt, surly, and pointed. Jakey's answers were short, precise and nervous. He noticed that Hercules did not write anything down. This confirmed his anxiety that the meeting was not about work, but about the future of the yard.

'You didn't show up for the meeting we arranged. I thought I made it fairly clear I needed an answer within the week.'

'I have no answer. John Hendry is dealing with it.'

'I thought I told you not to contact him.'

'You did, but I've handed it to him. I don't want anything to do with it. I know about fish. I know nothing about running a business.'

'There will be no business to run unless you give me an

answer.'

'So be it,' said Jakey and stood up to leave.

'Sit down!' ordered Hercules.

For a moment Jakey hovered over the chair, as if to sit down as commanded, then he straightened up and moved towards the door.

'I said, 'sit down!' Have you forgotten I run this place, and that you still work for me? Come back and sit down. I want to talk to you.'

'But I don't want to listen, Mr. Douglas. I've got work to do.'

'You walk out of that door, and you don't have any work at all,' growled Hercules.

Jakey turned and stared at his boss then, without taking his eyes off Hercules' face, stripped off his stained waterproof apron, folded it, and gently laid it on the desk in front of his boss.

Then he walked out.

Not long after, Hercules left the yard. When he reached Avignon, he rang John Hendry and asked him to attend him at the house that evening.

When John Hendry arrived, Hercules met him at the door without greeting him; in fact, without speaking at all. He motioned to John to follow him and led him into the lounge, the same room where they had met to discuss Latchlaw. Again, he offered John the low seat on the settee, again he hovered over him on an upright chair. On the low coffee table in front of him, John laid down his document case and unzipped it.

'There will be no need for that,' stated Hercules, 'I have asked you here for one purpose and one purpose only. That is to tell you, to instruct you, to stop interfering in my affairs. Unless I show clemency, you have cost Jakey his job. Do you understand that? I will not have you undermining my authority with my employees.'

John Hendry did not reply immediately. He looked at Hercules. This was no tactic. He sought a destination for his words, a door open to receive them in the spirit in which he had come; a spirit of conciliation. He did not want a fight, a verbal contest. He wanted to talk to the man, reason with him, find some common ground, agree a way forward.

'Harold,' he said quietly, 'we need to talk. You have a problem. It could be that I have an answer to it.'

Hercules snorted. He stood up and, surely deliberately, menacingly, stood over the old man.

'If I have problems, I do not need your help to solve them. Problem-solving is what I do. It is what I am. Now if you would leave. You may have time to chat but I do not. I have work to do.'

John Hendry closed his document case and heaved himself out of his seat. As he regained his feet, he staggered forward. Hercules moved out of the way to allow him to recover his balance but offered no hand to steady him.

'It's a shame we cannot talk, Harold,' John Hendry repeated, again quietly. 'I have been looking into the affairs of Anthony Douglas & Co Ltd which, I am sure you know is, in law, an entity in its own right. It is not, for instance, the same as Harold Douglas.'

Hercules had reached the door of the lounge and opened it to encourage John to leave. John moved slowly towards the door but did not stop talking.

'You also know that the company may only apply its assets to its stated purposes, and not, for instance, to some other purpose - of a director, say, or even of its principal owner.'

As he spoke, John Hendry kept his eye on Hercules to detect evidence of impact. He saw none. He stepped into the hallway. Hercules still seemed intent on hustling out of the house.

'Who would I go to,' asked John shortly but solemnly, 'if I had discovered that a yacht has disappeared from the assets of the company? Yet as far as I can determine it has never been sold. It is, I see, still in the harbour.'

Hercules shot a nervous glance at the old banker but did not halt their progress to the front door. John drove on,

'Would they also be interested in millions of pounds that have been transferred to a company called HD Investments for unspecified services?'

They had reached the front door. John caught Hercules' eye and held it. Hercules stared back, said nothing and ushered John Hendry out.

'Think it over, Harold and...'

The door slammed, cutting off the sentence.

John walked down the path feeling both excited and frustrated. He had made a mess of it, had he not? He used to be able to handle meetings like these; awkward meetings, where the other party is uncooperative, belligerent even. But this had gone badly. He hadn't found the right words.

He had wanted to find a way through to the man but he hadn't done so, had he? He hadn't put his message across - that he wanted to do a deal; that he actually, sincerely, wanted to help; help Hercules, as well as Jakey and the workers in the yard. There is a way, isn't there? But he hadn't reached Hercules, had he? He had fluffed it. Had Hercules something up his sleeve that he, John, didn't know about?

'I made a mess of it. Maybe if I had written to him, setting out what I know and what I propose. That might have been better. What do I do now?'

Of course, what Hercules has done with the yacht is technically theft; of course, he should not have lifted cash out of Anthony Douglas & Son Ltd to cover his losses in Golden Opportunities; of course, if John Hendry reported his misdemeanours to the authorities, they would be bound to investigate them, and, no doubt, in the end would find Hercules guilty. But how long would that take? What restrictions and distractions would plague the business while that happened? It could take years. Throughout those years the business would be starved of investment, starved of working capital, starved of attention.

Anthony Douglas & Son Ltd already lay on life support. An investigation and prosecution would kill it off. While smart-suited investigating officers, lawyers and liquidators, consultants and counsellors came and went in their Audis and BMWs, Jakey, Angela and Fiona, Nudge, Wullie, Elaine and Jen, the Poles and the Filipinos, wives and partners, just-married men and single mums would all trudge up the hill to sign on at the Benefits Office. Their Great Benefactor had collapsed taking with it their livelihood, their friendships, their pride and their purpose, their plans for a week in Tenerife, a new bathroom suite, or a decent pushchair for the bairn. Now 'The Yard' (for it is known as nothing else) would decay into inactivity. The clatter, chatter and conversations would cease; the great gates that lean idly against the wall would slam shut to entomb a silent yard, rusting vans and derelict buildings. Property Developers, Enterprise Agents and busybody prettifiers on the Regional Council would welcome that, but not John Hendry. He did not want tourists; he liked fish workers.

In addition, John Hendry did not want to see Hercules humiliated. He didn't like Hercules; he thought him bumptious and arrogant. He also reckoned that the man's financial troubles were of his own making.

When Hercules first thought of breaking into Wealth Management, he had talked it over with John Hendry. John Hendry was neither his personal banker nor the banker of the firm, but Hercules knew of his reputation as an astute money man. The consultation had not gone well. John Hendry had listened to Hercules carefully then told him to stay with what he knew best, with fish processing. John Hendry thought then and thought now that Hercules had neither the mental nor temperamental equipment to make a success of money management. In John Hendry's estimation, the young man (and Hercules was only twenty-seven at the time) wasn't bright enough, astute enough or connected enough to survive in the shark-infested waters he intended to enter. Unfortunately, John Hendry conveyed enough of his doubts to incur Hercules' displeasure. The man had come for support, had come to be stroked, had come to be told that with him at the helm the venture could not fail to be a success. John Hendry had poured cold water on the scheme and became thereafter, in Hercules assessment, an envious and mean-minded adversary.

The intervening years, years in which with brutal accuracy John Hendry's predictions had come to fulfilment, had hardened and soured Hercules' opinion of the old banker. John Hendry lay in no doubt about where he stood in Hercules' estimation.

Over the years John Hendry had not had a great deal to do with Hercules; by and large, they had avoided each other. John Hendry had given up the Treasurer's position with Rotary when Hercules became President, so they would not have to work together. He suspected that Hercules talked better than he delivered. However, as we heard him in the paper shop, he acknowledged that Hercules had kept Anthony Douglas & Co afloat and provided jobs for many of the town's men and women. He wasn't against the man, he just hoped that he did not have to deal with him. Now he was being forced to do so and was being given the cold shoulder. In the past he had been known to strike back, or to walk away; now he felt that would be a waste of energy. Life is short; not enough of it lay ahead to cultivate resentment.

The last few weeks had softened John Hendry's dislike

of Harold Douglas. Lately, when the man came to mind, he glimpsed, not a parading braggart, but a frightened refugee running from life. What had impressed John Hendry most of all was the hand he had grasped when leaving Avignon with Duncan. Hercules' face may still stare and snarl, but his hand spoke of insecurity and fear.

The man was down and John Hendry felt sorry for him. He had, is spite of his braggadocio, done much for the people of Hecklescar. As well as jobs, wages and free fish, he had supported other businesses and organisations in the town and had fought Hecklescar's corner in the wider community. For all his self-seeking, he could be generous, and not only because it earned him credit. Now, John Hendry believed, the folk of the town, particularly the Inas of the place, would drag him from his horse and haul him through the street, cheered on by those who had fawned over him and bragged that they were his friends.

Something else counted: age, or, perhaps, we should call it maturity, or even, as some have it, a softening of the brain. John Hendry, like the rest of us, when in the prime of life, had concluded that there should be room in the world only for certain people: decent people, responsible people, hardworking people, people married in their twenties with 2.4 children; people who liked a drink but didn't get drunk and enjoyed a meal but didn't gorge; people who spoke quietly and sensibly and listened to what we had to say; people who rose at a reasonable hour and ate off a plate at a table; people who kept their kids under control and cleaned up after their dogs; people who could be trusted with a bank account and didn't overspend on their credit card; people who showered regularly and didn't dress like scruffs; people of average height and disposition - people like us! The rest should come into line, go away or stay out of sight.

John Hendry's gathering years had produced a kindlier assessment of his fellow men and women. Increasingly aware of his own frailty, of his own failings and of his reliance on the patient love of Lizzie and the forbearance of others, he had opened the doors of his opinion to let more stragglers in, until there was scarcely anyone he did not admit. Favourite words of Lizzie, previously discounted, now often weighed in with persuasive force: '*We are all wrapped together in the same bundle of life.*' He now understood what she meant.

With this in mind, a further consideration troubled John Hendry: how would a man like Hercules cope with failure and disgrace?

'He couldn't deal with it, could he? It would overwhelm him. What might he do then? How would that lie on my conscience - that I had not done all I could? How has this landed on me, Lizzie?'

He resolved to do all he could for the man. To do so he must persuade Hercules to meet him. But how?

CHAPTER FORTY-SIX

The morning following his confrontation with Hercules, before he had confirmed that he was still alive, John Hendry jerked into life at the jangle of his phone. He groped for his glasses, consulted the clock, learned that it was half-past five, then scrambled out of bed to pick up the receiver.

He found himself on the end of an invective from an irate Hercules, or rather, an incandescent Hercules.

As his faculties rallied, he caught enough of the drift to understand what had upset the man.

Apparently, Grubs from Corpach had turned up at Avignon at quarter past five in a 44-tonne truck loaded with prawns from Mallaig. He had parked on the road outside Avignon, had rung the bell and loitered on doorstep until Hercules opened the door. According to Hercules, Jakey had sent him – as instructed by John Hendry.

The same John now had enough control of his senses to deny his part in the episode but undertook to come over to see what could be done. But it would take time. He suggested, only partly by way of retaliation, that Hercules invite Grubs in and make him a cup of tea. Hercules turned down the suggestion. At least, that is the polite way of describing what Hercules said.

John Hendry met Grubs on the pavement outside Avignon. The driver reported that he had arrived at the yard and found no-one there. The gates were closed and the yard silent. He had then gone to rouse Jakey who had told him that Hercules had sacked him. When Angela and the workers had heard what Hercules had done, they had downed tools and gone home. When Grubs asked Jakey what he should do with the prawns, he had said nothing but Ina had butted into the conversation to tell Grubs to take them to Hercules – they belonged to him. She had added that that's what John Hendry would say.

John Hendry told Grubs that he would go to see Jakey. When Grubs asked whether he should take the truck to the yard, John Hendry at first agreed, then changed his mind and said no. The longer the truck obstructed traffic outside Avignon, the more likely that Hercules would agree to come off his high horse and start talking.

John then went to see Jakey to persuade him to go back to the yard, round up the workers and start work on the load that Grubs had brought, as well as yesterday's fish that lay in the yard.

Jakey came to the door in his pyjamas, shepherded by Ina in her dressing gown. Jakey was not for compromise.

'He sacked me,' he stated bluntly; 'I'm not going back till he reinstates me and stops badgering me about taking over the yard.'

'And apologises,' put in Ina.

'Can I come in, it's cauld oot here?' asked John softly.

Jakey led him into their lounge and switched on the fire.

'A cup of tea would be nice,' John continued, 'I've not had my breakfast.'

Ina glanced at Jakey. Jakey nodded. Ina left the two men to make the tea. Once she had gone, John Hendry tackled Jakey.

'Look,' he said bluntly. 'If you don't get down to the yard and start work, you'll shut the place.'

'Just till he sees sense,' grumbled Jakey.

'Hercules, see sense? When have you known Hercules see sense? The man doesn't work on sense. He works on pride. If you stand off, he'll stand off. That will lead to only one conclusion: you'll shut the yard - and you and all your freends will be out of work. Is that what you want?'

'Naw, but he fired me?'

'Did he?'

'Yes.'

'What did he say?'

'I don't remember, but he sacked me.'

'Tell me what happened.'

This is not a reasonable request. Jakey is not a trained policeman or lawyer. He didn't take notes. His memory of the meeting is engulfed in red mist, blurring any detail. John Hendry knows this but is looking for some purchase to lever Jakey out of his bunker. Jakey told of his confrontation with Hercules as far as he could recall it. What he recalled was the anger in Hercules' eyes and the arrogance of his command. But he did remember laying down his apron in front of his boss.

'So, you walked out?'

'Yes.'

'And he hasn't said anything to you since?'

'No.'

'He hasn't confirmed that you are no longer an employee?'

'No'.

'Then you are not sacked. He'd have to issue you with a formal dismissal, give you notice and advise you of the reason for dismissal. Did he do any of that?'

'No.'

'Then you have not been sacked. You walked out. At any time, you can walk back in. You are still employed. I want you to go back in, open up the yard, call back the girls and start work on the fish.'

'He'll do no such thing' said a voice from the door, a voice carrying a tray with three cups of tea on it.

John Hendry turned and fixed her in his sights.

'Ina,' he pronounced, 'the future of the yard, the future of your husband's position in the town, the future of the livelihood of forty or fifty families in Hecklescar depends on what we decide here and now. If Jakey does not go back to the yard this morning. Anthony Douglas & Son will shut – for good. It is on its uppers. It has no money. It has nothing behind it. If the banks wanted, they could close it tomorrow. The only hope, as Jakey knows, is for Hercules to sell the company as a going concern. If your man doesn't go in - now - it will stop going.'

'That's what I said to Grubs. I said go and see. . . . . .'

'Shut up Ina,' ordered Jakey.

Ina did as she was told, served their tea and disappeared.

John Hendry continued.

'I'll contact Hercules and say that you are prepared to go back to work provided he talks to me about the future of the company. Will that do it?'

'It sticks in the craw, John. I've given that bugger my best, I've defended him, I've stuck with him through thick and thin. He's let me down. I've run the yard for him and then he threatens me.'

'He's a man in deep trouble, Jakey. He's on the edge. When people are on the edge, they lash out. He'll be sorry for what he said.'

'He'll apologise then?'

'No, he won't do that. But that's not the point. The point is to get the yard up and running and for that we need you. You're a better man than he is, aren't you? You can rise above pointless spats.'

Jakey sipped his tea for fully five minutes, John sipped his and let the man think. Then Jakey said quietly,

'I'll get ma claes on. Before that I'll ring Angela. She'll turn out the army.'

'That's it, Jakey, but don't contact Grubs yet. We need that truck outside Hercules' front door while I negotiate a meeting with the man.'

CHAPTER FORTY-SEVEN

Once Hercules agreed to deal with John Hendry, Grubs drove his truck to the yard, Jakey helped him to unload it, and the girls worked all day processing the fish for Nudge, Wullie, Elaine, Eddie and Jennifer to deliver to clients at home and abroad. The breath returned to the yard; it became once again a living whole.

Like a man told that he must lose both legs to survive Hercules faced his meeting with John Hendry. Everything in his nature and disposition cried out against negotiating with the man, but he knew he had to do it - or face bankruptcy, ignominy and quite possibly prosecution.

We know what the deal is, and Hercules doesn't need to be reminded of the painful detail. We will, therefore, merely report that at a short tense meeting Hercules agreed to sell the business – and its debts, to John Hendry for £1.

At John's quiet insistence they each put their signature to a letter of intent, but when John offered to shake hands Hercules turned away, and refused to take from John the token coin. John Hendry laid it carefully on the table. Before he left John told Hercules that he would now put the transfer into the hands of Cockburn Heath and his legal friends in Edinburgh.

******

The meeting with John Hendry was not the only one that Hercules attended in the dull days of mid-November. That very evening he found himself confronted by his daughter Sally. Her mother had tipped her off that her father was at home and she had taken the bus from Edinburgh to see him.

'Where is my home?' she asked bluntly once the pleasantries were over.

Bruised by his humiliation by John Hendry, Hercules lay in no mood for conciliation.

'Here, of course, with your mother.'

'But mother says you have not yet decided to let her have it. That you want to sell it and turn us all out of our home!'

'Don't be dramatic, Sally. I had no intention of leaving you without a home. Your mother and I are splitting up, so the house becomes surplus to requirements. And, to be blunt, though it is none of your business, I need the money for my future. I need somewhere to live too.'

'With Elvira, for instance,' Sally exclaimed.

Hercules fixed her with a stare.

'Don't play games with me, Sally. Say what you've got to say. Spit it out.'

'You have to sell the house to mum – for all of us. Alexander thinks that as well.'

'Oh, does he - he who never comes home; he who has not been seen inside Avignon for three years, he is telling me what I should do with it? And what about Hector? Did he attend the conference deciding what I should do?'

'No, I haven't seen Hector. He's got Christine, they're going to move into Latchly with Duncan's parents.'

'Oh, are they now? And here is me thinking that Latchlaw belongs to me. They've taken it over, have they and decided what I should do with it?'

'But Duncan and Janet are buying it. You agreed.'

'Oh, you're very well informed – or, perhaps not so well. I have listened to them and have agreed what the price would be should I sell it to them. But it is still mine. Until it belongs to them – if ever it does belong to them, they should not assume they can do what they like with it, or who might move into it. That's right, isn't it?'

Sally sat still and lowered her head.

'That is a question, my daughter. Have they said that it now belongs to them and not me?'

'No, but they expect that you are going to sell it to them; you promised – and I don't see any reason why you shouldn't. Duncan's mother is suffering from dementia and she needs somebody beside her. Christine has told me that her and Hector will move in.'

'Will move in! So, it is decided, is it? Never mind the owner; treat it as ours. Is that it?'

Sally suddenly realised that she had said too much – not once but twice. Not only had she assumed that her father had agreed to hand over Latchlaw to Duncan and Janet, but that she also knew that Christine intended moving into it with Hector. Christine had told her this in confidence but had not told her parents. They were not aware of Christine's intention to move into Latchly, there to keep an eye on Alice and Alistair. Christine's fallout with her mother had prevented her from telling her parents what she was planning, so they remained in ignorance. Christine had told Sally. Now Sally had told Hercules.

'Nothing's decided' she said lamely, 'it's just an idea.'

''Well, Sally, you can tell Christine – and her mother and her father, that nothing is settled on Latchlaw; we have a handshake, that's all. But it is not signed, sealed and delivered.

There is many a slip. ... Some better offer may come along. Tell Christine that – and her parents. Okay?'

Sally nodded her head but did not speak. She dared not speak; she was too upset for that. She had made a mess of it. She must tell Christine as soon as she could that she'd let the cat out of the bag.

Sally retreated from her father in failure but she had not failed. Her intervention had had a curious effect on her father. You may believe, as John Hendry believes, that Hercules is a man in the open with wolves snapping at his heels and vultures circling overhead; a man expecting at any moment to be engulfed by disaster. Certainly, a man of greater sensibility and sensitivity would have panicked and thrown in the towel. But Hercules is not such a man. Perhaps the day will dawn when the awful truth of his vulnerability will explode and blow his head off. But this is not that day. For the moment he does not see events as random happenings but as plans and modifications of plans. He does not think of his life as sailing in a sea of fickle circumstance, but as a calculated passage through the storms and reefs that sink lesser mortals. John Hendry had thrown a rock in his way and it had almost wrecked him. But now, Sally, in her retreat, had reassured him that he was still in control, still on track – 'on schedule' slipped into his consciousness, followed almost immediately by 'when the going gets tough, the tough get going'. He had strategies; he would drive them forwards. He knew where he wanted to be and he would go for it. Now!

But what was *it*? The yard at Hecklescar had gone. He had given up on Avignon; Olivia could have it for the two hundred thousand she had offered. He didn't have time to wrangle. Two hundred thousand pounds in the hand was better than months in court with lawyers draining the pot. Mallaig was in the bag – for one and a half million. That left Latchlaw. Latchlaw bothered him. The thought that Duncan and John Hendry had snatched it from him, had presumed on his generosity, rankled. They needed a tug on the choke chain. This was a metaphor Hercules loved and used regularly.

On the other hand, he needed cash in hand. Time was running out; November would soon be at an end and by then he must be away. He had heard no more about Peter Munro coming back. But he could not risk it. He must be away if, when, Peter stepped back into Hecklescar.

The following morning, before he set out for work, Hector was surprised to be summoned by his father into the holy of holies: Hercules' study. Hercules lost little time getting to the point. He had heard from Sally that he and Christine were planning to move into the farmhouse at Latchlaw. This surprised Hector but he confirmed that it was so. Hercules then repeated to his son what he had told his daughter. He had not agreed to sell it. He had agreed the price Duncan would have to pay *if* he sold it to them. He then added that Latchlaw was attracting a lot of offers and in the next few days he must decide which one to accept.

'And,' he stated, staring at the lad, 'if the best offer stipulates that the site must be clear, that means clear of the farmhouse, I will have to reconsider selling to Duncan Kerr. Do you understand that?'

Hector nodded.

Then Hercules added, 'I do not like my generosity being taken for granted. Perhaps you could pass that on to Christine.'

Hector told Christine, Christine told her father, Duncan, Duncan told Janet, Janet demanded that John Hendry be consulted. John Hendry counselled caution. Say nothing. Protest not at all. Let him bluster. Hercules is playing games. That is to be expected. We know what we agreed. It does not need to be re-negotiated.

CHAPTER FORTY-EIGHT

Sally's blunder and Hector's innocence did nothing to heal the hurt of Christine and her mother. It was bad enough that Christine had decided to move in with Hector. But move into Latchly? Where had that come from? Janet's questions had no answers. Christine had decamped to Latchly and had stopped speaking to her.

Duncan, a peaceable man, avoided controversy unless he could not step round it. Whenever he and Janet fell out, she did the shouting; he absorbed it, then walked down the pier to clear the air. By the time he came back the storm had usually abated, Janet had subsided and they ... (I almost wrote 'kissed and made up', but that's not what happened with this couple) ... they crept back from the discomfort they suffered into the steady affection that governed their life together. Almost always Duncan put out his hand first. He would hide round the corner for so long, then with cap in hand, he would knock at Janet's door. You must not treat this as weakness. Janet didn't; for she understood that Duncan could do what she could not. For her to admit fault ran against the grain. She acknowledged that Duncan had a kindlier nature and she admired - and loved, him for it. After a day or two of self-imposed exile, she would creep back home sure that the door would be opened to welcome her.

That his wife and daughter should be at loggerheads pained Duncan. It had always done so. Christine was Janet's daughter, made of the same tough stuff. From her teens up, he had watched from the ringside many a contest with the outcome never clear until the last few blows. But Christine never doubted her mother's integrity, and the mother had learned to admire her daughter's determination. This mutual regard had always rolled in shortly after the spat, and these two did kiss and make up.

Not this time. Janet had broken the concord that bound them: that each respected the other's dignity. That she should liken Christine's behaviour to gadabout Audrey was nasty. Duncan could see that. He had tried talking Janet round without success. His suggestion that Hector move into Latchly for the time being had softened Janet's inflexibility but he knew that she could not welcome back her prodigal daughter while Ina and company smirked from the garden fence. That lay beyond cajoling. Yet Christine's proposal made sense and showed compassion: Hector needed a home; she loved him and would provide it. What could Duncan do?

He had tried putting it to the back of his mind and getting on with his work. But what was his work? Today he laboured at Latchly alongside Hector, the unwitting villain of the piece, working in anticipation of he and Janet moving there to company and care for Alice and Alistair. Now Christine and Hector are planning to usurp them.

Duncan thrashed about seeking a way out. Doubts assailed him, solutions gleamed then faded, possible outcomes loomed and threatened. Escape seemed impossible. In Hector he had always seen himself when young; had anticipated that the lad would enjoy, had planned that the lad would enjoy, the same satisfaction of bending materials, bricks and building blocks, cement and tiles, frames and finishings into something handsome and useful, and now, with joinery added, into whole houses! Then go home, as he himself had gone home for the past twenty-five years to a good meal, to a wife and friend who would sympathise with his complaints and share in his achievements. These dreams and hopes had lodged in his mind without notice. Now they threw off their disguise and snarled at him. Now when he glanced at the lad as he bent over the bench, his heart sank and he dreaded what might lie ahead. Christine would go off with Hector. Janet would be humiliated. Christine would be miserable. His little bundle of life, carefully gathered and treasured over the years, would be ripped apart. Duncan found no refuge in his work.

There are times, humbling for the storyteller, and disconcerting for the reader, when circumstances take over the plot. That is what happened now. Duncan's dilemma, Janet's intransigence, Christine's resolve, Hercules' deceit and Sally's blunder all collided over a bowl of soup at Latchlaw one lunchtime in the first week of November. Christine had come to see Hector, but he had been sent by Duncan to the builders' merchants in Gainslaw to pick up materials. She found her father sitting disconsolately at the table in the kitchen at Latchly with a bowl of Alice's homemade leek and potato soup at the end of his spoon. At first Christine turned to leave, but Duncan persuaded her stay. Even then she remained standing until Duncan rose and poured a cup of tea for her and placed it on the table beside him. She sat down.

'How are you, hen?' he said when she was seated. He deliberately dropped into local dialect, using old familiar words and phrases.

'I'm a' right.'

'And you and yer mither are still . . . '

'No start, fither. Until she says sorry, I no' want to hear anything else from her. She had nae right tae say thae things.'

'Aye, ye're right; I agree wi' ye, but she's yer mither and she's upset. Could ye no'. . . .'

'Not until she apologises...'

'Well, ye'll wait a long time. Hev y'ever heard yer mither apologise?'

'She was wrong to say what she did.'

'Of course, she was – and she kens it.'

'She kens it? She told y' that?'

'Me? No.'

'Then how d'ye know'

'Because I've been married to her for twenty-five years.'

'Well, there's a first time for everything. Ye can tell her...'

'Now Christine, no. I'm no' gettin' 'atween the pair o' ye.'

'Well,...'

Duncan cut in.

'Look, Christine, I'm goin' tae tell y'something I promised yer mither I would never repeat. But needs must when the devil drives. The reason yer mither is so dead set against this scheme o' yours comes from when she first set fit in Hecklescar. She wis a young bit lass and she'd come wi' her boss.'

'I no kent that!'

'Well ye wouldn't, because we've never told you.'

'She came wi' her boss, an' she's talkin' aboot me and Hector!'

'Ye see, ye see, whit happens? Jumpin' to conclusions! Aye, she was propositioned, but she hated it and turned him doon flat and gave up her job as soon as she could. That's whit yer mither did. But the tittle-tattlers o' Hecklescar wouldn't let it lie and she wis saddled wi' it for years. Even after we were married, she heard that some of the locals were saying that she wis the boss's bit of stuff and took the chance to marry Duncan to get 'out from under.'

'Out from under.' laughed Christine, humourlessly. It grated on Duncan. He felt his anger surge, but he swallowed it and continued steadily,

'That's what they said. Of course, it wisna' true; it couldn't be true; not of Janet. That's what this is all about. Think of what they'd say. They'd rake it all up again and crow all over her. She would hate that. You are the apple of her eye. She brags about 'our Christine' when they are slagging someone off. And ye picked the wrong day, oor anniversary - when it all started all those years ago. D'ye see that?'

Of course, Christine saw it. But did she go running to her mother to say sorry? If you think that I have misled you about Christine's character. Certainly, Duncan expected no sudden conversion, but he hoped that if Christine came down off her high horse, she might find her mother waiting to give her a hand to dismount.

Duncan suddenly changed the subject.

'Whit's this that's Sally's saying? You and Hector moving in here to look after the auld yins.'

'We've talked about it.'

'That's guid o' you, Christine – and it's like you. It's a lot tae tak' on. D'ye think ye could cope?'

'I love ma granny. I hate to see whit's happening tae her. We could make her life easier.'

'I'm sure y'could, and I ken ye'd do it, but I think it's a job for yer mither an' me.'

'But ye'd hev to sell the house in Priory Road. If we moved in here ye wouldn't hev tae do that.'

'And where d'ye think we'd find the money for Latchly if we didn't sell the Priory Road hoose?'

'We thought we could take oot a mortgage.

'Christine, Christine, ye're the best daughter a man

could hev' but ye'd never raise a mortgage for this tumble-doon place. If ye did, it would cost a fortune to dae up.'

'We could tak' oor time. Hector could work at it.' She suddenly glanced at her father

'and you.'

Duncan laughed.

'Aye, hen, ye hev it all worked oot, but wis Sally not saying Hercules might turn us all oot? You, me, yer mither and yer granny and grandad.'

'Whit's that about granny bein' turned oot?' said an anxious voice from the doorway.

Duncan turned to face his mother.

'No, no, mither, it's no' you. It's somebody else's granny. It's no' here. Not this hoose. Yer a' right here. Christine and me were jist talkin' aboot someone else. Some ither hoose.'

Christine joined in to reassure Alice and she sat down at the table with them. She believed their little lie, didn't she?

CHAPTER FORTY-NINE

On the Friday of the last week of November, after a tetchy meeting with her Care Co-ordinator, Mrs. Rostowski returned home and rang Oliver.

The Care Co-ordinator had come to the office in a prickly mood. (Had she fallen out with her partner or upset the cat's milk?) She had made an issue of Peter Munro.

Had they not agreed a strategy? To let him run but keep track of him at arms-length, was it not? That is what Mrs. Rostowski thought she had been doing, but the Care Co-ordinator's chose to listen to her own exasperation rather than Mrs. Rostowski's explanations.

'You seem to have mislaid him,' she grumbled, 'you need to decide what to do. It is just trailing on. You must bring it to some sort of conclusion. You'll need to meet him. Report back next week. Okay?'

That is why Mrs. Rostowski rang Oliver. Did he know how she could reach Peter Munro?

'I can do better than that,' Oliver replied, 'I can deliver him! Can you be here tomorrow, about lunchtime?'

'At Long Eaton? Yes, but why?

'Because Peter Munro is coming to see me at two.'

Oliver's reply silenced Mrs. Rostowski for a few moments, then she asked,

'Will you tell him I'll be there?'

'No'

'Will that not surprise him?'

'I hope so.'

'He might walk out.'

'No, he'll not do that.'

'How do you know that?'

'Because I know the man. So, I can expect you when? About one?'

Mrs. Rostowski did not reply immediately. Surely, she shouldn't ambush Peter Munro. Surely, the client should decide whether he met his counsellor, not the counsellor, or an old work friend. Yet Oliver was a good man, a perceptive man who knew Peter well. If she didn't go, she might never see Peter again. How would she account for that to her Care Co-ordinator? Surely, she had a right... no, not a right, an interest, in knowing what happened?

'Alright, I'll come. But I don't like it.'

'What do you not like?' said a voice in the room as she put down the phone.

She explained to Greg what Oliver wanted her to do.

'I'm not at all sure about it,' sighed Mrs. Rostowski.

'As the man said when he jumped off Brighton Pier in a snowstorm.'

'That's not very helpful, my husband.' snapped Mrs. Rostowski.

'But your husband will jump with you, my dear,' he replied.

All the way along the A22, all the way round the M25,

all the way up the M1, Mrs. Rostowski yattered at Greg. All the way her husband assured her she was doing the right thing.

When Oliver's wife, Moira, opened the door Mrs. Rostowski said,

'I'm not sure I should be doing this.'

Moira gave her no comfort.

'When he gets an idea into his head, you cannot shift it.'

Then, detecting Mrs. Rostowski's alarm, she added with a smile, 'Mind you, he's usually right - but don't tell him I said so.'

This time, Mrs. Rostowski found Oliver, not lying in bed, but sitting in his wheelchair, his arm looped over one of its handles to prevent him falling forward. He welcomed Mrs. Rostowski and ordered up a cup of tea for them both. Greg retreated to the kitchen with Moira, and Oliver filled in Mrs. Rostowski on Peter Munro's visit, or rather didn't; at least not much. Peter had been popping over to see him from Dereham where he had mounted a sort of vigil, keeping an eye on Dylis without ever actually being able to see her.

'D'ye understand that?' asked Oliver, 'how can a man sit and watch a door for weeks hoping someone will come out of it – and that someone is his own wife?'

'Is that what he did: sit in the car and watch the door?'

'What else? He never said that's what he did. He wouldn't talk about it. When I asked what he did at Dereham he just said, 'leave it, I know what I'm doing'. Then – well you know what happened.'

'What has he said since?'

'He came over to tell me that Dilys had died but not afterwards. It's not long. What is it? About a month?'

'Yes, beginning of last month. Did he tell you how she died?'

'He did.'

'That is awful, is it not?'

'It is.'

'He'd be badly upset?'

Oliver thought for a few moments before answering. Then he asked Mrs. Rostowski to hand him his beaker for a drink. He sucked the straw a few times then said,

'Was he upset? I couldn't tell. He seemed very controlled – but then he always is. He told me about Daniel (isn't it - his son?) finding her on the floor. But it sounded as if he were telling a story he'd heard down the pub. However, I know him well enough to know that he had the dampers engaged. Whenever things turned nasty, he clamped down, went calm, unnaturally calm. The pan might be boiling but he would stay sitting on the lid.'

'You've never known him explode then?'

'No, have you?'

'Not explode, but he was upset when Dilys died.'

'Was he? What did he say?'

'No, not when she died, at the funeral. No, not even then. But the note she left upset him.'

'She wrote him a note? He didn't tell me that. What did that say?'

'She didn't leave a note for him. At least he didn't mention one. She wrote to Daniel and Dolinda.'

'The children? What did it say? Did it slag him off?'

'No, that's just it. It didn't. She wrote that they were not to blame their father.'

'Not to blame him! And that upset him?'

'Yes -and writing the note was probably the last thing she did.'

'Why should that upset him? You would think....'

He got no further. The doorbell rang, they fell silent and, in nervous anticipation, looked to the door. They heard the front door open and Moira greeting someone at the door. Then Moira entered the room followed by Peter Munro.

He stopped when he saw Mrs. Rostowski, then smiled and said to Oliver,

'Up to your old tricks, you auld bugger.'

'I thought you should see the woman,' replied Oliver in the same spirit.

Peter shook Mrs. Rostowski's hand and said, 'I'm glad to see you.'

He sounded as if he meant it.

We've waited a long time to meet the man that keeps butting into our story so we should take a moment to take a good look at him. Of average height, stocky, with a full face and close-cropped grey hair, he is, as Mrs. Flaherty told us, not much to look at. If you met him at a party you would not notice him unless you were told that that man over there in the grey suit and quiet tie is a millionaire several times over. Mrs. Flaherty is also correct about his appearance now: he looks ill. His face is pale, his hair lank and his eyes dull. He looks much older than his fifty-five years. When he takes off his coat to give it to Moira his clothes hang loose on his body. When he speaks, even in banter with Oliver, his voice is weary.

He sat down and leaned forward in the chair.

'I owe you an apology,' he said to Mrs. Rostowski, 'I should have been in touch. But what could I say?'

He paused as if searching for some sentiment just out of reach.

'I've taken up enough of your life with my ramblings.'

He paused again and studied his hands in his lap.

Mrs. Rostowski noted that he said 'your life', not 'your time'. As if he felt that life, hers and his, were running out.

Then he looked up at her and added, 'You got my letter, I hope.'

Mrs. Rostowski assured him she had received it and read it. She was about to discuss its contents but Peter drove on.

'I am not going back to Eastbourne, or London, or anywhere else. I've put all the businesses up for sale and am going back home.'

Peter Munro announced this as if he were reading from a prepared statement on the steps of the Guildhall.

It came over so full of intent, so utterly decided that Mrs. Rostowski set aside the questions that crowded into her mind and simply said,

'If that is what you think best.'

Peter smiled softly, shook his head and murmured,

'You are a good woman, Grace. How do I know what is best? It's not the best; it's the only.'

This proved too philosophical, too sentimental for Oliver.

'Stop feeling so sorry for yourself,' he declared. 'You don't know what 'only' means!'

He turned to Mrs. Rostowski.

'You might shift that cushion up a fraction,' he asked.

Mrs. Rostowski took hold of the cushion at his back and expected him to lean forward to let her shift it. She then realised, of course, that he could not move. She laid her hand behind his neck and pulled him forward. Then holding him, and bearing the full weight of his body, adjusted the cushion and gently lowered him back.

Did the cushion need shifting? Or did Oliver ask for it to demonstrate what 'only' meant? Peter glanced at Oliver, nodded and smiled. Her turned to Mrs. Rostowski.

'I have been unfair to you; very unfair. I realise that now.'

'Please, I don't think. . . . '

Peter cut her off.

'I have not been fair because I have been asking you to help me to do the impossible: to help put my life back together; all the shattered pieces.'

Again, Oliver sought to lift him.

'Come off it, Peter,' he remonstrated, 'You've had a good life; you ran a successful business. You got things done - honestly. Dilys was a trial, I know that. That wasn't your fault. You did everything a decent man . . . .'

'Shut up, Oliver,' commanded Peter bluntly.

Oliver screwed up his face, half-smiled at Mrs. Rostowski and fell silent.

'It had all come apart,' Peter continued quietly, his head still bowed, his eyes still focussed on his hands in his lap, 'and I was trying to re-assemble it. It couldn't be done. Some pieces were missing - and I was scrabbling around trying to find them and fit them back in. But it can't be done. Worse, I caught you up in it. You must have seen that; you must have known that. I'd rush off along one road then, when it ran out, come charging back and shoot off in another direction. You tried to follow me, trying to work out where I wanted to go. How could you keep track of that? How could you know where I wanted to go when I did not know myself?'

As this poured out, Mrs. Rostowski felt a shiver of recognition. Peter was describing precisely what she had experienced as she tried to help him. How often she had come away from their discussions confused and frustrated, not understanding what he wanted, not knowing what to advise or where he might find relief. There were occasions when she thought they were making progress, thought that finally he would reach the destination he wanted and could be at peace. Then he'd throw it all up and they'd be back where they started. She had always credited such lack of progress to her own incompetence; that she wasn't skilled enough or wise enough to find the road ahead. Yet here, now, she heard him confessing that there never was a way forward; that he had chased will o' the wisps, dreams without legs, a Shangri-La that lay always beyond the horizon no matter how far he travelled. She had trailed along after him carrying all the baggage for the new life beyond; the new life that could never be - largely because of the baggage she was helping him to carry.

Oliver's voice broke into her consciousness. This time he sounded unchallenging, gentle, friendly.

'Peter, ye're telling the woman she's failed. Mrs. Rowst . . ., look, can I call you Grace?'

'Of course.'

'Grace here, has been helping you all this time and now you're saying she's wasted her time.'

Peter looked first at Mrs. Rostowski then at Oliver.

'When you are lost you need a friend - most of all when you are lost. Grace has been to me, is still, that friend. She went along with me, into all the byways and dead ends – and never lost her patience. She gave advice that I rejected, pointed out directions I did not take. But she did not give up, nor did she shout or sulk. No matter what I did or what I said she never lost faith in me, and when you have lost faith in yourself you need someone to continue to believe in you. She did that. No, my good friend Oliver, she did not waste her time. I hope she understands that.'

He looked at Mrs. Rostowski with an enquiring smile.

Mrs. Rostowski smiled and murmured, 'Of course.'

She was going to add 'it's part of the job', but as the words formed in her mouth her heart told her that she had not done it because 'it's the job', but because she loved the man and pitied him. Is that professional? I hope so.

'What now?' said Oliver from the chair he could not leave unless someone shifted him.

'I am going to walk back home.'

'Walk?'

'Yes, walk. I will walk back to Hecklescar.'

'Where on earth is that?'

'Home,' said Peter, then added with short laugh, 'I'll send you a postcard if I make it and you can Google it.'

CHAPTER FIFTY

A few days after her accidental meeting with her father at Latchlaw, in the evening when she knew her father would be at home, Christine walked into the kitchen in Priory Road to make an announcement. She found Janet and Duncan finishing their meal at the kitchen table, and launched into her statement without ceremony. Clearly, she had rehearsed it, and clearly, she was overwrought.

She and Hector had found a little house on the Poplace Estate and had agreed to rent it for six months starting on the first of January next year. During that six months, Hector would work on the Latchly farmhouse so that they could move in beside Alice and Alistair in the summer.

Throughout this announcement, Christine had kept her eyes firmly on her father. Now she addressed him directly.

'Hector has asked me to ask you, fither, if you would help him fit the Latchly hoose out.'

'My god, Christine, you've got a flaming...,' cut in Janet.

'Wheesht, Janet, let the lassie finish,' cut in Duncan, then added calmly, 'I might well help ye wi' that – if it's required. But...'

Janet exploded. She slammed her hand down on the table making the crockery rattle.

'Oh, but you will not - and you, my girl...'

'Wheesht, Janet, wheesht, the lassie isn't finished yet. Have ye love?'

'I will not 'wheesht' while she insults me in my own...'

'Quiet, woman,' commanded Duncan at the top of his voice, a sound she had rarely heard in all their twenty-five years together.

'Now then,' he said to Christine, 'tell us the rest of what you have to say.'

'We've pit up oor names to get married – on the 11th of December.'

For the first time since she had entered the house, Christine looked at her mother. For a moment Janet sat stock still. Then she burst into tears, stood up, went to her daughter, and threw her arms round her. She said nothing, delivered no apology, but held her daughter close until Christine understood and accepted her regret.

When she had recovered, and Christine was sitting with a cup of tea in her hand. Janet turned on Duncan.

'You two cooked this up.'

'No, we did not,' protested Christine.

Duncan shook his head and said, 'No, Janet, no. I did not know what she was going to say.'

'You can't expect me to believe that. You knew about her gettin' married'

'No, he didn't,' asserted Christine.

'I just heard it the now, like you.'

'But you knew she hadn't finished when she talked about rentin' the Poplace house. You told me to keep quiet. So, you must have known.'

'I did not.'

'He did not.'

'So, what did you know?'

'I know my daughter, and I know that, in spite of her grit she wouldn't want to keep on hurting her mother. When she arrived today, I thought it must be a peace mission, otherwise she wouldn't have come. It cost her a lot, I know that - but she came. She wouldn't have come to torment us, not our Christine. So, I thought there must be more - and there was.'

His tone changed and he glanced from one to the other.

'Have you two any idea of what I've been through with the pair of you lobbing grenades at each other; the two people most precious to me in the whole world?'

He stopped, suddenly embarrassed by his own sentiment. He had said too much, had given too much away. He picked up his empty cup and drained it. Christine stood up and gave her dad a hug and a peck on the cheek. For moment Duncan feared that Janet would do likewise. To his relief, she stayed in her chair and simply patted his hand.

Their conversation then turned towards Latchly and who would move in with granny and grandad. The more they talked, the more rational seemed the thought that Christine and Hector should do so. They had to live somewhere, so why not Latchly? Could Christine cope with her granny? Of course.

Janet dreaded leaving her home in Priory Road. She had laboured on it for twenty-five years, knew every nook and cranny of it, knew where she had bought what for it; knew that the garret stored both memories and junk; anticipated that the junk would have to be thrown out, but which was which? Ask Duncan – or Christine, and they will tell you that Janet is a stickler for tidiness. They will say, if you catch them when she is not listening, that she harps on about 'a place for everything and everything in its place'. Clutter, indecision and uncertainty unnerve her, so she is fretting about the upheaval, and anxious about squeezing her well-ordered life into a strange house. All this disturbance and anxiety would be avoided if Christine and Hector moved in with Alice and Alistair. For them it would be an adventure; a challenge certainly, but an adventure with the possibility. never admitted by any of them yet, nevertheless entertained by them all, that should something happen to the two old folk, *when* something happened to them, the house would become Christine and Hectors' home; a home to grow into and make their own - not a rented lodging.

But the more attractive the proposition appeared the more impossible it became. Latchlaw had to be bought immediately. Now. Duncan and Janet had a house to sell to raise the purchase price. Christine and Hector had nothing. End of argument! End of speculation! End of hopes and dreams! End of relief for Janet!

Janet and Duncan would sell Priory Road and move into Latchly. The decision, approved by everyone, pleased nobody.

Then the phone rang. It was Alistair. Was Alice with them? She had disappeared. He'd been sitting dozing. One minute she was there, the next she had gone.

CHAPTER FIFTY-ONE

On the same day that Duncan, Janet and Christine met at Priory Road, a little earlier in the day, we would have found Hercules hovering over an offer that he has been advised to grab with both hands. Seated at a table in the offices of Proctor & Porteous in Edinburgh's George Street, The Doc had told him that Davenports, the big Manchester developers were prepared to offer £3 million for Latchlaw - well ahead of any other offer. Hercules read through the offer, excited not only by the prospect of such a lucrative return, but also by Davenport's desire to tie up the deal quickly. Watched by The Doc, he skimmed the various clauses and sub-clauses with increasing satisfaction. Then ground to a halt. The land had to be clear. The farmhouse and steading must go.

Hercules looked up and into the eyes of The Doc.

'I'm sorry,' The Doc said, 'That's the deal.'

'No chance of give,' grumbled Hercules.

'No, I've tried.'

'Have you explained about my commitment to A...'

'Alice' was the word that came into his mind, (and not only the word, but the gentle woman in her apron, in the lane handing him a bundle of runner beans) but he quickly changed it to 'the sitting tenants.'

'I've tried.'

'And the closing date?'

'December 11th, but if I were you, I wouldn't wait. I'd grab it now. It's half-a million more than the next best. Take it!'

Hercules stared at The Doc. He tried to clear his mind, tried to concentrate on his objective and to contain his commitment to Duncan. Duncan he could deal with, and John Hendry, but Alice troubled him. He needed time.

'Tell them I like the deal. Tell them I will sign on the 11th. There are few loose ends I need to tie up first.'

He met Elvira for a sandwich, told her of his good fortune, then drove back to Hecklescar through the dark wind and rain. His exhilaration at the deal and at Elvira's approbation of it carried him as far as the bleak road over Coldingham Moor. There the worms started crawling out of it. What about his offer to Duncan? He had shaken hands on it, hadn't he? What about John Hendry – what would he do now? Try to block it? What about a home for his own son, Hector? Could he have got more? What about Peter Munro? What about Alice?

It was after nine on a miserable November night when Hercules shook the rain off his coat in the porch of Avignon. Olivia emerged to make an announcement.

'You have a visitor,' she said blandly, 'in the lounge.'

'That snivelling little banker, I have no doubt,' Hercules snarled.

'No, my dear. Not him. A woman, an old woman. Alice, from Latchlaw has come to see you. She arrived over two hours ago and refused to go away until she saw you. I told her you would be glad to see her.'

We know why Alice has come. She overheard what her son had said to Christine and wants kind Mr. Douglas to re-assure her that she is not going to be turned out of her home.

We also know that Hercules is considering doing just that. What is he to do? What is he to say?

He knows what the book says: '*listen to the facts, not your feelings*'; has lived by it, has boasted about his clarity of vision and yes, his ruthlessness. Now he must choose between his own bright new dawn, and the dark shadows of this old woman's twilight years. How often, in similar circumstances, he has parroted lines learned at Fettes:

'*There is a tide in the affairs of men,*

Which, taken at the flood, leads on to fortune.'

Stirring words; often they had rolled in to lift him, but tonight they left him grounded. For now, as he sits looking at this old woman in her plastic raincoat and knotted rainmate, he sees, sees blindingly, that if he goes ahead and sells out to the builders, the tide may lead on not to fortune but to purgatory; not to wealth, comfort and liberty, but to betrayal, dishonour and shipwreck.

Alice is speaking. She has fished in her handbag and has pulled out a small notebook and is handing it to him.

'This is the rent book. You will see it is paid up. But if you're having a struggle, we could always pay a bit more.'

Hercules took the book into his hand. It felt alive, as if it were worming its way into his soul. He quickly handed it back. Alice carefully unclipped her bag, zipped open a pocket inside the bag, placed the book in the pocket, pulled along the zip and closed the bag. The concentrated effort Alice applied to this simple process silenced Hercules. When she had closed the bag, she looked at Hercules and smiled,

'I keep it safe', she said

Hercules felt compelled to say something.

'I didn't know you had a rent book. I thought it was handled through the bank.'

'Well, my granddaughter, that's Katie, no,'

'Christine,' prompted Hercules.

'Thank you – Christine; she writes it up. I asked her to do that, so we know it's being paid.'

'No, no,' mumbled Hercules, 'what you pay is fine.'

'That's good,' said Alice, 'I knew that it would be alright. I'll tell Alistair when I get home, that it's alright. I knew it would be.'

She stood up.

Hercules stood up with her.

'I'll run you back. It's a poor night.'

'No, no, I'll walk. I got here so I'll get back.'

'You'll not,' insisted Hercules, 'I'm taking you.'

When they drew up at Latchlaw, the door burst open and Duncan, Janet, Christine and Hector came rushing out.

'That's dad's Mercedes,' cried Hector

'Your father?' exclaimed Janet, 'What's he doing here?'

Her question was answered when Hercules handed Alice out to them.

'Where on earth have you been?' demanded Janet, 'We've been worried sick.'

'She turned up at Avignon,' explained Hercules, 'she came to see me. I thought I'd better bring her home.'

Janet made to ask about what they had talked about, but Duncan put a hand on her arm to prevent her. Then he thanked Hercules.

Alice, wrapped up in her family, hurried out of the drizzle into the warmth of her home. Hercules invited his son Hector to return with him but, on being turned down, made his way back to his house alone.

CHAPTER FIFTY-TWO

At Long Eaton, once Peter Munro had declared his intention of walking back to Hecklescar, the party descended from the lofty peaks of philosophy to the dull plain of particulars. They stopped asking themselves 'what is life for?', and 'why is he doing that?' and discussed arrangements for his long hike. In this Peter, Oliver and Mrs. Rostowski were greatly aided by Moira and Greg who joined them.

Peter did not intend making his journey a penance. He would dress comfortably, walk ten miles a day, or fifteen at the most, eat a hearty breakfast and arrive at his next lodging in time for dinner. Moira advised on snacks along the way and Greg volunteered to use his expertise and contacts to organise the transport of his luggage from one port of call to the next to save him carrying it. Peter graciously accepted the offer, but made it clear; insisted on it; that he did not want to be disturbed; no phone calls, no letters, no messages except those concerning the walk.

'There is not much in life,' he said, 'and nothing important, that cannot wait a fortnight.' When Greg started to ask him, pleasantly but quizzically, how a man walking ten miles a day can expect not to be disturbed, his wife cut him off. Later she explained that she knew precisely what Peter meant. The walk had to be a clean break; an emotional bath,

345

you might say.

Diverted, Greg darted down another track, offering to pick up Peter's belongings from his house in Eastbourne, and store them with M & Y Wegg at Crawley.

'Marney's place,' he said looking at Peter, then added, with a quizzical smile, 'or should we say, 'Peter's'?'

Peter responded with a short laugh, thanked Greg for the offer, accepted it, then changed the subject.

On the way back to Eastbourne, Greg returned to the subject. He didn't like silence, and Grace had been silent ever since they had left Long Eaton; silent because she had still not fathomed why Peter had decided to walk alone for days on end. A symbol of some sort; a sign? Of 'closure', or 'moving on'? If so, closure of what? Grief? Guilt? Remorse? Regret? Moving on - to where? Had he sorted himself out? Had he found the answer to his questions? Had he dealt with them? Where did hiking home appear in the pages of the Counsellor's manual? What would she report to the Care Co-ordinator?

Now Greg is talking in riddles – again!

'It belongs to him,' he pronounced.

'What belongs to him?' snapped his wife.

'Marney's place at Crawley.'

'He didn't say that.'

'Did the cat admit to the budgie?' said Greg cryptically.

'What cat?'

'The cat that killed the budgie'.

'What's that got to do with it?'

'Well, we don't always admit to what we've done – especially when we are ashamed of it.'

'Ashamed?'

'Well, guilty!'

'Guilty!? Are you saying that Peter Munro is guilty about taking over Marney Wegg's company?'

'Yes.'

'Why should he be guilty about that? I thought you said that he had done the firm a good turn by taking it over.'

'He did. It would have gone bust without the money he put into it.'

'Greg, would you stop talking in riddles? Why should he feel guilty about taking over a company and saving it?'

'It's the same as with her.'

'Who, Dylis, his wife?'

'Yes.'

'You've lost me, Greg, you'd better explain.'

'Well, I've been thinking.'

'Oh dear,' Mrs. Rostowski sighed.

Undeterred, Greg drove on.

'It's not regret that's wrong with him. That's why he's hiking back to Scotland.'

Mrs. Rostowski smiled and shook her head. He was off on a conundrum ride. Why stop him?

'Now then, my husband,' she said tersely, 'what is it that you understand that I do not?'

'Well, y'see, you don't do deliveries. I spend my days trailing all over the South of England. I go to some funny places, dangerous places, possibly – and, sometimes, the wrong places. Sometimes I'm lost; sometimes I know where I want to be but I can't find it. Sometimes I get snarled on the M25 or some other road and I can't move no matter how much I need to or want to. Sometimes I find a place and discover it's not there but somewhere else. Then you have people shouting at you. It's not your fault they haven't got what they ordered. It might be their own fault. But they shout at you. Sometimes the paperwork doesn't match the load, or some of the load, and sometimes the van breaks down (not that often now, I must say, since they gave me the Mercedes; best van I've ever had.) Then sometimes when its filthy weather and you've made a mess of it; like delivering the wrong thing to the wrong place, or when you're packing up at night you find something's still in the van that should have been delivered way back up the road, and you can't go back because it's too late. You see, the trouble with all this is that you can't put it right. You feel a failure and a wally - not in control. What do you say to yourself?'

He paused and, for effect, looked at his wife, hoping she would not attempt a reply and break the thread. She read the signal.

'You're going to tell me, I believe.'

He nodded. She settled back to listen to what she anticipates will be a long and rambling story.

'I say to myself: 'it's like the kite."'

'The kite?'

'Yes, the kite. My grandfather . . . ,'

'The one left behind, drunk, when his ship sailed away.'

'That's him! He spent a lot of time with us when we were kids. He used to take me to the park to feed the ducks and go on the swings. This day he'd picked up a kite from somewhere and took me to the park to fly it. He wasn't much good at it. As a matter of fact, grandad wasn't much good at anything. Granny always said that the only thing he was good at was keeping a chair warm and his plate empty. Too laid back, I think they call it. Back then they called it lazy but he always made an effort for us. Anyway, we went to the park and he let me fly the kite. For a while we managed fine, then it came crashing down. When we picked it up, we found that the string had tangled up with the tail. So, me and grandad sat down on a bench and tried to tease it out. But the more we tried the worse it got. We'd get one bit clear then find that another bit had knotted up again. This upset me because I'd been flying the kite when it happened. I kept blubbering, 'You can fix it, grandad, can't you,' He would say he could, so I kept on at him. But he didn't seem to be having much success. Then suddenly he picked the kite up and stuck it in a bin.'

"What are we going to do now?' I bawled.'

"I tell you what, son,' he said, 'we're going home."

'On the way out of the park, he stopped, look me by the hand and said, 'Look, son, remember this, whatever mess you make, if you can't sort it out, you can always go home."

'I've always remembered that: 'you can always go home!' It's been my comfort many a time. I think that's what your man's come to. He's failed to fix it, so he's going home.'

'That might work for kites,' replied his wife, 'but he hasn't just decided to go home. He told me months ago that he'd be back in Scotland by Christmas.'

Greg drove on for a while in silence, contemplating this leak in his argument. He then moved to plug it.

'Ah, but it's different now. He's walking. Before he was returning home a conquering hero, now he's going back like a dog without a tail. That's what the walking's about – and the incommunicado.'

'Incommunicado?' she laughed.

'To get his head round home. He's forgotten what it's like. Like the prodigal son. He's been in the far country.'

As it usually did, Greg's rambling warmed Mrs. Rostowski, and she patted him on the knee. Something he had said had lit a little light. Could he be right? That Peter had been trying to put everything in order before returning home in peace if not in triumph. Now he was just going home - leaving the mess behind; unfinished, unresolved, a tangle in the bin?

Greg had more to add; philosophy, you might say.

'Y'see' he expounded, 'in life there are no destinations, just depots.'

'Depots?' responded his wife, 'I thought depots were destinations.'

'Oh, no; you put stuff in, and you take stuff out; nothing stays there.'

Satisfied with his conclusion, Greg smiled. Mrs. Rostow-ski shook her head and smiled too.

We can readily understand, that Mrs. Rostowski did not include kites, depots or tailless dogs in her final report to the Care Co-ordinator; nor did she mention the word 'incommu-nicado'. What she wrote there was: *'client continues to work through his feelings of grief and regret, is coming to terms with his decisions, and will, I believe, find closure.'* That looked right – and professional. But she could not resist the urge to add: *'Peter Munro is going home.'*

CHAPTER FIFTY-THREE

Once Jakey had informed the men and women at the yard that John Hendry had taken over the yard, they regarded the company as saved and their jobs safe, so they turned their attention to what to buy the bairns for Christmas, ordering up the turkey and complaining about the price of Christmas stamps at the Post Office.

Such questions do not trouble Hercules. At Christmas, he intends being nowhere near Hecklescar; well out at sea in his yacht Olympian. Today we find him in his study at Avignon scraping together the remnants of his exit strategy.

He has missed his target dates. At the beginning, away back in June, he had, as we know, pencilled in 30th October. Then he had moved it back to 30th November. Now the calendar had flipped over into December and he was still behind his desk in Avignon. Equally he has failed to sell off Anthony Douglas & Son.

He is, however, not totally despondent. He has shuffled off his debts onto John Hendry ('shuffled off' is my term not his; he calls it 'retrenchment'.) His treasure chest is filling up. He has come to terms with Olivia over the house. From that he will pocket £200,000 in the next few days. (Where she has found the money he does not know, would like to know, but has no way of finding out). Even better, CoCarvers, who are handling the sale of the Highland Company, have advised him that the first tranche of the one and a half million for the company will be in his account by a week Monday.

Then there is the £3 million offer of Davenports for Latchlaw. To gain it he has to renege on his agreement with Duncan Kerr to sell him Latchlaw farmhouse and steading. He had shaken Duncan's hand, but has since persuaded himself that this was just an understanding, an indication, not an agreement; about the price, not the sale; about what Duncan *would* pay, if, *if,* he decided to sell it to him. Nothing has been signed.

After Davenports, the next best offer for Latchlaw is £500,000 light. Half-a-million is too big a price to pay, too big a loss to take, over the niceties of what is or is not a binding agreement. Were that all that concerned him it is likely that he would have driven on and toughed it out, mumbling under his breath that *'you can't make an omelette without breaking eggs'.*

But he is troubled. Alice troubles him. He can brazen out his duplicity with Duncan Kerr, can face down John Hendry with some satisfaction, can silence his daughter and disregard his son, but he is discovering to his frustration that he cannot unload Alice without anguish. Her simple act of handing him her rent book, of her smile of acceptance of assurances he had not given, gripes like a cramp in his innermost being.

Of course, he can call Proctor and Prentice and tell The Doc to go ahead with the sale. Commit, irrevocably, now! There is the phone; pick it up! Why not? Why the doubt? What stands in the way? Nothing but a door; the door in his imagination, the door at Latchlaw slamming shut behind a distraught Alice as she leaves her home for the last time, her rent book in her hand, calling out to Mr. Douglas to prevent her eviction. An incessant drama that will not switch off no matter what rationalisation and business jargon knobs he twists.

He has played for time; time is running out. He finds himself still hoist on the horns of his dilemma. He must either ditch Alice or lose at least half a million pounds. He must decide - by December 11th; scarcely a week away.

CHAPTER FIFTY-FOUR

Out of allegiance to Lizzie, John Hendry felt he should make an effort to enjoy Christmas, but neither heart nor head supported him. He sat at breakfast and tormented himself with the thought of what he had done. Technically, Anthony Douglas & Son Ltd now belonged to him – or would do so once the formalities had been completed. But what then? The company's debts soared above him like a tsunami. It could not be long before it crashed down. Once the banks and creditors learned of his potential ownership, they would expect to be relieved of some of their debt. He would need to meet them, talk to them, persuade them to keep the company afloat while he sought new investment. New investment? From where? From whom?

'How old are you Mr. Hendry?' 'Eighty-three!' 'And you have taken over the company?!'

'Do I have enough energy to turn this company round? Do I have enough life left?' No, I do not!

He then did what he always did when his despair threatened to overwhelm him: put it to work in his legs. He would walk round the Bantry, see the sea, breathe in the air, hopefully meet someone who would restore his hold on life.

He had barely entered the High Street when he encountered a gang of men putting up Christmas lights on the shops and premises along the street. As he approached, one of the men peeled off and came up to him: Nudge, one of the fish-yard's drivers.

'Just the man I wanted to see,' he said, cheerfully. 'Can we borrow a forklift truck from the yard? We're gettin' the cherry-picker from the boatyard to-morrow but for now we're havin' to use ladders and it's an awfy trackle. I asked Jakey, but he said I'd hev to ask you. He used tae ask Hercules. But Hercules is no more, we hear; you're the man now.'

John Hendry looked at him blankly for a few moments trying to find words to protest his innocence. 'No, no, it's not for me. . ..' What makes Jakey think I know anything about forklift trucks?

'No, no,' he replied urgently, 'I am not in for Hercules; it's just. . ..'

He stopped. He did not know what it was.

'Leave it with me. I'll see Jakey.'

At the yard, Jakey welcomed him. They all welcomed him; everyone in the yard. They smiled at him, greeted him, some of the women in the fish room cheered. Before he could ask Jakey about the forklift truck, Jakey shook his hand and said,

'Good to see you, John; I'll show you the office.'

Before John had time to object, Jakey had turned away and clearly expected him to follow.

They climbed a narrow stair into a long room that had been more or less hung from the rafters above and to the side of the fish room. Behind a desk immediately inside the door, there to deter intruders, sat Fiona, Hercules secretary, dibbing at the keyboard of a computer. When she saw John Hendry, she stood up.

'Your new boss,' mumbled Jakey to Fiona without looking at her.

'No, no,' John began, but Jakey ignored him and hustled him past Fiona, through the room to a broad executive desk, piled with papers. Behind it sat a large padded executive chair.

'Here's your chair,' announced Jakey. 'I've been waiting for you. The schedule's downstairs. You make yersel' comfortable and I'll bring it up.'

He had gone before John Hendry could prevent him. Not knowing what to do, he sat down in the chair behind the desk. Almost immediately, Fiona arrived, notebook in hand, and sat down in the chair at the front of the desk.

'Is there anything you need me to do?' she asked.

John Hendry looked at her and smiled. His heart thumped, he felt sick, his mind thrashed around in confusion, yet he smiled. It was ludicrous! He, boss of a Fish Merchants! He didn't know a thing about fish unless it was on a plate with chips!

'Yes, Fiona, explain to me what I am doing here.'

'You're the boss,' she said tentatively.

'No, Fiona, I am not the boss.'

The words were no sooner out of his mouth than he regretted them. Fiona's face fell and her eyes filled with tears.

'What is it that Fiona does?' they asked down the street. 'She's Hercules' secretary, ye ken; at the yard.'

Hercules' secretary! Bigsy, bombastic, bullying Hercules. Hercules, that despises his workers; that has run the yard into the ground; that has taken a lend of Jakey once too often. Fiona is his secretary! Fiona, who alone turned up for work the day they all walked out last week; Fiona, who has been snubbed down the street since; Fiona who has spent all her working life, all thirty years of it, in this office, serving at first Anthony and then Harold; fending off intruders and time-wasters, humouring the boss's whims, chasing their daft ideas, harbouring their secrets, covering up their mistakes, tholing their bad temper, doing their dirty work; keeping faith. Seeking each morning to anticipate their needs and trying each evening not to resent their selfishness. Fiona is, was, Hercules secretary.

She is plump and plain. She was chosen, not to adorn the office, but to manage it. She has never married and lives alone in a single bedroom flat in the Poplace Scheme with her cat and mementoes of holidays abroad. This Fiona now sits in front of him as smart as ever, with her shorthand book in her hand and tears in her eyes, asking if there is anything she can do for him.

'I tell you what, Fiona,' he said gently, 'bring me a cup of coffee and when Jakey has gone you can tell me what it is you do.'

When Jakey came up with the schedule, he found John Hendry sitting behind the boss's desk, drinking a cup of coffee.

'You've no idea what a relief it is for me to see you in that chair,' he said before galloping through the schedule: about prawns in and langoustines out, about shipments and deliveries, about fish and lobsters, crabs and scampi, about what drivers were where; about Angela's report on throughput and output, and that she is a bit short-staffed because Katie is expecting and is off with morning sickness, and Morag's got pains in her legs again, 'but Angela'll tell ye that when she reports the now.' About pallets and packaging, about boats and boxes, about clapped out equipment, dodgy vans and Brian wanting his money for the roof repairs he did six months ago. 'Fiona will tell ye about that and all the rest.'

Jakey concluded with a request to allow Nudge to use the fork-lift truck to put up Christmas Lights in the High Street. John Hendry asked Jakey what he thought. When Jakey said Nudge could borrow the forklift, John Henry agreed and thus made his first executive decision.

On Jakey's heels, came Angela who rattled through her report with enthusiasm but without pause. She then looked John Hendry full in the face and asked if he had any questions. John Hendry felt obliged to say, to ask, something.

'Yes, Angela,' he said. 'you mentioned prawns and langoustines. I always thought they were the same thing.'

Angela smiled benevolently, like a teacher who has just been told by a pupil that two and two equal five.

'A langoustine is a large prawn, once you've seen one there no mistaking them,' she said patiently, 'then there's crayfish; they're different again, more like a small lobster.'

John Hendry, although no wiser, smiled and thanked her.

After Angela left, he spent a couple of hours with Fiona discovering that while Jakey and Angela ran the yard, she ran the business. He learnt that, along with her assistant Lucy, she maintained contacts with suppliers and customers, handled quotations, issued invoices, chased up payments, dealt with the bank, paid suppliers, ordered up necessities, and calculated and paid out wages. She kept on top of tax and VAT, drew up monthly and weekly accounts on an IT system she had bought herself, handled all mail, facilitated the boss's correspondence and carried out many other tasks, the purpose of which John Hendry had not the foggiest idea.

When John Hendry asked about the company's creditors; the 'investors' who had lent Hercules money to prop up the company, he found her, as in all else, expert and organised. She would put together a folder for him to take home.

'There's quite a few,' she said.

'As I expected,' replied John Hendry smiling.

Encouraged by his smile, Fiona looked at him and decided she could trust him with a confidence she had dared not share with anyone else.

'Hercules wasn't all bad, you know', she uttered quietly. 'He was kind to me – especially when I lost my mother – and he helped me buy my house. I will miss him.'

'Of course, you will,' replied John gently.

As John Hendry prepared to leave, Angela marched into the office with a small polythene box. She placed it on the desk and lifted the lid. John Hendry peered into the box and saw three creatures locked in mortal combat. Deftly, Angela separated them and picked up the smallest of them. She plonked it on the desk and pronounced,

'That's a prawn.'

Then she grabbed the largest of them and held it in front of him. It did look like a small lobster.

'And that's a crayfish.'

That joined the prawn on the desk and made an instant bolt for freedom. Angela hauled it back into the box.

She lifted out the langoustine and handed it to John. John put out his hand then, as it spread its legs and opened its claws, his courage failed him.

'It's for you. Grill it with garlic butter and it will be delicious. Break the tail off before you eat it. I'll put it in a bag. There's one or two more in here.'

She hauled a bag from the front of her waterproofs and stuck the langoustine into it.

When he arrived home, John Hendry cooked the langoustines as instructed by Angela. As he ate it, (and enjoyed it) he complimented himself on his first executive decision (the fork lift truck) and concluded that Anthony Douglas & Son Ltd did not need a boss. Jakey, Angela and Fiona could run it; did run it. But if they needed somebody to sit in the big chair for a couple of hours each day, he would do it. For now.

He could sit in the chair but could he rescue the company? From Fiona's immaculate figures he discovered that each month the company washed its face, income on the whole covering expenditure. However, when he calculated the company's future cashflow (the money a company needs to fund its activities), he discovered the company lay in much worse shape that he had anticipated. Interest payments were crippling, but thanks to Fiona's grip on company finances, sustainable - just!

While he worked on the cashflow, Fiona's creditor file sat on his desk and glowered at him. No matter how often he assured it that he would deal with it when ready, it refused to back off and kept barging into his thinking. If they, the creditors, became aware of what he had just learnt they would start howling for their money back. The company lay on lifesupport. One shock: one missed payment, one major breakdown, even one load to the continent held up long enough for the langoustines to perish, and the company would follow. One of the creditors would call it a day, the rest would back off and the company would be tipped into administration. If that happened, John knew, the business could not be revived. The fishyard would die and those who depended on it for their daily bread would starve.

To the teetering cash flow, add a ramshackle plant, the result of neglect over the past ten years. The building, plant and equipment had been starved of maintenance and worked to death. Jakey had warned him that the large industrial walk-in freezers, essential to the business, were constantly breaking down and could not be kept going much longer. Each one would cost £8-10,000. Angela had complained that the stainless-steel benches at which the girls worked were now almost impossible to keep hygienically clean; they all need to be replaced, add in £5,000 for that. The asbestos roof of the processing shed had a Health and Safety Improvement Notice on it. It must be stripped out and replaced by the end of next year: £20,000 at least. Much of what lay beneath it (including the pitted concrete floor) needed similar treatment at a similar cost. Two of the large 44-tonne trucks were clapped out; (how much for those? £100,000 each?); three of the delivery vans had to be nursed through their MOTs every year and...

Stop, stop, stop! It is impossible! No-one in their right mind would put a penny into such a company. Better to let it go and start again – without the debt - and somewhere else! Hecklescar is too far from the markets. Set it up in Hatfield or Harlow or, if you want it by the sea, in Lowestoft or Great Yarmouth; even Devon would be better than here.

Stealing himself, John at last picked up the creditors' file, and opened it. Fiona had listed the lenders on a control sheet in the front of the file. There she had recorded the name and address of the lender and the amount they had lent the company. As well as the usual suspects, the bank and investment companies, he found a considerable list of small, some of them tiny, investors who, no doubt, had been tapped by Hercules in the Gullane Clubhouse.

One of the personal investors, however, jumped off the page, not only for the amount but also for the name. The amount: £1,500,000; the name: Raymond Munro. Raymond Munro! Peter Munro's father. The date of the loan was given as 3rd of March 1990, the year of Anthony's stroke; the year Hercules took over the firm.

Who had concluded the deal, Anthony or Hercules? If it were the father, did the son know? And, John wondered, is Peter Munro aware of it? Who in Hecklescar might answer such a question? Cockburn Heath. He would go and see him tomorrow.

John Hendry found comfort in these questions. He laid down his pen, closed his notebook and covered his laptop. He then walked into the back room and sat down at his organ. He opened it up and launched into 'The Holy City'. Why 'The Holy City' I don't know - and neither did he. Whatever, as he played it, a curious sense of reassurance warmed him and stayed with him as he made his way to bed.

CHAPTER FIFTY-FIVE

Of course, Hercules knew about the loan. He had not concluded it; his father Anthony had done that, but he knew about it. He suspected that Peter Munro did not, but that when he came back to Hecklescar he would discover it. Certainly, it could not be kept secret now; now that that nit-picking John Hendry had his nose in the records.

It gave Hercules a fleeting sense of revenge that the Munro debt now bore down on the banker's shoulders. Let Peter ask John Hendry for it when he comes back!

Hercules, however, knew that he could not hang around to savour John Hendry's embarrassment. When Peter arrived, he must be gone. The calendar had flitted past successive departure dates without paying any heed to them and had now clicked over into December. The Latchlaw deal would be concluded on the 11th, a week today. What had he planned for after that? Like his departure dates, the mode of his disappearance had gone through several modifications.

He had discovered that it is not easy to disappear. His original thought of retreat to a small estate in the Outer Isles had been scotched as his wealth shrank. Besides, he would still be in Scotland, still within reach of those who might want to ask him where their money had gone. Similarly, he had entertained then dismissed a move to a discreet flat in the South of England - Brighton, or Sittingbourne, or even somewhere in West London. Corfu had beckoned and faded as the Greek economy collapsed. Escape to Bermuda he had ruled out when he discovered at least two Hecklescar families had time-shares there.

Then one day in October, returning from the golf course, his yacht sailed into his attention. Olympian, he had often bragged, was an 'Ocean-going Yacht'. Why then should he not sail oceans in it? After talking it over with Elvira, or rather, after Elvira had listened several times to his scheme, he determined his strategy. He would equip the yacht and sail out of Hecklescar harbour one day and never return. For a fortnight now, he had been readying Olympian for his departure.

Such a scheme appealed to his Herculean sense of importance. His imagination played over the reaction on the streets of Hecklescar:

'He just jumped in his boat and sailed away. Out of the harbour and gone! What a man!'

However, no sooner had Hercules made his bold decision than he discovered with Hamlet that *'there is a divinity that shapes our ends, rough hew them how we will'*. The divinity in this case is a faulty gland in Olympian that is allowing the water to seep along the propeller shaft into the boat. Not only that, but Hecklescar boatyard can't fix it. The gland is a specialist part available only from the original boat builder whom, we know, builds his boats in Australia. The part will not be available for fitting until the second week in December.

Such a finding substantiates an already crushing sense of frustration. He is frustrated with Olivia, for not supporting him and for stealing half of Avignon; frustrated that Golden Opportunities has been undermined by the financial crisis; frustrated that he has had to surrender his company to that pernicious little banker; frustrated with Jakey, with Angela, with Fiona, traitors all. It all adds up to the crowning frustration: that the treasure chest he has so assiduously packed has been raided and depleted.

But deeper than his frustration is a sickening sense of his own vulnerability. Not that he has made a mess of it all: of Golden Opportunities, of his father's company, of his relationship with Olivia! Certainly, these all growled but he had blunted their bite by rationalisation and self-justification; none of them were his fault. What unnerves him is that he has not been able to untangle himself from Alice.

Often, during the past few days, he has reprimanded himself for being so stupid, so weak, so emotional, so pathetically amateurish, as to credit Alice's rent book with such importance. Several times he has picked up the phone to tell the Doc to go ahead with the deal and thus rid him of the dilemma, but every time he has put it down again without ringing. He'll think about it a little longer. Why? What's to think about? Either he sells Latchlaw to Davenports or he loses £500,000. He must accept Davenport's bid. He will accept it!

But the dilemma will not dissolve. It is a mere wraith, a phantom; of no substance, no significance; no leverage. Alice has no power over him; could do nothing to prevent him pocketing three and a half million pounds; yet he cannot clear her out of the way. Latchlaw is Alice's home. That is the playback loop he cannot switch off. It is not politic, not advisable, not clever, not economically sensible, not financially rewarding, but *right* that he should let her live on at Latchlaw. In the dark hours such a conviction haunts him; in the morning it stinks in his conscience like rotting fish.

December 5th, dark and cold. He will drive down to the yacht with a few more supplies. Because of the leaking gland he can't leave before the 11th anyway - and the mark of an astute manager is not to make a decision until you have to: *keep all options open; a week is a long time in business as in politics.* Such phrases once firm and bracing now shuffle into his consciousness and collapse on the floor. They afforded little defence against the relentless advance of the days. Time is running out. He must be away before Peter Munro arrived in Hecklescar.

* * * * *

The fifth of December also marked the day that John Hendry intended to seek out Cockburn Heath to discover what he knew about the loan that Raymond Munro gave to Anthony Douglas & Co. twenty years ago.

He bustled into the solicitor's office at nine to find that Cockburn had not yet arrived. Fortunately, as it turned out, Mrs. Somerville, his redoubtable Chief Clerk, was in residence and listened attentively as he told her about Raymond Munro's loan to Anthony Douglas.

'This rings a bell' she said cryptically when he had finished, 'Leave it with me. I'll speak to Mr. Heath when he comes in.'

Within an hour Cockburn rang John Hendry.

'I've got something to tell you about Latchlaw.' he said, in the excited voice of a schoolboy with a frog in his pocket. 'You'd better come down.'

Although Hercules was reconsidering the offer he had made to Duncan Kerr to sell Latchlaw to him, he had not told them of his change of mind. He has suggested it to Sally his daughter. She had told Christine and Christine had told her parents, Duncan and Janet. But, as far as they were concerned, the deal was still on and they have urged Cockburn Heath to tie it up before Hercules wriggled out of it. Cockburn had done what he always did with anything that needs speed and attention: he had handed it to Mrs. Somerville.

When John Hendry arrived at Cockburn's office, the solicitor hardly waited until John was in the door, before he blurted out his news.

'Mrs. Somerville says that she thinks that Latchlaw

might not belong to Harold Douglas.'

'What? Say that again. Latchly doesn't belong to Hercules!'

'Not 'doesn't. She doesn't say 'doesn't', she just says 'might not'.

"Might not,' what does that mean?'

Cockburn launched into an explanation, but excitement curdled what little understanding he had of the matter. John Hendry stopped him and asked him to slow down. Instead, he stood up and darted past John Hendry to the door.

'I'll bring her in. She can explain it better than me. Grab a pew.'

There were no 'pews' that were not piled with papers, so John Hendry cleared the documents from a chair and sat down.

Shortly afterwards, Mrs. Somerville sailed into the office followed by Cockburn resembling a flunkey minus the uniform.

'About Latchlaw,' she pronounced. John felt the urge to stand by his desk and say, 'Yes, teacher.'

'It's really quite straightforward', she proclaimed. 'To gain that loan from Raymond Munro, Anthony Douglas pledged Latchlaw as co-lateral. It was, I believe, to become the property of Mr. Munro if the loan were not paid back within ten years. They signed a letter of agreement, here in this office. Well, not in this office, in the old office, in old Mr. Heath's office. It was to be followed by a proper deed, but Anthony died before it could be completed.'

'Well, well,' said John Hendry, 'so Latchlaw belongs to Peter Munro.'

'Not at all,' rebuked Mrs. Somerville, 'the deed was never delivered. Raymond Munro didn't want to push the matter straight after Anthony passed away, then he himself collapsed on the golf course hardly two years later. In consequence it was left hanging. I have the draft deed on file. But it is not signed.'

'But you'll have the letter of agreement, signed by Anthony.'

'Unfortunately, I do not. I have a photocopy, but not the original. Someone must have taken the original out of the file, given it to someone and put back only a copy.'

As she stated this, she stared at Cockburn who, John Hendry observed, was attempting to sink beneath his desk.

'I gave it to Hercules to check against the one he had,' muttered Cockburn defensively. 'He must not have brought it back,'.

'When was this?'

'It would be sometime in June...'

'When, this year?'

'Yes,'

'When I was on holiday.' Mrs. Somerville interjected. 'He should have been given the copy, not the original.'

As Mrs. Somerville glowered and Cockburn squirmed, John Hendry tried to make sense of it all.

'So, what's the position legally?' he asked.

Mrs. Somerville knew the answer but gave Cockburn his place and smiled at the solicitor to induce him to answer.

'Well,' said Cockburn, glancing nervously at Mrs. Somerville, 'in the absence of a delivered deed, either the money belongs to Peter Munro or Latchlaw does.'

'And if the money is spent?'

'Then you could argue that Latchlaw belongs to Peter Munro - if, that is, he is the residual beneficiary of Raymond Munro's will.'

'Which he is,' stated Mrs. Somerville.

'Does Peter know about this?' asked John Hendry.

'I doubt it,' cut in Mrs. Somerville, an answer with which Cockburn heartily agreed.

'Then we must contact him,' said John Hendry urgently. 'As soon as possible. I have every reason to believe that Hercules is about to sell Latchlaw to a building contractor.'

'But he is selling the farmhouse and steading to Duncan and Janet, is he not? We're drawing up the contract now,' replied Cockburn.

'Let us hope he is, but what if it doesn't belong to him?'

'That would need to be tested in court.'

'Would that prevent the sale?'

'Most likely; if the action were raised before the sale went through. Duncan would not want to be caught up in a legal wrangle. Nor would the contractors. They'd want it cleared up before they signed on the dotted line, I would imagine.'

'Then we must raise an action – and quick!'

'Not we,' interjected Mrs. Somerville, 'Peter Munro must do it.'

'Then I will contact him,' said John Hendry. 'Do you have his address and phone number? He's been talking to you about buying a house here, hasn't he?'

'He has, but not to much effect. We're not sure what he wants. Is it a house, or a flat, or what? He keeps changing his mind. We thought we had found what he wanted; a nice little executive bungalow on Millerfield, but he pulled out saying he wanted something in the town, something that belonged the place – whatever that means. We just keep sending him details.'

'That's when we can find him,' put in Mrs. Somerville,

then left the room.

She returned shortly with an index card in her hand. She read it out.

'Peter Munro's phone number is 013237 54841. His address is: 43 Burleigh Square, Eastbourne. BN22 1YD'.

CHAPTER FIFTY-SIX

J ohn Hendry hurried home from Cockburn Heath's office to ring Peter Munro at Eastbourne. But we know that Peter isn't at Eastbourne – and that he is not going back there. We also know that his flat is now occupied by Florence.

After several unanswered calls John Hendry left a message on the answerphone pleading with Peter to speak to him on what is an urgent matter. He waited all day for a reply but none came. At eight that evening, he rang again and found himself speaking to Florence.

No, her father wasn't in. No, he didn't live here anymore. No, she didn't know how to contact him.

John in one last, desperate throw asked if there was anyone who did know where he was. She told him about Oliver. He rang Oliver and found himself speaking to Moira in the agitated tones of a man mucked about by telephone.

'I need to speak to Oliver,' he commanded.

'That is not convenient at the moment.' (Oliver is being bathed by a carer).

'Is he at home?' John asked sharply.

'Yes, but….'

'Look,' cut in John Hendry, 'this is urgent and important. Whatever he's doing please ask him to the come to the phone.'

For a second or two Moira, whom, we know, has frustrations of her own, thought about slamming down the phone but changed her mind and tersely informed John Hendry that she would not interrupt her husband, but that if John Hendry gave her his number, she would try to persuade Oliver to ring back later in the evening. Something in her tone conveyed to John Hendry that he had pushed her too far. He apologised and accepted her offer. He then sat beside the phone for an hour or more.

Eventually, at ten o'clock on the evening of the 3rd December, he spoke to Oliver – and discovered that Oliver did not know where Peter Munro was.

'He's walking back to somewhere in Scotland.'

'Where in Scotland?'

'Hackle or Heckle or something. It's a little place by the sea.'

'Hecklescar. That's where I am now.'

'Oh well, he'll be with you in a few days.'

'A few days! That'll be too late. How many days?'

'How long would it take him to walk The Pennine Way? That's what he's doing; walking back home, he says.'

This reply did nothing to soothe John Hendry. He became surlier than ever.

'That'll be too late. I must speak to him.'

'I'm sorry I can't help you.'

'There must be someone who knows how to reach him. It really is very important.'

'You could try Mrs. Rostowski, but I wouldn't hold my breath.'

'Look, Oliver, let me have her phone number, then you can get back to whatever you were doing.'

'Yes, I'll give you her number. But I'm not going anywhere. I'll be staying right here.'

John Hendry thought this reply peculiar until Mrs. Rostowski put him right about Oliver. He was then appalled at his crass insensibility.

Mrs. Rostowski held to the line that she had agreed with Peter. No, she wouldn't contact him, even if she could, which she couldn't. John Hendry explained to her why he needed to speak to him so urgently, but that just bolstered Mrs. Rostowski's determination.

'That is just the sort of thing he needs to keep clear of on his walk,' she said.

But we know Mrs. Rostowski is a sympathetic woman and she felt sorry for the old banker trying to do his best for his friends. She therefore put Greg on the phone and Greg was able to tell John Hendry that Peter Munro would be arriving at a place called Kirk Yetholm at the Northern end of the Pennine Way on the 10th of December, or it might be the 11th - depending on the weather - or anything else that might get in the way.

Would that be early enough to prevent Hercules closing a deal with Davenports? John Hendry's first thought was to contact Hercules to alert him to Mrs. Somerville's doubts, but dismissed it as soon as it stepped forward. If Hercules caught the merest whiff of their intention to block the deal, he would clinch it before Peter could stop it, wouldn't he?

Hercules must not know what they were up to, but what were his intentions? Could Cockburn use his legal contacts to find out when Latchlaw would be handed over to Davenports? Perhaps, Sally could find out from her mother, Olivia, or granny, Connie? Belt and braces! Try them all!

Within a few hours on the 6th of December, John Hendry learned what we already know: Latchlaw is to be handed over on December 11th. Cockburn had drawn a blank from his legal contacts – 'commercial in confidence' and all that. But Hercules had breathed something to Olivia. 11th of December, that's when the boat would be ready. On the same day, the last ashes of the Latchlaw dream would be buried. He had enjoyed telling Olivia that! 'Gloating', is how Olivia described him to her mother Connie.

It is not crucial to our story to know where Olivia laid her hands on the two hundred thousand pounds, she has given to Hercules to buy out his half of Avignon. But in Hecklescar, you lose face if you cannot tie up a story – even if it means guessing or making it up. Ina is hard at work investigating the mystery. She has already reported to the coffee ladies that she knows '*of a certainty*' that Olivia does not own that kind of money, for hadn't she come across Olivia's tax return and bank statement when the lid of the bureau fell open one day when she was dusting it.

We need no such subterfuge. I will tell you where the money came from: her mother Connie. You may recall that Connie had lived unhappily with Fordyce her husband in a nice little bungalow on Upper Seafield, but when he died, she sold the place and rented a flat from the local authority. Hercules had offered to invest the proceeds in Golden Opportunities. Instead she took the advice of her old bank manager, one John Hendry. He had suggested an ISA investment in Arriva, an up and coming insurance company. Her shares have done well and a sale of most of them, added to Olivia's smaller contribution will be sufficient to pay off Hercules.

Connie regards her investment in Avignon as a loan but anticipates that the capital will never be repaid. Olivia, in response to her mother's kindness, proposed that her mother give up her council flat to come and live with her at Avignon. Connie has turned this down. She knows Olivia too well to want to live with her.

CHAPTER FIFTY-SEVEN

The conjunction of dates comforted Hercules but scared John Hendry.

Hercules saw the clustering of events on the 11th as justification for his strategy. The fact that the eleventh of December had been thrust upon him by decisions and events outwith his control did not trouble him because they had not burst through the bulwark of self-deception behind which he has sheltered for the past thirty years. Alice and her rent book had breached his deceit, but lay, he believed, within control; to be dealt with later.

He had planned to leave Hecklescar: he would do that. He had planned to throw off the shackles of fish and function: he would accomplish that. He had planned to raise enough money for a comfortable future life: he had done that (not to the extent he had planned, but sufficient). He had decided to explore the world's oceans: he would set sail on the eleventh, a week today. A new day dawning; a new life beckoning.

John Hendry, on the other hand, regarded the day before, the tenth of December, as Doomsday. The day on which he would fail to reach Peter Munro in time to stop Hercules' Latchlaw deal going ahead; the day Duncan and Janet would be robbed of their plan to take over the farmhouse and steading; the day Alice would lose the right to her home; the day self-seeking would trump compassion and evil triumph over good. Where is God when you need him?

In such commotion, how could he think of Christmas and do what Lizzie expected of him? He had left too much to do in the days counting down to the feast. He looked out Lizzie's old Christmas lists of presents to be bought and cards to be sent, and tried to recall which of these always-to-be-remembered people he had forgotten, which of them had died, or from whom he had not received a card last year. Did that mean that they were no longer with us? Should he send one this year? Was there anyone new he should remember – like Oliver and what was Oliver's wife's name? Did I write it down? Should I send them a card? What would Lizzie have done? She would have sent a card: maybe a little present of some sort; to make up for my blunder. No, I can't cope with that!

He called up the discipline of years to force him to start what he did not want to do. For three days he worked at it, scouring local shops and the internet for presents, patronising the flower shop and Post Office for cards. When Gloria in the flower shop saw him slotting wrapping paper in and out of the bin in a fever of indecision, she first suggested what might be suitable, then taking pity on his desperation, offered to help him wrap up his presents; an offer he gladly accepted.

The cards he would do on his own; Lizzie would not allow him delegate that. He printed off address labels on his computer: eight pages of fourteen labels a page. Lizzie always wrote a short personal note on each card; he would try to do that. 'Recalling happy memories of you', 'Hope all goes well with you.' 'With love to all the family at Christmas.' (They do have a family, don't they? They haven't all fallen out?)

Hercules, Peter Munro, Latchlaw and Anthony Douglas & Son retired into the back room of his concern, until he came to 'Mr. and Mrs. Duncan Kerr – and Christine. Christine! She is marrying Hector, so she would become Christine Douglas. Should he send a separate card to the? When were they getting married? Before Christmas? Of course! When? He looked out the invitation and the date smacked into his face: Hecklescar Parish Kirk at 2 o'clock on Saturday 11th December. The eleventh! This Saturday! The day before - the 10th - he must be at Kirk Yetholm waiting for Peter Munro to finish his walk through the hills! So that Peter could sign a restraining order preventing the sale of Latchly to the Manchester builders. He'll be on time? Surely!

As that doubt alarmed him, he looked up and out of the window. A few lazy snowflakes floated down into the yard. 'Please don't snow,' he prayed, 'please!'

CHAPTER FIFTY-EIGHT

Kirk Yetholm is no place for a crucial meeting; not in December anyway. In summer it is a pleasant place to visit if you can find it - and don't mind driving along narrow country roads with the threat of a tractor or flock of sheep round every corner. The road from the south has trouble finding the village, meandering north, then west then south before coming across it tucked into the northern folds of the Cheviot Hills. Yet that is the most direct route. From any other direction the roads seem intent on avoiding the place. Mind you, it is worth reaching if you make the effort. A clean, green, settled sort of place – but not in December, and not if it is snowing or freezing. The council leaves it until last when clearing roads. After all, who wants to go to Kirk Yetholm in winter?

John Hendry wanted to go, though his presence was not strictly necessary. Cockburn Heath, as a Writer to the Signet, was the man to present the restraining document to Peter Munro and persuade him to sign it. Cockburn could then put it into the hand of Hercules to prevent the sale until the legal ownership of Latchlaw could be determined. Although he was not needed, John Hendry was resolved to drive the solicitor to Kirk Yetholm, not only because he had doubts about Cockburn's ability to find the place, but also because he genuinely wanted to meet Peter again and explain why blocking the sale of Latchlaw was so important to Duncan, Janet, Christine, Alice and Alistair - people that Peter knew.

On the tenth day of December, a watery sun clambered over the horizon at twenty past eight. Shortly afterwards, feeling jittery and not fully awake, John Hendry drove to Cockburn Heath's house. Cockburn bounced along his path into the car with the air of a man on a mission. He carried a briefcase. Before they set off John Hendry made him open it and demonstrate that he had the restraining letter they wanted Peter Munro to sign. Once he had signed it, they would hotrod it back to Hecklescar. Cockburn would deliver it into the hands of the named Harold Douglas of Avignon, Alexandra Drive, Hecklescar, forbidding him to conclude the sale until lawyers or courts decided who Latchlaw belonged to.

The roads were clear and empty and they arrived at The Border Hotel in Kirk Yetholm about ten and sat down to wait for Peter Munro. John Hendry could have done with silence but Cockburn, ever more interested in sailing than law, had blethered all the way; largely about Hercules' yacht; who made it, what type it was, how much it cost, how much canvas it could spread, how little it had been used. John made the mistake of enquiring about the fault that had developed and was treated to a half-an-hour's dissertation on propeller shafts, thrusters, hull integrity, membranes, glands and gaskets, bilges and ballast and other highly technical details that enthused Cockburn but left John feeling numb above the neck. Cockburn brought up the subject again when they were sitting at coffee in the Border Hotel, John Hendry having established from the receptionist that they had a booking for that night in the name of Peter Munro. At least they were in the right place.

As the day wore on, John Hendry became more apprehensive and less tolerant of Cockburn's incessant chatter. Several times he left the lawyer sitting in the lounge of the hotel and walked up the lane that led from the hill into Kirk Yetholm.

Late in the afternoon he spotted a lone figure striding round the corner, but just as John was about to approach the man, he was joined by a lady companion. Not Peter Munro. Had they seen a man walking on his own, a man in his fifties? Yes, they had passed him labouring up the track to the Auchope Cairn at the back of The Cheviot. He had asked them to inform the Border Hotel that he wouldn't be able to make it to them before nightfall. He would spend the night in the Mountain Refuge Hut below Auchope Cairn, and set out at dawn tomorrow to reach them at eleven or thereabouts.

What to do? Cockburn proposed staying the night, but John Hendry baulked. He wasn't prepared for that - no pyjamas, no shaving tackle, no pills, no fresh clothes – and no patience with Cockburn. It had run out and the thought of sharing a room with the loquacious lawyer made up his mind. While there was still light, they would drive back to Hecklescar and come back first thing in the morning.

It was dark by the time they reached Hecklescar and John Hendry settled gratefully into the peace and quiet of his own house for the night. He lit the log fire in the front room, buttered some toast, made a pot of tea, sat down in his chair, took out the crossword, and sought to lift his thoughts from the boggy ditch into which they had fallen. How had all this landed on him? Cockburn was enjoying it, but he did not feel the burden of commitment to Duncan and Janet, the hopes of Christine and Hector, or the needs of Alice and Alistair.

'It all depends on us reaching Peter before Hercules signs Latchlaw away, doesn't it?' he thought. 'Tomorrow that will happen in Edinburgh; we must get Peter to sign the restraint, then put it into the hands of Hercules before *he* signs.'

'How likely is that now? Say, Peter arrives in Kirk Yetholm at eleven. An hour from there to Hecklescar, twelve. Hercules will probably have left by then, perhaps by then the deal will have been signed already. Why couldn't that woman, that Mrs. Rowtski, or whatever they call her, have contacted Peter en-route to tell him how important it all is - and how critical the time? He might not then have delayed his arrival. But the man couldn't walk the hills in the dark. Don't be unreasonable! Unreasonable? I wish someone, I wish all of them, would be reasonable with me! I wish they'd either help me or leave me alone. God, I'm tired. Have I not done enough?'

'We're going to be too late! Even if the restraint is signed as soon as he steps through the door at Kirk Yetholm, I could fax it to Proctor and Porteous, couldn't I? That would do, wouldn't it? They don't need the original, do they? I'll have to ask Cockburn. If I can shift him off yachts. They'll have a fax machine at The Border Hotel, surely. I should have asked.'

'Then there's the wedding. Of Christine and Hector. At two in the kirk. I don't want to miss that. Mustn't miss it. We'll be back in time, surely. Peter arrives at eleven, signs the letter, say half-past, then back here for, (what?) twelve-thirty. That's time enough to get ready. It's not until two. Just. Even if Peter is late, say twelve, then here for half one. Can't be much later than that, can't be. So, twelve at the latest. But suppose he hasn't turned up by then? It'll be too late anyway. Hercules will have signed away Latchly by then, won't he?' What will we do then?'

The clamour of the phone scattered John's ramblings. Jakey; about nothing important; nothing that he needed John Hendry to decide, just a rapid run through of what they had done that day including with the shipment that had been delayed at the Channel Ferry. Something already dealt with and over. But Jakey rang; just to touch base; just to add another pound or two to the weight already bearing down on John Hendry's shoulders. Yet John Hendry thanked him and Jakey went to bed with the reassurance of a supportive boss and the satisfaction of good day's work behind him.

That night John Hendry prayed. Nothing rehearsed or religious, nothing particular; just the bleat of a weary sheep that had wandered into the waste-howling wilderness. Oh, and a fine day to-morrow. Please, no snow, no ice, no rain. Please, no heavy rain - and no tractors!

At twelve, John Hendry carried his troubles to his bed, yet slept soundly and the next morning arrived on the doorstep of Cockburn Heath before the sun reached it.

John's prayers were answered: a fine day, no snow, ice or rain, no tractors, no sheep. A gathering wind though, from the North-East, as forecast. They reached Kirk Yetholm and were only half way through their third cup of coffee when Peter Munro walked through the door to join them. John Hendry instinctively looked at the clock: quarter past eleven. Peter was surprised to see John Hendry and Cockburn but greeted them warmly and listened carefully to what they had to say.

He did not know about Latchlaw and the loan. Of course he would sign the restraining letter. But no, he would not accompany them back to Hecklescar today. The walk had been hard, especially the last two days. He was tired. He had arranged a bed for the night at the Border Hotel and a lift to take him to Gainslaw the following day.

'I am coming home,' he confessed quietly to John Hendry, 'I do not want to rush it. I want to. . . .'

He paused. Cockburn suggested the word 'enjoy'.

'No', he said firmly, 'not enjoy. In fact, I fear it.'

He stopped and for a while no-one spoke – not even Cockburn.

''Consider' is the word', he said at length, 'I want to take my time over these last few miles to consider and perhaps understand what I am doing as I make my way towards the old place. Am I going back or moving on?'

'I would say. . . .' began Cockburn. John Hendry cut him

off.

'We must be on our way. Peter. I think I understand you. But come round and explain it when you get back. Believe me, you will be welcome in Hecklescar. Not least by me. And, if you need a lodging for a little while, you'll not go past me, I hope.'

They left at twelve and reached Hecklescar at a quarter to one. John Hendry let Cockburn off at Avignon and the solicitor bounded up the steps to the front door. He rang the bell and waited. John Hendry watched from his car. After what seemed an age, the door opened and framed Olivia. John Hendry saw Cockburn talking to her, then he turned and scurried down the path.

'He's gone,' gabbled Cockburn. 'He left first thing this morning for Edinburgh.'

'Is he coming back for the boat?' asked John Hendry.

'No,' I don't think so. She didn't say.'

'Go back and ask her.'

Cockburn again scuttled up the steps and rang the bell. John Hendry watched as he once more interrogated Olivia.

'Well?'

'He's not coming back. Not to the house anyway. She thinks he's gone. She tried, well, sort of tried, I think, to get him to stay for the son's wedding, Hector, but he said he had to be off. It's not good between them, I would say.'

John Hendry was in no mood for marriage counselling.

'Quick,' he ordered, 'we'll go down to the harbour. See if the boat's still here.'

'Yacht!' corrected Cockburn as he scrambled into the passenger seat.

They knew before they reached the basin that they were too late. Nudge waved them down in Harbour Road.

'If you're looking for Hercules, you've missed him,' he announced. 'He sailed out about two hours ago. With Manuel and Edgardo, the Filipinos off the Bright Morn. Offered them a lift home, I expect.'

The humour was lost on John Hendry. He slumped back into his seat. Then Nudge added.

'They'll have a rough ride. Have y'seen the sea? It's making. There's been wind away out. The prawn boats hev come in early.'

'What'll I do with the letter?' asked Cockburn plaintively, as they drove back to his house.

'You are the lawyer,' replied John Hendry wearily. 'You tell me.'

'I think I should take it to Edinburgh to Proctor and Porteous. See if anything can be done.'

'Do that' muttered John Hendry. 'Do that! In the mean time I have a wedding to attend. I haven't told them about this check on the sale of Latchlaw – them or anyone else - and I don't intend telling them until the wedding is over.'

CHAPTER FIFTY-NINE

When it comes to money, Janet is cautious, but for her daughter's wedding, she would have pushed the boat out. She would have moved the ceremony to Beanston Kirk with its woodland setting (not cramped into a busy corner like Hecklescar's Parish Church). She would have hired Beanston Castle and had the photographs taken on its majestic lawns and held the reception in its magnificent ballroom. 'Nothing is too much for our Christine,' she would have said, '- and Hector.'

The expense of the move to Latchlaw had scotched all that. Of course, Janet and Duncan offered grandeur; of course, Christine rejected it and demanded economy. The service would be in the Parish Church, the photographs taken at the door and the reception held in the Golf Club. Jessie Mac would make the cake: two tiers but nothing fancy, Jessie. Only immediate family and close friends to be invited to the reception. The front pews would be reserved for them in the church. But others would be welcome further back.

John Hendry was the last of the invited to arrive at the church and was shown past Ina and other sightseers to a pew towards the front. He found himself sitting beside Connie and greeted her warmly.

'Sally is bridesmaid – and Alexander the best man,' she whispered once he was seated. (Sally, you will recall, is her beloved granddaughter, daughter of Olivia and Hercules, and sister of Hector. Alexander is Hector's brother.)

Then she added, 'Harold will not be here. He's set off to sail round the world, I believe.' She looked John in the face and smiled, and he could almost feel her satisfaction. John Hendry could not share the satisfaction but returned the smile. He had barely done so when Christine glided in on the arm of her father, Duncan. She wore what we later learned to be her mother's wedding dress let out, lengthened and re-covered with muslin. Duncan, polished up for the occasion, walked beside her, pride and delight bursting out of his best suit.

When they reached the waiting minister, Duncan released his daughter and she took her place beside Hector and grasped his shaking hand to steady him.

These simple acts of trust and devotion struck John Hendry forcibly. He felt a lump in his throat and a tear gathering in the corner of his eye. He looked away, and caught sight of a large wide-brimmed hat sitting in the second pew. Beneath the hat he detected Alice, bright with happiness. On one side of Alice, Janet; on the other, Alistair, unbelievably - and uncomfortably, in a suit.

In the opposite pew he picked out Olivia sitting on her own, arrayed in an elegant ensemble of understated blue with bright white trim. Although she smiled, she looked almost miserable, apprehensive certainly. John Hendry felt for her. She had caught the wrong train and now cowered in a cold waiting room, not knowing when the next train was due or where it might take her.

As he looked from one to the other, he felt more weight piling onto the burden under which he already buckled. He cared for these people - and was about to let them down.

By now Latchlaw had been signed away to Davenports.

Of course, it could be challenged; it would be challenged. But that would take years - and they'd be up against the might of a corporation with deep pockets and clever lawmen. If only he could have prevented that! What would Duncan and Janet do in the meantime – and Christine and Hector? All their plans blown up; or, at best, put on hold; the house and the steading all the while deteriorating. Worse, what about poor Alice?

Would Davenports claim the property to establish sitting rights to the site? Would they pull down the house before anyone could stop them? Would they put Alice and Alistair out of the house until the legalities were resolved? For the couple had no legal right to it. What would that do to Alice? She needed her home about her; familiar things in familiar places. She would be lost anywhere else. Where could she go if she had to leave Latchly? It would be the end of her, wouldn't it?

The ceremony had started and soon reached those solemn promises to love and cherish that he and Lizzie had tried and tested through fifty years and more. Such recollection provided a little temporary shelter from the storm that raged within him.

It is impossible, is it not? Latchly is now in the hands of an alien firm that cares nothing for Hecklescar and its people. Duncan and Janet's kindly plan is disintegrating, Christine's dream evaporating and Alice's life approaching dissolution. It is impossible!

In John Hendry, the spark leapt from Latchlaw to life; from impossibility to futility. Life is futile, is it not? Its course unpredictable; it's conclusion inevitable! Till death do us part! All our schemes, our plans, our ambitions and our aspirations, all our dreams, defences and devices, end in collapse, in disease, dwindling powers and dementia; in the pale face of death, the death of the one we loved, the death that parts us from life, from our life as well as theirs.

Then just as the storm reached its wild worst, a still
small voice directed him to see what he was looking at, and to
understand what he saw. He looked out and there were Christine and Hector: young, optimistic, forward-facing, eager for
the adventure of life together. Then he took in Janet and remembered her determination and discipline, then Duncan,
unflinchingly loyal and utterly dependable, then Alice in her
big brimmed hat gathering to herself her failing powers with
dogged courage. Were these qualities enough to challenge
the impossibilities they faced? Did they answer the futility?
Would they make it through?

He heard the answer in the mouth of his Lizzie - from all
those years ago, yet vivid now. In the mouth and the eyes of his
Lizzie when they were told that their wish for children would
not be granted.

'Could we find a way through life? A way up? We
searched for it together - for fifty years!'

'And found it, did we not, Lizzie?'

Is there a way through now for them? For Christine and
Hector, for Duncan and Janet, for Alice and Alistair? Surely!
The sun will rise tomorrow. They will rise with it and take up
the life they threw over the chair last night. Is there a way?
There always is.

But when to tell them that Hercules has reneged on his
promise and has sold off Latchly? At the reception? No, let
them have their cake and their dancing. Call on Duncan and
Janet once the couple are off on their honeymoon (to North
Berwick, would you believe? – in December!)? No, it has been
a busy day, they need their rest. His news would keep them
awake all night. Tomorrow? Yes, he must. It is not fair to keep
it from them any longer. Tomorrow – morning, late morning.

Then the photographs: on the steps of the kirk; and, to
the obvious irritation of Janet, in full gaze of the gawpers,
like Ina. The photographs: the bride and groom, the bride and

bridesmaid, the bride, groom, best man and bridesmaid; Janet and Duncan, the groom and best man, the bride and groom and best man and Olivia who tries to smile, then. ... but you know how it is, and if you don't the photographer does.

At the best of weddings, I'm sure you know, the photographs usually take longer than the ceremony and almost as long as the reception. Guests have been known to collapse with hunger at weddings where the happy couple have a lot of relatives. But this is not a proper photographer, not from Studio Elegans in Gainslaw with arty pictures in the window of the bride peeking out from behind an arbour and the groom searching for her in the bushes. No, they have asked Elaine, who dabbles in photography when not delivering fish for Anthony Douglas & Son.

Elaine has soon taken all the pictures she wants, and apart from the bridal party and Janet, Duncan, Alice and Alistair, Olivia and Connie, the guests make their own way to Golf Club for the reception.

The reception room at the Golf Club is upstairs and boasts a large picture window that, as the sign at the end of the road brags, provides 'stunning sea views'. The bride and groom have been seated with their backs to the window flanked by bridesmaid, best man and parents. The other guests populate tables running away from the ends of the top table into the heart of the room, thus forming the gathering into a wide U shape. In the space in the middle stands a small table on which stands Jessie Mac's version of a not too expensive Wedding Cake - and very splendid it appears too.

Hector and Christine leave their places and walk round their guests to cut the cake and are cheered and applauded for doing so. Janet comments that the cake looks quite rich and fruity inside.

Then the speeches. Christine has asked her father to say a few words and Duncan with his single sheet of notes shaking in his hand stands up and works his way through what he has written, though what he says not many catch, and, although everyone laughs, no one understands the joke about the parrot. Hector fares no better in his reply but remembers to propose a toast to the bridesmaid. Then Alexander, blessed with the self-assurance of his father, polishes off his reply with neat phrases and lofty sentiments.

Then it is John Hendry's turn. As he entered the reception room Christine had asked him to propose a toast of thanks to her mother and father, and he has scribbled a few words on the back on the menu. He stands up and is cheered. As he tries to read what he has written, the door at the back of the room bursts open.

You will readily understand that, with a large picture window at the other end, the back wall of the room is brilliantly lit. The door is in the centre of the wall. It is as if the door were lit by a floodlight. Out of the door and into this brightness, into the full gaze of all the guests, stumbles Cockburn. The guests laugh, Cockburn retreats then a moment later tries to sidle into the room without opening the door.

When he sees John Hendry on his feet, he first of all tries to signal to him, then when John Hendry glowers at him, attempts to fade into the wallpaper.

The guests subside, John Hendry recovers and pays tribute to Duncan and Janet, then excuses himself to rescue Cockburn from his embarrassment.

'What is it?' he urges.

'Come outside,' whispers Cockburn.

They step outside to the head of the stair.

'What is it?' John Hendry repeats.

'It's Latchlaw,' exclaims the solicitor. 'Hercules didn't sign. He hasn't sold it! He pulled out of the deal.'

CHAPTER SIXTY

Once John Hendry had calmed down Cockburn, the solicitor became coherent.

He reported that, after he had left John Hendry that morning, he had gone to Edinburgh to Proctor & Porteous. There he had sought out The Doc to see what might be done now the sale had been concluded. He had found The Doc somewhat tetchy.

Earlier in the day - apparently, with Davenports already in the building, but before Hercules had arrived - Gladys, The Doc's equivalent of Mrs. Somerville, had drawn his attention to what she called an anomaly; namely, that there was some doubt about the ownership of Latchlaw.

How did Gladys know? Mrs. Somerville had told her. Over the years, in the course of business, they had communicated regularly. They were not exactly friends but they shared similar doubts about the perspicacity of their masters and a confidence in each other's grasp of practicality. Mrs. Somerville, realising that Cockburn was unlikely to reach Peter Munro in time, had rung Gladys and told her about the letter casting doubt on the ownership of Latchlaw. Gladys thought it merited a mention to The Doc.

'So, Proctor and Porteous pulled the plug,' exclaimed John Hendry.

'No!' replied Cockburn,

'No! Davenports, then.'

'No, it never got that far. Hercules called it off.'

'Hercules, Harold Douglas! Called it off?'

'Yes, that's what's so strange. When Hercules arrived, The Doc had told him what Gladys had said about the letter, and expected Hercules to deny it, or rubbish it. That would have been enough for The Doc to proceed. They could go ahead; The Doc had advised; often there were snags. He reckoned that Davenports tackle that sort of detail all the time.'

'Hercules had smiled (grimaced was the word The Doc used), then asked The Doc if Davenports were still insisting on the whole site being cleared. When The Doc confirmed that they were adamant, Hercules shrugged his shoulders and told The Doc to scrap the deal.'

'What on earth?!' began John Hendry but Cockburn rattled on.

'The Doc was livid, but Hercules just stood up and walked out.'

'And that was all?'

'Yes – well, no! The Doc said that the only explanation that Hercules gave was to mumble something about an old lady and a rent book. It made no sense to The Doc. He thought Hercules must be suffering from stress. He was left trying to explain it to Davenports. They were not pleased.'

'I can imagine that! So Latchly still belongs to. . . Who does it belong to?'

'That will need to be tested.'

'If you had to give an opinion?'

For a moment Cockburn looked alarmed, then said slowly,

'It depends. Peter Munro, I would say, I think, yes, I think, I would say Peter Munro, probably.'

'So, what do Alice and Alistair do?' asked John Hendry.

'It depends,' said the lawyer as lawyers generally do. 'But they should sit tight. It's going to turn out all right for them – I would say, probably; well, almost certainly. But it's good for them, I would say, very good. They should stay put until we can ask Peter Munro what he wants to do. It'll be up to him, I would think, in the end, up to him. He's a good man. They'll be all right. He'll sell the house and steading to Duncan, I'm sure, if they still want it. It depends, but it'll be all right,'

'I'm sure it will,' agreed John Hendry, and that is what he told Duncan and Janet once the happy couple were off for their two-night 'Special Deal' honeymoon in The Marine at North Berwick.

CHAPTER SIXTY-ONE

Two days after Christine's wedding, Peter Munro came home.

By his own choice, he came by bus. With his knapsack on his back he dismounted at the old school and made his way to John Hendry's house in Hallyknowe Terrace, there to take up John Hendry's offer of a lodging. He would stay only for a few days, until he could move into one of the many holiday houses that Hecklescar provided. At this time of year many lie vacant and such a let would allow him time to decide what sort of house he wanted. He still was not sure what it was.

John Hendry found him a pleasant guest and enjoyed his company. Peter, on the other hand, found John a willing listener to the account of his long walk as well as of the long wanderings of his life. When John Hendry had heard Peter's story, he told him his own, particularly the boggy chapter through which he was now battling. Peter stayed with John Hendry no more than four days but, by the end of it, the two men had found friendship and common purpose.

On the day after his arrival, John took Peter down to the fishyard where Jakey gave him a Cook's tour of the facilities, Fiona gave him an insight into its management and Angela gave him fish. Of course, he would help to save Anthony Douglas & Son, though how and when and in what way must wait until he had examined the books and understood what restructuring and investment would be required. John Hendry returned home that day with a lighter step and an easier mind.

The next evening John took Peter round to Duncan and Janet's house to talk about what might be done about Latch-law and found with them the newly-married Christine. Peter listened carefully to their plans and dreams and assured them that one way or the other he would see Alice and Alistair set-tled safely in the Latchlaw farmhouse - and encouraged Dun-can and Hector to start immediately on the renovation of both house and steading.

When Janet reminded him that Hercules might wriggle out of his promise, Peter responded by saying that if Hercu-les disputed his right to the property, he would buy him out. Janet baulked at the proposal.

'What? Pay Hercules for what is rightfully yours! No way! Don't give him a penny! Not a penny! The man's a rogue. He tried to diddle Duncan out of £10,000. If it hadn't been for John Hendry here God knows what we would have done. No. You'll not pay him anything for Latchly. It belongs to you. Everyone says that.'

'Everyone?' put in John. 'How does everyone know about Latchly?'

Janet glanced at him and said, 'Ina knows.'

'Of course,' nodded John Hendry and explained to Peter Ina's interests and reputation.

Peter smiled and answered Janet.

'If it goes to litigation, it will take years and the lawyers will take more than I am prepared to offer Hercules.'

'Well, I don't think...' Janet made to continue her objec-tion, but Christine broke in.

'Mother,' she said, 'remember that Hercules is Hector's father – and Sally's. They are upset about the whole business. Hector says he doesn't think his father is as bad as folk are saying. He's given a lot of people a lot of work for a lot of years. He says he knows he's no saint but he was an okay father. They never wanted for anything and he took them places when they were young. He's not all bad. Look how he brought granny back that night she went to see him.'

'With her rent book, I believe,' put in John Hendry.

'With her rent book,' Christine repeated. 'And think, mother, that could be why he didn't sell the place to those builders. That's why he didn't go through with it; why he didn't fight it. Because he genuinely didn't want to put granny and granddad out. Perhaps he's kinder than folk think. Nobody's all bad.'

At this Duncan nodded and looked at Janet pleading silently with her not push the argument further.

'Listen to her,' agreed Peter; 'give him the benefit of the doubt, eh? Let me add something else about our man. We do not need to chase him. He has plenty of wolves snapping at his heels already.'

Peter went on to explain that claims would come piling in from those who had lost out on 'Golden Opportunities'. Then there is the snarling threat from the Fraud Office. They may well want to enquire into the transfer of funds from fish to finance, from Anthony Douglas & Son to HD Investments.

Janet retreated and, aided by Christine, provided them all with a glass of wine and a slice of wedding cake.

John Hendry accepted, at least as a possibility, that Alice's innocence had stirred Hercules' conscience. But, like Janet, Peter Munro's offer to pay Hercules for Latchlaw offended his sense of financial propriety, and he raised it with Peter when they reached home. Peter insisted that it was the simplest and quickest way to resolve any impasse. Money was the language Hercules understood. He would speak to him in it if it were necessary. When John Hendry pointed out that the yacht, the Olympian, in which Hercules is escaping, technically belonged to Anthony Douglas & Son, Peter persuaded John that little would be gained from trying to recover it.

John Hendry was not convinced.

Then Peter, looking intensely at the old banker, added, 'John, I have learned the hard way that there is a stark justice in circumstance. Being what Harold Douglas is, whatever it is, has its own consequences. We do not need to agonise over-much what they might be. Let him sail away from Hecklescar; he cannot sail away from himself. He will fetch up somewhere, not by anything we might do, but because of who he is. Let that content us. Who knows; it might save the man?'

John Hendry caught Peter's eye and fell silent. He recognised in the man an earnestness that precluded contradiction. Peter, he saw, had suffered enough to understand the human condition and had gathered enough sympathy for it to learn to forgive.

CHAPTER SIXTY-TWO

Ina had her own ideas on why Peter Munro did not want to claim back the yacht. Didn't it have to do with Olivia? We all know, she argued, that Peter Munro was gazumped (that's Ina's word, not mine) by Hercules. Now he's back he wanted Hercules out of the way so he could take up where he left off with Olivia.

If, at the coffee gathering that morning, she had taken a vote on her proposal she would have lost it. Most of the ladies looked doubtful. Then Ina opened up with both barrels.

'He's been round there already,' she said, 'and to the mother.'

She lowered her voice.

'Then of course, he's staying in one of Nudge's holiday houses. Hasn't got a place of his own. Now, why not? Well, it makes sense, doesn't it? He's hoping that Olivia takes him in. She has that muckle house all to herself. He told Nudge he wouldn't want the holiday house for long.'

It's true. Peter Munro has been to see them both. Connie, because he always went to see Connie, Olivia because he feels sorry for her. Will anything come of it? Flickers yet the old flame? Both having ventured into the wilderness and lost their way; will they risk a new expedition?

Questions without answers, at least in this story. Besides, we have Christmas to celebrate, and I cannot think of any of our characters, apart from Hercules, who will not seek to enjoy it.

It is barely a week away and the contradiction of Christmas has already overwhelmed almost everyone in the town. 'Contradiction' because everyone seeks the peace of Christmas in a frenzy that chases it away. Afterwards, if you ask folk what kind of Christmas they have had, they will all say, 'Oh, quiet, just the family, ye ken.' But quiet it will not be; 'frantic' is the word that comes to mind.

Yet there is a sort of peace; a cessation of the battling through that makes up the rest of the year: battling debt, battling illness, battling anxiety, battling poverty, battling boredom, battling regret and recrimination, fighting the neighbours, fighting flab. All are set aside at Christmas. In an impressive display of determination everyone dedicates themselves to enjoying the feast.

At the yard, Fiona, to everyone's surprise, has baked a Christmas Cake and brought it in for everyone to share. If you have never had a piece of Christmas cake flavoured with fish from the hands that hold it, then a tantalising taste awaits you. So popular it was that when Wullie returned from his deliveries there were only a few crumbs and a bit of icing left for him.

John Hendry has authorised (on Jakey's say so) a drop-in Christmas Party, to be held at The Old Barque on the evening before Christmas Eve, and Peter Munro has promised to pay for a buffet for them all, but not the drink. This last on the advice of Angela, who from many years' experience of company parties knows what happens when her older fish-gutters drink too much.

Peter has been invited to spend Christmas with daughter Dolinda and family in Guildford, but he has turned down the invitation, and will spend the season in Hecklescar. Of course, he will send his family cards loaded with cheques so they need not be short on their celebrations. He has remembered Florence too, and made sure that he addressed her as his daughter in his greeting. In addition, he has arranged for Christmas floral arrangements to be delivered to Mrs. Rostowski, and to Moira, the wife of Oliver. On the card to Mrs. Rostowski he expressed his thanks and apologised again for wasting so much of her time and leading her down so many blind alleys. He has also asked Greg to dispose of the Lexus which he had bought in the days of his vanity, but now lay unwanted and unvalued in a garage in Eastbourne.

John Hendry has managed (with the help of Gloria in the Flower Shop) to wrap up his presents and post off his cards. The card he has sent to his brother in Australia will not reach him until well after the New Year. He has also raked out Lizzie's old decorations from the chest in the garret and done his best to give the house a festive feel. He has tied a wreath on the front door, wrapped a pine garland through the bannisters, stuck holly behind the pictures and planted a spindly tree in the front room window. The effect is far short of what Lizzie achieved but he has done it with love – and not a little longing for the warm Christmases they enjoyed together. Oh! and one thing more, or rather two: a holly wreath for Lizzie where she lies – and one to deck the grave of Lizzie's folk; they too must join the feast. From the flower shop to be picked up on the day before Christmas.

No short measures will mar Janet's celebrations. Although menaced by their forthcoming move to Latchly she has decked out the house in Priory Road with meticulous care. A traditionalist, she despises brightly-lit reindeers stuck on walls, frantic fairy lights in windows and Santa climbing the chimney. If you are fortunate enough to visit Duncan and Janet at the end of December you will find yourself welcomed into the colour, light and comfort of Christmas Past.

Janet is also prepared for the Christmas day meal. It will be pork, not turkey; pork with crackling, ordered weeks ago from Pete the Butcher. He will also provide most of the vegetables and apples for the sauce, but not the sprouts; Alistair will bring those in from the garden at Latchly. That is where the meal will be served – at Latchlaw. Janet will allow Alice to help her prepare and serve it. Having the meal at the farm will be a considerable sacrifice for Janet. One of the highlights of her year is to present the Christmas dinner in her own dining room on her own old dining table, laid with a rich red cloth, bearing at its centre a polished candlestick, and, at each place, a holly placemat, silvered cutlery, and a linen serviette in cream and gold wrapped round with a glittering bow. When the meal is served it is on her treasured red and gold-rimmed bone china plates. But this year she will give it up, just as she is giving up her house for the love of her husband's mother and father. She will try to recreate for the old woman the rich, remembered Christmas dinners of her earlier years, for, who knows, by next year Alice may not remember anything at all.

Janet will not reckon her decision a sacrifice, and Duncan, although he understands what it is costing her, will not mention it.

Janet and Duncan have invited John Hendry to join them for the meal on Christmas Day, and he has accepted. They have also invited Peter Munro but he will not be with them for he has already accepted a previous invitation - from Olivia to join her at Avignon. Her mother Connie will be with her, as will Sally and Alexander. Hector will divide himself between the two parties, attending his mother's celebratory drinks before making his way to join his wife and in-laws at Latchly.

Ina will cook a splendid meal for herself, husband Jakey, her son and daughter-in-law from up the road at Brisset, and Nudge who otherwise would be on his own. He protested that he would quite enjoy being on his own, but Ina would have none of it and he will turn up at 3 for the feast – but not the drink. As we know, he is strictly teetotal.

Though not a churchgoer, Peter Munro has suggested to John Hendry that they attend the Parish Kirk for the service at midnight on Christmas Eve. John Hendry agreed to the occasion but not the location. He guessed, correctly, that Peter sought to penetrate the mystery of Christmas, and thus, of life. The brave absurdity of Christmas drew him, the absurdity that young children understand, careless adults throw away, and old folk spend the last of their lives trying to retrieve.

But Hecklescar Kirk would not do. There is no mystery about what goes on there. It is all bluster, bustle and blurb. John will take Peter to the Old Priory along the road and will hope that they have asked old Mr. Hamilton to conduct the service again. Mr. Hamilton is old enough and wise enough not to attempt to explain anything.

The old Priory is candle-lit for the midnight service, the soft light warming the old sandstone arches and pillars, the solemn organ hushing the gathering congregation to silence as they enter. They are in luck, (or should we say blessed?): Mr. Hamilton it is. He has the old stories read in the Authorised Version, accepts God's grace in his prayers rather than badgering Him about world affairs, and invites the congregation to sing old obscure carols. By such diversions he leads the congregation to understand what they cannot know and accept what they cannot prove.

'Comfort and Joy', they sing and as he sang John Hendry prayed that he could do with more comfort and would pass up on the joy if, in any way, it meant excitement. He'd had enough excitement for this year; more than enough.

Peter Munro, meanwhile, meditated on his homecoming and protested that it was not what he sought. As we know, he has anguished long and hard about his past life with its ups and downs, its achievements and disappointments, its opportunities and mistakes. He had anticipated sneaking back into his home town, buying a quiet house in a quiet street, throwing his tangled thoughts and unanswered questions into a lumber room and shutting the door. He would settle for that - and he had intended to tell Mrs. Rostowski so in a few months' time when the regular rhythms of a languid life had lulled his fears and doubts to sleep.

Now, unexpectedly, he found himself sucked back into the cross currents of commerce he had so deliberately abandoned. Unexpectedly - but not frighteningly; not, to his surprise, frighteningly. He had come home hoping, at best, to find in stagnant tranquillity enough comfort to soothe his troubled soul. Instead he had stumbled back into the turbulent mainstream of work; had met Jakey and Fiona and Angela, had been congratulated by Nudge and welcomed in the fish room; had discovered that they had placed their hopes and livelihoods in his hands, hands that he had concluded were not safe hands, not strong enough or skilled enough to carry such fragile freight. Yet, it did not frighten him, or depress him. He had found, to his surprise, that sitting in Hercules' big chair lifted his spirits. This was not the refuge he sought. He found himself still jostled in life's street, but by companions. He did not travel alone. He knew his fellow travellers – and they needed him as much as he needed them.

It gave him comfort and a gentle joy.

CHAPTER SIXTY-THREE

But where is Hercules?

Unst!

Where on earth is Unst?

In the Shetland Isles - as far north as you can go without falling off the edge.

We know this because on his way to Latchlaw for his Christmas Lunch, John Hendry ran into Jakey. Jakey had been called to the Fishermens' Mission, late last night to meet Edgardo and Manuel, the two Filipinos who had set sail with Hercules.

The yacht had sprung a leak (the old problem with the gland) and Hercules had had to put into Baltasound. Edgardo and Manuel, having lost faith in his seamanship and the boat, jumped ship and had come back to Hecklescar. Elvira, seasick and sick of Hercules, had also deserted and gone home.

Hercules is now stuck in Unst. The replacement gland will not be delivered for a fortnight and the boat has to be pumped out three times a day, so it cannot be left. Besides, he can't come back for there is nowhere for him to come back to. Even if there were, he wouldn't dare. There are too many angry people with too many awkward questions wanting to speak to him. He is therefore lying low, hoping the boat will be ready before those that seek him know where to find him.

His will be a lonely and miserable Christmas.

As John Hendry told the story to Duncan, Janet and family over their friendly Christmas table the words of Peter Munro came to mind:

'Hercules cannot sail away from himself. He will fetch up somewhere, not by anything we might do, but because of who he is.'

Also applies to Peter Munro, does it not . . and John Hendry?

... and Janet, Duncan, Christine and Hector, Alice and Alistair, Mrs. Rostowski and Greg, and Moira and Oliver - particularly Moira and Oliver,

... and Connie, Olivia and Sally, and Fiona, Angela and Jakey, even Ina, though she would dispute it?

........and the rest of them down the yard,

.... and all of us, would you say?

THE END

Printed in Great Britain
by Amazon